Come with me. The words were in slashing black ink on a page from a pocketbook. *I can get you away from this. You'll be safe.*

Lucy's head jerked up.

"Safe?" *With him?*

Domenico nodded. "Yes."

Around them journalists craned to hear. One tried to snatch the note from Lucy's hand. She crumpled it in her fist. He couldn't want to help her. Yet she wasn't fool enough to think she could stay here. Trouble was brewing and she'd be at the center of it.

Still she hesitated. This close, Lucy was aware of the strength in those broad shoulders, in that tall frame and his square olive-skinned hands. Once, that blatant male power had left her breathless. Now it threatened. But if he'd wanted to harm her physically he'd have found a way long before this.

He leaned forward. She stiffened as his whispered words caressed her cheek. "Word of a Volpe."

She knew he was proud. Haughty. Loyal. A powerful man. A dangerously clever one. But everything she'd read, and she'd read plenty, indicated he was a man of his word. He wouldn't sully his ancient family name or his pride by lying.

She hoped.

Dear Reader,

We know how much you love Harlequin®Presents®, so this month we wanted to treat you to something extra special—a second classic story by the same author for free!

Once you have finished reading *Captive in the Spotlight*, just turn the page for another beautifully innocent heroine from Annie West.

This month, indulge yourself with double the reading pleasure!

With love,

The Presents Editors

Annie West

CAPTIVE IN THE SPOTLIGHT

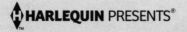

HARLEQUIN PRESENTS®

ISBN-13: 978-0-373-13133-4

CAPTIVE IN THE SPOTLIGHT

Copyright © 2013 by Harlequin Books S.A.

The publisher acknowledges the copyright holder of the individual
works as follows:

CAPTIVE IN THE SPOTLIGHT
Copyright © 2013 by Annie West

BLACKMAILED BRIDE, INNOCENT WIFE
Copyright © 2009 by Annie West

Recycling programs
for this product may
not exist in your area.

HARLEQUIN®
™ www.Harlequin.com

Printed in U.S.A.

CONTENTS

All about the author...
Annie West

ANNIE WEST spent her childhood with her nose between the covers of a book—a habit she retains. After years spent preparing government reports and official correspondence, she decided to write something she *really* enjoys. And there's nothing she loves more than a great romance. Despite her office-bound past she has managed a few interesting moments—including a marriage offer with the promise of a herd of camels to sweeten the contract. She is happily married to her ever-patient husband (who has never owned a dromedary). They live with their two children amongst the tall eucalypts at beautiful Lake Macquarie, on Australia's east coast. You can contact Annie through her website, www.annie-west.com, or write to her at P.O. Box 1041, Warners Bay, NSW 2282, Australia.

Other titles by Annie West available in ebook:

Harlequin Presents® Extra

201—UNDONE BY HIS TOUCH
190—GIRL IN THE BEDOUIN TENT
174—THE SAVAKIS MERGER

CAPTIVE IN THE SPOTLIGHT

In memory of our special Daisy, canine member of the family for almost sixteen years and ever-supportive writer's companion.

And with heartfelt thanks to Josie, Serena and Antony for your advice on Italian language, law and locations.

CHAPTER ONE

FOR FIVE GRIM years Lucy had imagined her first day of freedom. A sky the pure blue of Italian summer. The scent of citrus in the warm air and the sound of birds.

Instead she inhaled a familiar aroma. Bricks, concrete and cold steel should have no scent. Yet mixed with despair and commercial strength detergent, they created a perfume called 'Institution'. It had filled her nostrils for years.

Lucy repressed a shudder of fear, her stomach cramping.

What if there had been a mistake? What if the huge metal door before her remained firmly shut?

Panic welled at the thought of returning to her cell. To come so close then have freedom denied would finally destroy her.

The guard punched in the release code. Lucy moved close, her bag in one clammy hand, her heart in her mouth. Finally the door opened and she stepped through.

Exhaust fumes instead of citrus. Lowering grey skies instead of blue. The roar of cars rather than birdsong.

She didn't care. *She was free!*

She closed her eyes, savouring this moment she'd dreamed of since the terror engulfed her.

She was free to do as she chose. Free to try taking up the threads of her life. She'd take a cheap flight to London and a night to regroup before finishing the trip to Devon. A night somewhere quiet, with a comfortable bed and unlimited hot water.

The door clanged shut and her eyes snapped open.

A noise made her turn. Further along, by the main entrance, a crowd stirred. A crowd with cameras and microphones that blared 'Press'.

Ice scudded down Lucy's spine as she stepped briskly in the opposite direction.

She'd barely begun walking when the hubbub erupted: running feet, shouts, the roar of a motorbike.

'Lucy! Lucy Knight!' Even through the blood pounding in her ears and the confusion of so many people yelling at once, there was no mistaking the hunger in those voices. It was as if the horde had been starved and the scent of fresh blood sent them into a frenzy.

Lucy quickened her pace but a motorbike cut off her escape. The passenger snapped off shot after shot of her stunned face before she could gather herself.

By that time the leaders of the pack had surrounded her, clamouring close and thrusting microphones in her face. It was all she could do not to give in to panic and run. After the isolation she'd known the eager crush was terrifying.

'How does it feel, Lucy?'

'What are your plans?'

'Have you anything to say to our viewers, Lucy? Or to the Volpe family?'

The bedlam of shouted questions eased a fraction at mention of the Volpe family. Lucy sucked in a shocked breath as cameras clicked and whirred in her face, disorienting her.

She should have expected this. Why hadn't she?

Because it was five years ago. Old news.

Because she'd expected the furore to die down.

What more did they want? They'd already taken so much.

If only she'd accepted the embassy's offer to spirit her to the airport. Foolishly she'd been determined to rely on no one. Five years ago British officials hadn't been able to save her from the grinding wheels of Italian justice. She'd stopped expecting help from there, or anywhere.

Look where her pride had got her!

Lips set in a firm line, she strode forward, cleaving a path through the persistent throng. She didn't shove or threaten, just kept moving with a strength and determination she'd acquired the hard way.

She was no longer the innocent eighteen-year-old who'd been incarcerated. She'd given up waiting for justice, much less a champion.

She'd had to be her own champion.

Lucy made no apology when her stride took her between a news camera and journalist wearing too much make-up and barely any skirt. The woman's attempt to coax a comment ended when her microphone fell beneath Lucy's feet.

Lucy looked neither right nor left, knowing if she stopped she'd be lost. The swelling noise and press of so many bodies sent her hurtling towards claustrophobic panic. She shook inside, her breathing grew choppy, her stomach diving as she fought the urge to flee.

The press would love that!

There was a gap ahead. Lucy made for it, to discover herself surrounded by big men in dark suits and sunglasses. Men who kept the straining crowd at bay.

Despite the flash of cameras and volleys of shouts, here in these few metres of space it was like being in the eye of a cyclone.

Instincts hyper-alert, Lucy surveyed the car the security men encircled. It was expensive, black with tinted windows.

Curious, she stepped forward, racking her brain. Her friends had melted away in these last years. As for her family—if only they could afford transport like this!

One of the bodyguards opened the back door and Lucy stepped close enough to look inside.

Grey eyes snared her. Eyes the colour of ice under a stormy

sky. Sleek black eyebrows rayed up towards thick, dark hair cropped against a well-shaped head.

The clamour faded and Lucy's breath snagged as her eyes followed a long, arrogant nose, pinched as if in rejection of the institutional aroma she carried in her pores. High, angled cheekbones scored a patrician face. A solid jaw and a firm-set mouth, thinned beyond disapproving and into the realm of pained, completed a compelling face that might have stared out from a Renaissance portrait.

Despite the condemnation she read there, another emotion blasted between them, an unseen ripple of heat in the charged air. A ripple that drew her flesh tight and made the hairs on her arms rise.

'Domenico Volpe!'

Air hissed from Lucy's lungs as if from a puncture wound. Her hand tightened on her case and for a moment she rocked on her feet.

Not him! This was too much.

'You recognise me?' He spoke English with the clear, rounded vowels and perfect diction of a man with impeccable lineage, wealth, power and education at his disposal.

Which meant his disapproving tone, as if she had no right even to recognise a man so far beyond her league, was deliberate.

Lucy refused to let him see how that stung. Blank-faced withdrawal was a tactic she'd perfected as a defence in the face of aggression.

How could his words harm her after what she'd been through?

'I remember you.' *As if she could forget.* Once she'd almost believed… No. She excised the thought. She was no longer so foolishly naïve.

The sight of him evoked a volley of memories. She made herself concentrate on the later ones. 'You never missed a moment of the trial.'

The shouts of the crowd were a reminder of that time, twisting her insides with pain.

He didn't incline his head, didn't move, yet something flickered in his eyes. Something that made her wonder if he, like she, held onto control by a slim thread.

'Would you have? In my shoes?' His voice was silky but lethal. Lucy remembered reading that the royal assassins of the Ottoman sultan had used garrottes of silk to strangle their victims.

He wouldn't lower himself to assault but he wouldn't lift a finger to save her. Yet once long ago, for a fleeting moment, they'd shared something fragile and full of breathless promise.

Her throat tightened as memories swarmed.

What was she doing here, bandying words with a man who wished her only ill? Silently she turned but found her way blocked by a giant in a dark suit.

'Please, *signorina*.' He gestured to the open car door behind her. 'Take a seat.'

With Domenico Volpe? He personified everything that had gone wrong in her life.

A bubble of hysterical laughter rose and she shook her head.

She stepped to one side but the bodyguard moved fast. He grasped her arm, propelling her towards the car.

'Don't *touch* me!' All the shock and grief and dismay she battled rose within her, a roiling well of emotions she'd kept pent up too long.

No one had the right to coerce her.

Not any more.

Not after what she'd endured.

Lucy opened her mouth to demand her release. But the crisp, clear order she'd formulated didn't emerge. Instead a burst of Italian vitriol spilled out. Words she'd never known, even in English, till her time in jail. The sort of gutter Italian Domenico Volpe and his precious family wouldn't recognise. The sort of coarse, colloquial Italian favoured by criminals and lunatics. She should know, she'd met enough in her time.

The bodyguard's eyes widened, his hand dropping as he stepped back. As if he was afraid her lashing tongue might injure him.

Abruptly the flow of words stopped. Lucy vibrated with fury but also with something akin to shame.

So much for her pride in rising above the worst degradations of imprisonment. As for her pleasure, just minutes ago, that she'd left prison behind her… Her heart fell. How long would she bear its taint? How irrevocably had it changed her?

Despair threatened but she forced it down.

Fingers curling tight around the handle of her bag, she stepped forward and the bodyguard made way. She kept going, beyond the cordon that kept Domenico Volpe from the straining paparazzi.

Lucy straightened her spine. She'd rather walk into the arms of the waiting press than stay here.

'I'm sorry, boss. I should have stopped her. But with the media watching…'

'It's okay, Rocco. The last thing I want is a press report about us kidnapping Lucy Knight.' That would really send Pia into a spin. His sister-in-law was already strung out at the news of her release.

He watched the crowd close round the slim form of the Englishwoman and something that felt incredibly like remorse stirred.

As if he'd failed her.

Because she'd looked at him with unveiled horror and chosen the slavering mob rather than share a car with him? That niggling sense of guilt resurfaced. Nonsense, of course. In the light of day logic assured him she'd brought on her own destruction. Yet sometimes, in the dead of night, it didn't seem so cut and dried.

But he wasn't Lucy Knight's keeper. He never had been.

Five years ago he'd briefly responded to her air of fresh enthusiasm, so different from the sophisticated, savvy women in his life. Until he'd discovered she was a sham, trying to ensnare and use him as she had his brother.

Domenico's lips firmed. She'd looked at him just now with those huge eyes the colour of forget-me-nots. A gullible man might have read fear in that look.

Domenico wasn't a gullible man.

Though to his shame he'd felt a tug of unwanted attraction to the woman who'd stood day after day in the dock, projecting an air of bewildered innocence.

Her face had been a smooth oval, rounded with youth. Her hair, straight, long and the colour of wheat in the sun, had made him want to reach out and touch.

He'd hated himself for that.

'She's some wildcat, eh, boss? The way she let fly—'

'Close the door, Rocco.'

'Yes, sir.' The guard stiffened and shut the door.

Domenico sat back, watching the melee move down the street. A few stragglers remained, their cameras trained on the limousine, but the tinted windows gave privacy.

Just as well. He didn't want their lenses on him. Not when he felt…unsettled.

He swiped a hand over his jaw, wishing to hell Pia hadn't put him in this situation. What did the media frenzy matter? They could rise above it as always. Only the insecure let the press get to them. But Pia was emotionally vulnerable, beset by mood swings and insecurities.

It wasn't the media that disturbed him. He ignored the paparazzi. It was *her*, Lucy Knight. The way she looked at him.

She'd changed. Her cropped hair made her look like a raunchy pixie instead of a soulful innocent. Her face had fined down, sculpted into bone-deep beauty that had been a mere promise at eighteen. And attitude! She had that in spades.

What courage had it taken to walk back into that hungry throng? Especially when he'd seen and heard, just for a moment, the pain in her hoarse curses.

For all the weeks of the trial she'd looked as if butter wouldn't melt in her mouth. How had she hidden such violent passion, such hatred so completely?

Or—the thought struck out of nowhere—maybe that dangerous undercurrent was something new, acquired in the intervening years.

Domenico sagged in his seat. He should ignore Pia's pleas and his own ambivalent reactions and walk away. This woman had been nothing but trouble since the day she'd crossed his family's threshold.

He pressed the intercom to speak to the driver. 'Drive on.'

Twenty minutes till the bus came.

Could she last? The crowd grew thicker. It took all Lucy's stamina to pretend they didn't bother her. To ignore the cameras and catcalls, the increasingly rough jostling.

Lucy's knees shook and her arm ached but she didn't dare put her case down. It held everything she owned and she wouldn't put it past one of the paparazzi to swipe it and do an exposé on the state of her underwear or a psychological profile based on the few battered books she possessed.

The tone of the gathering had darkened as the press found, instead of the easy prey they'd expected, a woman determined not to cooperate. Didn't they realise the last thing she wanted was more publicity?

They'd attracted onlookers. She heard their mutterings and cries of outrage.

She widened her stance, bracing against the pushing crowd, alert to the growing tension. She knew how quickly violence could erupt.

She was just about to give up on the bus and move on when

the crowd stirred. A flutter, like a sigh, rippled through it, leaving in its wake something that could almost pass for silence.

The camera crews parted. There, striding towards her was the man she'd expected never to see again: Domenico Volpe, shouldering through the rabble, eyes locked on her. He seemed oblivious to the snapping shutters as the cameras went into overdrive and newsmen gabbled into microphones.

He wore a grey suit with the slightest sheen, as if it were woven from black pearls. His shirt was pure white, his tie perfection in dark silk.

He looked the epitome of Italian wealth and breeding. Not a wrinkle marred his clothes or the elegant lines of his face. Only his eyes, boring into hers, spoke of something less than cool control.

A spike of heat plunged right through her belly as she held his eyes.

He stopped before her and Lucy had to force herself not to crane her head to look up at him. Instead she focused on the hand he held out to her.

The paper crackled as she took it.

Come with me. The words were in slashing black ink on a page from a pocketbook. *I can get you away from this. You'll be safe.*

Her head jerked up.

'Safe?' *With him?*

He nodded. 'Yes.'

Around them journalists craned to hear. One tried to snatch the note from Lucy's hand. She crumpled it in her fist.

It was mad. Bizarre. He couldn't want to help her. Yet she wasn't fool enough to think she could stay here. Trouble was brewing and she'd be at the centre of it.

Still she hesitated. This close, Lucy was aware of the strength in those broad shoulders, in that tall frame and his square olive-skinned hands. Once that blatant male power had left her breathless. Now it threatened.

But if he'd wanted to harm her physically he'd have found a way long before this.

He leaned forward. She stiffened as his whispered words caressed her cheek. 'Word of a Volpe.'

He withdrew, but only far enough to look her in the eye. He stood in her personal space, his lean body warming her and sending ripples of tension through her.

She knew he was proud. Haughty. Loyal. A powerful man. A dangerously clever one. But everything she'd read, and she'd read plenty, indicated he was a man of his word. He wouldn't sully his ancient family name or his pride by lying.

She hoped.

Jerkily she nodded.

'Va bene.' He eased the case from her white-knuckled grip and turned, propelling her through the crowd with his palm at her back, its heat searing through her clothes.

Questions rang out but Domenico Volpe ignored them. With his support Lucy rallied and managed not to stumble. Then suddenly there was blissful space, a cordon of security men, the open limousine door.

This time Lucy needed no urging. She scrambled in and settled herself on the far side of the wide rear seat.

The door shut behind him and the car accelerated away before she'd gathered herself.

'My bag!'

'It's in the boot. Quite safe.'

Safe. There it was again. The word she'd never associated with Domenico Volpe.

Slowly Lucy turned. She was exhausted, weary beyond imagining after less than an hour at the mercy of the paparazzi, but she couldn't relax, even in this decadently luxurious vehicle.

Deep-set grey eyes met hers. This time they looked stormy rather than glacial. Lucy was under no illusions that he wanted her here, with him. Despite the nonchalant stretch of his long legs, crossed at the ankles, there was tightness in his shoulders and jaw.

'What do you want?'

'To rescue you from the press.'

Lucy shook her head. 'No.'

'No?' One dark eyebrow shot up towards his hairline. 'You call me a liar?'

'If you'd been interested in rescuing me you'd have done it years ago when it mattered. But you dropped me like a hot potato.'

Her words sucked the oxygen from the limousine, leaving a heavy, clogging atmosphere of raw emotion. Lucy drew a deep breath, uncaring that he noted the agitated rise and fall of her breasts as she struggled for air.

'You're talking about two different things.' His tone was cool.

'You think?' She paused. 'You're playing semantics. The last thing you want is to *rescue* me.'

'Then let us say merely that your interests and mine coincide this time.'

'How?' She leaned forward, as if a closer view would reveal the secrets he kept behind that patrician façade of calm. 'I can't see what we have in common.'

He shook his head, turning more fully. Lucy became intensely aware of the strength hidden behind that tailored suit as his shoulders blocked her view of the street.

A jitter of curious sensation sped down her backbone and curled deep within. It disturbed her.

'Then you have an enviably short memory, Ms Knight. Even you can't deny we're linked by a tie that binds us forever, however much I wish it otherwise.'

'But that's—'

'In the past?' His lip curled in a travesty of a smile. 'Yet it's a truth I live with every day.' His eyes glowed, luminous with emotions she'd once thought him too cold to feel. His voice deepened to a low, bone-melting hum. 'Nothing will ever take away the fact that you killed my brother.'

CHAPTER TWO

LUCY KNIGHT SHOOK her head emphatically and for one crazy moment Domenico found himself mourning the fact that her blonde tresses no longer swirled round her shoulders. Why had she cut her hair so brutally short?

After *five years* he remembered how that curtain of silk had enticed him!

Impossible. It *wasn't* disappointment he felt.

He'd spent long days in court focused on the woman who'd stolen Sandro's life. He'd smothered grief, the urgent need for revenge and bone-deep disappointment that he'd got her so wrong. Domenico had forced himself to observe her every fleeting expression, every nuance. He'd imprinted her image in his mind.

Learning his enemy.

It wasn't attraction he'd felt then for the gold-digger who'd sought to play both the Volpe brothers. It had been clear-headed acknowledgement of her beauty and calculation of whether her little girl lost impression might prejudice the prosecution case.

'No. I was *convicted* of killing him. There's a difference.'

Domenico stared into her blazing eyes, alight with a passion that arrested logic. Then her words sank in, exploding into his consciousness like a grenade. His belly tightened as outrage flared.

He should have expected it. Yet to hear her voice the lie strained even his steely control.

'You're still asserting your innocence?'

Her eyes narrowed and her mouth tightened. Was she going to blast him with a volley of abuse as she had Rocco?

'Why wouldn't I? It's the truth.'

She held his gaze with a blatant challenge that made his hackles rise.

How dare she sit in the comfort of *his* car, talking about *his* brother's death, and deny all the evidence against her? Deny the testimony of Sandro's family and staff and the fair judgement of the court?

Bile surged in Domenico's throat. The gall of this woman!

'So you keep up the pretence. Why bother lying now?' His words rang with the condemnation he could no longer hide.

Meeting her outraged his sense of justice and sliced across his own inclinations. Only family duty compelled him to be here, conversing with his brother's killer. It revolted every one of his senses.

'This is no pretence, Signor Volpe. It's the truth.'

She leaned closer and he caught the scent of soap and warm female skin. His nostrils quivered, cataloguing a perfume that was more viscerally seductive than the lush designer scents of the women in his world.

'I did not kill your brother.'

She was some actress. Not even by a flicker did she betray her show of innocence.

That, above all, ignited his wrath. That she should continue this charade even now. Her dishonesty must run bone deep.

Or was she scared if she confessed he'd take justice into his own hands?

Domenico imagined his hands closing around that slim, pale throat, forcing her proud head back…but no. Rough justice held no appeal.

He wouldn't break the Volpe code of honour, even when provoked by this shameless liar.

'Now who's playing semantics? Sandro was off balance

when you shoved him against the fireplace.' The words bit out from between clamped teeth. 'The knock to his head as he fell killed him.' Domenico drew in a slow breath, clawing back control. The men of his family did not give in to emotion. It was unthinkable he'd reveal to this woman the grief still haunting him.

'You were responsible. If he'd never met you he'd be alive today.'

Her face tightened and she swallowed. Remarkably he saw a flicker of something that might have been pain in her eyes.

Guilt? Regret for what she'd done?

An instant later that hint of vulnerability vanished.

Had he imagined it? Had his imagination supplied what he'd waited so long to see? Remorse over Sandro's death?

He catalogued the woman beside him. Rigid back, angled chin, hands folded neatly yet gripping too hard. Her eyes were different, he realised. After that first shocked expression of horror, now they were guarded.

The difference from the supposed innocent he'd met all those years ago was astounding. She'd certainly given up playing the ingénue.

She looked brittle. He sensed she directed all her energy into projecting that façade of calm.

Domenico knew it was a façade. Years of experience in the cutthroat world of business had made him an expert in body language. There was no mistaking the tension drawing her muscles tight or the short, choppy breaths she couldn't quite hide.

How much would it take to smash through to the real Lucy Knight? What would it take to make her crack?

'If you admitted the truth you'd find the future easier.'

'Why?' She tilted her head like a bright-eyed bird. 'Because confession is good for the soul?'

'So the experts say.'

He shifted into a more comfortable position as he awaited

her response. Not by a flicker did he reveal how important
this was to him.

Why, he didn't know. She'd already been proven guilty in
a fair trial. Her guilt had been proclaimed to the world. But
seeing her so defiant, Domenico faced an unpalatable truth.
He realised with a certainty that ran deep as the blood he'd
shared with his brother that this would never be over till Lucy
Knight confessed.

Closure, truth, satisfaction, call it what you would. Only
she could lay this to rest.

He hated her for the power that gave her.

'You think I'll be swayed by your attempts at psychology?'
Her mouth curled in a hard little smile he'd never seen in all
those weeks of the trial. 'You'll have to do better than that, Signor Volpe. If the experts couldn't extract a confession, you
really think you will?'

'Experts?'

'Of course. You didn't think I was living in splendid isolation all this time, did you?' Her words sounded bitter but
her expression remained unchanged. 'There's a whole indus-
try around rehabilitating offenders. Didn't you know? Social
workers, psychologists, psychiatrists.' She turned and looked
out of the window, her profile serene.

Domenico fought the impulse to shake the truth from her.

'Did you know they assessed me to find out if I was insane?'
She swung her head back around. Her face was blank but for
the searing fire in her eyes. 'In case I wasn't fit to stand trial.'
She paused. 'I suppose I was lucky. I can't recommend jail as
a positive experience but I suspect an asylum for the crimi-
nally insane is worse. Just.'

Something passed between them. Some awareness, some
connection, like a vibration in the taut air. Something that
for a moment drew them together. It left Domenico unsettled.

Any connection with Lucy Knight was a betrayal of Sandro.
Anger snarled in his veins. 'You're alive to complain about

your treatment. You didn't give my brother that option, did you? What you did was irrevocable.'

'And unpardonable. Is that why you spirited me away from the press? So you can berate me in private?'

She lounged back in her corner and made a production of crossing her legs as if to reinforce her total lack of concern. Even in her drab navy skirt and jacket there was no hiding the fact she had stunning legs. He was honest enough to admit it was one of the things that had drawn him the day they met. That and her shy smile. No wonder she'd always worn a skirt in court, trying to attract the male sympathy vote.

It hadn't worked then and it didn't work now.

'What a ripe imagination you have.' He let his teeth show in his slow smile and had the satisfaction of seeing her stiffen. 'I have better things to do with my time than talk with you.'

'In that case, you won't mind if I enjoy the view.' She turned to survey the street with an intense concentration he knew must be feigned.

Until he realised she hadn't seen anything like it for five years.

It was even harder than she'd expected being near Domenico Volpe. Sharing the same space. Talking with him.

A lifetime ago they'd shared a magical day, perfect in every way. By the time they'd parted with a promise to meet again she'd drifted on a cloud of delicious anticipation. He'd made her feel alive for the first time.

In a mere ten hours she'd fallen a little in love with her debonair stranger.

How *young* she'd been. Not just in years but experience. Looking back it was almost inconceivable she'd ever been that naïve.

When she'd seen him again it had been at her trial. Her heart had leapt, knowing he was there for her as she stood alone, battered by a world turned into nightmare. She'd waited day after day for him to break his silence, approach and offer a crumb of comfort. To look at her with warmth in his eyes again.

Instead he'd been a frowning dark angel come to exact retribution. He'd looked at her with eyes like winter, chilling her to the bone and shrivelling her dreams.

A shudder snaked through her but she repressed it. She was wrung out after facing the paparazzi and *him*, but refused to betray the fact that he got to her.

She should demand to know where they were headed, but facing him took all her energy.

Even his voice, low and liquid like rich dark chocolate laced with honey, affected her in ways she'd tried to suppress. It made her aware she was a healthy young woman programmed to respond to an attractive man. Despite his cold fury he made her aware of his masculinity.

Was it the vibration of his deep voice along her bones? His powerful male body? Or the supremely confident way he'd faced down the press as if he didn't give a damn what they printed? As if challenging them to take him on? All were too sexy for her peace of mind.

The way he looked at her disturbed, his scrutiny so intense it seemed he searched to find the real Lucy Knight. The one she'd finally learned to hide.

Lucy stifled a laugh. She'd been in prison too long. Maybe what she needed wasn't peace and quiet but a quick affair with an attractive stranger to get her rioting hormones under control.

The stranger filling her mind was Domenico Volpe.

No! That was wrong on so many levels her brain atrophied before she could go further.

She made herself concentrate on the street. No matter what pride said, it was a relief to be in the limo, whisked from the press in comfort.

Yet there'd be a reckoning. She'd given up believing in the milk of human kindness. There was a reason Domenico Volpe had taken her side. Something he wanted.

A confession?

Lucy pressed her lips together. He'd have a long wait. She'd never been a liar.

She was so wrapped in memories it took a while to realise the streets looked familiar. They drove through a part of Rome she knew.

Lucy straightened, tension trickling in a rivulet of ice water down her spine as she recognised landmarks. The shop where she'd found trinkets to send home to her dad and Sylvia, and especially the kids. The café that sold mouth-watering pastries to go with rich, aromatic coffee. The park where she'd taken little Taddeo under Bruno's watchful eye.

The trickle became a tide of foreboding as the limousine turned into an all too familiar street.

She swung around. Domenico Volpe watched her beneath lowered lids, his expression speculative.

'You can't be serious!' Her voice was a harsh scrape of sound.

'You wanted somewhere free from the press. They won't bother you here.'

'What do you call that?' The pavement before the Palazzo Volpe teemed with reporters. Beyond them the building rose, splendid and imposing, a monument to extreme wealth and powerful bloodlines. A reminder of the disastrous past.

Lucy's heart plunged. She never wanted to see the place again.

Was that his game? Retribution? Or did he think returning her to the scene of the crime would force a confession?

Nausea swirled as she watched the massive palazzo grow closer. Horror drenched her, leaving her skin clammy as perspiration broke out beneath the cloth of her suit.

'Stop the car!'

'Why? I wouldn't have thought you squeamish.' His eyes were glacial again.

She opened her mouth to argue, then realised there was

no point. She'd been weak to go with him and she had to face the consequences. Hadn't she known he'd demand payment for his help?

Lucy lifted one shoulder in a shrug that cost her every ounce of energy. 'I thought you wouldn't like the press to know we were together. But on your head be it. I've got nothing more to lose.'

'Haven't you?' His tone told her he'd make it his business to find her soft spot and exploit it.

Let him try. He had no notion how a few years in jail toughened a girl.

He fixed his gaze on her, not turning away as the vehicle slowed to enter a well-guarded entrance. The crowd was held back by stony-faced security men. Anxiously Lucy scanned them but couldn't recognise any familiar faces.

Surreptitiously she let out a breath of relief.

Then the car slipped down a ramp. They entered a vast underground car park. A fleet of vehicles, polished to perfection, filled it. She saw limousines, a four wheel drive, a sleek motorbike and a couple of sports cars including a vintage one her dad would have given his eye teeth to drive.

Out of nowhere grief slammed into her. She'd missed him so long she'd finally learned to repress the waves of loss. But she hadn't been prepared for this.

Not now. Not here. Not in front of the man who saw himself as her enemy.

Maybe grief hit harder because it was her first day of freedom. The day, by rights, when she should be in her dad's reassuring embrace. But all that was gone. Lucy swallowed the knot of emotion clogging her throat, forcing herself to stare, dry-eyed, around the cavernous space.

'How did you get permission to excavate?' She was relieved her voice worked. 'I thought this part of the city was built on the ancient capital.'

'You didn't know about the basement car park?' His voice was sceptical.

Finally, when she knew her face was blank of emotion, Lucy met his stare. 'I was just the au pair, remember? Not the full-time nanny. I didn't go out with the family. Besides, Taddeo was so little and your sister-in-law—' she paused, seeing Domenico's gaze sharpen '—she didn't want him out and about. It was a struggle to get permission to take him to the park for air.'

Gun-metal grey eyes met hers and again she felt that curious beat of awareness between them. As if he knew and understood. But that was impossible. Domenico Volpe hated her, believed she'd killed his brother. Nothing would change his mind.

'The car park was necessary for our privacy.' His shoulders lifted in a shrug that indicated whatever the Volpe family needed the world would provide. *Naturally.* 'There was an archaeological survey but fortunately it didn't find anything precious.'

Lucy bit back a retort. It wouldn't matter how precious the remains. The Volpes would have got what they wanted. They always did. They'd wanted her convicted and they'd got their way.

The car slid to a halt and her door opened.

Lucy surveyed the big man holding it. Her heart gave a flip of relief as she saw it was the guy who'd tried to strong-arm her into the car earlier. Not a spectre from the past. But embarrassment warred with relief as she recalled how she'd abused him.

'Thank you.' She slid awkwardly from the seat, not used to a skirt after years in regulation issue trousers.

Silently he inclined his head.

Damp palms swiping down her skirt, Lucy located the rest of the security staff. Her heart clenched as she thought she saw a familiar figure in the dim light but when he moved Lucy realised it was another stranger. Her breathing eased.

'This way, *signorina*.' The bodyguard ushered her towards a lift.

Minutes later she found herself in a part of the palazzo she'd never visited. But its grand dimensions, its exquisitely intricate marble flooring and air of otherworld luxury were instantly familiar.

Her skin prickled as she inhaled that almost forgotten scent. Of furniture polish, hothouse flowers and, she'd once joked, money. Memories washed over her, of those first exciting days in a new country, of her awe at her surroundings, of that last night—

'Ms Knight?' *Lucy*, he'd called her once. For a few bright, brief hours. Instantly Domenico slammed the memory of that folly into an iron vault of memory.

She spun around and he saw huge, haunted eyes. Her face had paled and her fine features were pinched.

The mask slipped at last.

He should feel satisfaction at her unease in his family home. But it wasn't pleasure he experienced. He had no name for this hyper-awareness, this knife-edge between antipathy and absorption.

Sensation feathered through him, like the tickle of his conscience, teasing him for bringing her here.

Lucy Knight had fascinated him all those years ago. To his chagrin he realised she still did. More than was desirable. It was one thing to know your enemy. Another to respond to her fear with what felt too much like sympathy.

As he watched the moment of vulnerability was gone. Her face smoothed out and her pale eyebrows arched high as if waiting for him to continue.

'This way.' He gestured for her to accompany him, conscious of her beside him as they headed to his side of the palazzo. She was a head shorter but kept pace easily, not hesitating for a moment.

He had to hand it to her; she projected an air of assurance many of his business associates would envy. Twice now he'd seen behind the façade of calm but both times it had been a quick glimpse and the circumstances had been enough to discomfit anyone.

In his study he gestured for her to take a seat. Instead she prowled the room, inspecting the bookcases, the view from the window and, he was sure, scoping out a possible escape route. There was none.

Instead of taking one of the sofas near the fireplace as he'd intended, Domenico settled behind his desk.

'Why have you brought me here?'

She stood directly before the desk, feet planted as if to ground herself ready for attack.

'To talk.'

'Talk?' The word shot out. 'You had your chance to talk five years ago. As I recall, you weren't interested in renewing our acquaintance.' Her tone was bitter and her eyes glittered with fury.

The difference between this Amazon and the girl he'd briefly known struck him anew.

'And to separate you and the press.'

'No altruistic rescue then.' She gave no indication of disappointment, merely met his gaze in frank appraisal.

'Did you expect one?'

'No.' She answered before he'd finished speaking.

Why did her readiness to distrust rankle? He hadn't expected doe-eyed innocence. The scales had been ripped from his eyes long ago.

'Feel free to sit.'

'No.' She paused. 'Thank you. I prefer to stand.' She swallowed hard.

Thanking him must almost have choked her.

As having her in his home revolted every sensibility. Was

Sandro turning in his grave? No. Sandro would have approved of his actions.

'For how long?' She watched him closely.

'As long as it takes.'

She frowned. 'As long as what takes?'

Domenico leaned back in his chair. He sensed it was too early to reveal his full intent. Better proceed slowly than rush and have her refuse out of hand.

'For the press to lose interest in this story.'

'There *is* no story. It happened so long ago.'

Domenico's belly clenched. 'You think what happened means nothing now? That it's all over?'

Her head shot up. 'It *is* over. I've served the sentence for manslaughter and now I'm free. If there was anything I could do to bring your brother back I would.' She heaved a deep breath that strained her breasts against the dark fabric. 'But there's not.'

'You cut off my brother's life in his prime.' Anger vibrated in his words and he strove to modulate his voice. 'You made my sister-in-law a widow before her time. She was barely a wife, still struggling to adapt to motherhood, and suddenly she was alone.'

Sky blue eyes met his unflinchingly.

Did none of it matter to her?

'Because of you my nephew will never know his father.' The words grated from a throat scraped raw with anger. 'You denied them both that. You left a gaping hole in his life.'

As she'd ripped a hole in Domenico's life. Even now he found it hard to believe Sandro was gone. The older brother who'd been his friend, his pillar of strength when their parents had died and Domenico was still a kid. His mentor, who'd applauded his tenacity when he'd branched out as an entrepreneur, building rather than relying on the family fortune and traditions.

He wanted her to know the pain she'd caused. To *feel* it. The civilised man he was knew she'd paid the price society saw fit for her crime. The wounded, grief-stricken one wanted more. Remorse. Guilt. A confession. *Something*.

'You can't control the press.' She spoke as if nothing he'd said mattered, brushing aside so much pain.

For a full thirty seconds Domenico stared at the woman who'd destroyed so much, yet felt so little. He couldn't understand how anyone could be so devoid of compassion. He wished he'd never sullied himself by helping her, even if it wasn't for her benefit.

But he refused to let Sandro's family suffer any more because of Lucy Knight.

'I can starve them of fresh news.'

'But there *is* no news.'

'You're out of jail. The murderess set free.'

Her chin jutted. 'The charge was manslaughter.'

Domenico bit down the need to tell her legalistic quibbling didn't change the fact of Sandro's death. Instead he reached for the glossy pages on his desk.

'There's still a story. Especially after this.'

'What is it?' She stepped forward, her expression closed, but he read the rigidity of her slim frame, as if she prepared for the worst.

For a second Domenico hesitated. Why, he didn't know. Then he tossed the magazine across the gleaming surface of the desk.

She tilted her head to read it where it lay, as if not wanting to touch it. He couldn't blame her. It was the sort of trash he avoided, but Pia, his sister-in-law, was obviously a fan. She'd brought it to his attention, hysterical that the sordid tragedy was being resurrected.

Eventually Lucy Knight reached out and flipped the page with one finger. The story spread across both pages. Her likeness featured beside the text. Another picture of her and an older man, her father. Then more of a rather hollow-eyed woman and a gaggle of children.

He watched Lucy Knight's eyes widen, heard her breath hitch, then a hiss of shock. She'd turned the colour of ash. Even her lips paled. Rapidly she blinked and he could have sworn tears welled in those remarkable eyes.

Then, with a suddenness that caught him off guard, the woman he'd thought as unfeeling as an automaton swayed off balance and he realised she was going to faint.

CHAPTER THREE

LUCY STARED AS the text blurred and dipped. She blinked, torn between gratitude that she couldn't make out all the snide character assassination and desperation to know the worst.

She thought she'd experienced the worst in prison. With the loss of her father, her friends, freedom, innocence and self-esteem.

She'd been wrong.

This was the final betrayal.

She struggled to draw breath. It was as if a boulder squashed her lungs. She slammed a hand on the satiny wood of the desk, her damp palm slipping as she fought to steady herself.

Darkness rimmed her vision and the world revolved, churning sickeningly like a merry-go-round spinning off kilter.

There was a pounding in her ears and a gaping hole where her heart had been.

Hard fingers closed around her upper arm.

It was enough to drag her back to her surroundings. She yanked her arm but the grip tightened. She felt him beside her, imprisoning her against the desk.

From somewhere deep inside fury welled, a volcanic force that for a glorious moment obliterated the pain shredding her vitals.

Driven by unstoppable instinct Lucy pivoted, raised her hand and chopped down on the inner elbow of the arm that captured her. At the same time she jabbed her knee high in his groin. Her hand connected with a force that almost matched the strength in that muscled arm. But her knee struck only solid thigh as he sensed her attack and shifted.

Yet it worked. She was free. She stood facing him, panting from adrenalin and overflowing emotions.

Gimlet eyes stared down at her. Glittering eyes that bored deep into her soul, as if he could strip away the self-protective layers she'd built so painstakingly around herself and discover the woman no one else knew.

Her chest rose and fell as she struggled for air. Her pulse thundered. Her skin sizzled with the effervescence in her bloodstream.

The muzzy giddiness disappeared as she stared back at the face of the man who'd stripped away her last hope and destroyed what was left of her joy at being free.

Far from fainting, she felt painfully alive. It was as if layers of skin had been scored away, exposing nerve endings that throbbed from contact with the very air in this cloistered mansion.

'Don't touch me!'

Instead of backing off from her snarling tone he merely narrowed his eyes.

'You were going to faint.' The rumble of his voice stirred an echo inside her.

'I've never fainted in my life.' She shoved aside the knowledge that he was right. Until the shock of his touch she'd been about to topple onto his pristine parquet floor.

'You needed support.' His words betrayed no outrage at her attack. It was as if he, like she, was no longer bothered by social niceties. As if he understood the primitive intensity of her feelings.

That disturbed her. She didn't want him understanding anything about her. She didn't like the sense that Domenico Volpe had burrowed under her skin and was privy to her innermost demons.

Something shifted in his gaze. There was a subtle difference in those deep-set eyes that now shone silver. Something in the line of his lips. Her eyes lingered there, tracing the shape of a mouth which now, relaxed, seemed designed solely for sensual pleasure.

A gossamer thread of heat spun from her breasts to her pelvis, drawing tight—a heat she'd felt only once before.

Had his expression changed, grown warm? Or had something inside her shifted?

Lucy bit her lip then regretted the movement as his gaze zeroed in on her mouth. Her lips tingled as if he'd reached out and grazed them with a questing finger.

A shiver of luxurious pleasure ripped through her. Fire ignited deep within, so hot it felt as if she were melting. Her pulse slowed to a ponderous beat then revved out of control.

She'd known Domenico Volpe was dangerous. But she hadn't known the half of it.

She swallowed hard and found her voice, trying to ignore her body's flagrant response.

'You can move back now. I can stand.'

He took his time moving. 'Yet sitting is so much more comfortable, don't you think?'

He said no more but that one raised eyebrow told her he saw what she'd rather not reveal. That her surge of energy was short-lived. Lucy felt a dragging at her limbs. Her knees were jelly and the thought of confronting him here, now, was almost too much to bear.

Had he guessed her visceral response to his flagrant masculinity? That would be the final straw.

She grabbed the magazine, crushing its pages.

'Thank you. I will take that seat now.'

He nodded and gestured to a long sofa. Instead she took the black leather swivel chair that looked like something from an exclusive design catalogue, a far cry from the sparse utilitarian furniture she'd grown used to. It was wickedly comfortable and her bones melted as she sank into it. It was massive, built to order, she guessed, for the man who took a seat across from her. Lucy tried to look unfazed by such luxury.

'You didn't know about the article?'

Lucy refused to look away from his keen gaze. Confrontation was preferable to running. She'd learned that in a hard school. But looking him in the eye was difficult when her body hummed with the aftermath of what she could only describe as an explosion of sexual awareness.

'No.' She glanced down at the trashy gossip mag and repressed a shiver. It was like holding a venomous snake in her palm. 'I had no idea.'

'Would you like something? Brandy? A pot of tea?'

Startled by his concern, she turned to find Domenico Volpe looking almost as surprised as she was, as if the offer had slipped out without volition.

It was no comfort to know she must look as bad as she felt for him to offer sustenance.

'No. Thank you.' Accepting anything from him went against every instinct.

Already he moved towards the desk. Obviously it didn't matter what she wanted. 'I'll order coffee.'

Lucy's gaze dropped to the magazine. How could Sylvia have done this? Did she despise Lucy so much?

Silently her heart keened. Sylvia and the kids had been Lucy's last bright hope of returning to some remnant of her old life. Of having family again. Of belonging.

Quotes from the article floated through her troubled mind. Of her stepmother saying Lucy had 'always been *different*', 'withdrawn and moody' but 'hankering after the bright lights and excitement'. That she put her own needs first rather than those of her family. There was nothing in the article about Sylvia's resentment of her husband's almost grown daughter, or the fact that Lucy had spent years as unpaid nurserymaid for Sylvia's four children by a previous marriage. Or that Sylvia's idea of bright lights was a Saturday night in Torquay and a takeaway meal.

Nothing about the fact that Lucy had left home only when her dad, in his quiet way, had urged her to experience more of the world rather than put her life on hold to look after the younger children.

She'd experienced the world all right, but not in the way he'd had in mind.

As for the article, taken from a recent interview with Sylvia, it was a lurid exposé that painted Lucy as an uncaring, amoral gold-digger. It backed up every smear and innuendo that had been aired in the courtroom. Worse, it proved even her family had turned against her.

What would her stepsiblings think now they were old enough to read such malicious gossip?

Lucy's heart withered and she pressed a hand to her throat, trying to repress rising nausea. Sylvia and she had never been close but Lucy had never thought her stepmother would betray her like this. The article's spitefulness stole her breath.

Until now she'd believed there was someone believing in her. First her father and, after he died, Sylvia.

She felt bereft, grieving all over again for her dad who'd been steadfastly behind her. Never having known her long-dead mother, Lucy's bond with her father had been special. His faith and love had kept her strong through the trial.

Lucy had never been so alone. Not even that first night in custody. Even after the conviction when she knew she had years of imprisonment ahead. Nor facing down the taunts and jeers as she'd learned to handle the threats from prisoners who'd tried to make her life hell.

The magazine was a rag but an upmarket one. Sylvia had sold her out for what must be a hefty fee.

Lucy blinked stinging eyes as she stared at the vile publication in her lap.

She thought she'd known degradation and despair. But it was only now that her life hit rock bottom.

And Domenico Volpe was here to see it.

She shivered, chilled to the marrow. How he must be gloating.

'The coffee will be here soon.'

Lucy looked up to find him standing across from her, watchful. No doubt triumphing at the sight of her down and out. Framed by the massive antique fireplace and a solid wall of books, he looked the epitome of born and bred privilege. From his aristocratically handsome features to his hand stitched shoes he screamed power and perfection.

Once the sight of him had made her heart skip with pleasure. But she'd discovered the real Domenico Volpe when the chips were down. He'd sided with his own class, easily believing the most monstrous lies against her.

Slowly she stood, pride stiffening her weary legs and tilting her chin.

'It's time I left.'

Where she'd go she had no idea, but she had to escape.

She had just enough money to get her home to Devon. But now she had no home. Her breath hitched as she thought of Sylvia's betrayal. She wouldn't be welcome there.

Pain transfixed her.

'You can't leave.'

'I'm now officially a free woman, Signor Volpe, however much you resent it. If you try to keep my here by force it will be kidnap.'

Even so a shiver of apprehension skated down her spine. She wouldn't put anything past him. She'd seen his cadre of security men and she knew first hand what they were capable of.

'You mistake me for one of your recent associates, Ms Knight.' He snapped the words out as if he wanted to take a bite out of her. 'I've no intention of breaking the law.'

Before she could voice her indignation he continued. 'You need somewhere private; somewhere the press can't bother you.'

His words stilled her protest.

'And?'

'I can provide that place.'

And pigs might fly.

'Why would you do that?' She'd read his contempt. 'What do you get out of it?'

For the longest moment he stood silent. Only the hint of a scowl on his autocratic features hinted he wasn't used to being questioned. Tough.

'There are others involved,' he said finally. 'My brother's widow and little Taddeo. They're the ones affected the longer this is dragged through the press.'

Taddeo. Lucy had thought of him often. She'd loved the little baby in her care, enjoying his gurgles of delight at their peekaboo games and his wide-eyed fascination as she'd read him picture books. What was he like now?

One look at Domenico Volpe's closed face told her he'd rather walk barefoot over hot coals than talk about his nephew with her.

'So what's your solution?' She crossed her arms over her chest. 'Walling me up in the basement car park?'

'That could work.' He bared his teeth in a feral smile that drew her skin tight. 'But I prefer to work within the law.' He paused. 'I don't have your penchant for the dramatic. Instead I suggest providing you with a bolthole till this blows over. Your bag is already in your room.'

Her room.

Lucy groped for the back of the chair she'd just vacated, her hand curling like a claw into the plump, soft leather. She tried to speak but her voice had dried up.

Her room.

The memory of it had haunted her for years. Ever since arriving here she'd been cold to the core because she knew that room was upstairs, on the far side of the building.

'You can't expect me to stay there!' Her voice was hoarse with shock. 'Even *you* couldn't...' She shook her head as her larynx froze. 'That's beyond cruel. That's *sick*.'

His eyes widened and she saw understanding dawn. His nostrils flared and he stepped towards her, then pulled up abruptly.

'No.' The word slashed the clogged silence. 'That room hasn't been used since my brother died. There's another guest room at your disposal.'

Relief sucked her breath away and loosened her cramped muscles. Slowly she drew in oxygen, marshalling all her strength to regroup after that scare.

'I can't stay in this house.'

He met her gaze silently, not asking why. He knew. The memories were too overwhelming.

'I'll find my own place.'

'And how will you do that with the press on the doorstep?' He crossed his arms over his chest and leaned a shoulder against the fireplace, projecting an air of insouciance that made her want to slap him. 'Wherever you go they'll follow. You'll get no peace, no privacy.'

He was right, damn him. But to be dependent on him for anything stuck in her craw.

The door opened and a maid entered, bearing a tray of coffee and biscuits. The rich aroma, once her favourite, curdled Lucy's stomach. Instinctively she pressed a hand to her roiling abdomen and moved away. Vaguely she heard him thank the maid, but from her new vantage point near the window Lucy saw only the press pack outside. The blood leached from her cheeks.

Which was worse? Domenico Volpe or the paparazzi who'd hound her for some tawdry story they could sell?

'If you don't mind, I'll take you up on the offer of that room.

Just to freshen up.' She needed breathing space, time away from him, to work out what to do.

Lucy swung round to find him watching her. She should be used to it now. His scrutiny was continual. Yet reaction shivered through her. What did he see? How much of what she strove to hide?

She banished the question. She had better things to do than worry about that. Nothing would change Domenico Volpe's opinion. His reluctant gestures of solicitude were evidence of ingrained social skills, not genuine concern.

'Of course. Take as long as you like. Maria will show you up.'

Lucy assured herself it wasn't satisfaction she saw in that gleaming gaze.

'No! I said I can't talk. I'm busy.' Sylvia's voice rose and Lucy thought she discerned something like anxiety as well as anger in her stepmother's words. She gripped the phone tighter.

'I just wanted—'

'Well, I *don't* want. Just leave me alone! Haven't you done enough damage to this family?'

Lucy opened her mouth but the line went dead.

How long she sat listening to the dialling tone she didn't know. When she finally put the receiver down her fingers were cramped and her shoulders stiff from hunching, one arm wrapped protectively around her stomach.

So that was it. The severing of all ties.

A piercing wail of grief rose inside her but she stifled it. Lucy told herself it was better to face this now than on the rose-covered doorstep of the whitewashed cottage that had been home all her life.

Yet she couldn't quite believe it. She'd rung her stepmother hoping against hope there'd been some dreadful mistake. That perhaps the press had published a story with no basis. That

Sylvia hadn't betrayed her with that character assassination interview.

Forlorn hope! Sylvia wanted nothing to do with her.

Which left Lucy with nowhere to go. She had no one and nothing but a past that haunted her and even now wouldn't release its awful grip.

Slowly she lifted her head and stared at the panelled door separating the bedroom from the second-floor corridor.

It was time she laid the ghost of her past to rest.

She wasn't in the room he'd provided but she hadn't tried to leave. His security staff would have alerted him. There was only one place she could be, yet he hadn't thought she'd have the gall to go back there.

Domenico's stride lengthened as he paced the corridor towards the side of the palazzo that had housed Sandro's apartments. Fury spiked as he thought of Lucy Knight there, in the room where she'd taken Sandro's life. It was an intrusion that proved her contempt for all he and his family had lost. A trespass that made his blood boil and his body yearn for violence.

The door was open and he marched across the threshold, hands clenched in iron fists, muscles taut and fire in his belly.

Then he saw her and stopped dead.

He didn't know what he'd expected but it wasn't this. Lucy Knight was huddled on the floor before the ornate fireplace, palm pressed to the floorboards where Sandro had breathed his last. Domenico remembered it from the police markers on the floor and photos in court.

Her face was the colour of travertine marble, pale beyond belief. Her eyes were dark with pain as she stared fixedly before her. She was looking at something he couldn't see, something that shuttered her gaze and turned it inwards.

The hair prickled at his nape and he stepped further into the room.

She looked up and shock slammed him at the anguish he

saw in her face. Gone was the sassy, prickly woman who'd fought him off when he'd dared touch her.

The woman before him bore the scars of bone-deep pain. It was clear in every feature, so raw he almost turned away, as if seeing such emotion was a violation.

A shudder passed through him. Shock that instead of the anger he'd nursed as he strode through the house, it was something like pity that stirred.

'I'm sorry.' Her voice was a rasp of laboured air. 'It shouldn't have happened. I was so young and stupid.' Her voice faded as she looked down at the patina of old wood beneath her hands. 'I should never have let him in.'

Domenico crossed the room in a few quick strides and hunkered beside her, his heart thumping.

She admitted it?

It didn't seem possible after all this time.

'If I hadn't let him in, none of it would have happened.' She drew a breath that shook her frame. 'I've gone over it so often. If only I hadn't listened to him. If only I'd locked the door.'

Domenico frowned. 'You had no need to lock the door against my brother. I refuse to believe he would have forced himself on you.'

The idea went against everything he knew about Sandro. His brother had been a decent man. A little foolish in his choice of wife, but honourable. A loving brother and doting father. A man who'd made one mistake, led astray by a beautiful, scheming seductress, but *not* a man who took advantage of female servants.

That blonde head swung towards him and she blinked. 'I wasn't talking about your brother. I was talking about the bodyguard, Bruno.' Her voice slowed on the name as if her tongue thickened. Domenico heard what sounded like fear in her voice. 'I shouldn't have let Bruno in.'

Domenico shot to his feet. Disappointment was so strong he tasted it, a rusty tang, on his tongue.

'You still stick to that story?'

The bruised look in her eyes faded, replaced by familiar wariness. Her mouth tightened and for an instant Domenico felt a pang almost of loss as she donned her habitual air of challenge.

A moment later she was again that woman ready to defy the world with complete disdain. Even curled up at his feet she radiated a dignity and inner strength he couldn't deny.

How did she do it? And why did he let it get to him? She was a liar and a criminal, yet there was something about her that made him wish things were different.

There always had been. *That was the hell of it.*

His gut dived. Even to think it was a betrayal of Sandro.

'I don't tell stories, Signor Volpe.' She got to her feet in a supple movement that told him she hadn't spent the last years idle. 'Bruno killed your brother but—' she raised her hand when he went to speak '—don't worry, you won't hear it from me again. I'm tired of repeating myself to people who won't listen.'

She made to move past him but his hand shot out to encircle her upper arm. Instantly she tensed. Would she try to fight him off as she had downstairs? He almost wished she would. There'd be a primitive satisfaction in curbing her temper and stamping his control on that fiery, passionate nature she hid behind the untouchable façade.

Heat tingled through his fingers where he held her. He braced himself but she merely looked at him, eyebrows arching.

'You wanted something?' Acid dripped from her words.

Domenico's eyes dropped to her mouth, soft pink again now that colour had returned to her face. The blush pink of rose petals at dawn.

A pulse of something like need thudded through his chest. He told himself it was the urge to wring her pretty neck. Yet his mouth dried when he watched her lips part a fraction, as if she had trouble inhaling enough air. There was a buzzing in his ears.

Her eyes widened and Domenico realised he'd leaned closer. Too close. Abruptly he straightened, dropping her arm as if it burnt him.

'I want to know what you plan to do.'

He didn't have the right to demand it. Her glittering azure gaze told him that. But he didn't care. She wasn't the only one affected by this media frenzy. He had family to protect.

'I want to find somewhere private, away from the news hounds.'

He nodded. 'I can arrange that.'

'Not here!' The words shot out. A frisson shuddered through the air, a reminder of shadows from the past.

'No, not here.' He had estates in Italy as well as in California's Napa Valley and another outside London. Any of them would make a suitable safe house till this blew over.

'In that case, I accept your generous offer, Signor Volpe. I'll stay in your safe haven for a week or so, until this furore dies down.'

She must be more desperate than she appeared. She hadn't even asked where she'd be staying. Or with whom.

CHAPTER FOUR

LUCY WOKE TO silence.

Cocooned in a wide comfortable bed with crisp cotton sheets and the fluffiest of down pillows, she lay, breathing in the sense of peace.

She felt…safe.

The realisation sideswiped her.

Who'd have thought she'd owe Domenico Volpe such a debt? A solid night's sleep, undisturbed till late morning judging by the sunlight rimming the curtains. She couldn't remember the last time she'd slept so long or so soundly.

Lucy flung back the covers, eager to see where she was. Last night she'd left from the helipad on the roof of the palazzo and headed into darkness. Domenico Volpe had said merely she'd go to one of his estates, somewhere she could be safe from press intrusion.

After yesterday's traumas that had been good enough for her. She desperately needed time to lick her wounds and decide what to do. With no friends, no job and very little money the outlook was grim.

Till she pulled back the curtains and gasped. Strong sunlight made her blink as she took in a vista of wide sky, sea and a white sand beach below a manicured garden.

It was paradise. The garden had an emerald lawn, shade trees and sculpted hedges. Pots of pelargoniums and other

plants she couldn't identify spilled a profusion of flowers in a
riot of colours, vivid against the indigo sea.

Unlatching the sliding glass door, Lucy stepped onto a balcony. Warmth enveloped her and the scent of growing things.
Birds sang and she heard, like the soft breath of a sleeping
giant, the gentle shush of waves. Dazzled, she stared, trying
to absorb it all. But her senses were overloaded. Tranquillity
and beauty surrounded her and absurdly she felt the pinprick
of hot tears.

She'd dreamed of freedom but had never imagined a place
like this. Her hands clenched on the railing. It was almost too
much to take in. Too much change from the grey, authoritar-
ian world she'd known.

A moment later she'd scooped up a cotton robe and dragged
it on over her shabby nightgown. She cinched the tie at her
waist as she pattered down the spiral staircase from her balcony.

Reflected light caught her eye and she spied a huge infin-
ity pool that seemed to merge with the sea beyond. Turf cushioned her bare feet as she made for the balustrade overlooking
the sea. Yet she stopped time and again, admiring an arbour
draped with scented flowers, a pool that reflected the sprawling villa, unexpected groves and modern sculptures.

'Who are you? I'm Chiara and I'm six.' The girl's Italian
had a slight lisp.

Lucy turned to meet inquisitive dark eyes and a sunny smile.
Automatically her lips curved in response to the girl's gap-
toothed grin, stretching facial muscles Lucy hadn't used in
what seemed a lifetime.

'I'm Lucy and I'm twenty-four.'

'That's so old.' The little girl paused, looking up from her
hidey-hole behind a couple of palm trees. 'Don't you wish you
were six too?'

Unfamiliar warmth spread through Lucy. 'Today I do.' How

wonderful to enjoy all this without a care for the future that loomed so empty.

It had been years since she'd seen a child, much less talked with one. Looking into that dimpled face, alight with curiosity, she realised how much she'd missed. If things had been different she'd have spent her life working with children. Once she had the money behind her to study, she'd intended to train as a teacher.

But her criminal record made that impossible.

'Will you play with me?'

Lucy stiffened. Who would want her daughter playing with an ex-con? A woman with her record?

'You'd better talk to your mummy first. You shouldn't play with strangers, you know.'

The little girl's eyes widened. 'But you're not a stranger. You're a friend of Domi's, aren't you?'

'Domi?' Lucy frowned. 'I don't know—'

'This is his house.' Chiara spread her hands wide. 'The house and garden. The whole island.'

'I see. But I still can't play with you unless your mummy says it's all right.'

'Uncle Rocco!' The little girl spoke to someone behind Lucy. 'Can I play with Lucy? She says I can't unless Mummy says so but Mummy's away.'

Lucy spun round to see the stolid face of the big security guard she'd lambasted outside the prison. Did it have to be him of all people? Heat flushed her skin but she held his gaze till he turned to the little girl, his features softening.

'That's for Nonna to decide. But it can't be today. Signorina Knight just arrived. You can't bother her with your chatter.' He took the child by the hand and, with a nod at Lucy, led her to the villa.

Lucy turned towards the sea. Still beautiful, it had lost some of its sparkle.

At least Rocco hadn't betrayed his horror at finding his

niece with a violent criminal. But he'd hurried to remove her from Lucy's tainted presence.

Pain jagged her chest, robbing her of air. Predictable as his reaction was, she couldn't watch them leave. Her chest clamped around her bruised heart and she sagged against the stone balustrade.

Lucy had toughened up years ago. The naïve innocent was gone, replaced by a woman who viewed the world with cynicism and distrust. A woman who didn't let the world or life get to her any more.

Yet the last twenty-four hours had been a revelation.

She'd confronted the paparazzi, then Domenico Volpe, learnt of Sylvia's betrayal and faced the place where her life had changed irrevocably. Now she confronted a man's instinct to protect his niece, from *her*.

All tore at her precious self-possession. It had taken heartache, determination and hard-won strength to build the barriers that protected her. She'd been determined never to experience again those depths of terror and pain of her first years in prison. Until now those barriers had kept her strong and safe.

Who'd have thought she still had the capacity to hurt so much?

She leant on the railing, eyes fixed on the south Italian mainland in the distance.

Domenico took in her slumped shoulders and the curve of her arms around her body, hugging out a hostile world.

It reminded him of the anguish he thought he'd spied yesterday in her old room at the palazzo. She'd hunched like a wounded animal over the spot Sandro had died. The sight had poleaxed him, playing on protective instincts he'd never expected to feel around her.

Almost, he'd been convinced by that look of blind pain in her unfocused eyes. But she'd soon disabused him. It had been an act, shrewd and deliberate, to con him into believing her story of innocence.

Innocent? The woman who'd seduced his brother then killed him?

He'd once fancied he felt a connection with the girl who'd burst like pure sunshine into his world. But before he could fall completely under her spell tragedy and harsh truth had intervened, revealing her true colours.

A breeze flirted with her wrap, shifting it against the curve of her hip and bottom.

She didn't look innocent.

He remembered her trial. The evidence of Sandro's Head of Security and of Pia, Sandro's widow, that Lucy Knight had deliberately played up to Sandro, flirting and ultimately seducing him.

When it became clear her relationship with Sandro was core to the case against her, Lucy Knight had offered to have a medical test proving her virginity.

You could have heard a pin drop in the courtroom as all eyes fixed on her nubile body and wide, seemingly innocent eyes. Every man in that room had wondered about the possibility of being her first. *Even Domenico.*

The prosecution had successfully argued it was her intentions that mattered, not whether the affair had yet been consummated. In the end a medical test was deemed immaterial but for a while she'd cleverly won sympathy, despite the rest of the evidence.

Having seen her in action, Domenico had no doubt she knew exactly how to seduce even the most cautious man.

He traced the shapely line of her legs down to her bare feet and something thudded in his chest. Was the rest of her bare beneath that wrap?

His body tightened from chest to groin as adrenalin surged. His pulse thudded. Physical awareness saturated him and he cursed under his breath.

Hunger for Lucy Knight was *not* to be contemplated.

Yet the hectic drumming in his blood didn't abate.

As if sensing him, she turned her head. 'You! What are you doing here?' She spun to face him, legs planted wide and hands clenched at her sides, a model of aggressive challenge.

Except for the robe's gaping neckline and the flutter of cotton around bare thighs that highlighted her femininity.

Domenico reminded himself he liked his women accommodating. Soft and pliant. Warrior queens with lofty chins and defiance in every sinew held no appeal.

Till now.

His body's wayward response angered him and guilt pricked. This woman had destroyed Sandro.

'This is my property. Or had you forgotten?'

'You implied I'd be here alone.'

'Did I? Are you sure?' Of course she wasn't. He'd chosen his words carefully. Even to his enemies, Domenico didn't lie. Seeing her skittishness, he'd deliberately neglected to mention he'd arrive here today. 'I fail to see what my travel plans have to do with you.'

He waited for her to splutter her indignation. But she merely surveyed him through slitted eyes. He sensed she drew her defences tight, preparing for battle.

Was she like this with everyone or just him?

'You came to make sure I don't steal the silver.' The sarcastic jibe almost hid her curiously flat tone. Yet he heard that hint of suppressed emotion, as if she was genuinely disappointed.

As if what he thought mattered.

Domenico frowned, instinct and intellect warring. He *knew* what she was, yet when he looked at her he *felt*…

Abruptly she pulled her robe in tight, as if only now realising the loose front revealed the shadow of her cleavage. Methodically she knotted the belt, all the while holding his gaze. Why did it feel as if she were putting on armour, rather than merely covering herself?

Did she know, with the light behind her, the wrap revealed rather than concealed her curves? Was it a deliberate ploy to distract him?

His voice was harsh. 'I leave it to my security staff to watch for thieves.'

Did she flinch? He remembered her rosy flush in court when evidence had been presented about the jewellery she'd either been given or had stolen from Sandro.

No sign of a blush now.

'What do you want?' Her insolence made his hackles rise.

It was on the tip of his tongue to deny he wanted anything, but pragmatism beat pride. He was here for one reason only and the sooner he fixed it the sooner he could put Lucy Knight firmly in the past.

'I do have some business to discuss with you but—'

'Ha! I knew it!' She folded her arms and Domenico had to force his gaze above the plump swell of her breasts, accentuated by the gesture.

'Knew what?' To his chagrin he'd missed something. He who never missed a nuance of any business negotiation.

'That it was too good to be true.' Her lip curled. 'No one gives anything for nothing. Especially you.' Her gaze flicked him from head to toe as if she read his body's charged response to her. His skin drew tight. Fury spilled and pooled. At her dismissive tone. At himself for the spark of arousal he couldn't douse.

'You're here, aren't you? Safe from the media?'

'But at what price?' She stepped close, eyes flaring wide as if she felt it too, the simmer of charged awareness, palpable as a caress against overheated flesh. 'There are strings attached to this deal, aren't there? A price I have to pay?'

Domenico looked down his nose with all the hauteur six centuries of aristocratic breeding could provide. No one doubted his honour. Ever.

'I'm a man of my word.' He let that sink in. 'I offered you sanctuary and you have it. There are no strings.'

Yet if she hadn't been so stressed yesterday she'd have made sure of that before agreeing to his offer.

Domenico muffled a sliver of guilt that he'd taken advantage of her vulnerability. The stakes were too high, the trouble she could cause too severe for him to have second thoughts.

Her perfectly arched eyebrows rose. 'I'm free to leave?'

Domenico stepped back and gestured to the boats moored in the bay. 'I will even provide the transport.'

He wished she'd take him up on the offer. Yes, he wanted more from her but instinct warned him to be rid of her. He didn't relish the discordant tumble of his reactions to her. There was nothing logical or ordered about them. She made him feel…things he thought long dead.

Her eyes bored into his, as if she sought the very heart of him. 'But you want me out of the limelight.'

'Of course.' He shrugged. 'But I'm not keeping you prisoner. There are laws in this country.'

Her breath hissed and she stiffened, reading his implication. That one of them at least was honest and law-abiding.

Her mouth tightened but otherwise her face was blank. So much for vulnerability. Lucy Knight was as tough as nails.

'If you're staying…' He looked at her expectantly but she said nothing. 'We can discuss business when you're dressed.' He glanced at his watch. Eleven o'clock. 'Shall we say midday?'

'Why delay? I'd rather know what you want now.'

She spoke as if he hid something painful from her. He almost laughed at the idea. Once he made his offer she'd be eager enough.

'You're hardly dressed for business.'

She stuck her hands on her hips, her pose challenging and provocative. 'You'd be more comfortable if I wore a suit? Why can't you tell me now?' Again those delicate eyebrows rose, as if she silently laughed at him.

Something snapped inside.

He stalked across till he stood close enough to inhale the scent of soap and fragrant female flesh. Close enough to hook an arm round her and haul her flush against him if he chose. Instead he kept his hands clenched at his sides.

She refused to shift. Even though she had to tip her head back to look at him, exposing her slim throat. Heat twisted in his belly, part unwilling admiration at her nerve, part implacable fury.

His gaze held hers as his pulse thumped once, twice, three times. The artery at her throat flickered rapidly and she swallowed. Yet she didn't look away.

Charged seconds ticked by. Her pupils dilated. His senses stirred. Did he imagine that hint of musky arousal in his nostrils? The quiver of anticipation in the air?

Her breasts rose with her rapid breathing, almost but not quite brushing against him. The woman staring back defiantly was no modest, unprotected innocent.

The thought pulled him up. He'd almost forgotten this was about her, not him.

She wasn't as unaffected as she pretended. He saw the fine tremor running under her skin. Her tongue flicked out to swipe her lips and he bit back a smile. For it wasn't a consciously slow, seductive movement but sure evidence her mouth had dried. Nerves or arousal?

Domenico leaned close, letting the heat of her body drench him. Her lashes flickered and her trembling pulse accelerated. His quickened too.

Holding her gaze, he reached out and snagged her belt. Instantly she stiffened, but she didn't retreat.

Was that a challenge in her eyes?

Her breath was a warm, sweet sigh against his chin as he tugged the bow undone, loosening the fabric around her.

Domenico bent his head and her pursed lips softened. Her eyes widened and something flickered there. Fear or anticipation?

'My office in an hour. You'll be less easily distracted if you're fully dressed.'

He straightened, spun on his heel and left her.

Lucy's breath came in great gulps. Her heart pumped so hard she thought it might jump out of her ribcage.

Domenico Volpe strolled back to the villa with an easy, loose-limbed grace that made her want to hurl something at his broad back. In dark trousers and an open-necked shirt he was the picture of elegant ease. He looked casual, sexy, utterly unaffected by the charge of erotic energy that hammered through her.

She shivered despite the molten heat inside. Her nipples were tight buds of need and she was wet between the legs. Because of the way he'd *looked* at her. Just looked!

How was that possible?

She shook her head, torn between shock, fury and shame. Her body betrayed her. *And he knew it.*

She'd read triumph in his eyes when he'd undone her belt. Had he sensed the voluptuous shiver she couldn't suppress? The tension in her body that had as much to do with fighting her traitorous desire as standing up to him?

With fumbling hands she pulled the wrap tight, as if it made any difference now. He didn't even look back. He was so confident he'd made his point.

That she was vulnerable to him. That she…desired him.

The realisation blasted Lucy's ragged confidence. She wanted to pretend it wasn't true. But hiding would get her nowhere. She had to face it.

Yet surely the fledgling attraction she'd once felt for him was dead, crushed by his cruel assumption of her guilt. She assured herself this wasn't about Domenico Volpe. It was what he represented—hot animal sex. Despite his shuttered gaze and his insultingly casual contempt, there was no mistaking the virile male beneath the expensive clothes.

Who wouldn't be affected by such a potently masculine man?

Lucy had been celibate so long, so cut off from attractive men. This was her body's way of reminding her she was female, that was all.

She shoved aside the fact that she'd felt nothing like this around Chiara's Uncle Rocco.

Maybe her distrust of Domenico Volpe, the fact that her emotions were engaged because of the past, gave a piquancy to her response.

Whatever it was, she had no intention of succumbing to weakness. As he'd soon learn.

He was seated at an enormous desk when she entered his study. Of course he'd take the position of power. Lucy had dealt with enough officials to recognise the tactic.

He was like the rest. Predictable.

He turned from the computer to survey her, taking in her denim skirt and the blue shirt that matched her eyes. It was the nicest one she owned and had always made her feel confident. Now it was years out of date and a snug fit around the bust but it was the best she could do.

His appraising glance told her he wasn't impressed. Or was he recalling her standing, spellbound, as she let him undo her robe? The idea stiffened her resolve and she crossed the room, leaving the door open.

'You had business to discuss?' She sat in the chair before his desk and crossed her legs in a show of nonchalance.

He seemed riveted to the movement and she suppressed a surge of satisfaction. So, he wasn't as remote as he appeared. The knowledge gave her a sliver of hope.

'Yes.' He cleared his throat. 'I have a proposition for you.'

'Really? I'd have thought I was the last woman you'd ever proposition, Signor Volpe.'

His gaze darted to her face and she read simmering anger there. She could deal with anger. She clung to her own like a lifeline. It was preferable to the other feelings he evoked.

'Do tell,' she purred. 'I'm all ears.'

She had to bite back a smile when a frown furrowed his brow. She liked the fact that she pricked his self-possession. It wasn't fair that even scowling he still looked lethally gorgeous. Not that she cared.

'You want privacy and peace from the press. I want you out of the limelight. Our interests coincide.'

'So?'

'So I'd like to make the situation permanent.'

It was Lucy's turn to frown. 'I don't understand.'

He pushed a typed document towards her. 'Read that and you will. I've had it drawn up in English.'

'How considerate.' Perhaps he thought her Italian, learned behind bars, was inadequate. He had no idea the hours she'd spent poring over Italian legal documents.

She slid the paper towards her. It was a contract. She turned the page, heart racing as she read what he planned. She could barely believe it.

Finally she sat back. 'You really are desperate to keep me quiet.'

His dark eyes gleamed. 'Hardly desperate.'

'No? A lot of people would be fascinated to know how much you're offering to stop me talking.'

His look turned baleful. His voice when it came was a lethal whisper scudding through the silence. 'Is that a threat?'

'No threat, Signor Volpe. An observation.'

His eyes pinioned her and her breathing grew shallow. But she refused to be intimidated.

'I want peace for my family.' Yet his eyes didn't plead, they demanded. 'You can't say the offer isn't generous.'

'Generous?' The money on the table was stupefying. Enough to fund that new start in life she'd longed for. Enough to establish herself immediately, even though what was left of her family rejected her. Looked at that way, it was tempting.

'On condition that I don't talk about your brother, his wife, their son, their household, you or anyone associated with your family or the court case.' She ticked the list off on her fingers. 'Nor could I discuss my time in jail or the legal proceedings.'

Indignation settled like a burning ember, firing her blood. 'I'd be gagged from making any comment, ever.'

'You have to earn the money I'm offering.' He shrugged those powerful shoulders, leaning back behind the massive desk, symbol of the power he wielded.

'Earn!' Lucy was sick of being the one ground down by those in authority. The one forced to carry the blame.

Searing anger sparked from that slow burning ember in her belly. She pushed the document across the desk.

'No.'

'Pardon?'

Lucy loved his perplexed expression. How many people said no to this man? She bet precious few women ever had.

'I'm not interested.'

'You've got to be joking. You need money.'

'How do you know that?' She leaned forward. 'Don't tell me you managed to access my private bank details.' She shook her head. 'That would be a criminal offence.'

His teeth bared in a grimace that told her he fought to retain his temper. Good. Goading him was the closest she'd get to revenge and she was human enough to revel in it.

'If you expect a better offer you'll have a long wait. My price is fair.'

'Fair?' Her voice rose. 'No price is *fair* if I can't tell my side of the story. You really expect me to forget what happened to me?' Disbelief almost choked her. 'If I took your blood money it would be tantamount to admitting guilt.' The thought made her sick to the stomach.

'And so?'

'Damn you, Domenico Volpe!' Lucy shot from her chair and skewered him with a glare that should have shrivelled him to ashes in his precious executive chair. 'I refuse to soothe your conscience or that of your sister-in-law.'

He rose and leaned across so his face was a breath away from hers.

'What are you implying?'

'Don't play the innocent.' She braced her hands on the table, firing the words at him. 'Your family's influence was what convicted me.'

'You have the temerity to hint the trial wasn't fair? Because of us?'

She had to give him credit. He looked so furious he'd have convinced anyone. Except someone who'd been behind bars for years because of his precious family.

'Come *on*! What chance did I stand with an overworked public defender against your power and influence?'

'The evidence pointed overwhelmingly to you.'

'But it wasn't true.' Her breath came in uneven pants as she faced him across the desk.

'You'd be well advised to sign.' His look sent a tremor of fear racing through her.

But he couldn't hurt her. Not now. She was free. She had no one and almost no money, but she had integrity. He couldn't take that.

'Now who's making threats?' She stared into eyes that glowed like molten steel.

Deliberately she leaned across his desk, her lips almost grazing his cheek, her nostrils filling with the heady spice scent of him. His eyes widened in shock and she wondered if she'd looked like that out in the garden when he'd come close enough to kiss her.

'I don't respond to threats,' she breathed in a whisper that caressed his scrupulously shaved jaw. 'The answer is still no.'

CHAPTER FIVE

DAMN THE WOMAN.

Domenico paced his study, furious he hadn't broken the deadlock. Lucy Knight still rejected his offer.

It stuck in his craw to give her anything but it was the only way to stop her selling her story. Then what privacy would Pia and Taddeo have? The scandal could go on for years, dogging Taddeo as he grew.

Money was the obvious lever to get what he needed. She was desperate for cash. If she'd had funds she'd have spent it on a top-flight defence team.

A splinter of discomfort pierced him, remembering her inexperienced, under-prepared lawyer. Watching his ineffectual efforts had made Domenico actually consider intervening to organise a more capable defender.

To defend the woman who'd killed Sandro!

Perhaps if he hadn't known she was guilty he would have. But how could he doubt the overwhelming evidence against her?

A mere week before Sandro's death Lucy Knight had bumped into Domenico, literally, at an exhibition of baroque jewellery. He was supervising the inclusion of some family pieces but had been distracted, outrageously so, by the charms of the delightful young Englishwoman who'd blushed and stammered so prettily. She'd looked at the gems with unfeigned delight and at him with something like awe.

Yet it was her hesitation to accept his spur of the moment invitation to coffee that had hooked him. How long since a woman had even pretended to resist him?

Coffee had turned into a stroll through the Forum, lunch at a tucked away trattoria and an afternoon sightseeing. He'd enjoyed himself more than he could remember with a woman who was just Lucy to his Domenico. A woman whose eyes sparkled with unconcealed awareness, yet who trembled with innocent hesitation when he merely took her hand. She was smart, fun and refreshingly honest. Enough to make him believe he'd found someone special and rare.

She'd evoked a slew of emotions. Passion, delight and a surprising protectiveness that had kept him from sweeping her off to his bed then and there. For the connection between them had been sizzling, each touch electric.

She'd been different from every other woman, her impact so profound he'd suggested meeting again when he returned to Rome.

In New York he'd counted the hours to his return.

Till he'd seen Lucy in a news report, doused in his brother's blood as she was led away by the police.

His heart stuttered at the memory.

Then piece by piece he'd heard from Pia and Sandro's staff the truth about Lucy. How she'd seduced his brother and flaunted her power over him.

She must have known who Domenico was at the gallery and engineered the meeting. Why stick with Sandro, whose wife was already making a fuss about his affair, when his brother—just as rich and single to boot—was available? *And just as susceptible.*

Domenico thrust a hand through his hair. He'd fallen for her with an ease that shamed and angered him.

No. She'd brought on the result of the trial herself.

Yet he couldn't douse his awareness of her. The delicacy of

her features snagged his attention again and again, as did the proud, wilful angle of her jaw that appealed even as it repelled.

All afternoon he'd watched her. She appeared fascinated by the grounds, apparently content with the tranquillity here. Which made him wonder what her life had been like behind bars that she should revel in solitude.

There it was again. This unholy interest in the woman. She should mean nothing to him but a problem to be solved. Instead he found himself…intrigued.

And that tiny dead of night niggle was back, disturbing his rest.

He strode to the window, hands jammed in his pockets.

She gave him no peace. There she was at the end of the garden. The afternoon sun burnished her hair, making it glint like gold as she tipped her head back. Her obvious sensual delight was far too alluring, the way she held her arms open to embrace the heat, her deep breaths that drew his eyes to her delectable breasts.

She stiffened, head turning and arms folding in a classic defensive pose. Her tension was obvious as a figure approached from the villa. Rocco, his Head of Security.

Rocco held out a broad-brimmed hat. For a moment she stood stiff, as if unwilling to accept it. Then Rocco spoke and her defensive posture eased. She took the hat and put it on. Rocco spoke again and she shook her head. Was that laughter he caught in the distance?

Domenico stared, fascinated. Lucy Knight was so wary, stiffening the instant he or his security staff came near. To see her relaxed and laughing… Why? Because Rocco had offered her protection from the sun? It was a simple consideration anyone would offer.

Yet look how she responded. Now they were in conversation. She must be asking about landmarks for he pointed to the mainland and she nodded, leaning close.

Domenico frowned, not liking the swirl of discontent that rose as he watched them together.

The difference in her was remarkable. Domenico recalled the way her face had lit up at lunch when the maid served a delicious tiramisu, saying it was the cook's speciality, prepared to welcome the new guest. Lucy's eyes had widened then softened with appreciation and shock before she realised he was watching and looked away. Later she'd made a point of telling the maid how much she'd enjoyed the dessert.

The tiramisu was a little thing, a familiar courtesy to a guest, yet Lucy Knight had responded with surprised delight.

Was she so unused to consideration or kindness?

Given how she'd lived for the past several years it wasn't surprising.

What had she said when she'd rejected his offer out of hand? That she didn't respond to threats?

Domenico's brain snapped into gear. He'd seen her proud defiance, her cool calm and her haughty, almost self-destructive need to assert her independence. Look at the way she'd faced the paparazzi.

If the threats didn't work…what *would* she respond to?

Perhaps there was another way to get what he needed.

Instead of demands, persuasion might be more effective. Didn't they say you could catch more flies with honey than vinegar?

Lucy shut her eyes and listened to the drowsy hum of bees in the garden and, below, the soft shush of waves. She was so incredibly lethargic, mind and body reacting as if, for the first time in years, she didn't need to be constantly on guard. It was easy to relax here, too easy, given she had a future to organise and decisions to make. She should—

'I thought I'd find you here.' The deep voice swirled across her nerve ends, jerking them into tingling life.

She sat up abruptly in the low sun lounger. Standing between her and the sun was her host. For a moment she saw only an imposing silhouette, rampantly male with those broad shoulders, long legs and classically sculpted head. Her heart quickened with something other than surprise.

She scrambled to rise.

'Don't move.' He put his hand out to stop her and sank onto a nearby seat.

She subsided, then gathered herself. Obviously he was here to demand she sign his contract. So much for the peace he'd promised!

She sat straight, knees together, watching suspiciously.

'I thought I'd take you on a tour of the grounds.'

Lucy stared at him, but he returned her disbelieving look blandly.

'Why?'

His black brows arched infinitesimally and ridiculously she felt a sliver of jab at her brusqueness. As if she cared what he thought of her manners. Once upon a time she'd have bantered polite words but not now. He'd forfeited her trust.

'If you're going to stay you should learn the lie of the land.'

He sounded so reasonable. So civilised.

But then he was a civilised man. Look at the way he'd invited her to sit at his table today, as if she was a guest, not the enemy. She'd seen the tension in him, had felt its echo in her own discomfort, but if he was able to bear her company she refused to let him know how confused and edgy she was in his.

'You don't want to spend time with me.' The words grated from her tight throat. 'Why suggest it?' The words sounded churlish, but it was the truth.

She waited for his annoyance to show, but his face remained impassive. What was he thinking?

'You're a guest in my villa and—'

'Hardly.' Her fingers curved around the edge of her seat. 'More a burden.'

'I invited you here.' He paused as if expecting her to interrupt. 'As your host I have an obligation. I need to ensure your safety.'

'Safety?' Incredulous, she surveyed the delightful garden. 'Don't tell me, you have meat-eating killer ants that prey on people who fall asleep on the lawn?'

Was that a smile she saw, quickly suppressed? The fleeting hint of a dimple in that lean cheek was ridiculously attractive. Her response to it scared her. 'Or rabid guard dogs who can sniff out an ex-convict if they stray near anything precious?'

No smile now with that blatant reminder of reality. Lucy told herself she preferred it that way. The last thing she needed was to find the man appealing again.

'No animal dangers but there are things you need to be wary of, including an old well and some sink holes.' He paused, obviously waiting for her assent.

What could she say? His offer sounded reasonable, though the chances of her falling down a hole were nil.

He wanted something. Why else seek her out?

To badger her into signing his contract? She was strong enough to withstand threats.

Besides, she was curious. She hated to admit it but it still felt as if there was unfinished business between them. Surely a little time in his company would erase that unsettling notion? Then she could leave without that niggle at her consciousness. It would be a relief to banish him from her thoughts.

'If you think it necessary, by all means show me the dangers of your island.'

'*Va bene.*' He stood and extended a hand.

Lucy pretended not to notice. The last thing she needed was physical contact with a man whose presence threw her senses into overdrive.

She stood quickly, brushing down her skirt.

'The first thing you must remember is to wear a hat at all times.'

'Like you do?' She stared pointedly at his dark hair, bare to the blazing sun.

Again that hint of a dimple marked his cheek, playing havoc with her insides. Lucy drew herself up, quenching the memory of how his smile had once made her heart skip and her mind turn to mush.

Clearly she'd been a passing amusement. Had he laughed at her gaucheness and wide-eyed wonder at Rome? And at being escorted by a stranger so handsome and attentive he'd all but made her swoon?

'I'm used to southern summers and I've got the skin for it.' He was right. His olive skin was burnished a deep bronze that enhanced the decisive contours of his face. 'Whereas you—'

'Have been behind bars.' Her chin jutted.

He shook his head slowly. 'You shouldn't finish other people's sentences. I was going to say you have a rare complexion. Cream and roses.' He leaned closer. 'And quite flawless.'

His eyes roved her face so thoroughly she felt his regard like the graze of a hand, making her flesh tingle. Her breath quickened and something unfamiliar spiralled deep inside, like the swoop and dip of swallows on the wing.

'Your English is good but the phrase is peaches and cream.' As if she believed he meant it! Prison pallor was more like. She looked away, needing to break the curious stillness that encompassed them.

'I say what I mean.' His voice was a low rumble from far too close. He raised his hand as if to touch her, and then let it drop. 'Your skin has the lustre of new cream, or of pearls, with just a hint of rose.'

Lucy swung round to face him fully, hands on hips as she leaned forward to accuse him of making fun at her expense. She was no longer a gullible young thing to be taken in by smooth talk.

But the look on his face stole the harsh response from her lips.

It stole her breath too.

There was no laughter in his expression. He looked stunned, as if shocked at his own words.

Burnished pewter eyes met hers, making her blood pound.

Something arced between them, something like static electricity that drew the hairs at her nape erect and dried her mouth.

Abruptly they moved apart.

She wasn't the woman he'd thought he knew.

Domenico watched her navigate the dusty path at the far end of the island with alacrity, as if exploring a semi-wilderness was high on her list of things to do. Her head swung from side to side as she took in the spectacular views and the countryside he always found so restful.

What had happened to the girl who thrived on bright lights and male attention? Who hankered after expensive jewellery and the excitement of a cosmopolitan city filled with boutiques, nightclubs, bars and men?

Was she hiding her boredom? She did a good job.

She'd even forgotten to scowl at him and her face had lost that shuttered look in the last half hour. Relaxed, she looked younger, softer.

Dangerously attractive.

There was a vibrancy about her he hadn't seen since the day they'd met.

Perhaps she'd been seduced by the warmth of the afternoon and the utter peace of the place. She'd changed. The tension radiating from her like a shield was gone.

She paused, eyes on a butterfly floating past, as if its simple beauty fascinated her.

As she fascinated him.

The realisation dropped into his thoughts like a stone plummeting into a calm millpond.

How could it be? He carried Sandro's memory strong within him. Any interest in her should be impossible.

Yet why had he chosen to oversee her stay here? It wasn't necessary. A lawyer could witness her signing the contract.

The truth was Domenico was here because something about Lucy Knight made him curious even now. Something he couldn't put his finger on. Something he needed to understand before she walked out of his life for ever.

'Is that a ruined *castle*?' The husky thread of pleasure in her voice brought Domenico back to the present.

'It is.'

'Yet you built your villa on the opposite end of the island.'

He shrugged. 'The aspect is better there. This was built to defend, not enjoy.'

'Strange,' she mused as they stopped to take in the scene. 'I had pegged you as someone who'd rather rebuild the old family estate than start afresh. After all, you live in the family palazzo in Rome.'

She shifted abruptly and he had the impression she wished she hadn't spoken. The palazzo conjured memories of what lay between them.

'You think I'm bound by tradition?'

She lifted her shoulders. 'I have no idea. I don't know you.'

That was the problem, Lucy decided. She'd thought she knew Domenico Volpe. All those weeks during the trial he'd been like an avenging angel, stonily silent and chillingly furious, waiting for her to be convicted. His eyes, cold as snow yet laser-hot when they rested on her, had told her all she needed to know about him.

Yet now she found him approachable—courteous and civilised. As if his lethal anger had never existed. She caught glimpses of the man she'd been wildly attracted to all those years ago. The man who'd made such an impression that in her innocence she'd thought she'd found The One.

Lucy stole a look as he stared at the tumbled stones. His severe features held a charisma that threatened to steal her breath. Abruptly she looked away, hating her quickened pulse.

'Because I honour family tradition doesn't mean I live in the past.'

He lounged against a stone wall beyond which was a deep ravine. A moat, she supposed, staring at the castle beyond. But though she kept her eyes on the view, she was supremely aware of her companion. In faded denim jeans that clung to powerful thighs and a dark short-sleeved shirt that revealed the sinewy strength of his tanned forearms, he looked far too real. Too earthy and sexy. She'd never seen him like this.

Lucy told herself a change of clothes meant nothing. Yet she couldn't suppress the idea that she was closer to the real Domenico Volpe than in his city mansion.

She shied from asking herself why she wanted to know him at all.

Lucy shrugged. 'I thought you'd prefer the castle.'

'To lord it over my subjects?'

She shook her head. This man didn't need external proof of his authority. It was all there—stamped in the austere beauty of his face. He'd been born to wealth but he'd grown into a man used to command.

'Since family tradition means so much, you could restore the place.'

'Ah, but this is an acquisition, not an inheritance. I bought it years ago to celebrate my first success.'

Lucy turned to meet his gaze. 'Success?'

'Si.' His brows rose and she caught a flash of steel in his eyes. 'Or did you think we Volpes have no need of work? That we sit on our inherited wealth and do nothing?' His tone bit.

Once she'd have thought that was precisely what his family did, after seeing the ultra-luxurious way his brother and sister-in-law lived. Pia had never lifted a finger to do anything for herself, or her child.

Instantly guilt flared, twisting Lucy's stomach. Pia might have been completely spoiled but her lack of involvement with little Taddeo had stemmed from her inability to bond with the baby. Lucy knew how much guilt and shame, not to mention fear that had caused the poor woman. No wonder she'd been insecure.

'I see that's exactly what you think.'

'Sorry?' Lucy blinked and turned, surprised to find herself so close to the man who now loomed over her.

'You view us as lazy parasites, perhaps?' His voice was low and amused but Lucy knew in her bones that amusement hid anger.

'Not at all.' She tilted her chin to meet his stare unflinchingly. 'I know your wealth began with your inheritance but you struck out on your own as an entrepreneur, risking your capital on projects others wouldn't touch. Your flair for managing risk made you the golden-haired boy of the European business world when other ventures were collapsing around you. You have a reputation for hard work and phenomenal luck.'

'It's not luck,' he murmured. 'It's careful calculation.'

Lucy shrugged. 'Whatever the reason, the markets call you *Il Volpe*, the fox, for good reason.'

'Fascinating that you should know so much about me.' His voice brushed across her skin like the touch of rich velvet. A ripple of pleasure followed it.

Instinctively Lucy made to step back, then stopped.

Never back down. Never retreat. Weakness shown was an invitation to be walked over.

'It seemed prudent to know what I was up against.'

His eyebrows soared. '*We* weren't in conflict.'

'No?' She shook her head. 'Your family's influence put me behind bars.'

His eyes narrowed to deadly slits. Heat sizzled at the look he gave her.

'Let's get this straight. My family did no more than wait the outcome of the trial.'

Lucy opened her mouth to protest but his raised hand stopped her.

'No! You imply *what*? That we rigged the trial? That we bribed the police or judiciary?' He shook his head in a fine show of anger. 'The evidence convicted you, Ms Knight. Nothing else.' He paused and she watched him grapple for control, his strong features taut, his muscles bunched.

He drew a deep breath and Lucy saw his wide chest expand. When he spoke his voice was crisp. 'You have my word as a Volpe on it. We live within the law.'

There was no mistaking his emotion. It was almost convincing.

'You don't believe me?' His eyes narrowed.

In truth she didn't know. There was no doubt she'd been disadvantaged by the quality of her legal team compared with the ruthless efficiency and dogged determination of the prosecution. And it was obvious that sympathy lay with Pia, the beautiful grieving widow and young mother. Lucy knew that sympathy had given Pia's evidence more weight than it deserved. At Lucy's expense.

Plus Bruno Scarlatti, Sandro's bodyguard and the prosecution's chief witness, was ex-police. He'd shone in court. His evidence had been clear and precise, unclouded by emotion. That evidence had damned her and swayed the court. She was sure his ex-police status had weighed with the investigators too, though she had no proof.

'I…don't know.' For the first time confusion filled her, not the righteous indignation that had burned so long.

'I'm not used to having my word doubted.' Hauteur laced Domenico's tone.

Lucy's lips curled in a sour half smile. 'Believe me, it doesn't get any easier with time.'

His eyes widened as he realised she was talking about herself. She almost laughed, but there was nothing funny about it.

Even after all this time, bearing the burden of public guilt was like carrying an open wound. She wondered if she'd ever feel whole again while she carried that lie with her. It had changed her life irrevocably.

Now the dreams she'd cherished about starting afresh seemed just that—dreams. How could they not, with Sylvia's cruel betrayal and the eager press waiting to scoop more stories? How would she find the peace she craved to build a new life?

She turned away, her joy in the place forgotten.

'Wait.' The word stabbed the silence.

'What?' Reluctantly she faced him.

'This—' his hand slashed between them '—isn't helpful.'

'So?'

'So—' his nostrils flared as he breathed deep '—I propose a truce. You're my guest. I'll treat you as such and you'll reciprocate. No more accusations, by either of us.'

Was this to soften her up so she'd sign his paper? Or was it, a little squiggle of hope tickled her, because he had doubts about her guilt?

No. That hope died as it was born. He'd shown no doubt in court. Not once. He'd spurned her as if she were unclean. He didn't want to absolve her, just strike an accord that would give them peace while they shared the villa.

Peace. That was what she craved, wasn't it?

'Agreed.' Lucy put her hand out and, after a surprised glance, he took it.

She regretted it as soon as his fingers enveloped hers. Fire sparked and spread from his touch, running tendrils of heat along her arm to her cheeks, breasts and belly. Even down her legs, where her knees locked against sudden weakness.

She sucked in a shocked breath at the intensity of that physical awareness.

Did he feel it? His eyes gleamed deep silver and his sculpted lips tightened.

His next words were the last she expected to hear.

'So you will call me Domenico, *si*? And I'll call you Lucy.'

Time warped. It was as if they were back in Rome, chance met strangers, her heart thundering as their eyes locked for the first time.

His gaze bored into hers, challenging her to admit the idea of his name on her lips discomfited her. Or was it the sound of her own name, like a tantalising caress in his rich, deep voice, that made her pulse falter?

'I don't think—'

'To seal our truce,' he insisted, his gaze intent as if reading the thrill of shock snaking through her.

'Of course.' She refused to let him fluster her, especially over something so trivial.

Yet it didn't feel trivial. It felt... Lucy groped for a word to describe the sensations assailing her but failed.

With a nod he released her and stepped away. Yet Lucy still felt the imprint of his hand on hers and her spine tingled at the memory of him saying her name with that delicious hint of an accent.

She had the uncomfortable feeling she'd just made a huge mistake.

CHAPTER SIX

THEY WERE SILENT as they walked along the beach to the villa. Late afternoon light lengthened their shadows and for the first time in weeks Domenico felt something like peace, listening to the rhythm of the sea and their matched steps.

Peace, with Lucy Knight beside him!

His business negotiations had reached a crucial phase that would normally have consumed every waking hour. On top of that was Pia's near hysterical response to the latest press reports, and his own turbulent reactions to the release of his brother's killer.

And here he was walking with her in the place that was his refuge from the constant demands on his time. Was he mad letting her in here?

Yet the stakes were too high. He had to convince her—

Beside him she stopped. He turned, wondering what had caught her attention.

In the peachy light her hair was a nimbus of gold, backlit by the sun that lovingly silhouetted her shape. She'd taken off her sandals and stood ankle-deep in the froth of gentle waves. She looked…appealing.

His pulse thudded and he realised she was watching him. Her gaze branded his skin.

Instinctively he moved closer, needing to read her expression. What he saw made premonition jitter through him. Was she going to agree to his terms? He schooled his face, knowing better than to rush her.

'Lucy?' Her name tasted good on his tongue. Too good. This was business. Business and the protection of his family. It was his duty to protect Taddeo and Pia now Sandro wasn't here to do it. The thought of Sandro renewed his resolve.

'I...' Her gaze skated away and he leaned in, willing her to continue. She drew a deep breath, straining her blouse across ripe breasts. Domenico berated himself for noticing, but he noticed everything about her. Was that an asset or a penalty?

'You?' Expectation buzzed. It wasn't like her to hesitate. She was aggressively forthright.

Her eyes met his and something punched deep in his belly. Gone were her defiance and her anger. Instead he read something altogether softer in her face.

'I never told you.' She paused and bit her lip, reminding him in a flash of blinding memory of the girl he'd met all those years ago. The one whose forget-me-not eyes had haunted him with their apparent shock and bewildered innocence. Who'd been a conundrum with her mix of uncertainty and belligerent, caustic defiance.

His belly tightened. There was no logic to the fact she unsettled him as no other woman had.

'Sorry. I'm usually more coherent.'

'You can say that again.'

Her lips twisted. Then she straightened, her jaw tensing as she met his eyes head-on.

'We agreed not to make accusations and I understand there's no point protesting my innocence.' She inhaled through flared nostrils. 'But there's something you need to hear.' She paused as if expecting him to cut her off, but Domenico had no intention of interrupting.

'I'm sorry about your brother.' Her gaze didn't waver and Domenico felt the force of her words as a palpable weight. 'His death was a tragedy for his wife and child, for *all* his family.

He was a good man, a caring one.' She released a breath that shivered on the air between them. 'I'm sorry he died and I'm sorry I was involved.'

Stunned, Domenico watched her lips form the words.

After all this time...

He'd never expected an apology, though he'd told himself an admission of guilt would salve the pain of Sandro's loss.

She didn't confess, yet, to Domenico's amazement, her words of regret struck a chord deep inside. He stared at her and she didn't try to hide, even lifted her face as if to open herself to his scrutiny.

For the first time he felt the barriers drop between them and he knew for this moment truth hovered. Truth and honest regret.

'Thank you.' His voice was hoarse from grief that seemed fresh as ever. But with the pain came something like peace.

The cynic in him stood ready to accuse her of an easy lie, a sop to his anger. Yet what he saw in Lucy's face drowned the voice of cynicism. 'I appreciate it.'

Her lips twisted in a crooked smile. 'I'm glad.' She paused then severed eye contact, turning towards the sea. 'I wrote to your sister-in-law some time ago, saying the same thing. I'm not sure she even read the letter.'

'You wrote to Pia?' It was the first he'd heard of it and usually Pia was only too ready to lean on him for emotional support.

He stared at the woman he'd thought he understood. How well did he know her after all? She confounded his certainties time and again.

She made him feel so many unexpected emotions.

A day later Domenico stood at his study window, drawn from his computer by the sound of laughter.

On the paved area by the head of the stairs to the beach were Rocco's niece, Chiara, and Lucy, neat in her denim skirt and blouse. Lucy bent to mark the flagstones in a square chalk pattern and Domenico fought to drag his eyes from the denim tight around her firm backside.

Heat flared as his gaze roved her ripe curves.

Too often he found himself watching Lucy with distinctly male appreciation.

He switched his gaze to Chiara as, shaking her head, she took the chalk and drew her own patterns, circular this time. As she finished, understanding dawned. They were playing a children's game: Mondo. Watching Chiara gesticulate he guessed she was explaining her game rather than the English Hopscotch, that Lucy had marked.

'You wanted me, boss?' Rocco tapped at the door.

Did he? Domenico couldn't recall. Frustration bit. He'd been distracted all morning. Lucy and her refusal to sign his contract undermined his focus.

'Have you seen who your niece is playing with?' His voice grated as he realised it wasn't Lucy's obstinacy that distracted him. It was the woman herself—prickly, proud and, he hated to admit it, intriguing in ways that had nothing to do with the danger she posed to his family.

'They're good together, aren't they?'

Domenico frowned. 'You have no qualms about Chiara playing with a woman who served time for killing a man?'

Not just any man. His brother. Domenico's breath was harsh in his constricted lungs.

There was a long silence. He turned to find Rocco regarding him steadily. 'The past is the past, boss. Even the court said it wasn't premeditated. Besides, she loves children. Anyone can see that.' He nodded to the garden and Domenico turned to see Lucy ushering Chiara, who'd grown boisterous with excitement, away from the steps.

Domenico felt a sliver of something like shame, seeing her concern for Chiara. Even the prosecution at her trial had acknowledged she'd been a reliable carer for little Taddeo.

'Mamma trusts her with Chiara. You can't say better.'

Rocco's *mamma* was a redoubtable woman, canny and an excellent judge of character. As housekeeper to the Volpes for over thirty years, she and Sandro between them had brought Domenico up when his parents had died.

'Maybe Signorina Knight isn't the woman you think.'

Domenico stiffened. He didn't need Rocco's advice, even if he was the best security manager he'd ever had.

Yet once lodged in his brain, his words couldn't be dismissed.

Was she the same woman he'd heard about all those years ago? Greedy, self-centred, luring his brother into indiscretion under his wife's nose? If he hadn't experienced first-hand the powerful tug of her innocent seductress routine he'd never have believed Sandro would be unfaithful.

She had been only eighteen then; had the last years changed her?

He saw glimpses of a far different woman. One with surprising depths—an inner core of strength and what he suspected was her own brand of integrity. One that reminded him a little of the golden girl who'd once snared his attention, but far, far tougher and sassy. Besides, that girl had been a mirage.

Frustration rose. He wasn't used to uncertainty, either in business or with women. Usually his instincts for both served him well.

Was he seeing what he wanted to see?

More important, did he see what *she* wanted him to see? Unfamiliar tension coiled in Domenico's belly. She'd got under his skin, inserting doubt where previously there'd been certainty.

Why maintain her innocence after all this time? Unbidden, he recalled again her inexperienced legal representative. Would the trial's outcome have been different with a better lawyer?

A twinge of discomfort pierced him.

Domenico's mouth tightened. His curiosity had as much to do with attraction at a primal level as it did the need for understanding. This was about more than gagging Lucy Knight from spreading stories that would harm his family.

The stakes were far more personal.

Lucy was walking back to the villa when a figure loomed before her.

'How would you like to come snorkelling?'

Suspicion welled as she looked into Domenico's unreadable grey eyes. True, they'd agreed a truce. True, he let her have the run of the estate, even access to the Internet so she could trawl fruitlessly for jobs—as if anyone would take her on with her history. But taking her on an excursion?

Lucy shook her head. 'I should check my email.' As if there was a chance some employer had bothered to respond to the dozens of queries she'd sent. Given the poor economic climate, attracting an employer's interest would be a miracle. Even if she managed that, there were the hurdles of character and criminal record checks.

'You can do that when we return. Come on, it will be good to get off the island.'

'Why?'

What did he want? Remembering his glowering scowl when they'd first met, a fatal boating accident seemed possible. But lately… No, he wasn't a violent man, just one used to getting what he wanted. And he wanted her to sign his contract. Was he trying to soften her up?

He shrugged and to her chagrin she followed the movement of those wide, straight shoulders with a fascination she still couldn't conquer.

'Because I'm fed up with emails and performance indicators and financial statements. It's time for a break.' His lips curved in a one-sided smile that carved a long dimple in one cheek and snared her breath before it could reach her lungs.

The man was indecently attractive.

'I really should—'

'You're not avoiding me, are you, Lucy?'

Stoically she ignored the way his hint of an accent turned her ordinary name into something delicious. It had made her weak at the knees the day they'd met.

'Why would I do that?'

His eyes sizzled pure silver—the colour of a lightning bolt against a stormy sky. She could almost feel the ground shake beneath her feet from its impact.

Again he shrugged. This time she kept her eyes on his face. 'Perhaps I make you nervous.'

He was dead right. No matter how often she told herself Domenico had no power over her, instinct eclipsed logic and fear shivered through her. A fear that had nothing to do with his wealth and influence and everything to do with him as a potently attractive, fascinating man.

She'd washed her hands of him long ago. She'd seen him in court and her heart had leapt, believing he was there for her. Instead he'd cut her dead, so sure of her guilt before the trial even began. She'd been gutted.

Why did she still respond to him?

'Why should I be nervous?'

'I have no idea.' Yet his expression was knowing, as if he read her tension.

Did he guess the shockingly erotic fantasies that invaded her dreams each night? Fantasies that featured Domenico Volpe, not as disapproving and distant, but as her hot, earthily sexy lover? Lucy swallowed hard, reassuring herself that if he knew the last thing he'd do was invite her to spend time with him.

'I don't have a swimsuit.' Her voice emerged husky and she watched his attention shift to her mouth. Her lips tingled and heat bloomed deep in her belly.

He smiled. A fully fledged smile that made her heart skip a beat and alarm bells jangle.

'Be my guest. Find yourself a new one in the pool house.'

Lucy shook her head before she could be tempted. 'No, thank you.'

'Why not? Don't you want to go out there?' His gesture encompassed the azure shimmer of sea that had lured her since the moment she'd arrived.

How she'd love to do more than paddle in the shallows for once! She'd even toyed with the idea of a midnight skinny dip but it would be just her luck to be found by his security staff.

'I don't accept handouts.' She wasn't a charity case.

Domenico watched her for long seconds with a look that in anyone else she'd call astonished. When he spoke his voice had lost its teasing edge.

'It's not a handout. It's what we do for our guests. Rocco's *mamma* has a lovely time buying hats and wraps and swimsuits for guests. You'd be surprised how many people forget them on a seaside stay.'

Not like her. Lucy had been shuffled out of Rome in a hurry with no idea where she was heading. She wasn't like his other guests. She opened her mouth to say so when he spoke again.

'Come on, Lucy. Set your pride aside and enjoy yourself. I promise it won't make you obligated to me.'

That was what she hated, wasn't it? Feeling indebted to Domenico Volpe for this respite when she most needed it.

Of course he had his own agenda. He wanted to buy her silence.

Was she too proud? Self-sufficiency was something she'd learnt in a hard school. Did she take it too far?

The sound of the sea behind her and the tang of salt on the air reminded her that the only person to suffer for her pride was herself. Swimming in the Med was something she'd always wanted to do. When would she have the chance again? When she finally found a job she'd be too busy making ends meet to travel.

'Thank you,' she said at last. 'That would be...nice.'

Was that a flash of pleasure in Domenico's eyes? Not triumph as she'd half expected. Her brow puckered.

'Good.' He pointed her to the pool house. 'You'll find what you need up there. Don't forget a hat. I'll meet you at the boat.'

Fifteen minutes later Lucy hurried down the steps to the beach. She'd rifled through a treasure trove of designer swimwear, finally selecting the plainest one-piece she could find. No way was she flaunting herself before Domenico in a barely there string bikini. Nevertheless she felt strangely aware of the Lycra clinging to her body under her skirt and shirt. It reminded her of the flicker of heat she saw in his eyes, and her body's inevitable reaction—a softening deep inside.

So often she found him watching her, the hint of a frown on his wide forehead, as if she was some enigma he had to puzzle. Or was he calculating how long she'd hold out against the fortune he offered?

On condition she stopped proclaiming her innocence.

She set her jaw. The first thing she'd do when she found work was pay back the price of this swimsuit. Even if it took her months on the basic wage!

Lucy stepped into the boatshed, trying to calculate how much a designer swimsuit would set her back.

It was dim inside and it took a moment for her eyes to adjust. She blinked at the sleek outline of the speedboat moored inside. Was this the boat they were taking?

She turned, wondering if she should wait outside, when movement caught her eye.

On the far side of the boat a man came towards her—thickset with a bullish head and broad neck that spoke of blatant strength. He moved with surprising agility. His dark suit blended with the shadows but, as her eyes adjusted to the gloom, she caught the crooked line of a broken nose and hands the size of dinner plates.

The hair at her nape stood on end and terror engulfed her. She froze, recognition filling her.

The rusty taste of blood on her bitten tongue roused her. She drew a shuddering breath and catapulted towards the door. With every step she imagined one of those heavy hands grabbing her, capturing her, punishing her.

Lucy's breath sawed through constricted lungs as she reached, hands outstretched, for the door. Her legs seemed to slow as if in a nightmare. She knocked over some tins that clattered to the floor and almost fell but kept going, eyes on the sunlit rectangle of freedom ahead, desperation driving her.

With a sob of fear she plunged outside, blinded by light, only to find her flight stopped by a hard, hot body.

He'd never held her but she knew it was Domenico. The scent of warm spice and pine, and something else, something so profound she had no name for it, told her it was him in the millisecond before his arms came round her, hugging her close.

'Please,' she gasped. 'Watch out! He's here. He's—'

She struggled to turn, but Domenico's grip was firm. She was plastered to him, her face pressed to his collarbone. One hand held her head against him and his other arm lashed protectively around her waist.

Lucy felt heat, strength and solidity. Safety. His heart beat steadily against her raised palm and, despite her fear relief weakened her knees. Tendrils of heat invaded her ice-numbed body, counteracting the horror that filled her.

'Lucy? What is it?' His deep voice ruffled her hair and wrapped itself around her.

She shook her head. 'Be careful! He—'

'I'm sorry, sir.' An unfamiliar voice came from behind her. 'I was putting provisions in the boat. I didn't mean to scare the lady.'

Lucy turned her head, eyes widening at the man who emerged from the boatshed.

He was a stranger.

Her heart leapt even as reaction set in and her knees buck-led. She clung to Domenico. His grip tightened, holding her against him as if she belonged there.

Later she'd regret clinging to him, but now she was too over-whelmed by a sense of deliverance from danger.

It wasn't him.

The knowledge beat a rapid tattoo in her blood. She took in the worried face and bright eyes of the stranger. What she'd thought a bodyguard's suit was a casual uniform of dark trou-sers and shirt. The man was an employee, but not the one she'd feared. Even the crooked jut of his nose was different and his eyes held none of the gleaming malice she remembered.

In face of the stranger's concern Lucy tried to summon a reassuring smile but it wobbled too much.

'Lucy?' Domenico's broad palm rubbed her back and com-forting heat swirled from the point of contact. She pressed closer, arching into him.

'I'm sorry.' Her voice was husky. She turned as far as she could within Domenico's firm embrace. She should step free but couldn't dredge the strength to stand alone. 'I…overreacted. I saw someone coming towards me in the darkness and…'

'I'm sorry, *signorina.*' The big man looked solemn. 'I didn't mean—'

'No. Don't apologise.' Lucy's smile was more convincing now, though it felt like a rictus stretch of stiff muscles. 'It was my mistake.'

'It's okay, Salvo.' Domenico's deep voice was balm to shred-ded nerves. 'Everything's fine. You can leave us.'

With one last troubled look the man left and Lucy sagged. The rush of adrenalin was fading. She felt almost nauseous in the aftermath.

'Lucy? Come and sit in the shade.'

Suddenly, as if her brain had just engaged, she became fully conscious of how intimately they stood. The press of hard muscle and solid bone supporting her. The reassuring beat of his heart beneath her palm. The need to lean closer and lose herself in his embrace. The flare of pleasure at the differences between them—he was so utterly masculine against her melting weakness.

That realisation made her snap upright on a surge of horrified energy.

'I'm sorry.' Humiliation blurred her words as she struggled to remove herself from his hold. What must he think of her, clinging to him?

Bile churned her stomach. She knew what he must think. The prosecution at the trial had painted her as a femme fatale, using the promise of her body to win expensive favours from her indulgent boss. Domenico probably thought she was trying a similar tactic to win sympathy.

A shudder of self-loathing passed through her and she broke free. How could she have turned to him?

Her pace was uneven but she managed the few steps to the boatshed, putting her hand to its wall for support.

Stifling her shame and embarrassment, Lucy forced herself to turn. He stood, frowning, the line of his jaw razor-sharp and his grey eyes piercing.

'Now we're alone you can tell me who you thought you were running from. Who are you scared of?'

CHAPTER SEVEN

'SCARED?' LUCY GAVE a shaky laugh. Her hand dropped from the wall and she straightened. She swayed and Domenico discovered the heat curling through his belly had turned to anger.

It was a welcome change from the surge of hunger he'd known as she'd melted against him.

'Tell me, Lucy.' His tone was one his business associates obeyed without question.

Her chin jutted obstinately. 'There's nothing to tell. I saw someone coming towards me in the dark and panicked.'

Domenico shook his head. 'You don't panic.'

'How would you know? You're hardly an expert on me.'

But he was.

He'd spent the weeks of the trial trying to learn every nuance of her reactions—not that it had got him far. She'd been an enigma. But in the days since her release he'd been able to concentrate on little but her and he'd learned a lot. Enough to make him question his earlier, too easy assumptions.

'You're no coward. You faced the paparazzi.' He added quietly, 'You faced *me*.'

Her eyes widened, acknowledgement if he'd needed it, of just how hard she'd found the last several days.

He remembered her hunched on the floor in the palazzo, her hand splayed where Sandro had breathed his last. Her blind pain had been almost unbearable to witness. What strength of character had it taken to face the place? The same strength it took to face him with an air of proud independence despite the tremors racking her.

Something hard and unforgiving inside him eased. Something that had already cracked when she'd expressed regret for Sandro's death. When he'd seen her playing with little Chiara. When he'd held her close and been torn between protectiveness and an utterly selfish desire for her soft, bountifully feminine body.

'There's nothing to tell.' But her eyes were clouded and her mouth white-rimmed. Her tension reignited the protectiveness that had enveloped him as he held her and felt the waves of fear shudder through her.

'Liar.'

She flinched, her face tightening.

'I thought we'd agreed to leave the accusations behind.' There was desperate hauteur to her expression but she couldn't mask her pain.

'I'm not talking about the past. I'm talking about now. Here.' His slashing hand encompassed the scene that had just played out. 'You were scared out of your wits.'

Her pale eyebrows rose. 'Nothing scares me. After the last few years I'm unshockable.'

Looking into her unblinking gaze he almost believed her. Yet her desperate panting breath against his throat, the clutch of her hands and the feel of her body's response to overwhelming fear had been unmistakable.

Domenico stepped close and she stiffened. He kept going till he stood a breath away. Her face tilted up to his as he'd known it would. Lucy had proven time and again that she was no coward. She faced what she feared.

Until today. In the darkness of the boatshed.

His heart beat an uneven rhythm as he realised only true terror would have made this woman run.

'Who is he, Lucy?' He lifted a hand to her jaw, stroking his thumb over her silken flesh, feeling the jittering pulse. 'Who are you afraid of?'

Her eyelids flickered. She pressed into his touch and pleasure swirled deep inside.

'Bruno.' The word was a whisper. 'Bruno Scarlatti. Your brother's Head of Security.'

Domenico read her fear and knew she spoke the truth. He wanted to assure her she was safe. He wanted to tug her close and not let her go.

Because she was scared?

Or because he wanted an excuse to touch her?

He dropped his hand. 'Why are you afraid of him?'

'It doesn't matter.' Her mouth flattened.

'Did he visit you behind bars?' Had he threatened her?

'Him! Visit me? You've got to be kidding. In five years my only visitors were a couple of criminologists writing a book on female offenders and crimes of passion.' Sarcasm dripped from her voice. 'They found me such a *fascinating* study.'

She shouldered away from him, into the sun. Yet she rubbed her hands up her arms as if to warm herself.

Stunned, he let himself be distracted. In five years she'd had no personal visitors? What about her family and friends? Then he remembered the tawdry exposé interview with her stepmother. Lucy's family relationships were strained. But to be alone so long?

He felt no triumph, only regret as he read her grim tension, the way she battled not to show emotion.

'Tell me, Lucy.' His voice was gruff. 'Why are you afraid of Bruno Scarlatti?'

His gaze held hers and almost he thought he'd won. That she trusted him enough to tell him.

She shrugged but the movement was stiff as if her muscles had seized up. 'We agreed not to talk about the past. Let's abide by that. You wouldn't appreciate what I have to say.'

She turned towards the water.

There was no point trying to force her to talk. She'd proved time and again that she didn't bow to pressure.

But her terror couldn't be denied.

Something had happened. Something that frightened one of the most composed, self-sufficient women he knew.

He thought of her evidence at the trial. She'd claimed it was Bruno Scarlatti, not Sandro, who'd come to her room that night. He'd heard about the scene between Sandro and Lucy when earlier that day she'd pleaded for immediate leave to visit her sick father. Understandably, Sandro had refused, concerned that with Pia unwell and the nanny off work due to illness, they needed the au pair, Lucy. The meeting had ended with Lucy shouting she'd find a way to leave despite her contract.

Her story was that Bruno had said he'd help her persuade the boss to give her leave and she'd innocently let him into her room. Once inside, he'd allegedly attacked her, tried to rape her. Sandro had heard the noise and come to her aid, but in the scuffle with Bruno he'd knocked his head against the antique fireplace and died.

Domenico rubbed a hand over his tense jaw, remembering all the holes in her story. The court had dismissed it. There was too much evidence of her guilt.

Pia had given evidence, backed by diary notes, that Sandro and Lucy had had a passionate affair. Bruno's evidence had been the same. He'd revealed her as a seductive tease who knew her power over men and bragged about twisting the boss around her little finger. He'd seen her and Sandro together, given dates and times.

Sandro had given her expensive treats, like the exquisite jewellery found in her room the night he died. The household had heard her threaten Sandro when he'd refused to let her go.

That night he'd been drinking, torn no doubt between concern for his wife and the fight with his mistress. He'd gone to Lucy's room with an expensive gift to salve her anger. But they'd fought again, she'd shoved him and, unsteady on his feet, he'd fallen and cracked his skull. As for Lucy blaming Bruno—he had an alibi.

Pia had found Sandro bleeding to death, cradled in Lucy's arms.

Domenico shivered, recalling the moment he'd discovered Lucy's identity—the image of her in a bloodstained nightdress with a blanket around her shoulders, being escorted to a police car outside the palazzo. Sandro was dead and she'd been arrested.

Domenico hadn't even been able to blame Sandro for his fatal attraction to the young Englishwoman. He knew how difficult Pia could be and guessed that in the months following childbirth she'd been particularly demanding.

More importantly, Domenico had first-hand experience of Lucy's power. He'd fallen under her spell in just a few hours. What must it have been like for Sandro, facing such temptation in his own home every day? That didn't excuse the affair. But Sandro was only human.

Who was Domenico to judge when he'd felt attraction sizzle the moment he'd looked into Lucy Knight's eyes? That knowledge had twisted guilt deep in his gut ever since.

He shifted his focus to the woman walking along the beach. Her head was bowed and her arms were wrapped tight around her body.

Confusion filled him as he recalled the fear that had racked her as he'd held her.

Because she thought she'd seen Bruno Scarlatti.

Because he'd killed Sandro?

The thought stopped the breath in Domenico's lungs. It wasn't possible. The court had been through all the evidence, right down to Lucy's fingerprints on the expensive necklace Sandro had given her that night. It had been a lovers' quarrel. And there was a witness who put Scarlatti elsewhere when Sandro died.

And yet… Again that frisson of unease stirred. That sense that something wasn't right.

Domenico forced himself to concentrate on proven facts. The evidence supported Lucy's guilt yet she was scared of Scarlatti. Had one part of her story been true? Had he tried to force himself on her?

There'd been an avid hunger in Scarlatti's eyes whenever he'd looked across the courtroom at Lucy. Domenico had noticed immediately, ashamed as he was of his own response to her.

Domenico's hands clenched so hard he found himself shaking. Could that be it? The idea hollowed his belly.

He wished Scarlatti was here now. Domenico needed an outlet for his churning fury.

'Scarlatti no longer works for the Volpe family.'

Lucy spun to find Domenico a few paces away, eyes shaded by wraparound sunglasses. She felt at a disadvantage, wondering what the lenses hid from view.

'Why not?'

'He was dismissed years ago. Rocco found evidence that he'd…bothered one of the maids.'

'Bothered?' Why wasn't she surprised? Bruno was a slime ball who wouldn't take no for an answer.

'She complained he was pestering her. A bit of digging revealed she wasn't the first.'

Lucy bit her lip. The temptation to spill her own story about Bruno was strong. But Domenico had heard it in court. He hadn't believed it then and wouldn't now. Defeat tasted sour on her tongue.

Why should it matter after all this time that he didn't believe her? Instead of getting easier to bear, it grew harder.

Nothing had changed. She'd let herself be lulled into believing it had.

Domenico was weakening her, subtly undermining her ability to keep the unsympathetic world at bay.

'Don't worry, he's long gone.'

She nodded. What was there to say?

'Now, let's get out on the water.'

'I've changed my mind. I'll stay ashore.'

'Why? So you can hide in your room and brood?'

Lucy's eyes widened. 'I *never* hide!'

'Isn't that what you're doing now?'

She knew Domenico's tactic. He deliberately baited her, yet she couldn't resist the challenge. The one thing, the only thing she'd had on her side all these years had been her resolute strength. An ability to tough out the worst the criminal justice system could throw at her and pretend it didn't matter.

She'd forced herself to morph from a scared, desperate teenager into a woman who could look after herself no matter what.

There was more than pride at stake. It was her faith in her one tangible asset—strength in the face of adversity.

Without that, how could she face the future that loomed like a black hole? She had no family now. No friends. No prospects, as each day's job-hunting proved. If she let herself weaken she'd never survive.

Lucy met Domenico's gaze, reading anticipation in his stillness. He expected her to make a run for it, damn him.

'Where's your boat?'

Three hours later she was a different woman. The mutinous set of her mouth had eased into a smile that made Domenico's belly flip over. Her haunted expression had disappeared. Now her eyes shone pure forget-me-not blue, rivalling the sky for brightness.

He'd only once before seen a woman lit from within like this. It had been Lucy then too. Her enthusiasm was contagious.

He shook his head, unable to believe her avid enthusiasm was anything but real this time. There'd been no primping, not

even a comb or mirror in the bag she'd brought. No coy looks
or subtle feminine blandishments. Her focus had been on the
boat and the sensation of speed as they circled the island. Her
husky laughter still echoed in his ears. She'd been like a kid
on a roller coaster for the first time—delighted and delightful in her glee.

'Did you *see* the size of that octopus?' She surfaced beside
him, grinning as she removed the snorkel's mouthpiece. 'It's
amazing, and the way it moves!'

'Do you like octopus? I could catch it for our dinner.' Like a
smitten youth showing off for a pretty girl. Like the man he'd
been that first day in Rome. He'd turned from a cabinet of ornate jewellery and fallen into the cerulean depths of her gaze.

Yet even that thought couldn't dim Domenico's good mood.
He'd enjoyed the last couple of hours more than any he could
remember in months.

She was a pleasure to be with. Her questions had stimulated
rather than bored him. She'd made him see the place through
fresh, appreciative eyes.

How long since he'd enjoyed such simple pleasures? Usually
when he visited he was busy, finishing work or entertaining
guests who were too sophisticated to get excited about snorkelling or a speedboat ride.

'No.' She reached out and put a restraining hand on his
shoulder when he would have dived back under. 'Thank you,
but I'd rather you let it be.'

'Squeamish about seeing your dinner before it appears on
your plate?' He kept his eyes on her face though it was her slim
hand on his shoulder that stole his attention.

'Maybe.' Her smile turned wistful. 'Can't we just leave him
alone? Free?'

Something about the way she said that last word made him
pause. Was that what she'd enjoyed so much? The freedom of
their afternoon on the water?

It struck him that this was a massive change from the restrictions she'd known behind bars. He couldn't imagine such a life. How had she coped?

He wasn't in the business of feeling sorry for her. Yet seeing her so different from the touchy, self-protective woman he'd known, Domenico couldn't completely suppress a sense of connection between them.

His motive in being with her had been to soften her into accepting his deal—her silence for a big chunk of money. But somewhere in the past days he'd found himself *wanting* her company. He'd told himself he needed to understand the woman who threatened his family, but that wasn't all. Not any more.

He wanted to be with her. He wanted…

'In that case we'll leave it be.' He looked at the westering sun. 'It's time to stop. Come on.'

Lucy wrapped an oversized beach towel around herself, conscious of Domenico's gaze lingering as he'd helped her aboard. His eyes had shone silver as he took in the swimsuit moulding her body. It had only been for a second before he'd looked away, but that had ignited a slow, curling heat inside. His look had seared her to the core and shivers still rippled across her skin.

The trouble was, though they were on opposing sides, the old attraction was back, stronger than before.

Worse, she'd begun to *like* him.

He put her at ease and made her smile, and it wasn't just about him trying to persuade her to sign his contract. There was the way he was with little Chiara—like an honorary uncle instead of the man who employed half her family. The way he treated Lucy—always straight down the line. The way he'd held her this afternoon.

It scared her how much his concern had meant to her.

'Why did you never speak to me at the trial?'

Horrified, she heard the words slip out. Did she really want to break the afternoon's spell by dredging up the past? It seemed she did. 'I thought you'd talk to me at least. Acknowledge me.'

There. It was out in the open finally.

She turned her gaze on him. To her amazement, colour flushed his tanned face, rising high on those lean cheeks.

'Would it have changed anything?'

Lucy's lips firmed. It wouldn't have changed the trial's outcome but it would have meant everything to her.

'When I saw you there I thought you'd come to support me.' Her mouth twisted. She'd felt utterly alone, her family so far away. 'Until I found out who you were.'

His eyes widened, something like shock tensing his face.

'Surely you knew that already.'

'How could I? I only knew your first name, remember?'

They'd had such a short time together, less than a day. Her chest tightened. It wasn't his fault she'd fallen under his spell so utterly. That she'd read too much into simple attraction. She'd been so inexperienced. Domenico was the first man to make her heart flutter.

She looked into his stunned eyes and realised what a little fool she'd been. What had her claim on him been? An afternoon's pleasant company compared with supporting his family in crisis.

All this time she'd blamed him for not hearing her out. How could he, with Pia clinging hysterically to him? With the weight of his brother's death weighing him down?

How could she have expected him to leave those responsibilities for her, a woman he barely knew? Simply because she'd woven juvenile fantasies about him! Suddenly she felt a million years older than the immature girl who'd stood in the dock.

She raised her hand when he went to speak.

'Forget it, Domenico. It doesn't matter now.' To her surprise, it was true. Clinging to pain only held her back.

If this afternoon had shown her one thing it was that life was worth living—here, now. She intended to grab it by the throat and make the most of it. No point repining over what couldn't be changed.

'I'm thirsty. Do you have anything?'

Still Domenico stared, a strange arrested look in his eyes. 'There's beer or soft drink.' He stepped closer and now it wasn't his expression that held her.

He'd wiped the excess water away but hadn't wrapped a towel around himself. She drank in the sight of his gold-toned body, powerfully muscled and mouth-wateringly tempting. His low-slung board shorts emphasised his virile masculinity.

'Juice?' she croaked.

He poured her a glass then collected a beer and sat down.

'We're not going ashore?'

He shrugged and Lucy couldn't help but watch the way muscle and sinew moved across his shoulders and chest. In Rome he wore a suit like a man bred for formal dress. But his tailored clothes hid a body that spoke to her on the deepest, most elemental level. A level that made her forget herself.

'Not unless you're in a rush. Sunset over the island looks terrific from here. I thought you'd enjoy it.'

Lucy had no doubt she would, if she could tear her eyes from him.

'Thank you for this afternoon,' she said brightly. 'I've never done anything like this before.' Better to babble, she decided, than to gawk silently. Why didn't he cover himself?

'You've never been snorkelling?'

'Or for a ride in a speedboat. I've never been in a boat.'

His eyebrows rose. 'Never?'

Lucy smiled. She couldn't help it. His look of amazement was priceless. 'I'm a landlubber. I've never even been in a canoe.'

'But you can swim.'

'Even in England we've got public indoor pools, you know.' She paused. 'That's why I jumped at the chance to work in Italy, to see the Mediterranean.' Pleasure rose at the sight of the azure sea, the sky turning blush pink over Domenico's island and, when she turned, the dazzling view of villages clinging to the mainland.

It was the embodiment of those fantasies she'd had as a girl: sun, sand and an exotic foreign location. Even a sun-bronzed hunk with mesmerising good looks.

How naïve she'd been, yearning for adventure.

'You lived far from the sea?'

She sipped her juice. 'Not far. But our interests were all on dry land.'

'Our?'

'My dad and me.' She paused, registering the familiar pang of loss, but with her attention on the breathtaking view, the pain wasn't as sharp as usual. 'He was a bus driver and mad about vintage cars. I spent my childhood visiting displays of old automobiles or helping him fix ours.' She smiled. 'He'd have loved that one you have at the palazzo.'

Her smile faded and her throat tightened as it often did when she thought of her dad and the precious time they'd lost. 'He died just after the trial.'

She turned to find Domenico looking as grim as she'd ever seen him. This time the shiver that ran through her wasn't one of pleasure but chill foreboding.

'I'm sorry for your loss, Lucy.' He stood and moved towards her, then shifted abruptly away.

'It's no one's fault,' she murmured, refusing to listen to the little voice that said she should have found some way to see her beloved dad before he passed on. The voice of guilt, reminding her of all she'd put him through when he was so ill.

'But you wanted to be with him.'

Surprised, she looked up and saw understanding in his eyes. Of course. He'd been overseas when his brother had died. He knew how it felt to be far away at such a time.

'Yes.' Her voice was hoarse.

'He would have known. He would have understood.'

'I know, but it doesn't make it easier, does it?'

He was silent so long she thought she'd overstepped the mark, referring however obliquely to his own loss.

'No, it doesn't.' His mouth twisted. 'I was in New York when Sandro died. I kept telling myself it would never have happened if I'd been in Rome.'

Lucy bit her lip but finally let the words escape. 'It wouldn't have made any difference.' Did he want to hear that from the woman he thought responsible?

His eyes darkened, then he nodded. 'You're right. It's just that Sandro was—' he frowned '—special. Our parents died when I was young and Sandro was more than a big brother.'

'He was a good man,' she said. He hadn't been perfect. She'd wished he'd got specialist help for his wife's depression. Yet though she didn't agree, she understood his reluctance not to upset her when she saw outside help as proof she was a bad mother.

As an employer he'd been decent. Looking back, she realised what a quandary she'd put him in with her hysterical demand to leave immediately for England. Of course he'd put his family's needs first. She'd been young and overwrought, convinced a delay of a few days would make a difference to her father.

'Sandro was the one who taught me to swim, and to snorkel.' Domenico smiled wistfully. 'And, come to that, how to drive a speedboat.'

'My dad taught me how to strip down an engine.' Her mouth curved reminiscently. 'And how to make a kite and fly it. He even came to ballet classes when I was little and too shy to go alone.'

'He sounds like a perfect father.'

'He was.'

'You never wanted to be a mechanic or a driver like him?'

'No. I wanted to be a teacher. Working with children was always my dream. But that's not possible now.' She kept her voice brisk, refusing to wallow in self-pity.

'What will you do?' He sounded grave, as if her answer mattered.

Lucy looked at the sunset glowing amber and peach, rimmed with gold, then across to the mainland, where the dying sun gilded the coastline into something fantastic. It was the most exquisite view. She stored the memory against the empty days ahead, when life would be all struggle.

'I took a bookkeeping course. I thought there'd be more chance of getting a job working with figures than with people, given my record.' Except she doubted she'd be left alone long enough to find a job. This was a temporary respite. Once she left, the press would hound her. Who would employ her?

Abruptly she put her glass down and stood. 'Isn't it time we headed back?' She needed to be alone, to sort out the problems she'd avoided while she was here. She'd been living in a fantasy world. Soon she'd face reality.

Lucy spun away. But the deck was slick where she'd dripped seawater. Her foot shot out beneath her. She flailed but was falling when Domenico grabbed her and hauled her to him.

She told herself it was the shock of almost falling that made adrenalin surge and her heart thump. It had nothing to do with the look in Domenico's stormy eyes or the feel of his hot, damp body against hers.

'You can let me go.' Her breasts rose and fell with her choppy breathing.

Lucy put her hands on his arms to push herself away. Instead her fingers curled around the tensile strength of his biceps as if protesting the need to move.

'What if I don't want to let you go?' His voice was so deep its vibration rumbled through her.

Bent back over his arm, she watched his face come closer. His gaze moved to her mouth and her heart gave a mighty leap as she read his intent.

'No!' Her voice was breathless. 'I don't want this!'

He shook his head. 'I thought we'd agreed, Lucy. No more

lies.' For a moment longer he watched her, waiting for the protest they both knew she wouldn't make.

Then slowly, deliberately, he lowered his head.

CHAPTER EIGHT

DOMENICO'S LIPS BRUSHED hers in a light, barely there caress that made her mouth tingle and her blood surge. Twice, three times, he rubbed his mouth across hers, sending every sense into overdrive, till finally impatience overwhelmed caution and she clamped her hands to his wet hair and kissed him back.

There! No more teasing, just the heat of his mouth on hers. Her fingers slid around his skull, cradling him. The reality of him, the unyielding strength of bone and bunched muscle, of surprisingly soft lips making her blood sing, was everything she'd imagined and more.

His tongue slipped along the seam of her lips and it was the most natural thing in the world to open for him. For him to delve into her mouth and swirl delight through her veins. For her to respond with an honesty that eclipsed any vague thought of restraint.

She felt as if she'd waited a lifetime for this.

It didn't matter that she was a novice and he a master at this art. Eagerness made up for inexperience as she met his need with her own. Their tongues tangled, slid, stroked and goose bumps broke out across her flesh.

Domenico sucked her tongue into his mouth and her pulse catapulted. He nipped her bottom lip and Lucy sighed as pleasure engulfed her.

She leaned back, supported only by his embrace but she had no fear of falling. His arms were like steel ropes, lashing her close. His chest slid against hers and she gasped as electricity sparked and fired through her body, to her nipples, her stomach, the apex of her thighs. Behind the shocking heat came a melting languor that liquefied her bones and stole her will.

She tilted her head, accommodating him as desire escalated and their kisses grew urgent, hungry. She was burning up and so was he, his flesh on fire beneath her hands.

Yes! This was what she wanted from him, had always wanted. Even when she'd spat and snarled, she'd fought this chemistry between them.

Why had she tried to fight it? It was delicious, addictive.

Domenico tasted of the sea and dark, wickedly rich chocolate—a seductive mix. She shivered in sensual overload as he devoured her with a thoroughness that matched every long-suppressed need.

Had he yearned for this too? Had he lain awake, imagining this moment?

The slide of their bodies was pure magic. The thin fabric of her swimsuit was negligible against the heated promise of his body. Lucy pressed closer, revelling in his powerful musculature, the heady scent of his skin and a deeper, musky note of arousal.

He kissed her throat and she arched back, feeling her feminine power even as she knew herself caught in a web of desire. She was utterly open to his caresses, unprotected against his strength. Yet Lucy felt no doubt or fear. Each kiss he pressed to her skin was homage to the spell woven between them.

Rousing herself from drugged delight, Lucy pulled herself higher, rubbing her cheek against his. The friction of his sandpapery jaw sent another shaft of lightning straight to her groin and she shivered in delicious arousal.

She nipped his ear lobe and heard him growl, low in his throat. It was the sexiest thing she'd ever heard. She smiled and did it again, eager at the thought of Domenico reacting to her at the most primal level.

Large hands wrapped around her waist and he lifted her high to sit on something. Domenico pushed her thighs apart and stepped between them, lodging himself at her core.

'Domenico.' Her voice was a rasp of pleasure as the fire spread, overriding a belated voice of warning.

She wanted him. Had done for so long. Even in the days when she'd hated him, she'd secretly yearned for this delight. This affirmation. She'd given up trying to puzzle the attraction that smouldered between them. It was enough to let glorious pleasure sweep her away.

Lucy felt the power of his erection between her legs and against her belly and her breath faltered. They felt so *right* together. It was all she could do not to rock against him, lost in the need for sensual satisfaction.

With an effort of willpower that almost undid her, she opened her eyes and met the mercurial glitter of his. Heat and shimmering silver fire engulfed her.

His hand palmed her breast and she gasped, overloaded with exquisite sensation. It was too much to bear.

She grabbed his neck and pulled him to her, wanting his lips on hers. Needing the dark mystery of their kisses. Needing *him*.

Long fingers thrust through her hair, tipping her head back as he tasted her in a long, luxurious kiss that curled her toes. His other hand teased her nipple. Darts of heat arced from the spot, making her move restlessly.

Immediately Domenico slid his hand from her scalp, down her spine, to splay over her bottom and drag her up tight against him. He kissed her hard, his tongue delving as his blatantly aroused body surged against hers.

The world tumbled and re-formed. Her blood sizzled like molten metal swirling in a crucible of pure need. Her lips moved against his and her dazed brain almost stopped functioning.

Domenico eased away a fraction as he slipped his hand over her bare thigh to brush the Lycra at the juncture of her thighs. A bolt of lightning slashed through her, jolting every nerve end, concentrating every sense on that point of contact. She grabbed his shoulders.

Wide-eyed she looked up. His face was pared to austere lines that spoke of raw hunger. Gone was his sophistication, stripped to something more elemental.

More dangerous. The words surfaced in her foggy brain as long fingers teased the band of fabric at her inner thighs, sending whorls of fiery pleasure through her.

Desire warred with shock as she realised how far their kisses had taken her. To the brink of fulfilment. To the brink of giving herself to the man she'd called enemy. To the point of baring herself emotionally as well as physically. *That* was what scared her.

Her hand clamped his as he moved to insinuate his fingers under the fabric. He froze, his eyes turning blindly to hers. His other hand still cupped her breast.

Lucy watched realisation dawn. His eyes lost that unfocused glitter and widened a fraction.

'I think it's time to stop.'

It was a wonder he heard. Her voice was hoarse, a frayed thread of sound. Yet he understood. An instant later he'd backed away, his hands furrowing through his thick hair as if he didn't trust himself not to touch her again.

Lucy swayed, perched on the edge of the boat. Without his support she felt bereft. She bit her tongue to stop herself calling him back. Her eyes ate him up, from the hard jut of his jaw to the dusting of hair across his broad pectoral muscles and the swell of his biceps as he lifted his arms. From the heavy arousal to the storm-dark glint of his hooded eyes.

She wanted him still. Wanted him to step back and obliterate her doubts with the caress of that clever mouth, seduce her into delight with that big, hard body. Every nerve ending danced in anticipation, undermining her resolve.

Fear surfaced. She'd never known how compelling the need

for sexual gratification could be. Domenico tempted her to forget everything. She'd thought herself strong and self-sufficient. Yet all it had taken was one kiss to undo every barrier she'd spent years erecting.

What did it mean?

'You're right. It's late.' He turned away and, to her consternation, Lucy felt disappointment swell.

After an evening apart breakfast the next morning was full of silences and stilted conversation.

What had got into him?

Oh, he knew what had got into him. He'd desired Lucy from the moment he'd set eyes on her all those years ago.

How could he have come so close to sex, raw and unvarnished, with the woman convicted of killing Sandro? Guilt churned in his belly. Where was his family loyalty?

Gone the moment he held her. Evicted by sexual desire and the conviction Lucy Knight was a mystery he'd just begun to unravel. An enigma who'd haunted him for years. He desperately needed to understand her for his peace of mind.

It wasn't only desire she triggered. He'd been beside himself with thwarted fury when he realised she'd been attacked by a family employee. His need to protect had been as strong as if she was his responsibility. *His woman.*

A frisson of warning crept down his spine.

Yesterday's revelations had rocked him to the core.

For years he'd believed Lucy had engineered their initial meeting. How unlikely a coincidence that she'd literally bump into him, on his fleeting visit to Rome, when she already worked for his brother?

When the revelations had come thick and fast about Sandro's uncharacteristic weakness for his au pair, the way she'd twisted him round her little finger and milked him for expensive gifts, it hadn't taken a genius to work out she'd tried out the same wiles on Domenico.

He'd picked up the tension in his brother's household that very morning on his visit, only later realising it was due to a love triangle.

Or was it?

She'd said yesterday she hadn't known his identity before the trial. It was tempting to think Lucy lied but there was no reason now. Besides, he'd seen real hurt in her face when she'd asked why he'd avoided her. Hell! He no longer knew what to believe.

Could she be innocent?

His blood froze. The idea that he'd misjudged her so badly, letting her suffer for a crime she didn't commit, didn't bear thinking about.

He looked across to where she sat, eyes riveted on her breakfast as if it fascinated her.

Never before had she refused to meet his eyes.

He wanted to demand she look at him. He wanted to kiss that sultry down-turned mouth and unleash the passion that had blasted the back off his skull yesterday. Behind that reserve lurked a woman unlike any he'd known. More alive, more vital, more dangerous.

Was he out of control, ignoring what he owed his dead brother? Or were his doubts valid?

'Mail, sir.' The maid entered with a bundle of letters. To his surprise she placed an envelope beside Lucy's plate.

'For me?' Lucy frowned. 'Thank you.'

Who knew she was here? Someone she'd corresponded with via email? He forced himself to take another sip of fresh juice rather than demand to know who'd sent it.

She slipped a finger under the seal and withdrew a sheet of paper, discarding the envelope. That was when he saw a bold, too-familiar logo. It belonged to the magazine that had run her stepmother's interview.

He clenched his jaw, forcing down bile. Obviously Lucy was making the most of her opportunities, accepting his hospitality while negotiating with the gutter press for a better financial deal.

It shouldn't surprise him.

So why did he feel betrayed?

So much for the wronged innocent. How often would he let her dupe him?

'Is it a better offer?'

'Sorry?' Lucy looked up into eyes of gun-metal grey, piercing in their intensity.

She blinked, stunned by the change in Domenico. His eyebrows slashed in a V of disapproval and he looked as if he'd bitten something sour.

True, she'd shied away from contact this morning, still shocked by her response yesterday. But there'd been no venom in his voice, no ice in his stare when she'd entered the breakfast room.

'I assume from your absorption they're offering better terms than I did.'

Belatedly understanding dawned as he stared at the paper in her hand.

Pain sliced down, sharp as a blade of ice. It tore through her heart, shredding the bud of hope she'd nursed since yesterday. Making a mockery of that warm, sunshine glow Domenico had put there with his protectiveness, his acceptance and his desire.

What an idiot she'd been! How pathetically gullible.

Hadn't life taught her not to believe in miracles?

Domenico Volpe caring for her, trusting her even a little, would be a miracle. Yet against the odds she'd hoped some of the emotions she'd read in him yesterday had been real.

She'd almost given herself to him!

Lucy cringed at how far she'd let herself be conned.

Crazy, but even more than his sexual hunger or his protectiveness, Lucy missed their camaraderie as they'd snorkelled and watched the sunset. The sense of acceptance and liking.

That had been precious. They'd shared things that were important to them both. Memories of their loved ones.

For those few hours Lucy had felt genuine warmth, a spark of liking. Of trust.

Fool, fool, fool. He'd buttered her up to get what he wanted.

'I said—'

'I heard.' She looked from him to the letter in her clenched fingers. There was nothing to choose between them. At least the press was upfront about what they wanted. Domenico had tried to distract her with a show of friendliness.

And she'd fallen for it.

What was one more deceit in a world of disappointment? Yet this one gouged pain in a heart she'd told herself was too well protected to hurt again.

'It's an attractive offer,' she said at last. As if the idea of selling her story to those hyenas didn't make her flesh crawl. They'd done more than destroy her reputation. They'd harried her poor dad in his last weeks. 'I'll have to consider it carefully.'

Distaste burned but maybe she didn't have the luxury of saying no any more. If she sold her story she'd get enough to start fresh. Hadn't she earned the right to profit after the terrible price she'd paid?

Maybe if she co-operated they'd leave her alone and she could pretend to be the woman she'd been before.

And pigs might fly. The press would never let her go whilst there was a story to be sold. Lucy squeezed her eyes shut, imagining lurid revelations about her attempts to live a normal life. Shocked reactions from neighbours when they discovered a killer living in their midst.

It would never end. Not for years.

She snapped open her eyes and glared as Domenico looked down his aristocratic nose at her.

A silent howl of despair rose. She'd wanted to trust him. She'd begun to open up, to believe he cared.

'Perhaps I could canvass the other media outlets and see what they're offering.'

His scowl was a balm to her lacerated feelings. Let him stew!

'You haven't already done that? Isn't that why you spend so long on the computer? Negotiating the best deal?'

'Actually, no. But of course you won't believe me.'

He leaned across the table, his eyes flashing daggers. 'If you haven't contacted the press, how do they know where you are?'

Lucy shoved her chair back and stood.

'Perhaps they took an educated guess,' she purred. 'Since they knew I was at your palazzo it wouldn't take much to suppose I'd be at one of your properties. Maybe they've written to me at each one. Who knows? Maybe this is the first of a flurry of offers.' She smiled, injecting saccharine sweetness into her tone. 'A bidding war. Wouldn't that be fun?'

He looked as if he wanted to strangle her with his bare hands. They clenched into massive fists before him.

Lucy's bravado ended as she recalled the stroke of those hands across her body. He'd touched her as if she were the most precious thing on earth.

She'd *felt* precious, desirable, special.

She forced down welling pain.

'Here.' She slowed as she walked past, letting the letter flutter to his lap. 'See what the opposition is offering. Maybe you'll increase your bid.'

Lucy strode out of the door before nausea engulfed her.

'Excuse me, boss. Have you seen Chiara?'

Domenico looked up from his email to find Rocco at the door, concern etched on his face.

'Isn't she with Lucy? They spend half the day together.'

'Chiara said Miss Lucy couldn't play today. She said she looked upset.' He paused and Domenico's stomach dipped. A finger of guilt slid across his neck as he remembered the pain he'd seen on Lucy's face when he'd confronted her.

After what they'd shared yesterday, and in light of what they'd *almost* shared, her anguish had been a knife to his gut. It made him feel like a jerk. Even though he was trying to protect his family, he'd been in the wrong.

Maybe because his anger wasn't about protecting his nephew but himself? Because he'd overreacted when he'd seen her correspondence as he'd felt his illusions shatter?

Lucy Knight got under his skin as no other woman. He'd lashed out because emotion had overridden his brain.

Certainty had become doubt. But was it because he wanted her for himself or because she was innocent? He circled again and again round the puzzling truths he'd discovered about her.

She had him so confounded he didn't know what to believe. He'd felt so betrayed this morning, discovering he couldn't rely on his instincts where she was concerned.

Then he'd read the letter and realised she'd told the truth. The magazine had taken a chance on finding her here.

He'd been boorish and in the wrong. The knowledge didn't sit well.

'Chiara didn't come in for lunch.' Rocco interrupted his troubled musings.

'That's not like her.' Domenico frowned, anxiety stirring.

'No. She hasn't been seen in any of her usual haunts for hours. I'm just about to search for her.'

'Where's Lucy?' Domenico shoved his chair back.

'She's already searching.'

Most of the staff was scouring the shoreline, though no one had voiced their deepest fears, that Chiara had got out of her depth in the water. Domenico strode along the path at the wilderness end of the island, knowing someone had to check the less obvious places. That was how he ran into Lucy. Literally. She catapulted around a curve in the track and into his arms.

Domenico grasped her close. The summer sun lit her hair to gold and he inhaled her sweet fragrance. Yesterday he'd imprinted her body on his memory and now he didn't want to let her go. Crazy at it seemed, it felt as if she belonged there against him.

'Please,' she gasped, her hand splaying against his chest. It trembled. 'Please, help me.'

'Lucy?' He tilted her head up. 'What is it?'

She was breathless, barely able to talk. Her cheeks were flushed and there was dirt smeared across her cheek as if she'd fallen. Domenico tensed.

'Is it Chiara?'

She nodded. 'Up ahead.' She grabbed his shirt as he made to go. 'No! Wait.' She gulped in air and he forced himself to wait till she could speak.

'You'll be faster than me. We need rope and a torch. A medical kit too.'

'The well?' His heart plunged into a pool of icy fear.

'No. A sinkhole. I found her hair ribbon on the edge of it and some marbles.'

Domenico's breath stopped. If she'd been playing too close to the edge and then leaned in…

'I'll go and check it out.'

Lucy shook her head, her hands clutching like talons. 'No! I've done that. There's no sound from below. We need a rope to reach her. Every minute counts. Please, trust me on this.' He read her desperation.

He thought of the way she'd cared for Chiara as they played together, and her careful nurturing of Taddeo all those years ago.

He couldn't waste precious time. He had to trust her judgement. A second later he was gone, pounding down the dusty path to the villa.

When he returned, laden with supplies, Lucy had disappeared. He found her half a kilometre on, at the edge of the narrow hole. She was leaning down, talking. As he sprinted to her he realised she was telling a story about a brave princess called Chiara who was rescued in her hour of need.

'She's spoken to you?' He shrugged off the rope looped across his shoulder and put down the medical kit.

Lucy's face was solemn. 'No. But I thought if she comes to and hears a familiar voice she won't be so scared.' Her mouth was white-rimmed and she blinked hard. Domenico squeezed her shoulder.

'Thank you, Lucy. That's a great idea.' He wasn't sure he'd have thought of it.

'Where are the others?' She looked beyond him.

'Still at the shore. They'll be here soon. Chiara's grandmother will have got the message to them by now.' He looked around. 'I'll have to tie this to that old olive tree. You keep a look out while I'm down there.'

'No. I'll go.'

Domenico dropped to his knees and shone the torch down the hole but he couldn't see anything. His heart sank but he quickly uncoiled the rope.

'I said I'll go down.' As if he'd let her risk her neck down there. 'My property. My risk.'

'Have you seen the size of that hole? Your shoulders are too wide. You'll never fit.'

Domenico turned to scrutinise the sinkhole.

Damn! She was right. In his youth he'd done some caving but the squeezes had become difficult as he'd grown. This hole was so narrow he wasn't sure a grown woman could get down.

Nevertheless he opened his mouth to protest.

Lucy's fingers pressed his lips. He tasted dust and salt and the familiar sweet flavour of her skin. His nostrils filled with her scent. Despite the crisis his body tightened.

'Don't argue, Domenico. If I'd come out to play with her this morning this wouldn't have happened.'

'It's not your fault.' Already he was looping the rope around her, securing it firmly. 'You didn't do anything wrong.'

Deep blue eyes met his and a flash of something passed between them. Something that pounded through his chest and into his soul.

'Thank you, Domenico. But that's how it feels. Now, how do I lower myself?'

'Don't worry. I'll take care of it all.'

The next hour was pure nightmare for Lucy. She'd never been fond of small, dark places and being confined in a claustrophobically narrow hole evoked panicked memories of her first nights behind bars, when life had been an unreal horror.

She scraped off skin getting through the entrance but to her relief, the hole widened as she progressed.

Even better, she found Chiara conscious, though barely. Lucy's heart sped as she heard her whimper.

'It's all right, sweetie. You're safe.'

Nevertheless it took an age. First to undo the rope so Domenico could send down the medical kit. Then to assess Chiara's injuries—grazes, a nasty bump and a broken wrist. Then to bind her wrist and reassure her while she secured the thick rope around her.

Lucy wished she could go up and hold her close but there wasn't room for two. Finally, an age later, she tugged the rope so Domenico could lift Chiara free. Lucy bit her lip, hoping her assessment of minor injuries was right. They couldn't leave her here much longer; already she was shivering from shock and cold. Goodness knew how long it would take to get a medic from the mainland.

The shadows had lengthened and the sky clouded over by the time Lucy entrusted herself again to Domenico's strong arms. She was breathless with relief as he hauled her up to sit on the ground. A crowd of people was there, huddled around Chiara.

Lucy gulped lungfuls of sweet air, hardly daring believe she was on the surface again.

'How is she?' Her voice sounded rusty.

'She'll be fine, but she's going to the mainland for a check up.' The deep voice came from close by. Powerful arms pulled her higher then wrapped her close. A sense of belonging filled her, and sheer relief as she sank into Domenico's hold.

Weakness invaded her bones and Lucy let her head drop against his chest. Just while she collected herself. Her heart pounded out of sync as she breathed deep, absorbing the peace she found in his embrace.

How could it be? He'd berated and duped her. He'd raised her up till she felt like a goddess in his arms, then reduced her almost to tears with cruel taunts.

Her body betrayed her. It never wanted to move again.

Dimly she became aware of noise and lifted her head to applause and cheers. They were all looking at her, smiling and clapping.

'Thank you, Lucy.' Rocco came forward and, turning her in Domenico's arms, kissed her on both cheeks. 'You saved our special girl.'

His mother came next, the friendly woman who'd been so kind to her, then a string of others, some she knew and some she didn't. One by one they embraced her and kissed her cheeks. And all the while Domenico supported her as if he knew her shaky legs couldn't keep her upright unaided.

Warmth stirred. A warmth Lucy hadn't known in what seemed a lifetime of cold, miserable isolation. It radiated out till her whole body tingled with it. Something deep inside splintered and fell away, like ice from a glacier. Its loss made her feel raw and vulnerable and yet closer to these welcoming people than she'd felt to anyone in years.

Finally they moved away, bustling around Chiara.

Lucy stayed in Domenico's arms, too exhausted, too stunned to move. A smile stretched her muscles yet she felt the hot track of tears down her cheeks. She didn't understand why she cried, but she couldn't seem to stop. A sob filled her chest then broke out, shocking her.

Domenico's arms tightened.

'It's all right, Lucy. We'll have you home soon.'

Home? Bitterness drenched her. She was the eternal outsider. She had no home, nowhere to belong. Then she stiffened. She had to get a grip.

Lucy blinked and saw Domenico looking down at her, no arrogance, no hauteur, no accusation on his face. There was an expression in his gleaming eyes that made another splinter of ice crack away. She shivered, realising how defenceless she was against him now.

'Thank you, Lucy, for saving Chiara.' He lifted his hand and wiped her cheek. She'd never seen him look more serious. 'You risked your life for her.'

Lucy shook her head. 'Anyone would have—'

'No! Not anyone. Lots wouldn't have dared. If it hadn't been for you I dread to think how long it would have been before we found her and got her out.'

His thumb swiped her cheek again, then rubbed across her lip. She tasted the subtle spice of Domenico's skin through the salt tang of tears.

'I was wrong about you.' His voice had lost its mellow richness. Instead she heard strain. 'You're not the woman I thought. What I said this morning… I apologise.' He drew a deep breath. 'Can you forgive me?'

Numb with shock, Lucy nodded.

Then sweet wonder filled her as he dipped his head. Their gazes meshed, their breaths mingled and something like joy swelled in her breast.

Domenico leaned in and kissed her gently, tenderly, with a reverence that filled her heart with delight and eased her wounded soul.

CHAPTER NINE

'OF COURSE TADDEO is welcome here as usual. Nothing will ever change that. He's my nephew and as precious to me as a son.'

Domenico thrust his hand through his hair in frustration as his sister-in-law squawked her outrage down the phone line. She was family and, for his nephew's sake especially, Domenico put up with her.

'Yes, Lucy's here. Far better she stays here away from the press than selling her story. Isn't that what you wanted?'

He eased the phone from his ear as Pia unleashed a torrent of objections. Mouth flattening, he strode to the wide terrace and inhaled deep of the fresh sea air. Pia had read about Domenico rescuing Lucy from the press and demanded to know why she was still with him.

As if he had to clear his actions with Pia!

He'd only got involved in this situation because Pia had pleaded for him to intervene.

Though this had passed well beyond a simple business negotiation. He was…personally involved.

He thought of his overwhelming relief when Lucy had emerged from that dark hole. For heart-stopping minutes panic had filled him as it seemed to take a lifetime to haul her up. Domenico tasted rusty fear, remembering.

He'd gathered her close and hadn't been able to release her even when her well-wishers crowded around. He'd needed her with him.

Domenico scrubbed a hand over his jaw. He and Lucy had unfinished business. Business he'd delayed. It had nothing to do with Sandro or Pia or the press.

'Calm down, Pia, and hear me out.'

Lucy heard Domenico as she entered the house. She stopped, not to eavesdrop but because he had that effect on her. She'd given up pretending. She might be weak where he was concerned but she refused to lie to herself.

The sound of that rich macchiato voice pooled heat deep in her body. The memory of his tender kiss, as if he treasured her, made forbidden hope unfurl.

'I understand your concerns, Pia, but she's not the woman the press have painted.'

Lucy started, realising Domenico was talking to his sister-in-law about *her*. She went rigid, torn between curiosity and protecting herself. Since the rescue it had been hard to keep him at arm's length. Yet she needed to because he could hurt her badly.

She was moving away when he spoke again.

'That was years ago, Pia. People change. *She's* changed. Did you get her letter?'

Lucy's steps faltered.

'You shouldn't have destroyed it. She wrote to say how much she regretted Sandro's death. She was genuine, Pia. I'm sure of that.'

Lucy's heart hammered against her ribs, her hand clenching on the door handle.

Domenico was standing up for her against his sister-in-law! She could scarcely believe it.

'I understand, Pia. But it's time we moved on. For Taddeo's sake.' He paused as if listening. 'We can't change the past, much as we wish it. I know Lucy wishes she could. She's genuinely sorry for what happened to Sandro.'

Lucy clung to the door handle as her knees wobbled.

'That's your choice, Pia. But think about what I've said. Living in the present is the best thing for your son. He's a fine boy, one Sandro would have been proud of. You don't want him growing up bitter and fearful, do you?'

Domenico's voice dipped on his brother's name, reminding Lucy this was a private conversation.

She released the door and crossed the foyer. Confusion filled her but it didn't dim her smile and her step was light.

Domenico had stood up for her!

Sunlight filtered through spreading branches and Lucy leaned against her cushion with a sigh of contentment.

'More?' Domenico lifted a bunch of dark grapes with the bloom of the vineyard still on them.

'I couldn't.' She patted her stomach. 'I've eaten like a horse.'

His eyes followed the movement and fire licked her. She stiffened then forced herself to relax as his gaze grew intent. Domenico saw too much, especially now when her skill at hiding her feelings had disintegrated.

'I'll have some.' Chiara skipped across the clearing. The plaster on her wrist was the only reminder of last week's ordeal.

Lucy met Domenico's rueful gaze and realised they shared the same thought. She smiled, sharing the moment of relief, and he smiled back. It was like watching the sunrise after endless night, warming her with an inner glow.

Her breathing snagged then resumed, quicker and shorter as she watched his eyes darken. Her skin shivered as if responding to the phantom brush of his hand.

'Domi? Can't I have some?'

Domenico dragged his attention to Chiara. 'Of course, *bella*.' He handed over the bunch then leaned back on his arms. Lucy's heart pattered faster. If he shifted again they'd be touching.

Domenico hadn't touched her since Chiara's accident. That made her wonder if she'd imagined the strength of his embrace that day, or the way his hands had trembled as he held her. Her breath eased out in a sigh.

She'd never forget the magic of his kiss. Her fingers drifted to her mouth as she relived the brush of his lips.

It worried her how much she longed for him. How readily she responded now he treated her as a welcome guest. After hearing him defend her to Pia she hadn't been able to quell effervescent excitement, or the conviction that things had changed irrevocably between them.

She looked up to find his hooded eyes gleaming with heat. It arced between them, pulsing darts of sizzling awareness to her breasts, her belly and beyond.

Lucy shivered and his mouth curled in a lopsided smile that carved a long dimple down his lean cheek. She curled her fingers into the grass, fighting the impulse to reach out and touch.

'So, Lucy.' He paused, glancing across to where Chiara sat with the flowers she'd gathered. 'You approve of Italian picnics?'

'I *adore* Italian picnics.'

'You've only been on one.'

She shrugged and felt the soft breeze waft over her bare arms, the melting laxness in her bones. 'What's not to like? Sunshine and food fresh from the farm.' She gestured to the remains of home baked bread, bowls of ricotta and local honey, prosciutto, olives and a cornucopia of summer fruits. 'It's heaven. Almost as good as our picnics back home.'

His eyebrows slanted high. 'Almost?'

'Well, there's nothing like a sudden English rainstorm to liven up outdoor eating.'

He laughed, the deep rich sound curling round her. An answering smile hovered on Lucy's mouth.

Smiling had become second nature lately. Because she'd been made to feel she belonged. By Chiara's warm-hearted family and by Domenico. Gone was his judgemental frown, replaced by easy-going acceptance that banished so many shadows. He'd taken her snorkelling again, taught her to waterski and whiled away more hours than he needed to in her company, never once mentioning his brother or the story she might sell to the press. *As if he trusted her.*

Lucy could relax with him now.

No, that wasn't right. This tingling awareness wasn't relaxation. It was confidence and excitement and pleasure all rolled together.

Risky pleasure, when it lulled her into fantasy. When she found herself hoping the horrors of the past would vanish and leave them untroubled in this paradise.

A chill frisson snaked up her backbone.

It can't last.

One day soon the real world would intrude.

Lucy marvelled that Domenico had taken so much time out from what must be a heavy work schedule. He'd have business elsewhere. And she…she'd have to go too.

Regret lanced her and she twisted towards Chiara rather than let Domenico glimpse her pain.

Its intensity shocked her. It ripped through her, stealing the breath in her lungs.

Lucy pressed a hand to her chest.

'Are you okay?' Domenico moved abruptly as if sensing her discomfort.

'I'm fine.' This time her smile was a desperate lie. 'Just a little too much indulgence after all.'

Panic stirred. This wasn't just regret that the vacation was almost over. She'd known it would be tough trying to create a new life. She'd spent the last weeks facing the unpalatable facts of a future without family, friends, a job or anywhere to call home.

But the dread that made her skin break into a cold sweat owed nothing to that. It had everything to do with Domenico Volpe and what she'd begun to feel for him.

She felt…too much.

On a surge of frantic energy Lucy shot to her feet. Domenico was just as quick, his expression concerned as he broke his own unspoken rule and encircled her wrist with long fingers.

Instantly Lucy stilled, willing her pulse to slow.

'What is it, Lucy?'

'Nothing. I just wanted to move.'

Grey eyes searched her face and she held her breath, praying he couldn't read her thoughts. She could barely understand them herself. Amazing as it seemed, she *cared* for Domenico in a way that made the idea of leaving him send panic spurting through her.

'Liar.' To her addled brain the whisper sounded like a caress.

The stroke of his thumb against her wrist *was* a caress. She clamped her hand on his to stop it, looking down to see his dark golden fingers cradle her paler ones.

They held each other, fingers meshing. Strength throbbed through her. How could she give this up?

Because she must.

'You promised—'

'I promised not to revisit the past.' His breath was warm on her cheek. 'But this isn't about the past, is it, Lucy? This is about the present. Here. Now.'

Unable to stop herself, she turned her head and met his eyes. Molten heat poured through her as their gazes locked. The world receded, blocked out by the knowledge she read there, the awareness.

'I can't—' Words clogged in her throat.

'It's all right, Lucy. You don't have to do anything.'

'Domi? Lucy? What's wrong?'

Domenico looked down at Chiara and Lucy felt the sudden release of tension as if a band had snapped undone around her chest. She breathed deep, trying to find equilibrium. But Domenico still held her, his touch firm and possessive. A thrill of secret pleasure rippled through her.

'Everything's fine, little one. I've got a surprise for you both.'

* * *

The surprise was a trip to the mainland, to a town that climbed steep hills in a fantasy of pastel-washed houses. Lucy wished she had a camera. Everywhere she turned were amazing vistas and intriguing corners.

'Come on, you're so slow.' Chiara tugged her hand.

'I've never seen any place like this.' Lucy lifted her gaze past a tree heavy with huge golden lemons to the view of green hilltops above the town. 'It's beautiful.'

The little girl tilted her head. 'Isn't it pretty where you come from?'

Instantly Lucy had a vision of grey concrete and metal, of bare floors and inmates scarred by life. It seemed like a dream as she stood here in the mellow afternoon sunlight.

'Yes, it is pretty.' She thought of the village where she'd grown up. 'The bluebells grow so thick in spring it's like a carpet in the forest. Our house had roses around the door and the biggest swing you ever saw underneath a huge old tree in the garden.'

Summers had seemed endless then. Like this one. Except it had to end.

She'd have to forget trying to find a bookkeeping job. Instead she'd look for casual waitressing when she got to England. Something that didn't require character references.

'Come on.' Chiara tugged her hand again. 'Domi said we can have a *gelato* in the square.'

Lucy let herself be led back towards the centre of town. Domenico would have finished his errand for Chiara's *nonna*. He'd be waiting. Her heart gave a little jump that reminded her forcibly that it was time to leave for England.

Yet her smile lingered. For this afternoon she'd live in the moment. Surely she could afford to store up memories of one perfect afternoon before she faced the bleak future?

They were passing some shops, Chiara hopping on one leg then the other, when a shout yanked Lucy's head around.

'Look! It's her!'

A thin woman on the other side of the narrow street pointed straight at Lucy and Chiara.

'I *told* you it was her when they walked up the hill, but you didn't believe me. So I went in and got this. See?' She waved a magazine, drawing the attention not only of the man beside her, but of passers-by.

Lucy's heart sank. She took Chiara's hand. 'Come on, sweetie.'

But the woman moved faster, her voice rising.

'It's her I tell you. She's a killer. What's she doing with that girl? Someone should call the police.'

Nausea roiled in Lucy's belly as she forced herself to walk steadily, not break into a sprint. That would only frighten Chiara. Besides, fleeing would only incite the crowd. She remembered how a mob of inmates reacted when they sensed fear in a newcomer.

Skin prickling from the heat of so many avid stares, she tugged Chiara a little faster. Around them were murmurs from a gathering crowd.

The woman with the magazine came close but not close enough to stop their progress. But the malevolent curiosity on her sharp features spelled trouble. For a moment Lucy was tempted to snarl a threat to make her shrink back.

But she couldn't do it. She couldn't bear to regress to that hunted woman she'd been, half-savage with the need to escape, ready to lash out at anyone in her way.

It had only been a few weeks since her release but they'd altered her. She'd lost the dangerous edge that had been her protection in prison. Besides, what sort of example would that set? She squeezed Chiara's hand and kept walking.

'Why doesn't someone stop her?' the woman shrieked. 'She's a murderer. She shouldn't be allowed near an innocent child.'

Out of the corner of her eye, Lucy saw the picture in the

magazine she waved like a banner. It was a close-up of Lucy getting into Domenico's limousine. The headline in blood-red said, 'Where Is Sandro's Killer Now?'.

Her heart leapt against her ribcage as fear battered her. The nightmare would never end, would it? Now Chiara was caught in it. She felt the child flinch as the woman screeched. Anger fired deep inside.

She stopped and turned, tugging Chiara protectively behind her.

The woman shrank back apace. 'Don't let her hurt me! Help!' Instantly others surged forward, curious.

'Signora—' Lucy dredged up a polite tone '—please don't shout. Can't you see you're frightening my friend? It would be much better for everyone if you didn't.'

The woman gawped, opening then closing her mouth. Then she hissed, 'Listen! She's threatening me.'

'Lucy?' Chiara's voice was unsteady, her eyes huge as Lucy turned to reassure her, stroking her hair and plastering what she hoped was a confident smile on her face. But inside she trembled. This was turning ugly.

'Grab her, someone. Can't you see she shouldn't be with that child?'

There was a murmur from the crowd and Lucy sensed movement towards her. She spun around to confront a sea of faces. Her stomach dived but she drew herself up straight.

'Touch me or my friend and you'll answer to the police.' She kept her tone calm by sheer willpower, her gaze scanning back and forth across the gathering.

The words were loud even over the mutterings of the crowd. And enough to hold them back...for now.

Domenico took in the defiant tilt of Lucy's head and her wide-planted feet, as if she stood ready to fight off an attack. But she couldn't fend them off. Her hands were behind her back, holding Chiara's.

She looked like a lioness defending her young.

A lioness outnumbered by hunters.

Something plunged through his chest, a sharp purging heat like iron hot from the forge. His hands curled into fists so tight they trembled with the force of his rage. He wanted to smash something. Preferably the shrewish face of the woman stirring the crowd.

He strode up behind Lucy.

She must have sensed movement for she swung round, her face pale.

Her eyes widened. She gulped, drawing attention to the tense muscles in her slender throat and the flat line of her mouth. She looked down, murmuring reassurance to Chiara, but not before he'd seen the fear in her eyes. Half an hour ago those eyes had danced with pleasure at the sight of the pretty town and its market stalls.

Naked fury misted his vision.

Domenico stalked the last pace towards her. In one swift movement he scooped up Chiara and cuddled her close. He looped his other arm around Lucy and pulled her to him. She was rigid as a board and he felt tension hum through her, an undercurrent of leashed energy.

'I don't know who you are,' he growled at the harridan in the thick of the crowd, 'but I'll thank you not to frighten my family.'

Beside him Lucy jerked then stilled. He heard her soft gasp and rubbed his palm up her arm. It was covered in goose bumps. *Damn him for leaving them alone!*

'But she's—'

'It doesn't matter who she is, *signora*. But I'll have your name.' His voice was lethal. 'I'll need it for my complaint to the police. For public nuisance and harassment.' He watched the woman wilt. 'Possibly incitement to violence.'

He turned and glared at the gathering, which had already thinned substantially.

'And the names of anyone else involved.'

He turned to Chiara, giving them time to digest that. 'Are you all right, *bella*?'

She nodded. 'But Lucy isn't. She was shaking.'

'It's all right, little one. I'm here now and Lucy will be fine.'

Domenico felt Lucy shudder and held her tighter, wishing he had both arms free to hold her. Wishing he hadn't dispensed with security support today. He turned back to the street. Only a couple of people remained, watching wide-eyed. He heard the woman at the front whispering.

'He's the one in the magazine. The one whose—'

'Basta!' He scowled. 'One more word from you and I'm pressing charges.' He gave her a look he reserved for underperforming managers. A moment later, she and her companions had scuttled away.

'Right, girls.' He turned towards the main square, his arms tight around Chiara and Lucy, his tone as reassuring as he could make it over simmering fury. *'Gelato* time. I'm having lemon. How about you?'

CHAPTER TEN

Lucy shoved her spare shoes into her bag. Just as well she didn't have much to pack. She'd be done in no time.

Then what? the little voice in the back of her head piped up. *Back to the town where you almost caused a riot simply walking down the street?*

She'd talk to Domenico—

No, not him.

She'd talk to Rocco. Surely a security expert could suggest how she could get away and lose herself in the crowds of a big city in England. Anonymity was all she asked. She had no hope of ever getting that in Italy. Not with the press hot on her trail.

Unless she gave in and sold her story.

Her stomach cramped at the idea of lowering herself like Sylvia, her stepmother. That betrayal cut deep. How could Sylvia have done it?

Lucy needed the money, now more than ever. But she needed her self-respect too.

She grabbed a shirt and slapped it on top of the shoes, fighting the hot prickle of tears.

What was happening to her? She hadn't cried in years, not till Chiara's accident. Now she wanted to curl up and blub out her self-pity. It was as if her defences had collapsed, leaving her prey to weakness she'd thought she'd conquered years before.

She looked at the winking lights of the mainland.

A few hours ago she'd been *happy*. Happier than she'd believed possible. The day had been glorious, the surroundings spectacular, and she'd basked in Domenico's approval and solicitude. She'd blossomed into a woman she barely recognised, who actually believed good things might come to pass. Who believed Domenico saw beyond the surface to the woman she was at heart, or was before the last years had scarred her.

She dragged a deep breath into constricted lungs.

He'd been kind, caring, fun. She'd enjoyed his company. More, she'd believed he'd enjoyed hers. And though he hadn't kissed her again, she'd felt the weight of it between them, a potent presence. A promise.

But there could never be more between them. She tried to tell herself he was softening her up to convince her to sign his contract. But she rejected the idea.

Why?

Because she'd fallen for him.

Her hands clenched so hard the nails bit crescents into her flesh.

Pathetic, wasn't she? As if he'd ever care for her.

Maybe those years in jail had warped her judgement—made her ready to succumb to the tiniest hint of caring. She was ready for passion and more, for tenderness, because they'd been denied her so long. That had to be the reason. How else could she explain the way she'd fallen for Domenico like a ripe plum?

She was doing the right thing, getting on with life. This time tomorrow she'd be in anonymous London.

'What do you think you're doing?'

His voice slid like a finger of dark arousal down her spine. Lucy trembled and clutched her clothes tight. Her heart pounded so hard it seemed in danger of bursting free.

'Packing.' She didn't turn. This was difficult enough already. Domenico made her weak in too many ways.

Her pulse thundered as she waited for his response. Maybe he'd turn and leave, glad to be rid of her.

When he spoke again he was so close his words wafted warm air on her neck. She shivered with longing.

'No, you're not.'

Lucy spun round, dropping clothes from nerveless fingers.

'I *beg* your pardon?' She drew herself up. 'Don't tell me what to do.'

But her defiance was hollow. Her heart wasn't in it. Especially when the sight of his arrogant, endearing, brooding features clamped a different sort of pain around her chest.

She yearned for him to pull her into his embrace as he had earlier and convince her that everything would be okay.

Except it wouldn't. Nothing could make this right.

'You're not the sort to run away when things get tough.'

Lucy's eyes widened at the compliment.

Or did he just see her as prison-tough and able to weather anything?

'Watch me!' She turned to her case but he grabbed her upper arm and hauled her round towards him.

Shock froze her. Some part of her brain rehearsed the quick, violent action that would make him break his hold, yet she made no move to free herself.

'You're not a coward.'

He was so close his words caressed her forehead. Unbidden, rills of pleasure trickled across sensitive nerve endings.

'This isn't just about me. What about Chiara? She got caught up in this.'

'You're using Chiara as an excuse.'

'Excuse?' Her voice rose to a screech as guilt and despair filled her. 'Don't you understand what happened back there?' She waved an arm towards the mainland. 'I've seen what a mob can do. I don't want Chiara or anyone else put in danger because of me.'

Lucy yanked her arm free and marched to the door, gesturing for him to leave. He followed, but only to stand before her, hands on hips and mouth stern.

'Our business isn't finished.'

'*Your* business, not mine!'

Cold washed through her as she realised that was what mattered to him. Signing that contract. Selling her soul and her chance to prove her innocence.

That was all she was. A problem to be sorted.

That was the only reason he'd been so nice to her. Nice enough for her to weave foolish dreams all over again.

Lucy thought she'd dredged the depths of despair but Domenico opened up a whole new chasm of it. She trembled on the brink of a vast void of anguish.

'I'm leaving.' Her words were clipped by welling emotion.

'You're going because you're scared.'

'Scared? Me?'

Her eyes rounded as he reached out one long arm and pushed the door shut with a decisive click.

'Oh, yes,' he purred in a low, menacing tone that made the hairs on her nape rise. 'You.' His face was implacable. Fear rippled through her.

Or was it excitement?

She stared, unable to break his gaze. What she saw unnerved her. Those hooded eyes were dark as a stormy sky, piercing as a dagger to the chest. She tried to fill her lungs and couldn't.

'*I'm* the menace to society, remember? People are scared of *me*.'

The bitter twist to her lips and the wretched, jarring note in her voice tore through Domenico's good intentions.

He pressed forward till she was flush against the wall.

Something wrenched in his gut at her retreat. He read her haunted expression, the jut of her chin and the shadows in her eyes.

Silently he cursed.

He refused to let her retreat into her shell again. She'd just let him discover the warm, vibrant woman behind the sassy attitude and touch-me-not air.

Briefly he thought of his family responsibility but nothing had the power to pull him back now. What was between Lucy and himself was every bit as important as his reverence for Sandro's memory.

'What have I got to be scared of?' It was pure bravado speaking but he heard the pain beneath. His heart clenched even as anger and anticipation surged.

'This.'

He took her jaw in his left hand, splayed his right on the wall beside her head and kissed her with all the force of his pent up fury and desire.

His senses convulsed in an explosion of pleasure. The sweet scent of her filled him, and her body against his was pure enticement. He swallowed her gasp of shock and heard it turn to a mewl of pleasure that revved his need higher. A shiver rippled through her and she arched against him, tearing away his last coherent thought.

He tasted her on his tongue, tart and sweet, like citrus and sugar syrup. Deeper he delved, needing more. Needing all she had.

The world tilted then righted itself as, with a groan of surrender, Lucy opened her mouth, luring him deep with the flick of her hungry tongue against his.

Instantly heat ignited in his groin. He pressed her to the wall, ravaging her mouth. Days of desperate longing had built need so deep one kiss couldn't satisfy. Domenico swept his hand down her arm and across to the swell of her breast. She stiffened, then desperate fingers threaded his hair, holding him to her as she kissed him with a passion that made his senses swim.

He squeezed her breast, rejoicing as its lush weight fitted his palm. His grip tightened and he wondered dimly if he should ease his hold but Lucy pressed closer, sending the last of his control spiralling into nothingness.

He was burning, fire instead of blood running in his arteries, hunger humming through each nerve and sinew.

Tearing fingers wrenched her shirt undone so he could tug her bra down beneath her breast. Her skin was silk and heat. His hand shook as he toyed with her nipple and heard her gasp of surrender.

He wanted to feast on her breast, lave her nipple and watch her writhe in pleasure. But he didn't have the patience.

One touch had sparked the powder keg of desire he'd guarded so long. Bending his knees, he ground his hips against hers, rejoicing in the friction against the warm centre of her womanhood. Lightning filled the blackness behind his eyelids.

'More!' Lucy gasped against his mouth, her hands almost painful against his scalp as she strained higher against him.

In his arms she grew frantic, her breath coming in little hard pants as she pulled her mouth from his and nuzzled his collar aside to bite the curve between his neck and shoulder.

Domenico shuddered as a bolt of jagged fire transfixed him.

He rocked into her again and she lifted one leg, wrapping it around his thigh as she tried to climb him.

A man could only withstand so much.

Hands at her waist, he hoisted her high, satisfaction rising as she wrapped him in her thighs, locking her ankles hard as if closing a trap.

She had no need to trap him. He was only too eager. He surged, wedging her back against the wall. His skin was too tight to hold the rising tide of need.

Through slitted eyes he saw the flush of arousal on her cheeks, the long line of her throat as she tilted her head back and her pure alabaster breast, tipped a delicate rose pink.

He'd never seen anything so arousing in his life. Or so beautiful. For a heartbeat he stilled, drinking in the sight of her, tenderness vying with pure animal lust at the way she opened herself to him.

Then her hand brushed the straining zip of his trousers and his body's needs banished all else. Between them they fumbled his zip down. Somehow Domenico freed himself of his underwear, not even bothering to wrench his belt undone.

He let his palms slide up the smooth invitation of her thighs, rucking up her skirt as he went. Quickly he reached for her panties, meaning to haul them aside just enough, but he misjudged his grip. They tore and fell, leaving her completely open.

'Lucy.' His voice clogged deep in his throat but she heard because she opened heavy eyes. Her blue gaze was feverish and he couldn't mistake the desire he saw there.

Yes! *This* was what he wanted from her. Total abandonment. His blood sang with triumph.

With a last shred of sanity Domenico reached for his wallet. Was there a condom there? He wasn't into one-night stands but the habits of youth, or of caution were ingrained. Hopefully...

Lucy kissed him hard, her tongue swirling, drawing him towards oblivion as she tightened her legs. His erection surged, brushing soft hair and even softer skin.

Domenico's pulse drummed a rough staccato beat as they moved together in an age-old rhythm. Arousal escalated to breaking point. One hand at Lucy's breast, he clamped the other around her calf, loving the feel of her encompassing him.

With each slide of their bodies against each other combustible heat rose. She felt so *good*. So perfect against his needy erection. He tilted his hips, enjoying the way she shivered against his shaft. Once more then he'd reach for...

Lucy hoisted herself higher, and on the next slow surge Domenico found himself positioned perfectly. Too perfectly, he realised as he slid a fraction into tight, slick pleasure.

He gritted his teeth, moving his hands to her hips, ready to withdraw and keep them safe. All he had to do was summon the willpower to withstand temptation. It would only be for a moment and then—

Lucy moved against him again, but this time it was a jerky rock of the hips. Her legs clamped tight as a hoarse gasp of shock filled his ears. She shuddered around him. Her body convulsed and Domenico felt her muscles ripple, urging him on. His eyes snapped open and he caught her gaze as she came apart, wonder in her eyes.

Need destroyed thought. He reacted instinctively, thrusting deep. For a teetering moment her body resisted, impossibly tight. So tight there could be only one reason for it. One that blew everything he'd heard about her out of the water. Stunned, he grappled to make sense of it.

Then coherent thought was obliterated as, with a sudden rush he was there at the heart of her, deep enough to feel the last of her shudders against his sensitive flesh.

The sensations were too much, especially with Lucy abandoned and delicious around him. With a cry of triumph he arched high and hard, pumping into her welcoming warmth.

Behind his closed eyes stars and planets whirled, whole constellations and galaxies burst into life and showered light in a dazzling, mind-blowing display. The ecstasy of release was so intense he wondered if he'd survive.

Through it all he felt Lucy's ragged breath on his face, her hands clutching as if she'd never release him.

When Lucy came to she was lying on the wide bed, under a sheet. She had no recollection of Domenico crossing the room and stripping the sheet back. She'd been dazed and disoriented by that cataclysmic orgasm. Remembering made her shiver, reawakening muscles she hadn't realised she possessed.

'Cold?' Domenico's voice rumbled from the other side of the bed.

She smiled slowly. Did she have the energy to speak?

'Lucy? Are you okay?' The strain in Domenico's voice puzzled her.

'Never better.' Her words slurred as if she'd been drinking. She felt marvellous. Wonderful. She sank into the feather pillow. This was utter bliss. Only one thing was missing. 'Hold me? Please?'

Silence.

'Domenico?'

'You should rest.'

Something in his voice made her drag her eyes open.

He stood on the far side of the bed, fully dressed, the picture of urbane sophistication but for the frown creasing his brow.

Gone was the out-of-control lover. This man didn't have so much as a hair out of place.

For the first time Lucy realised she was naked beneath the sheet. She vaguely recalled her buttons scattering as he'd tugged her shirt open. Her panties were history, a torn scrap on the floor somewhere. But the rest of her clothes? How could she not have noticed him undressing her?

Uneasily she shifted and felt moisture between her legs. Fire scorched her cheeks. She was wet from Domenico. Her belly clenched at the memory of him pumping into her. The power and stark beauty of what they'd shared overwhelmed her.

Looking at his closed face now, she saw Domenico didn't share her joy. He looked as if he'd just made the worst mistake of his life.

In a rush all her pleasure bled away.

'Good idea,' she murmured through frozen vocal cords. 'I think I'll rest.' She rolled away from him, wincing as tender muscles protested.

'Lucy?' His voice came closer. She shut her eyes. She'd never felt more vulnerable.

'Go away. I don't want to talk.'

The bed sank as he sat beside her, making her roll forwards. Putting out an arm to steady herself, she touched solid muscle beneath his cotton shirt. Instantly she dragged her hand back as if stung. She sucked in a shocked breath as skittering aware-ness filled her. How could that be when she was completely spent after that no-holds-barred loving?

Sex, she reminded herself. Domenico would call it sex. She refused to consider what she'd call it.

She thrust to the back of her mind the feelings she had for him. The ones that grew stronger daily. The ones that had burst into full bloom when he'd called her his family and hugged her in front of that crowd. He'd acted like a man who'd defend her no matter what it cost.

That one act had shattered the last of her fragile defences.

Her mouth trembled as she acknowledged how much he meant to her. How much his good opinion mattered.

This had nothing to do with her years of sexual abstinence and everything to do with Domenico the man.

'Lucy?' A light touch on her forehead stilled her heart. 'I'm sorry.'

'Sorry?' Her eyes popped open.

'What I did just then…'

'What *we* did.' That was the magic of it.

'I was stupid and selfish.'

'What?' She'd lost track of their conversation.

He leaned close and Lucy inhaled the addictive scent of him, layered with something warm and spicy. The scent of sex, she realised.

'I didn't use a condom.' His glittering eyes held hers as she processed what he said. 'There's no excuse for what I did. But believe me, it wasn't deliberate.'

How could she not have noticed? Not even spared a thought for her safety?

Biting her lip, she sat up, dragging the sheet with her. She thought she'd matured—no longer the naïve girl who'd made the mistake of letting a predatory male into her room. She'd prided herself on her ability to protect herself. Yet she'd had unprotected sex.

'If it's any help, I can tell you I have no infectious diseases.'

She nodded, avoiding his eyes. After what they'd shared it was stupid to feel embarrassed but she was. 'Me too.'

But that left the risk of pregnancy.

Her heart crashed against her ribs. Pregnant with Domenico's baby?

The complications would be enormous. The divided loyalties, the sheer impossibility of it. And yet… Lucy pressed her palm to her stomach. Was it even possible?

Wonder filled her and a niggling sensation that felt like hope.

She'd always wanted children. Nothing had changed that, not even her stint in prison. If anything, that had consolidated her need for a family of her own now her dad was gone.

'You're not on the Pill, are you?'

The hope on his face soured her pleasure. 'No. Surprisingly, I wasn't planning on sex with the first man I met when I left prison.'

Except it was more than sex. It was liking, caring, and something she didn't want to name.

'If there's a baby—'

'Yes?' She felt herself freeze. Yet who could blame him for not wanting her to carry his child? Her heart dipped as she braced herself.

'If there's a baby you won't be alone.'

Her head jerked up and his silvery gaze snared her.

Did he have any idea how much his words meant? Imagine the scandal if she of all people bore his child! She'd half expected him to talk about a termination, not to reassure her.

She opened her mouth then found she couldn't speak. She nodded, dazzled by the warmth his words evoked. For the first time in ages she wasn't alone.

'I didn't hurt you?' His words were abrupt, scattering her thoughts.

Hurt her? He had to be kidding.

'I'm no china doll, you know.'

For a fleeting instant she thought she saw a smile, a masculine smirk of satisfaction quiver on his lips then disappear. She must have imagined it. When she reached out to touch him he shot to his feet as if scalded.

Lucy frowned, watching him pace across the room. He looked out of the window.

'But you were a virgin.' He ploughed his hands through his crisp dark hair. In a man so controlled it was a sign of major turmoil.

A presentiment of fear scudded through her.

Ridiculous! What was there to fear?

Yet why make such a big deal about her inexperience? It hadn't stopped them. She'd wanted him and he'd wanted her and the result had been glorious.

'It doesn't matter, Domenico. Really.'

Her words made no difference. He held himself ramrod stiff, tension in every line of his body.

'It matters.' His tone was harsh.

He swung round, his expression shuttered, no sign of warmth. His eyes were steely, devoid of the connection she'd imagined there.

'I…' Her words trailed off as realisation smashed into her in a sickening blow. She pressed a hand to her belly. Her heart nosedived as her last meal surged upwards.

It couldn't be true. It couldn't!

She jack-knifed out of bed, yanking the sheet around her with shaking hands.

'Why does it matter, Domenico?' Her voice was a scratch of sound, barely audible over her pounding heart.

In vain she waited for him to assure her it didn't. That he was just concerned he hadn't hurt her.

He said nothing.

The shaking in her legs worsened.

She couldn't drag her eyes from his. Domenico's expression was impenetrable. He didn't want her reading his thoughts.

There could only be one reason for that. One reason why the knowledge of her virginity turned him to stone.

Her blood ran cold.

'You utter bastard!' She heaved in a shuddering breath. Only sheer willpower kept her on her feet. 'You wanted proof, didn't you? Proof that I was telling you the truth?' She pulled herself up as straight as she could despite the cramping pain in her stomach.

'That's what this was about! You couldn't let me leave without knowing once and for all if I lied when I said I wasn't your brother's lover or killer.' She drew a breath so sharp it sliced straight through her ribs. 'When I claimed in court to be a virgin.'

Lucy marched across the room on stiff legs, kicking aside the dragging sheet. He stood still as a graven image.

'You had sex with me to find out if I was innocent or guilty! Didn't you?'

She raised her hand and smacked him across the cheek with such force her hand smarted and her arm ached. But it was nothing to the raw, bleeding anguish of her lacerated heart.

CHAPTER ELEVEN

HE DESERVED THAT slap, and more.

Not because he'd had sex with Lucy as some test, but because of the hurt ravaging her features.

He'd known she was stretched to breaking point by what life had thrown at her. She'd confounded the odds and stayed strong despite everything. But he'd seen behind the bravado to the woman who'd faced down disenchantment, betrayal, injustice and pain. The woman who bled inside but would rather die than show it.

Her prickly defensiveness hid a vulnerability that had first intrigued but latterly worried him.

Now he'd added to her pain.

Because he couldn't keep his trousers zipped!

She spun around, the sheet flouncing as she made to stalk away.

His hand snapped out and imprisoned her wrist, jerking her to a stop.

'Let me go. Now!' She had her back to him but Domenico knew she spoke through gritted teeth.

'Not yet. Not till you've heard me out.'

'Heard you explain why it was necessary to get naked with me?' A shudder racked her. 'Oh, that's right. You didn't get naked, did you?' Her voice dripped sarcasm. 'That would be taking it too far, wouldn't it? Why go to so much effort when all you had to do was—'

'*Basta!*'

She whipped round to face him, her eyes burning like embers, her colour high. 'No! That's *not* enough. You can't silence me.'

'Not even to hear what I have to say?' God help him, but seeing her so passionate, so vibrant, he wanted her again. More urgently than before. Heat drenched him and his body hardened.

He wanted to smother her anger and her protests with his mouth, strip away that damned sheet and take her again and again till she was boneless and didn't have the strength to snark at him.

He wanted to conquer her even as he revelled in her strength and defiance.

Ma che cavolo! What she did to him! What had happened to his ordered, structured life, where sex was simple, satisfying and civilised?

He stepped in and saw her eyes widen. Something other than fury flickered in those blue depths. Disappointment? Pain?

His urgency deflated to manageable levels.

'I didn't have sex with you to check if you'd slept with Sandro.'

'As if I'd believe that now. You heard me say in court I wasn't your brother's lover. If you'd *believed* me it wouldn't have been a shock to you.'

Domenico swallowed. 'It's not that simple.'

'Not simple?' Her voice rose. 'Either you believed me or you didn't.'

He shook his head, for the first time he could remember, floundering.

How did he explain he'd compartmentalised his thoughts—separating his strengthening belief in Lucy's innocence from the harsh fact of Sandro's death? In his heart he'd been convinced Lucy wasn't the woman they'd all believed. Yet he hadn't followed through to formulate the alternative in his mind. He'd been too busy reacting to her to think logically.

He'd been too addled by lust and all the other wild emotions she dragged from him.

And too horrified at what he'd have to confront if she *was* innocent—the enormity of how he'd failed her.

'I knew you weren't the woman we'd thought. I knew you weren't totally guilty.'

'Totally guilty.' Her voice was flat. 'That's nice. So I was just a little guilty. Which bit? Maybe I didn't kill Sandro but slept with him for money? Is that what you thought?'

'No! Don't talk like that.' The idea of her and Sandro together had eaten like acid in his belly for too long. Even now when he knew the truth, Domenico couldn't stomach the idea of her with anyone else.

He might be bigger and stronger than her, he might hold her in an unbreakable grip, but she had him reeling.

'I wasn't thinking! All right?' Tension crackled along his spine, augmented by the hefty dose of guilt weighing his belly. 'I wasn't planning to prove anything except how good we'd be together. Satisfied?'

His belligerent tone concealed the fear he'd felt, watching her pack. The thought of her leaving had gutted him, forcing him into actions that weren't planned but driven by his soul-deep instinct not to let her go.

'No, you weren't thinking.' Her face was pale and set. 'If you had been you'd have realised my virginity—' she said the word as if swallowing something nasty '—isn't proof I'm not a killer. The court rejected my offer of a virginity test, remember?'

Fire branded her cheeks and Domenico swallowed hard, remembering the day in court when the relevance of her virginity had been debated back and forth. His stomach dropped. How hard it must have been for an eighteen-year-old innocent, with no one but an impersonal lawyer to support her.

'I'm sorry.' His touch gentled on her wrist. 'That must have been horrific.'

Lucy blinked and stared as if seeing him for the first time. 'It was like being violated while the world watched.'

He felt her skin prickle and smoothed his thumb over her wrist. Guilt soured his tongue and sliced through what was left of his self-respect. How had he got it all so wrong and let her suffer so?

'My inexperience doesn't prove I'm innocent.' She spoke softly now, as if the fire in her belly had died.

Domenico wanted to wrap her in his arms and haul her to him, but one false move would have her lashing out. His cheek still burned from that slap. Not that he cared about being hurt. What he cared about was not hurting her.

Hell of a rotten job he'd done so far.

'For all you know,' she went on, 'I was leading your brother on, like they said, holding out the promise of sex for jewellery and money. Whether I'd actually spread my legs for him doesn't matter.'

'Don't talk like that!' Domenico's voice was hoarse.

'Why not?' She tilted her jaw in challenge. 'It's what I did just now—'

'No. It's not.' She *couldn't* reduce what they'd shared to something so crude. It had been wild and out-of-control, but it had been anything but casual sex. It had been… Dammit, he didn't understand what it was, but he knew it was *something*.

Domenico grabbed her other hand, regardless of the sheet slithering to the floor between them.

Fifteen minutes ago he'd been unable to tear his gaze from her luscious naked form. Now, though his predictable body stirred, his gaze meshed with hers. She looked back with a hauteur that chilled him to the marrow. She was so furious he wondered if she even noticed the loss of the sheet.

He threaded his fingers through hers, entwining them together. 'What just happened wasn't like that.'

'What was it like then?' Her fine brows arched. 'When you didn't even believe me?'

'I believed.' Not coherently, not consciously, because he'd put such effort into hiding from what his instincts told him. He'd shied from connecting all the dots. Because if Lucy was innocent she'd suffered all these years because of a mistake and his family's need for justice.

Because he'd let himself be swayed by hurt pride into believing the worst when others claimed she'd seduced Sandro.

He'd taken the easy route and avoided confronting his doubts head-on. He'd found comfort in his cosy role of righteous brother.

He'd been too comfortable, too long.

Domenico had never thought himself a coward. Now, seeing how he'd wounded her, he knew himself less than the man he'd always believed himself. His stomach churned.

'Liar,' she whispered.

'I knew you weren't the woman the prosecution painted you.' He sounded desperate. 'I knew you were warm and caring, that your instincts are decent, not self-centred. Look at the way you saved Chiara. The way you faced down a mob to protect her rather than leave her and take to your heels.'

She shook her head. 'Not good enough.'

He knew it wasn't. Shame blistered him as he realised it was the best he could do. He should have been sure *sooner*.

He'd wanted to believe she was innocent. He'd wanted to think her fear of Sandro's old bodyguard pointed to him, not her, being responsible for Sandro's death. But Domenico hadn't made that final leap of faith. Even when he'd felt her virginal body welcoming him home the truth hadn't hit. He'd been completely absorbed in the heady pleasure of potent, white-hot sex more intense than anything he'd known. His own pleasure had ruled him.

It was only afterwards, watching her go limp in his arms that the enormity of what he knew about her struck.

It had fallen into place, everything he felt, knew and guessed about her.

Every instinct had been attuned to Lucy since she'd bent at his car door and stared at him in frozen horror. Fear of being disloyal to Sandro had stopped him seeing clearly. Or was he simply used to the world fitting his expectations? Had he grown so used to his rarefied world he couldn't see the truth before his eyes?

Heat seared his face.

Domenico gestured to the wall where the world had shuddered as they came together. 'I wasn't thinking about your virginity.' Desperation made him speak the unvarnished truth. 'All I could think about was being inside you, filling you till you screamed my name as you came. Filling you till I finally found my own release.' His lungs hurt as he dragged in air. 'Do you *know* how I've hungered for you?'

Her eyes widened as if his words shocked her. A trickle of heat circled in his belly at the idea of shocking her some more, with actions this time, not words.

It was strange how innocent she was in some ways while she was so tough and worldly in others.

'I didn't have some grand plan to seduce you.' He held her gaze, wondering if he had any hope of convincing her. 'It's you who's been seducing me all along.'

'I have not!' She jerked back in his hold. 'You make it sound like I connived—'

'You didn't have to. All you had to do was be yourself.' That was what had hooked him from the start. Her fascinating, richly layered character. Her strength and fiery independence and her warm-hearted generosity, especially with Chiara. Her courage, her pleasure in simple delights, her straight-down-the-line honesty. She was so uncompromising in her truthfulness that even now he found her a challenge. How had he ever believed her deceitful?

Because he'd wanted someone to suffer for Sandro's death.

Because in his grief and rage he'd been too ready to accept the image painted by the prosecution.

Because he'd been jealous of his brother.

'You're like those lawyers, making out I—'

Domenico tugged her to him so her naked body pressed against his. His senses jangled into overdrive.

Yet Lucy apparently felt none of the seductive friction between them. She held herself proud as a princess.

He fought to keep his mind on what mattered. 'What happened had nothing to do with the trial.' He searched her troubled gaze, frustration filling him when he couldn't read her thoughts. 'You have to believe me.'

'I don't have to do anything.'

That was the hell of it.

He had no right to expect anything, especially after what had been done to her in the name of justice. Yet he wanted her, still, again, more than before.

Any minute now she could wash her hands of him and leave. Who would blame her?

He gathered her closer, one hand shackling her wrist and the other encircling her bare back. Heroically he strove to ignore the silken invitation of her nakedness. He was torn between so many conflicting emotions.

'I know you didn't kill Sandro, Lucy.'

He felt the almighty tremor race through her at his words, saw her eyes pop wide as she stared up at him.

'You can't know it.' She shook her head emphatically, distrust in her gaze. 'You have no new proof. Nothing. I told you, the fact that I didn't sleep with Sandro—'

'I understand.' He released her hand and lifted his fingers to her cheek, hesitating a moment before sliding his fingers into her hair. 'Technically it doesn't prove your innocence.'

But he knew in his gut, with every instinct, that she was innocent. Finding that she was a virgin had simply been the shock that made the pieces fit together.

No wonder he'd been plagued by doubts. Nothing about the

woman he'd come to know fitted with the woman the prosecution had portrayed in court.

'I won't ask you to forgive me for doubting you so long.' That would be asking too much. 'But you must know I'm sorry for what happened. More sorry than I can say.'

He recalled how she'd watched him in court, waiting for him to go to her. And he, blind fool, had been so wrapped up in prejudice and hurt pride, he'd spurned her instead of listening to his instincts. Even though an extramarital affair was out of character for Sandro, Domenico had believed it because Lucy had knocked him off his feet and he was scared by the conflicting emotions she aroused. In his neat world, no woman had the power to unsettle him.

'And I'm going to prove you didn't kill Sandro.' That wouldn't erase the last five years, but he owed her.

He read something that might have been wonder in her face. Hope dawned on her fine features. Her lips trembled and she swallowed hard. His throat dried as he saw her struggle with emotion.

How alone she'd been, with no one on her side. She deserved better.

Then she blinked and her mask of indifference dropped into place. The one she used to keep the world, and him, at bay. The one he was beginning to hate. He wanted to strip it away and smash it, so she couldn't hide from him any longer.

His pulse drummed at the intensity of what he felt.

He was so caught up in his thoughts he didn't move to stop her when she backed away, scooping up the sheet and wrapping it tight around her.

He tried not to notice the way the cotton moulded her ripe breasts and pebbled nipples. Impossibly, the flimsy cover only made him more aware of her delectable body beneath.

'Why would you try to prove my innocence?' Suspicion filled her voice and he was struck anew by how hard it was for her to trust.

'Because of the wrong done you.' Wasn't it obvious?

'That's not your problem.'

Domenico frowned. Didn't she want his help?

It didn't matter; she was getting it whether her pride revolted at the idea or not.

'I should have questioned earlier. Instead an injustice has been done in the name of my family. To ignore that would be cowardly. Not to act would bring shame on my family and me. I owe you.'

Lucy looked up into that dark, proud face, honed by a centuries-old aristocratic gene pool and the assurance born of success, wealth and privilege.

Despite the intimacies they'd just shared—maybe because of them, with him smartly dressed and her naked beneath a sheet—she felt the yawning chasm between them more than ever.

He spoke of family honour as if that was all that mattered.

Her heart dived. She'd thought for a moment his concern was for *her*. Instead it was for the precious Volpe name. She knew how devoted he was to it after he'd gone to such lengths to preserve it. He'd even brought her from prison to his home.

He hadn't done it for her. It was for his family.

She'd been right. He'd had sex. He hadn't made love.

'I'm not interested in preserving your family's honour.'

His eyes narrowed to glittering slits. 'This is about clearing *your* name. Rehabilitating you in the eyes of the world.'

Despite all logic, hope leapt in her chest. But only for an instant.

'That's something even you can't do.' If she'd had evidence to prove her innocence she'd have used it.

His head reared back as he folded his arms over his broad chest, the epitome of male confidence. 'Watch me.'

He spoke with the assurance of a man who took on disastrous financial markets and won. Who'd built an empire against all known trends. Who succeeded where so many others crashed and burned. A man who never failed.

But he'd learn as she had. The task was impossible. She'd hoped to clear her name but she'd accepted now she couldn't.

'Good luck with that, Domenico. But I don't care to stay around and watch you fail.'

Fire sizzled in those slitted eyes. Anger or challenge?

He paced towards her and to her horror Lucy found herself retreating.

'One way or another we're going to reintroduce you to society. You will *not* be on the run from troublemakers like that harridan this afternoon.' She opened her mouth to protest but he kept right on talking. 'If it's humanly possible, I'll find a way to overturn the court's ruling.'

Lucy wrapped her arms around herself, torn between wanting to believe he meant it and worry that he did. She didn't have the strength to keep fighting, much less go through another bout with the criminal justice system. The thought of it made her flesh crawl.

'You're not going anywhere, Lucy, till we've made this right.'

That's what he was good at, wasn't it? Fixing things, overcoming obstacles. Look at the way he'd risen to the challenge of keeping her from selling her story.

Only now he saw it as family duty to rectify the wrong done in their name. He'd do what he could to put things right because honour demanded it and then… What?

He'd walk away.

Better to make the break now, while she could. For no matter how she tried to deny it, her emotions were engaged. What she felt for Domenico petrified her.

'You haven't thought this through.' She wrapped the sheet more securely and walked to the bed where her case now rested on the floor. She lifted it onto the bed. 'Any scheme to "rehabilitate" me will attract press attention. The media circus would get worse and your family privacy would be a thing of the past.'

Guilt or no guilt, that would make him leave her alone. In a contest between family and the woman he'd lusted for briefly, family would win every time.

She bit her lip and reached for a shirt to put in the case. To her horror, her hand shook visibly.

A long arm reached around her and took the shirt from her grasp. He stood so close behind her she felt the blazing heat of his body warm her. Lucy stiffened.

'I don't care.' His words brushed her nape and shivered around her. 'I have to do this, Lucy. Don't you understand? Everything has changed.'

She stood transfixed as his words sank in.

How she wanted them to be true.

His hand wrapped around hers but this time his touch was infinitely gentle. Slowly he turned her towards him. For the life of her, Lucy couldn't resist.

When he demanded, she could stand up to him. But his tenderness? It undid her.

'Nothing has changed. Don't you see?' Her chest was too tight as she looked into eyes the colour of soft mist in the morning. 'I've lived with this. I *know*.'

'Cara.' The simple endearment stole her breath, or maybe it was the way he looked at her. As if he saw only *her*, not some debt of honour. 'You have to trust me, at least for a little longer.'

'I—' His thumb brushed her bottom lip as he cradled her jaw, the heat of his hand pure comfort after the inner chill she'd battled so long. It made her forget that she no longer knew how to trust.

'Let me help you, Lucy. Let me try to make amends.' He leaned forward till his mouth almost brushed her cheek. Her eyelids grew heavy as that riot of sensations started up inside. 'Please?'

The rich timbre of his voice detonated explosions of delight across her senses. Her head swam.

Domenico leaned closer, his lips brushing hers with a tenderness that almost undid her. Lucy's heart pounded and she jerked her head back.

'Don't do that!' If only she sounded as if she meant it. 'I don't want you to kiss me.' She shoved her palm against his chest but that only brought her in contact with his muscled heat.

'Liar,' he whispered in her ear, sending sensual pleasure spiralling through her. His mouth grazed her cheek, then his lips were at the corner of her mouth.

'I said no!' With a supreme effort she pulled out of his hold to stand, panting with exertion as if she'd run a marathon. That was how strong the sensual current of awareness she fought. 'You don't have to seduce me, remember? You already know all about my sexual experience. You've got nothing else to prove.'

Meeting his eyes was one of the most difficult things she'd done. Lucy felt stripped bare, the memory of her passion, her complete sexual abandon, glaringly proclaiming her weakness for him.

'You have no idea, do you, *cara*?' He shook his head, his mouth a grim line. 'This isn't about proving anything, except how much I want you. How perfect we are together.'

In a sudden, shocking movement, he tugged his shirt free of his trousers, pulling it over his head and away.

Lucy's throat narrowed and the air hissed from her lungs as she surveyed his chest—a dusting of dark hair over golden skin, a torso full of the fascinating dips and bulges that proclaimed his body's muscled power.

'I want you, Lucy. The same way you want me.' He kicked off his shoes and bent to strip away his socks before she could formulate a reply.

She stepped back, horrified, as her resistance crumbled at those simple words. Was that all it took to make her putty in his hands? The backs of her legs hit the mattress. Dazed, she thought of escape, but couldn't summon the energy to try.

Or maybe she didn't want to. The memory of ecstasy held her still.

As she watched, he made short work of his belt and zip, only pausing to retrieve his wallet before letting his clothes drop to the floor.

She'd seen him in bathers, with water plastering the fabric to his strong thighs and taut backside. But she'd never seen him naked. She wanted to reach out and trace the lines of his body. She wanted...

Domenico let the wallet drop and tossed a foil packet onto the bedside table. The sight of it made her skin prickle and heat swirl deep in her womb. He swept her bag off the bed and, dazed, she saw her belongings scatter across the floor.

She couldn't believe she stood, unmoving, waiting for his touch.

Except it was what she wanted—Domenico's passion and warmth. She craved the sense of being linked not just bodily but soul to soul. It almost didn't matter that it was an illusion. What he did to her was magic and, despite every argument common sense mustered, she couldn't turn her back on it. On him.

Not yet.

'Carissima.'

He took her in his arms as if she were fragile gossamer. Only the glitter in his eyes and the tremor in his touch revealed how hard it was for him to take his time.

Yet take his time he did, learning her body with a thoroughness that made her squirm in ecstasy and increasing desperation. Along the way she discovered some of his weaknesses. When she trailed her fingertips across his hip and down to his groin he sucked in his breath. When she nipped at his throat he groaned aloud and when she took his shaft in her hand he rolled her onto her back and pinioned her with the full weight of his body. She revelled in the sense of his powerful frame blanketing her.

'Do that again and this will be over in seconds,' he growled.

'Don't treat me like a piece of porcelain.' She stared up into stormy eyes, loving that she'd made him lose his cool. 'I want you. Now.'

Domenico's sudden feral smile should have scared her. Instead, fire licked her veins. She wriggled, her thighs opening wider, and he sank onto her.

His smile faded and her breath hitched.

What followed was testament to Domenico's iron control and sexual prowess. He brought her to not one but several peaks of ecstasy, till she thought she'd die from the force of the pleasure pounding through her.

Then at last he joined her, reaching his climax just as Lucy's world shattered in a whirling kaleidoscope of fractured colours and pleasure-drenched senses that surely would never recover from the onslaught.

For the longest time they clung together, hearts pounding in sync, gasps mingling and bodies so entwined it seemed they were one entity.

Lucy never wanted it to end. She never wanted to let him go.

She squeezed her eyes shut, imprinting the moment on her memory, knowing this couldn't last.

Finally, mumbling about being too heavy, Domenico rolled away. Instantly cold invaded her body. Even when he hauled her close, his arm around her and her head pressed to his thundering heart, she couldn't recapture that moment of perfect communion.

Lucy reminded herself that sexual pleasure was fleeting. The sense of let-down was natural.

But it was more than that.

She listened to Domenico's breathing slow, felt his heart beneath her cheek return to its normal beat. But even when her pulse slowed too, she felt anything but normal.

That was what petrified her.

She'd lost part of herself to Domenico Volpe. A part she could never get back.

CHAPTER TWELVE

'I STILL THINK this is a huge mistake.' Lucy stood in the vast dressing room of Domenico's master suite in the Roman palazzo, staring at the plastic-draped clothes lining one wall.

Exquisite designer clothes. All for her.

She clasped her hands as nerves snaked through her. This wasn't just a mistake, it was looming catastrophe.

'How could you even *think* this would help?'

'Because attack is the best form of defence, didn't you know?' Domenico's voice came from the adjoining bathroom. She gritted her teeth at his casual tone.

Didn't he know how much she risked, being seen in public with him?

Of course he did. When this backfired it would smear his name as much as hers. The thought made bile churn and she pressed her hand to her stomach.

She had to find calm.

Calm! The last three weeks had been anything but calm.

Lucy fought down the pleasure that always hovered at the memory of Domenico's loving. Anyone would think they'd be sated now, worn out by the amount of time they'd spent naked together.

Instead she felt energised. When she was with him she almost believed she could take on the world. Especially as she'd decided to make the most of each precious moment.

This interlude couldn't last. When he'd done his best to

clear her name they'd go their separate ways. If she'd learnt anything in scouring the press reports it was that he moved in a world far beyond hers. One that collided with hers only due to the circumstances of Sandro's death.

Domenico favoured elegant brunettes who fitted that world as she never could. Socialites and celebrities who took luxury as their due.

Lucy had no illusions. She was a novelty, a wrong to be righted. Domenico felt only lust, guilt and a determination to do right. Tellingly, he never spoke of a future for them beyond that.

When he failed, as inevitably he would, he'd turn to some gorgeous woman from his own rarefied world and Lucy would go far away to start again. All she'd have was memories.

Pain seared, banishing her nerves.

Who knew how long she had with Domenico? Tonight could be the beginning of the end.

Lucy tried to tell herself it had been worth it, these weeks of indulgent delight. She'd made her choice and settled for fleeting joy. She was strong and aware of the consequences. She simply chose to enjoy pleasure while it lasted, rather than wallow in self-pity.

Time for that later.

There could be no future for them, even if she did…*care* for Domenico.

Lucy grimaced at the way she avoided even thinking the alternative word.

What choice did she have? Domenico might be a wonderful lover, passionate and heart-stoppingly demanding. He might be single-minded in pursuing proof of her innocence, but that was guilt at work and his obsessive drive to make things right.

He might be tender with her but only in the way a man treated his current temporary lover. He never spoke of *them*, or of the future, only of clearing her name. He felt guilty because he hadn't trusted her all those years ago.

Domenico was a decent man, a good man, despite his arrogant certainty that the world would bow to his will, but there was no chance he could ever love her.

'Still not dressed?'

Lucy whipped around to find him leaning against the doorjamb, resplendent in a dinner jacket, his fresh-shaved jaw pure temptation to a woman who couldn't get enough of him.

She curled her fingers into fists and looked away, ignoring the inevitable jangle of awareness that cascaded through her.

'I still think this is nonsensical. What will it achieve, being seen in Rome with me? Nothing but more scandal.'

'What it will achieve—' he crossed to stand beside her '—is to prove I'm proud to be with you. That the past is the past. That's a first step.' He dragged a finger across the sensitive skin beneath her ear and she shivered.

'But it will do no good, don't you see?' She looked up at him. 'There'll be a rash of stories about me moving from one brother to the other.' She swallowed hard, trying to rid herself of the bitterness on her tongue.

'Ah, but there'll be far more revealed, just you wait and see. Soon things will seem a lot brighter.' He looked suspiciously pleased with himself.

'What do you know? Is there something?' She couldn't help the surge of hope that dawned.

'Soon, *tesoro*. I promise you, soon this will all be over.'

Logic told her there could be no proof unless Bruno confessed. But Bruno Scarlatti had been happy to let her bear his punishment. That wouldn't change.

Besides, Domenico was right. If by some miracle he did prove her innocence all this would be over. Not just the public burden of guilt, but their time together.

He stroked her again, lingering where the neckline of her T-shirt dipped. His eyes turned smoky dark and Lucy's pulse accelerated. One fleeting touch and she wanted so much more!

It was the knowledge of her neediness that gave her strength to step back.

'You don't trust me with your news?'

The sexy smile curving his mouth died. 'It's not that. I need to have it confirmed. It should be soon.' He paused, raking her face as if searching for something. 'But there is *some* definite news. As soon as you're ready we'll go downstairs and you'll hear all about it.'

'Why don't you tell me now? It's my name you're trying to clear, damn it!' She jammed her hands on her hips. She wasn't used to standing back and relying on others. It made her uneasy.

Domenico leaned in, the glint in his eyes pure devilment.

'Because I know, *cara*, that if I don't give you a reason to get changed and come downstairs, we'll have another argument about you accepting my charity.' He waved a hand towards the wardrobe stuffed full of expensive clothes. 'But now you know the only way to discover what I've found out is to do what I want…'

His smile was all arrogant male satisfaction. Exasperation filled her.

Lucy pressed her hand to his dinner jacket, feeling the steady beat of his heart. She let her fingers slide down the lapel, her fingers brushing his shirt. His muscles contracted beneath her touch.

She let a knowing smile play on her lips. The sort of smile she'd learned from *him*. It hid her skittering fear. Fear that she wanted too much from him.

'I wouldn't say it's the only way I could find out.' Her voice dropped to a husky note as she rose on tiptoe and pressed her lips to a point at the corner of his jaw.

He couldn't hide the way his muscles clenched tight, or the slight hitch to his breathing.

'Witch!' He stepped back, putting space between them.

'Coward,' she purred, pleased more than she should be. Sexually, there was no denying her power over him.

'A wise man knows when to retreat. I'll wait downstairs.' He made for the door then turned, his mouth curling in a piratical smile that turned her knees to jelly. 'But there'll be a reckoning later, *cara*. You can be sure of that.'

Domenico looked up at the sound of heels tapping on the travertine floor. He moved to the door of the drawing room, only to stumble to a halt.

Shock slammed into him. Shock and what felt remarkably like awe.

He knew every inch of Lucy's delectable body, each dip and curve and enticing hollow. Her face was the last thing he saw at night and the first thing he saw in the morning.

And yet she had the power to stun him.

Per la madonna!

A fine sweat broke out on his brow and heat misted his vision.

He thought he'd known, but he'd had no idea!

A vision stalked towards him in killer heels that made her hips sway in an undulating rhythm that took his pulse and tossed it into overdrive. A full-length gown in glittering gold clung like sin. It scooped low from tiny jewelled shoulder straps to skim the upper swell of her high breasts. The skirt accentuated the long, delicious curve of hip and thigh, hugging close before swirling out around her ankles.

Domenico hitched a finger inside his collar to loosen its suddenly constricting pressure.

'Lucy.' The word was a croak of shock. 'You look...' words failed him '...beautiful.'

More than beautiful. She was luminous. Her eyes were bigger than ever, her lips a glistening, tinted promise of pleasure to come.

He wanted to haul her back to bed.

What was he thinking, planning to show her off to the hungry wolves of Roman society? What madness possessed him?

'I told you it was too much.' She gestured to the dress as she stopped before him and he read the doubt in her eyes.

How could she doubt for a moment how fabulous she looked?

But he'd learned the woman behind the bravado was full of surprises. His chest tightened at the lack of confidence her words revealed. Only now was he beginning to understand how imprisonment had scarred her.

His belly hollowed with guilt.

How could he ever make it up to her?

Domenico reached out and took her cold hand, raising it to his lips as he held her gaze. He turned her hand and pressed a kiss to the soft underside of her wrist, then another, and was rewarded by her shiver of pleasure. Colour tinged her cheeks and her eyes turned slumberous.

'You look perfect,' he murmured in her ear. 'The most beautiful woman in Rome.'

And even now she might be carrying his child.

He'd relegated the idea to the back of his mind, but seeing her so beautiful yet vulnerable loosened the guard he placed on his thoughts.

A surge of protectiveness filled him.

He forced himself to step back.

Looking into her stunned face, Domenico had an unsettling feeling he'd strayed out of his depth. He'd never experienced anything like it.

He thought he'd known what he was getting into but at each turn Lucy confounded him. Uneasily he banished the suspicion that he, not she, was the one who needed help.

'Come, there's someone here to see you.' He hooked her hand through his and covered her fingers. 'And remember, I'm with you.'

His hand closed around hers in a gesture of reassurance.

She couldn't drag her gaze from his. For the first time ever she felt truly beautiful, because of the admiration in his eyes.

Domenico ushered her into the spacious sitting room. Walking in breakneck heels was much easier with his support. She could get used to—

Lucy stumbled mid-step, her hand clawing his arm. Her spine set as she fought a primitive instinct to flee.

How could he have done this to her?

'You remember my sister-in-law, Pia.' His voice was smooth, his manner urbane, as if he hadn't just introduced the woman who'd once screamed abuse at her for killing her husband.

Lucy swayed. Her knees weakened and she feared she'd crumple till Domenico wrapped an arm around her.

His hold was all that kept her upright.

Pia was pale and perfect, from her expertly cut dark hair to her exquisite designer shoes. Huge dark eyes surveyed her as if trying to read her soul. Slowly she crossed the room.

Lucy tried to drag in air. She couldn't breathe. Maybe the oxygen had been sucked from the room by the intensity of Pia's stare.

The other woman raised her hand and Lucy flinched.

It took a lifetime to recognise the gesture. A handshake? From Pia Volpe?

Hysterical laughter rose and Lucy bit her lip to stop it bursting out. She shook her head in disbelief.

'You won't shake my hand?' The other woman's face was tight as she shot a look at Domenico. 'I told you, didn't I?'

'Don't be hasty, Pia. Lucy's surprised. She didn't know you were here.'

Because if she'd known she'd never have agreed to come!

Lucy couldn't look away from the face of the woman before her. 'What's going on?' Her words were a rough whisper but at least her larynx worked.

'Come and sit down.' He urged them towards a group of leather sofas. 'There's no need for formality.'

Again that inappropriate gurgle of laughter threatened. He

thought they could be casual? She and the woman who blamed her for her husband's death?

Yet she found her legs moving stiffly. A moment later she plopped onto a sofa as her knees gave way. Domenico held her, his body crammed close. If she had the energy she'd elbow him away, but she was hollow with shock.

Pia subsided gracefully into an armchair. She didn't look happy.

'Pia, perhaps you'd explain why you're here?' Domenico's voice was smooth but held a note of steel. Lucy watched Pia shift and realised it hadn't been her idea to come here.

What was going on?

'I came to…' The brunette darted a look at Domenico then turned to Lucy. Her fingers went to her throat in a nervous gesture. 'To apologise.'

Lucy's breath stopped but her heart pounded on. She opened her mouth to speak but nothing came out.

Pia crossed her legs then uncrossed them, clearly ill at ease.

'I don't understand,' Lucy croaked.

'Domenico told me what he'd found out.'

Lucy jerked in shock, her head swinging round to Domenico. He *couldn't* have told her, could he? Fire scorched her face at the idea of him informing Pia she'd been a virgin.

As if reading her thoughts he shook his head. 'Not that,' he whispered. His hand closed on hers but she shook it off.

'He explained there was new evidence,' the other woman went on, 'about Bruno being the guilty one.'

Lucy darted a look at Domenico but his face was inscrutable.

'I never liked him, you know,' Pia said. 'He was always a bit too smooth. But I never thought…' She shook her head. 'You must believe me, Signorina Knight. I didn't know he lied. All I knew was Sandro was in your room, with you cradling his head, and he was dead.' She sobbed and lifted a handkerchief to her eyes.

'It's all right, Pia. Lucy understands you didn't know the truth.' Domenico's hand touched Lucy's again and this time she was too distracted to move it.

'Of course,' she said, trying to digest this news.

What new evidence?

'You understand?' Pia looked up through tear-glazed eyes.

Lucy nodded. 'I didn't know what Bruno was really like either. If I had I'd never have let him into my room.' She shuddered, thinking how gullible she'd been.

Domenico squeezed her shoulders and she had no desire to shake him off.

Pia's hand went again to her throat. 'It was a shock when Domenico told me the truth.' Her mouth curled in a trembling smile as she looked at her brother-in-law. 'You gave Sandro back to me with your news. You have no idea what that means after all this time.'

'It took me too long.' Domenico's voice was grim. 'I should have thought of it years before.'

Lucy looked from one to the other, curiosity mounting. 'Thought of what?'

The other woman turned to her. 'My jewellery, of course.' Her eyes widened. 'Domenico, you didn't tell her?'

'No one has told me anything.' Frustration rose. Everyone knew more than her!

'I thought Lucy would appreciate hearing it from you,' he said.

Lucy bit down a demand for someone, anyone, to tell her what was going on.

'Domenico found the artisan who made my jewellery.' Pia extended her arm. On her wrist was a bracelet of enamelled flowers, exquisitely executed and interspersed with lustrous pearls.

Lucy leaned forward, identifying primroses and forget-me-nots in a design she'd never expected to see again. Her stomach clamped down as icy fingers danced on her spine. Nausea rose and she breathed hard through her mouth, forcing it down.

Abruptly she sat back, shutting her eyes in an effort to regain control.

When she opened them she saw Pia's hand caressing the matching necklace at her throat. Lucy had been so preoccupied she hadn't recognised it.

'That was the necklace they found in my room.' Lucy's voice was hoarse. Stupid to be so affected but it brought back that night in too-vivid detail. More, it evoked memories of how it had been used against her in the trial. 'I didn't know there was a bracelet too.'

'Nor did I,' Pia said, smiling as she looked at her brother-in-law.

Lucy turned in his hold. Domenico's eyes were fixed on her with an intensity that banished the cold prickling her backbone. 'You knew there was a bracelet?' Why was that important? She still didn't see.

'No, I just tried to track down the maker. I was desperate for any leads that might give me a better picture of what happened back then.' His hand tightened on hers.

Her heart dipped. He'd tracked the maker down because he'd sought the impossible—something to prove she wasn't a killer.

'The police were only interested in the fact you had the necklace, not where it was made.'

'Because everyone assumed he'd bought it for me.' Lucy shivered, remembering how the prosecution had made so much about the match between the enamelled flowers and the colour of her eyes. Plus the fact that, beautiful as the piece was, it was nothing like the glittering emeralds and rubies Sandro had previously given his wife. The implication was that he'd got something expensive for his new lover, but nothing to rival the grandeur of the jewels he'd bought his wife.

'But they were wrong. See?' Pia undid the bracelet and held it out.

Lucy couldn't bring herself to touch it. Instead Domenico took it and laid it across his broad palm, revealing the engraved lettering on the back: *To my beloved Pia, light of my life. Always, Sandro.*

'I don't understand.' Lucy's head whirled.

Domenico passed the bracelet back.

'Sandro had commissioned a matching set but only had the necklace the night he was killed. According to the maker, when he came to collect them he decided to have the inscription engraved on the bracelet, but he didn't want to wait to give the necklace to Pia. He took it and said he'd be back for the second piece. When he didn't return and the artisan discovered he'd died, he didn't know what to do with the bracelet. He had no idea of its significance to the case. He thought of removing the inscription and selling it on, but was superstitious enough to think it might bring bad luck.'

'Why didn't your brother wait for both pieces?'

'Because of me.' It was Pia who spoke. The glow of happiness dimmed and her features were sharp with pain.

'I wasn't…well.' Her eyes met Lucy's before shifting away. 'I didn't know at the time. It wasn't till after that night, much later, that Domenico arranged for me to get help.' She swallowed and Lucy felt sympathy surge for the other woman's obvious pain.

'I…' Pia paused and dragged in a deep breath. 'I wasn't myself after Taddeo was born. I was…troubled.' She worked the bracelet on her wrist. 'I was so miserable I accused Sandro of not caring for me and of infidelity.'

Guilt-filled eyes rose to meet Lucy's.

Lucy remembered how difficult and moody Pia had been all those years ago. How she hadn't liked it when Lucy could calm little Taddeo so easily, and how she'd jumped to conclusions when she'd found Lucy and her husband talking together. Poor Sandro had been worried about his wife and son, checking with Lucy about his concerns. He'd been torn between placating his wife and getting help for what Lucy thought could be Pia's severe depression.

'At the trial I said things about you and Sandro.' Pia sucked in a shaky breath. 'Things I believed at the time, but things that looking back I realise I didn't *know*.'

Like stating emphatically that Lucy had been Sandro's lover, saying under oath she'd found them in compromising positions.

'It wasn't till Domenico came to me with his news, and *this*—' she looked at her bracelet '—that I realised what I'd done.' She paused. 'Sandro and I met in spring, you see. For all his money, Sandro courted me with primroses and forget-me-nots. When he ordered this he was trying to remind me of those early days when we were happy. He was bringing the necklace to me that night, not you. It must have fallen from his pocket when he...when he...'

Lucy leaned across and touched the other woman's hand. 'Your husband must have loved you very much. It was there in his face whenever he mentioned you.'

Pia's eyes filled but she smiled. 'I know that now. But at the time I was so unhappy. That's why I said those things—'

'It's all right, truly.' Even at eighteen Lucy had understood enough to realise Pia hadn't deliberately slandered her. She'd been hysterical with grief and misery, falling easily into supporting Bruno's damning evidence that tied so well with her own imaginings. He'd painted Lucy as an immoral opportunist, no doubt feeding Pia's worst fears. 'I'm sure it made no difference to the case.'

'You think so?'

No. Lucy wasn't certain. She'd seen the court moved by the beautiful grieving widow. But pity was stronger now than any desire for revenge. Pia's regret was genuine, as was her joy at rediscovering her husband's love.

Would Lucy ever know love like that? Her heart squeezed.

'I know it,' she murmured.

'Thank you.' Pia took her hand. 'That means a lot.'

A third hand joined theirs. Then Pia's touch dropped away as she sat back in her seat and Domenico's fingers threaded through Lucy's. Warmth spread from his touch. Not the fire of physical desire but something more profound.

Was he congratulating himself on the reconciliation? One step closer to the day he could wash his hands of his obligation to her?

He looked up at the antique clock above the mantelpiece then rose, tugging her to her feet. 'Come on, ladies. It's time we left.'

Pia rose and reached for a gossamer-fine wrap. It was left to Lucy to ask, 'Where are we going?'

'To the opera, then supper.' He tucked her hand into his elbow. 'We have a reservation at Rome's premier restaurant.'

'But the press! They'll see—'

'They will indeed,' he murmured. 'They'll see that far from shunning you, you're our guest. It will prime them for more news to come.'

CHAPTER THIRTEEN

'IT'S NOT AS bad as I expected.'

Lucy's murmured comment made Domenico smile.

He surveyed the ultra modern restaurant that was Rome's latest A-list haunt and thought of the other women he could have brought here. Women who'd toy with the exquisitely prepared food while making the most of the chance to see and be seen. Who'd have spent the day getting ready to come here.

By contrast he'd had to force Lucy into her glamorous new clothes. She shunned the avid gazes sent their way, concentrating on her food with an unfashionable enjoyment that would endear her to the chef.

'I'm glad you think having supper with me isn't too much of a burden.'

Her gaze darted to his face and her lips quirked in the first genuine smile he'd had from her all night. He couldn't believe how good it felt, seeing that. He'd even wondered, for about half a minute, if he'd done the wrong thing, thrusting her into the limelight again.

Earlier at the opera with Pia, Lucy had stood stiffly as they mingled in the foyer, sipping champagne and chatting with the many acquaintances who'd approached them. The three of them had been a magnet for attention. Yet only he, holding Lucy close, knew what it cost her to appear at ease in the glittering crowd. She'd projected a calm, slightly aloof air that fitted the setting perfectly and she'd held her own with a poise that made him proud.

She truly was a remarkable woman.

'If you're fishing for compliments you're out of luck, Signor Volpe.' But her eyes sparkled. 'It's not *you* I was worried about. It was everyone else.'

'You handled them beautifully.'

She laid her spoon down and licked a stray curl of chocolate from her upper lip. Desire twisted in Domenico's belly, sharp and powerful, and he sucked in his breath.

She aroused him so easily. Each time he had her he wanted her again. Every day he needed more, not less.

How long would it take to have his fill?

'*You* handled them beautifully, not me. No one dared say anything outrageous with you beside me. But they wondered what was going on.'

Domenico spread his hands. 'Of course they wondered. What do we care for that? Tonight is about making it clear the Volpes accept you. That's why Pia came to the opera. If we champion you, who in society will deny you?'

'It's not Roman high society I'm worried about. It's everyone else. The press, for a start.' She reached for her water glass and drank deeply. It was the only outward sign that she wasn't completely at ease.

'Let me take care of the press, Lucy.' Strange how he found himself deliberately using her name so often. As if he got pleasure from its taste on his tongue.

'Don't you see?' She leaned forward, face earnest. 'You can ward them off with your bodyguards. But when I'm on my own it will be different. They'll bay for my blood even more than before.'

Domenico covered her hand. 'It will be all right. You just need to be patient. If all turns out as I intend, soon you won't have to worry about the press.'

The media would have another victim in its sights. There'd

be a spike of interest in Lucy as victim, rather than criminal, but eventually it would die down.

Triumph filled him. After weeks of intense work, they were on the brink of success.

This particular success brought a satisfaction greater than any business coup. Because his pleasure in this was *personal*.

It would salve his battered conscience, clearing Lucy's name. The Volpe family would pay its debt by redressing the wrong done her. More specifically, it would be some small recompense for the way he'd rejected her out of hand.

But there was more. He'd been surprised at how tonight's meeting between Pia and Lucy had affected him. How he'd felt both women's pain.

He'd always thought Pia over-emotional and needy. Now he realised her belief in Sandro's betrayal had fed that neediness. She really had loved his brother. Believing Sandro no longer loved her had undermined her fragile self-worth. Now perhaps she could face the world with a little more confidence.

As for Lucy—he watched her watching him from under lowered lashes and his hold tightened possessively. It might have been responsibility, obligation and guilt driving him to clear her name. But he wasn't just acting out of duty.

He felt *good*, knowing Lucy would be in a better place when this was over.

In the past he'd confined his philanthropy to large charitable donations. Maybe in future he'd take a more hands-on role. He'd discovered he enjoyed righting wrongs and seeing justice done.

But there was another, more personal dimension to this—an undercurrent that flowed deeper and stronger than any do-gooder intentions.

Domenico stroked his thumb across Lucy's palm and felt her shiver. Her lips parted. He wanted to kiss her with all the pent up passion he kept in check.

But he preferred privacy for what he had in mind.

He stroked her palm again, this time drawing his finger past her wrist and along her forearm, watching with satisfaction the tiny telltale signs of her pleasure.

'What do you think you're doing?'

He loved the way her voice dropped to that husky note when she was aroused.

'Nothing.'

He looked up and her sultry gaze caught him. His heart thudded and urgency filled him.

'Liar,' she whispered. 'I know your game.'

'Good.' He drew her from her seat. 'Then you won't mind leaving the rest of your dessert.'

She leaned forward so her breath feathered his cheek. 'Not if you're offering something better.' She turned, collected her shimmering evening bag and headed towards the door with a slow, sexy sway that drew every male gaze.

Domenico was torn between appreciation and dog-in-the-manger jealousy that she flaunted herself in front of others.

In mere weeks she'd blossomed from artless innocent to a siren who turned him into a slavering idiot.

She really *was* remarkable.

Eyes glued to her, he summoned a waiter and had the bill put on his account.

He smiled as she slowed to wait for him at the door.

What more could he want from life? He had the anticipation of success, the satisfied glow that came from redressing past wrongs, and the bonus of Lucy in his bed.

Life was excellent.

It was over breakfast that news came.

Lucy was enjoying a platter of summer fruit when she heard Domenico on the phone. She looked up as he entered the room. Their eyes met and, as ever, her skin tingled.

'I see,' Domenico said into the phone, his eyes dark with

secrets. Images of their loving last night surfaced and she felt an unfamiliar blush rise.

Last night had been…phenomenal. She tried to tell herself it was just reaction, having survived the evening without falling in a heap or being accosted as a criminal. But she knew the magic came from far deeper feelings.

The efforts Domenico went to in order to clear her name were amazing. She owed him a debt she could never repay. He'd achieved more in a few short weeks, with his discovery of the jewellery, than the police had. Presumably because they'd been only too ready to accept Bruno's evidence and blame the outsider—her.

More, he was the one who'd cracked open the brittle shell she'd built to separate herself from the world. It was scary being without it, but wonderful too. These last weeks had been crammed with precious pleasures she'd remember all her life.

She looked away from those penetrating grey eyes.

If only she could feel simply gratitude. But she felt far more. Domenico touched her deep inside. He'd changed her for ever.

'When did this happen?' He paused and Lucy's head jerked up at his tone. 'Excellent. You've done well.' A smile split his face and Lucy caught her breath.

Domenico put the phone down and sat, looking smug.

'What is it? What's happened?' Even as she spoke something tempered her impatience, an atavistic fear of upsetting the good life they shared. Tension scrolled down her spine, like a premonition of cold, hard change to come.

'Good news. The best news.'

Yet, unaccountably, Lucy felt that tension eddying deep inside. Slowly she wiped her fingers on a linen napkin.

Domenico raised his eyebrows as if expecting her to burst into speech.

'The police have taken Bruno Scarlatti in for questioning in the light of new evidence. They're reviewing the investigation into Sandro's death.'

Lucy's heart pounded. 'New evidence?'

'Remember Scarlatti had an alibi for the time of Sandro's death? A colleague who claimed to have been with him on the other side of the palazzo?'

'How could I forget?' Lucy clasped her hands together, old bitterness welling.

'That colleague has come forward, saying he'd got the times wrong. He was with Bruno fifteen minutes earlier rather than at the time of the killing, as he said. There was always forensic evidence Bruno had been in the room but only your word for it he'd been there before Sandro died, not just later.'

'The witness admitted to lying?' It seemed too good to be true.

Domenico shrugged. 'He was young. Bruno was his mentor and friend. He thought he was doing him a favour, giving an alibi for a crime he couldn't believe Bruno committed.'

'You know a lot about this.' Lucy felt strangely disconnected from the news, as if it affected someone else.

'Rocco tracked the witness down and filled him in on Bruno's record since then.'

'He's got a record?' That was news.

'A conviction for assault and a string of complaints. Plus dismissal for questionable behaviour.'

Lucy sat back, her mind awhirl at the implications. 'You did all this.' It boggled her mind.

She waited for elation to hit.

'It was nothing. I had the resources to uncover the truth, that's all.'

Lucy shook her head, her heartbeat loud as a drum. 'It's more than anyone else did.'

'But I knew the truth. That made it easier.' He reached out and took her hand. His felt hard and capable. She looked into his eyes and read satisfaction there. The satisfaction of a man who'd solved a puzzle no one else had. The satisfaction of a man who'd achieved justice, no matter how belated. Who'd restored his family honour by redressing the injustice done in their name.

She slid her hand from his grip and laced her fingers together in her lap.

Dazed, she grappled with what he'd told her. She'd be able to reclaim her good name. It was what she'd longed for and fought for all this time.

Yet instead of euphoria, a sense of anticlimax enveloped her. It all seemed too…easy.

'So you threw resources at it and hey presto, the truth is revealed?' She couldn't hide her bitterness. 'If only the police had done that in the first place—really *listened* and investigated thoroughly…' She shook her head, a wave of anger and frustration engulfing her. '*Five years* of my life gone. Five years in hell.'

When Lucy looked up it was to see Domenico's grim expression.

'You're right. It should never have happened like this. Can you forgive me?'

She frowned. 'Forgive you? I'm talking about the way the investigators latched on to Bruno's evidence and didn't want to hear anything against it because he was one of them, ex-police.'

Domenico's mouth tightened. 'If I'd taken time to hear you out instead of assuming your guilt it would have been different.' His shoulders rose and fell in a massive shrug that spoke of regret and pain.

Suddenly she saw him clearly, right to the shadows in his soul. He expected her condemnation.

So it was true, his actions had been driven by guilt all this time. She sucked in a breath, trying to find calm.

Domenico was many things but, she knew now, he wasn't responsible for her conviction. That notion had been a sop to her anger and pride in the dark days when she'd needed it most.

She didn't need it now. She'd held on to anger and cynicism for too long and she didn't like the woman it had made her.

'Don't talk like that.' Her voice was husky. 'You're the man proving my innocence.'

'But too late. I should have—'

'No, Domenico.' She raised her hand. 'It devastated me when you cut me loose but it didn't make a difference to the trial. It hurt.' She faced him squarely, letting him read the truth. 'But that's all. No one could blame you for doubting me in the face of the other evidence.'

For a long moment searching grey eyes held hers. 'You're some woman, Lucy Knight. Thank you.'

She smiled, though her heart wasn't in it.

She told herself this was the beginning of the rest of her life, the beginning she'd wanted so long, but with it came sadness that her dad hadn't survived to see her innocence proven. And welling dismay over what this meant for her and Domenico.

Lucy rubbed her forehead, trying to ease the ache beginning there.

'Lucy? What is it? Are you all right?'

She looked down at the luscious fruit on her plate and her stomach roiled.

'Of course. I'm just…stunned. It's taking a while to process.'

Could she be pregnant? Was that what made her nauseous and maudlin instead of happy at this brilliant news? The possibility had sat at the back of her mind ever since she'd learned he hadn't used protection that first time.

Joy and fear filled her at the idea of carrying Domenico's child. Despite his assurances, she knew he wouldn't be happy. Innocent she might be, but it had become clear last night, seeing the glitz of the rarefied world he moved in, that she didn't belong. She'd had to call on every ounce of courage to face the calculating gazes of the uber-wealthy and the paparazzi.

She'd even been gauchely enthusiastic about her first opera when the rest of the audience displayed only polite appreciation. She'd been so obviously an outsider.

'It's okay, Lucy.' His tone was encouraging, kind. 'We achieved what we set out to do. It's all over now.'

Her gaze darted to Domenico's face. In it she read self-satisfaction that, melded onto his superbly sculpted features, gave an air of ingrained superiority.

It's all over.

Hadn't she told herself that what they shared would end soon? She could barely call it a relationship, despite the blinding moments of connection. It was based only on sexual pleasure and convenience. Not once had he spoken of a future beyond 'rehabilitating' her.

As if she was some project instead of a woman with feelings!

Feelings. Oh, she had those in spades.

She tried to dredge up gratitude. Instead a writhing knot of emotion wedged in her chest.

'Thank you,' she said finally. 'Without you, this would never have happened.'

He gestured dismissively. Obviously it had been nothing mobilising vast resources to revisit every aspect of the prosecution case.

Lucy swallowed, not wanting to ask, but needing to know. 'What now, Domenico? What will we do?'

Last night, basking in his closeness, she'd let herself dream what it would be like if he truly cared for her. If he *loved* her.

She snatched in her breath on a desperate gasp. Until now she hadn't used the L word. Coward that she was, she'd avoided even thinking it. But she couldn't pretend any longer. She wanted to be more to Domenico than a project.

She wanted to be in his life permanently. She wanted his laughter, his tenderness, his loving, the way he made her feel precious and special. She wanted to be the woman she'd become on his island, where she'd learned about compassion and trust and…love.

Her stomach dipped at the enormity of what she wanted.

She'd gone from total, self-absorbed isolation to knowing she wouldn't be whole without him.

She swallowed hard. She'd fallen in love.

'Now?' His brows drew together.

'Now it's over.'

She waited, longing for him to tell her it would never be over. That he felt this overwhelming sense of belonging with her too, despite the differences between them.

'Nothing more is necessary. The legal experts can take it from here.' He gave her a reassuring smile that did anything but. 'We'll continue the strategy of showing you out and about, accepted by the family and everyone who counts. My security staff will protect you.'

'Of course.' She felt like an inanimate object to be exhibited. Lucy told herself she was unreasonable. It didn't help.

'There'll be a spike in interest once it's clear you're innocent. But in the long run I'm hopeful you can start that new life you want so much.'

His smile was benevolent, like an adult giving a child a long awaited treat.

Except she didn't want it as she once had. Not if it meant leaving Domenico.

But it wasn't her choice to make.

She waited for him to say more. To talk about *them*.

He said nothing.

She read the satisfaction in his eyes and the way he sprawled in his chair. He'd done what he'd set out to do against the odds. Wasn't that his speciality? Succeeding where everyone failed? She'd been one more challenge to a man who revelled in beating the odds.

Lucy's stomach clenched. She wanted to be more.

'Where will you be, Domenico?' She was proud of her even tone when inside she shook like a leaf in a gale.

'Me?' He looked surprised she'd ask. 'I'll stay in Rome for

a while to help you through the media attention. You won't have to cope alone.'

No, he'd made it his business to look after her. She told herself she should appreciate it more. She *did* appreciate it, except she felt like a problem to be managed rather than the woman in his life.

Miserably, she reminded herself she'd never really been his woman, just conveniently available.

'And after that?'

He shrugged and reached for his coffee. 'I've got business in New York I've delayed for a couple of weeks.' Delayed because of her.

'And then?' She laced her fingers, willing him to say something, anything about *them*. About coming back to her or taking her with him. 'What about after that?' Even a promise to see her in England would be something.

Domenico frowned, clearly not used to being quizzed.

'It depends on a number of things. Perhaps Germany for a week or two.'

'I see.'

Finally, she did.

This *was* the end.

She'd known it was coming. How could she not, when despite the precious moments of communion, she didn't fit in his world or he in hers?

He'd support her for a week or two more, squiring her and protecting her from the press. And he'd be happy, no doubt, to share his body with her, while he was in town.

After that she was on her own.

Pain stabbed, transfixing her. She breathed slowly through her mouth, willing the searing heat, like a red-hot knife in her midriff, to ease. It didn't, but she couldn't bear to sit here with him surveying her like his latest trophy of success—proof that Domenico Volpe could achieve anything he set his heart on.

When she'd set her heart on—

No! She'd known this couldn't last. She'd resolved to enjoy every minute Domenico gave her and not look back. It was she who'd broken the rules by wanting more.

She prayed she still had the power to hide her feelings from him.

'I never believed you could do it, Domenico.' She let his name roll around her mouth, savouring it one last time. 'Thank you.' She met his gaze, felt that familiar sizzle of heat, then looked at her hands threading together in her lap. She'd have to do better than this if she was to leave with dignity.

'It was my pleasure, Lucy.' The rumble of his voice reminded her of the intimacies they'd shared, not just in bed, but when they'd laughed together, talked, and played with Chiara.

Her shiver of response was the catalyst she needed. She could stay but each day would draw her further into his thrall till she wouldn't have the strength to go. She couldn't wait for the day he decided it was time for her to leave.

Lucy's chair scraped the polished floor as she stood.

'If you'll excuse me I'll go and pack.' She lifted her head and looked at a point just over his shoulder. 'I appreciate your help, but I'd rather not stay in Rome.'

Domenico froze, his coffee halfway to his mouth.

'*Prego?*' What did she mean, she'd rather not stay?

'It's time I went home. I'm sure you understand.'

The cup rattled as he put it down. Understand? Like hell he did. As for going home, he knew as well as Lucy that she had no home. Her she-wolf of a stepmother had sold Lucy's privacy for a fistful of cash.

'No, I don't understand! Perhaps you'd explain.'

How could she be so eager to leave? Indignation stirred and with it male pride. Only hours ago she'd lain in his arms, crying out his name as they found bliss together. Heat stirred, remembering.

She didn't meet his eyes.

Fear prickled the hairs on his nape. He didn't understand it, but he did trust his instincts. Something was wrong. Badly wrong.

'I'm English, Domenico. I want to go to England.'

'You haven't mentioned returning in weeks.'

She shrugged. 'Because it was obvious I'd be hounded by the press. You gave me a place to lie low and I appreciate it.'

Was that all he'd given her? She short-changed them both implying it was.

'I've been in Italy since I left prison. I want to go home.' Her hands twisted. 'Do you realise that, even out of jail, I haven't chosen where I stayed? Not even for a night?'

She complained about the way he protected her? Or did she complain about being with him? Domenico's mind whirled. It wasn't possible. She'd welcomed him into her bed so eagerly.

'You'd rather I'd left you to the press?' He spoke through gritted teeth. He told himself he didn't want her gratitude but he sure as hell expected better than this. Anger stirred. 'You know it was for your own good.' Even if at first it had been for his convenience.

She nodded. 'I appreciate all you've done. And the way you came to my aid that day we went ashore. But it's time I stood on my own two feet.'

Domenico's jaw jammed shut. He hated that note of finality in her voice. He wanted to rail at her and tell her she couldn't leave.

But what right had he to stop her?

Only the fact that he wasn't ready to let her go. Not while the passion they shared burned so bright.

Didn't she feel it too?

Or had she simply taken advantage of what he offered, ready to discard him as it suited her?

Domenico's jaw tightened.

Never had a woman dumped him. And never had one left

with such little regret. He hated this dark roil of emotions. They made him feel…alarmingly out of control.

He strode around the end of the table, ready to reach out and grab her, only to stop when she faced him with that cold mask of disdain he'd thought she'd ditched for good.

'I'm a free woman now and it's time I acted like one.'

'The press will be after you.' She needed him, couldn't she see that? Something akin to desperation racked him. 'With the case reopened the press will be more eager.'

'I don't care. At least now they won't call me a murderess. They won't stop me getting a job.'

'You want to work?'

Her eyes, like blue stars, met his head-on and the impact rocked him back on his heels.

'Of course I want to work. What choice do I have?' Her expression was dismissive.

'You could always sell your story. They'd pay even higher money for your inside story now you've been in my bed.'

Even as he said it, Domenico regretted the words. She'd goaded him into a quagmire of bitter, unfamiliar emotions, announcing she was leaving. He felt betrayed and he lashed out.

Lucy looked at him as if she'd never seen him before. Her eyes were laser-sharp as they raked him, scraping his flesh raw. Had he really imagined she cared for him?

'Perhaps I will. After all, I didn't sign that gag contract of yours, did I?'

It was a physical blow to the gut, watching her turn back into the ice-hard woman she'd once been.

He wanted to beg her not to do it. But Volpes never begged. Besides, she was beyond listening to him.

'Goodbye, Domenico.' She spun on her foot and left.

CHAPTER FOURTEEN

AUTUMN CAME EARLY to London. Wind gusted down the city street, grabbed Lucy's second-hand jacket and flapped it around her.

The chill didn't bother her. She'd grown used to feeling cold, ever since that day in Rome when Domenico had washed his hands of her.

She tilted her head down and put one weary leg in front of the other. It had been a long day and she needed this short break to regroup before her busy evening shift. Jobs weren't easy to come by, not even casual waitressing jobs, and she had rent due. She couldn't afford to be anything but on the ball when her shift began again.

A cup of tea and twenty minutes with her shoes kicked off beneath a table would be bliss.

She was calculating if she had enough cash for food too when a dark figure loomed before her. Automatically she stepped to one side. So did he. Lucy stepped the other way to find he'd made the same manoeuvre.

That was when she took in the glossy, beautifully tooled shoes blocking her path.

Her nape prickled as she raised her gaze over an exquisitely tailored suit and cashmere overcoat. She gasped and sucked in a spicy scent she'd never forget if she lived to be a hundred.

'Domenico!'

Gun-metal grey eyes met hers from under straight black

brows. The shock of him in the flesh rocked her back on her heels. She'd imagined him often, dreamt about him every night, but had forgotten how incredibly magnetic that deep gaze was.

Hungrily she took in those high cheekbones, the strong nose and hard jaw, the sensuous mouth. So familiar, so dear. Her heart bumped then catapulted into a gallop. She buried her hands deep in her pockets lest she reach for him as she did in her dreams.

He looked utterly gorgeous, but there were lines of strain around his eyes and the groove in his cheek scored deeper than before. He'd been working too hard.

'Lucy.' Just two syllables and her nerves danced a shimmy of delight. No one said her name as he did. No one made it sound half so appealing.

'What are you doing in London?'

'I have an important meeting.'

Of course he did. Domenico's world was full of important meetings. She'd followed his progress in the press these last couple of months, from the USA to Germany, China and back to Rome. Nothing had stopped his spectacular business success. Certainly not regret over her.

Still she couldn't bring herself to move. She stood, drinking him in, like a shaft of Italian sunshine on this grey English day.

'With you.'

'Sorry?' She'd lost the thread of the conversation.

'It's you I'm here to see.'

She shook her head. Of course she wanted to see him, but self-preservation cautioned it could only lead to catastrophe. She didn't have the willpower to say goodbye again. Getting over Domenico Volpe was even harder than she'd feared.

'It's true.'

'How did you find me?'

His eyebrows rose and she thought of the vast resources he'd used to find the truth about her past. He'd probably just clicked his fingers and hey presto!

'Why track me down?' What could he want after all this time?

Then it struck her. Domenico put family above all. He was big on duty and making things right. Why else would he come?

She made herself meet his eyes, not letting him see her disappointment. 'You don't have to worry. You didn't get me pregnant.'

Domenico stared into her brilliant blue gaze and felt a knife slash of pain. The chances had been slim but still he'd hoped.

He made himself nod as if her news hadn't all but gutted him. 'Thank you for telling me.'

Crazy to have hoped so hard. He should have known nothing about this would be easy.

Looking into her wary face, having her so close, was more difficult than he'd imagined. She looked the same, more beautiful if possible, but the warmth was gone from her gaze and there was no sign of that rare wondrous smile he'd come to believe she saved for him. No sign of the cheeky, confident woman who'd brought him to his knees with her sexy flirting. Lucy held herself back as if expecting more pain.

Something plunged deep in his belly. Guilt sharpened its claws on his vitals.

'So there's no reason for us to meet.' She gave him a cool smile but he saw beyond it to her bewilderment. Either her mask of unconcern wasn't as good as it used to be or he was getting better at reading her.

Yet it was far too early to feel anything like hope.

'But we have things to discuss.' He reached for her elbow. 'Come. My hotel is just around the corner. We can talk there.'

He breathed in her honey and sunshine scent and pleasure slammed into him. His fingers tightened on her arm as he drew her along.

'I don't want to talk in your hotel suite.'

He should have known she'd resist. When had she made

things easy? Nervous tension battled pleasure at her familiar obstinacy.

'Fine. We'll use the public rooms.' He managed a smile, despite the nerves tightening his belly. Surely if she didn't trust the privacy of his suite it was because he could still tempt her? The notion charged his hopes.

He eased his grip and he tucked her arm in his. She didn't resist and anticipation rose as he led her around a corner towards a familiar brick building decorated with flags.

'Signor Volpe. Madame.' The top-hatted doorman welcomed them and they stepped inside.

Instantly Domenico felt Lucy stiffen. He liked the quiet and the excellent service here but he took for granted its hushed opulence.

'We can go to my rooms if you'd prefer.' His lips brushed her hair as he leaned close. The scent of her drove his careful plans into a tangle of lust and nerves. He prayed she'd say yes.

'No. This is fine.' He felt her stand taller, taking in the elegance of the area before them. It reminded him of her spunk when faced with the glitterati at the opera in Rome. Lucy had stiffened her spine, kept her head up and won the admiration of many.

Minutes later they were seated in a secluded corner of the vast reception room. The décor was opulent—huge arched mirrors, enormous pillars with gilded capitals and the scent of hundreds of roses from the massed arrangements. Yet here at their small table, seated comfortably in the glow of a nearby lamp, they had an illusion of privacy.

Lucy avoided his gaze, rubbing at a stain on her black skirt.

Domenico dragged his eyes from the short skirt that revealed her stunning legs. He had to focus.

Panic stirred and he forced it down. This was the most important negotiation of his life and he couldn't let nerves wreck his chances.

'Your stepmother contacted me.'

Lucy jerked her head up. 'Why you?'

He shrugged. 'She'd read about me collecting you from prison, and you being with me in Rome. It was the only place she could think of to reach you.'

Wariness was writ large on Lucy's face. 'What did she want? Money?'

'No.' He paused, remembering that difficult conversation. 'She wanted to talk with you.'

Lucy shook her head. 'I can't imagine why.'

'Apparently she wants to apologise.'

'And you believed her?' Lucy's face was taut with outrage but with something else too. Something that might have been hope.

Domenico's heart lightened. Lucy tried so hard to be tough and cold, yet always she responded with a good heart. Look at the way she'd taken to Chiara and the way she'd let him into her life. She'd given Pia a second chance. Maybe she'd do it again.

'I believe she was genuinely sorry for that article. She said she needed the money and thought she could handle the media. According to her, the reporter twisted most of what she said and conveniently removed any positive comments.'

He paused, waiting for her to consider.

'She said she didn't want to talk with you before because she felt so ashamed of what she'd done.'

Lucy gnawed her lip and he wanted to reach out and stop her. But he didn't have the right. She'd walked away from him and who could blame her? Even now he couldn't believe he'd let her go. Twice now he'd missed his chance with Lucy. Finally he'd learnt his lesson!

'I'll think about calling her.'

'Good.' He nodded and sat back as a waiter appeared with their afternoon tea. He was glad for a distraction despite the urgency coiling his belly tight. For the first time he could remember he was *scared*, not able to predict the outcome of this meeting.

'So, is that all?' Her tone was brisk, yet she cradled her celadon-green cup as if needing warmth. He didn't even bother taking his tea. He wouldn't be able to hold it steady. Too much rode on this and he'd lost the facility to pretend it wasn't important.

'No. There's more.'

Her brows arched. 'What? Is there something wrong with the case against Bruno?' For the first time she looked truly shaken.

'Nothing like that. It's all going smoothly.'

Her relief was palpable, yet it struck him that she hadn't looked directly at him. Not since that moment on the street when he'd read shock and something he couldn't name in her eyes.

'And so?'

'And so.' He swallowed and leaned forward. 'I want to talk about us.'

'There is no *us*, Domenico.' Her expression was cool. Yet the way she said his name in that scratchy voice gave him hope. He might be fooling himself but he'd take all the encouragement he could get.

She put her cup down and he snatched her hand up. It trembled.

'Liar,' he whispered. 'There's always been an us. Even when I didn't trust myself to believe what I felt for you in the beginning. I felt the world crumble around me because I wanted you so much it hurt. I wanted you so much I cursed my brother for having you first. Can you believe it?'

'Domenico!' Her voice was a hoarse gasp. 'You can't be serious. Back then you hated me.'

'I thought I hated you because of the bolt of emotion I felt whenever I looked at you. It shook me to the core and it wasn't just lust. It was a…link I couldn't explain. A link I pretended didn't exist because I let myself be swayed by lies and my own jealous pride.' He heaved in a tight breath.

'You felt it too, didn't you, Lucy?'

Her eyes were huge in her pale face. With her blonde hair long enough now to brush her shoulders, she looked more like the innocent who'd stood in the dock all those years ago and stolen his soul.

She shook her head. 'No. I knew you hated me and I felt…'

'What? What did you feel, Lucy?' Urgency made him grip her hand harder.

'I can't explain it.' She looked away. 'A link, I suppose, from the start. But it wasn't right. It was just lust.'

Was that what she thought? He grimaced, knowing it was his fault she believed it.

'No, *carissima*, it wasn't just lust.'

She tugged her hand. 'Please, let me go.'

'Not until you look at me, Lucy.'

Reluctantly she turned her head and he felt again that blast of heat surging through his veins as their gazes melded. Domenico lifted her hand and kissed it. He turned it over and pressed his mouth to her palm and felt her shiver delicately.

With a sigh he released her hand and watched her cradle it in her lap as if it burned her. Just as his lips tingled where he'd caressed her sweet flesh.

'I was a fool to let you leave, Lucy. I've regretted it from the moment you went.'

'It wasn't a matter of you *letting* me go. It was my decision.'

'Only because I couldn't see what was before my eyes.'

'What are you saying, Domenico?'

'I'm saying what's between us is more important than lust. It always was, though I was too shallow to trust my instincts. I'm saying I want you with me, Lucy. In Rome, or here in Britain if you prefer. I want you in my life.'

There. He'd said it. He'd never asked that of any woman.

'I don't believe you.'

She looked like a queen surveying a troublesome subject.

So proud. So feisty. So hurt. Seeing the pain etched around her pursed lips, shame rose.

'I was a fool to let you walk away but I was too proud to plead with you to stay.'

'I can't imagine you pleading for anything.'

'Can't you?' His lips twisted bitterly.

'No. You're too arrogant. Too sure of yourself.'

'Remind me never to come to you for a character reference. You know me too well.'

'What is it you want, Domenico? Is this some sort of game?'

'I was never more serious in my life.'

'Domenico?' Her eyes rounded as he slipped from his chair and knelt before hers. 'What are you doing?'

'Pleading, *carissima*.' And the hell of it was he didn't give a damn who saw him. All he cared about was convincing Lucy.

'I don't understand.' She blinked, her eyes overbright and he reached to take her hand.

'Nor did I, in Rome. I was too full of myself. Too pleased with my success in setting things right, and too full of relief that finally I was doing right by you after all those wrongs. I didn't question what was happening between us.'

For the first time since he'd known her Lucy looked lost for words.

'I thought I had it all—the satisfaction of seeing justice done, and you in my bed, in my life.' He paused, the words harder now. 'I thought that was all I wanted, to enjoy the moment, to have your company and the phenomenal sex, as long as it lasted.'

Her hand clenched in his. 'I hadn't thought past that. When you called me on it I wasn't ready to face what I really wanted. Because what I wanted scared me.'

'Liar.' The whispered word shivered through him. 'You're never scared.'

Again he lifted her hand to his mouth, inhaling her warm

scent, absorbing her taste. He couldn't bear the thought of not being allowed to touch her again.

'I was absolutely petrified. So petrified I couldn't think straight. It wasn't one of my finer moments. But when you reminded me you hadn't really been free from the moment you got out of jail, how could I stop you? You deserved the right to the life you wanted.'

He searched her face but couldn't read her thoughts. Fear coursed through his bloodstream and his breathing came in short, hard stabs.

'Cut to the chase, Domenico. What *is* it you want? Do you want me as your lover while you're in England? Or in Rome—' she paused as if searching for words '—till you've had enough?'

'No! I want more. I want everything. I fell for you years ago on one magic day in Rome. Then later you were so beautiful and so stoic in the face of all that horror, I couldn't get you out of my mind.'

His heart pounded as he pressed her palm to his chest. Her touch gave him courage to go on.

'When we met again I fell for you all over again.'

She shook her head. 'You're talking about sex.'

'That too.' He smiled at her prim expression, remembering her in his bed. 'But actually I fell for the woman who made me feel like a new man.'

He sliced his free hand through the air. 'I can't explain, but with your honesty, your generosity and your pleasure in everything around you, I became different too. A man who didn't calculate every last item, who remembered what it was to enjoy life and to *feel*. I learned there's more to life than balance sheets and takeovers. There's caring and forgiveness.'

His words echoed into silence. His pulse drummed a staccato tattoo that surely convinced her as nothing else could, that he was genuine.

'I want to be with you. I want to live my life with you, wherever you are. I want to make a family with you and be with you always. I love you, Lucy.'

Finally the words ran out. He'd bared himself utterly. In his former life where control meant everything, that would have been unthinkable.

'Lucy? Say something.' His voice was hoarse.

'I say you're very long-winded, Signor Volpe. But I wouldn't have missed a moment of it.' She leaned forward and there were stars in her eyes. 'You could talk the birds from the trees if you wanted.'

Hope spilled as he saw her glorious smile. 'You're the only one I'm interested in. Will you have me, *tesoro*? Will you be mine?'

'Domenico—' she murmured his name as if savouring each syllable and every muscle cinched tight '—I've been yours for so long I can barely remember what it was like before you burst into my life.' She sighed and whispered in his ear, 'I love you, Domenico.'

'Carissima!'

Finally he was free to do what he'd longed to from the moment he'd seen her in the street. He scooped her into his arms and kissed her so thoroughly he almost forgot to breathe. Breathing was overrated. With Lucy in his arms, who needed oxygen?

Eventually something, a faint noise, caught his attention. He lifted his head, smiling at the beatific glow on his beloved's face, and turned.

'Champagne, sir?' The waiter held a vintage bottle of his favourite bubbly.

'Excellent idea. In my suite. Now.'

The waiter nodded and melted discreetly away.

'Lucy?'

'Mmm?' She snuggled into his arms as he lifted her. 'How do you feel about having our honeymoon right here?'

Eyes the pure blue of an Italian summer sky met his and a

pulse of emotion beat through him. 'I think first you need to persuade me to marry you.' Her smile was that of a temptress.

Domenico turned and carried her out of the room, oblivious to the stares and smiles of the other patrons. The world had never been so right.

'Ah,' he whispered in her ear. 'You know how I like rising to a challenge.'

* * * * *

BLACKMAILED BRIDE, INNOCENT WIFE

To all the readers who have enjoyed my stories.

To the many who have taken the time to contact me about my books.

And especially to Sofia, Cindy, Gena and Dottie, who were the very first to encourage a brand-new author on her debut.

Thank you all!

CHAPTER ONE

ALISSA STEPPED OFF the tram just as the leaden Melbourne sky opened, releasing a downpour. She had no umbrella. The weather had been the last thing on her mind today.

Thunder cracked so close she expected the pavement to shatter before her. The temperature plummeted. Alissa shivered, suddenly chilled to the marrow.

It's a sign, an omen.

She grimaced, refusing to heed the superstitious inner voice. The voice of foreboding that had plagued her all day. The storm had been predicted days ago. It wasn't an omen of disaster. It was mere coincidence.

Alissa ignored the way the hairs on her neck prickled. She hunched her shoulders and darted along the pavement, heedless of the rain's drenching needles.

She'd planned this afternoon meticulously. Nothing, not a storm or her own doubts, would stop her when so much was at stake. Success was so close.

All she had to do was…marry.

Her pace faltered as her heel jammed against uneven pavement. She was doing the right thing, the *only* thing she could. Yet fear slid like an icy finger down her spine at the idea of marriage.

Tying herself to a man.

It didn't matter that this wedding was her idea. That Jason was unthreatening. Safe. Or that the marriage would be short-lived. Experience had taught her the danger of being in a man's power. All the logic in the world couldn't stop the atavistic dread freezing her veins.

But this was no time for caution. Donna needed her. This was her sister's last chance.

Alissa would do *anything*, even tackle her darkest terrors, to save her beloved sister. No one else could do this. The burden rested on her shoulders.

Setting her jaw, she climbed the steps of the looming public building. One leaden foot in front of the other.

It will be all right…unbidden, the old mantra filled her mind.

Of course it would be all right. She and Jason would marry and after six months they'd go their separate ways, unencumbered but for the money they'd receive. The money that would save Donna's life.

It was a simple business arrangement. No power play. No threat. A win-win situation.

Nothing could go wrong.

She hurried through the entrance, plunged into the gloomy foyer and tripped over something.

'Careful there!' an abrupt voice commanded.

Large hands grasped her elbows, holding her away from the solid body her momentum had flung her against. Heat encircled her, the smell of spicy, warm male skin and citrus aftershave. Alissa's pulse skittered at the understated yet unmistakable invitation of that heady scent.

She leaned away to see what she'd fallen over.

Shoes. Large enough to match the hands holding her so firmly. Glossy black handmade shoes that had never seen a scuff in their privileged life. The sight of that perfect footwear, of elegant suiting stretched over long, powerful legs, unsettled her as much as the stranger's silence.

She stepped back but his hands didn't fall. Annoyance skated through her.

Alissa raised her eyes. Past the exquisitely cut jacket, custom-made to accommodate broad shoulders and a rangy frame. Up to an angular jaw, scrupulously shaved. A firm mouth, wide and superbly sculpted, a slash of sensuality across an otherwise hard face. A long, decisive nose, bracketed by high cheekbones that gave him an aristocratic air of disdain.

The air hissed through Alissa's teeth as she drew a sharp breath. His face was lean, harsh, arrogant. With his black hair combed back from a widow's peak he looked impossibly elegant. But his eyes... Alissa reeled as she stared into a charcoal gaze ripe with disapproval.

Heaven help the woman he'd come here to marry.

With those looks—male model meets pure testosterone— his bride was probably too besotted to realise what she was in for. But one moment's collision with his piercing, censorious gaze told Alissa everything. He had an ego big enough to match those shoes. More, there was danger in his superior look, his air of latent power.

Trouble. That was what he was. Why any woman would shackle herself to a man like that...

'I'm sorry,' she muttered when she got her tongue to move. 'I was in such a hurry to get out of the rain I didn't see you there.'

Silence.

His brows arrowed down in a V of displeasure.

Alissa lifted a hand to her soaked hair. A dribble of rain slid down her nape. Her suit clung to her breasts, back and legs. Even her toes were damp. She shivered as cold sliced through her.

What was wrong with him? Did he disapprove of the way she looked? Or the fact that she'd run into him?

Uncontrollable, unladylike little hoyden. The words rang so loud and clear Alissa jumped. But it was her grandfather's hoarse voice she heard. The stranger's cold gaze had evoked an unexpected memory. The realisation shook her to the core. She must be even more nervous than she'd realised to hear the old man from the grave.

'Look, I—'

'Do you usually burst through doors like that? Without looking where you're going?' His voice was low, deep, with a husky edge that made her skin prickle, but not with fear or cold this time. It was a bedroom voice, made for seducing women to mindless compliance. A slight accent lengthened the vowels, producing a tantalising drawl. To her annoyance, she felt the zap and tingle of nerves reacting to the masculine timbre of that voice.

'I didn't burst anywhere.' She stood straighter, yanking her arms free. To her chagrin she barely reached his shoulder. Typical! That excess height no doubt added to his belief in his own superiority.

Those frowning brows rose in supercilious disbelief. He'd probably never been caught without an immaculately cut raincoat, or perhaps a lackey hovering with an umbrella.

'My apologies for interrupting your…reverie. I'll leave you in peace.'

Alissa spun round and strode away. She felt his glare graze the bare skin of her neck and the sway of her hips as she shortened her stride to accommodate her heels.

But she didn't mistake his stare for male admiration.

His regard was contemptuous, sharp as a blade. Why, she had no idea. But she had enough experience of disapproving men to recognise his animosity.

Perhaps his fiancée was late and he wasn't used to waiting so he'd taken out his impatience on her.

Alissa tilted her chin and stepped through a doorway into the corridor she needed. She had a marriage to attend and no time for speculating over strangers.

'He said what?' Her voice rose in breathless disbelief. Alissa shook her head, wondering if the soaking had somehow affected her hearing.

The clerk shrugged and spread his hands. 'That he couldn't make the appointment.'

The appointment! Alissa stared, numb with shock, hearing the loud thrum of her pulse in the silence. This was hardly an *appointment.* This was a *wedding.* Jason's wedding as well as hers. Was this a joke?

No, not a joke. Jason was as eager for this marriage as she. Well, as eager for the money they'd get when they inherited her grandfather's Sicilian estate then sold it. He'd jumped at the idea of a convenient wedding with an alacrity that surprised her. His need for cash was greater than she'd first thought.

Surely this was a mistake. Jason must be running late, that was all.

'What, exactly, did he say?' she asked through stiff lips.

The clerk darted a speculative glance at her before reading the note in his hand. 'Mr Donnelly rang thirty minutes ago and said he wouldn't be able to come. He'd changed his mind.'

Another sharply curious glance accompanied the words. Yet Alissa was beyond feeling embarrassed that her bridegroom had done a runner. The news was too devastating for humiliation even to register. This was disaster on a cataclysmic scale.

She linked her fingers tight together, willing herself to be calm. Her heart thudded out of control as panic edged her thoughts. Her stomach descended into freefall.

She couldn't afford to fail. The very idea knotted her stomach with dread.

What would she do if Jason really had jilted her?

Alissa *had* to marry. If within the next thirty-one days she wasn't Mrs Someone-or-other, married as required by the terms of her grandfather's will, she could kiss goodbye to the chance of getting Donna to the States for the treatment she needed.

Contesting the will would take too long and her solicitor had warned the outcome of such legal action wasn't certain. As for getting a loan to cover the astronomical costs…the banks had disabused her of that possibility. There were no other options but to do the one thing she'd vowed she never would—comply with her despised grandfather's last wishes in order to inherit part of his estate. The old so-and-so would be chortling in hell if he could see the fix she was in now.

She pinned a tight smile to her face and drew a slow, calming breath. 'Was there anything else?'

'No.' The clerk couldn't hide the inquisitive glimmer in his eyes. 'That was all.'

'I see. Thank you.' But she didn't see. This made no sense.

She turned away and drew out her cellphone. Punching in Jason's number with an unsteady hand, she lifted it to her ear, only to hear the infuriating engaged signal. Had something terrible happened or was he avoiding her? It took a moment to realise he could have phoned her instead of the marriage registry. So yes, he was avoiding her.

Alissa put a hand to her brow, flummoxed. What was she going to do? Panic edged her whirling thoughts. She'd go to Jason's, but she felt an unnerving certainty he wouldn't be at his flat or anywhere else she looked.

'Miss Scott?' The clerk's voice made her swing round eagerly. Had Jason turned up?

Hope died instantly. There was only the clerk and, with him, the tall stranger from the foyer.

Why was he here? She cast a swift glance at those narrowed eyes and looked away, feeling again that *frisson* of reaction to his blatant stare. The man made her supremely uncomfortable.

'Yes?' She stepped forward, concentrating on the clerk, not the stranger beside him.

'This gentleman is here to see you.'

'To see *me*?' She forced herself to look up into that beautiful, arrogant face and ignore the tremor of consternation that ran through her.

'If you are Miss Alissa Scott?'

She nodded. 'I am.'

'Affianced to Jason Donnelly?'

'That's right.' Her mouth dried. He had the deliberate, enigmatic tone of a judge pronouncing sentence.

'Granddaughter of Gianfranco Mangano?'

She nodded jerkily, her lips primming at the mention of her late, unlamented grandfather.

'We need to talk. I have news for you.'

'From Jason?' Was that why he'd been loitering in the foyer? To explain Jason's absence? Why hadn't he said so?

'*Si.*' The single word was curt, his expression sombre, and Alissa felt a presentiment of trouble, deep trouble.

He gestured for her to accompany him, not waiting to see if she complied before striding away. Alissa scurried to keep up, her feet sliding in her damp shoes.

He'd reached the foyer, heading for the main door, when she caught him up.

'Where are you going?'

He paused and turned his head, eyes narrowing on her. 'My limousine is outside. We can talk privately there.'

She shook her head. She was going nowhere with a man she didn't know. Especially not this man. Especially not into some anonymous vehicle. She was desperate, not a fool.

'We can talk here.' She angled her chin up.

'You wish to discuss your private affairs *here*, in such a public place?'

She met his gaze steadily. Better to err on the side of caution. 'You said you had news for me?'

Dario looked into that upturned oval face and felt it again—the stab of physical awareness. Despite everything, his hatred of the Mangano family, his contempt for this woman, his fury at the steps he'd been forced to take to secure what was his, there was no mistaking her impact on him. An intense jolt of desire carved a hole right through his belly. Its burning trail was hot as flame.

A similar, unexpected surge of need had held him still when

she'd run into him five minutes ago. He'd been stunned by its intensity—far stronger even than his disgust.

This was the woman who'd rejected his offers, rejected *him* not once but twice now, not even deigning to meet him in person. That alone was an insult for which he required satisfaction. No woman had ever denied him what he wanted. More, she connived to thwart his plans to recoup what was his. She'd schemed behind his back, collaborating with Donnelly to prevent Dario winning back his birthright.

She wanted it all for herself. If she'd planned to marry for love he might have understood. But this was a greedy, calculating attempt to keep the old feud alive and stop him acquiring the one thing that meant everything to him. The *castello* in Sicily her grandfather had stolen from Dario's family.

He breathed deep, suppressing a lifetime's hatred.

This woman was everything he despised. Shallow, conniving, spoiled. She'd grown up with every advantage money could buy yet she'd squandered her opportunities, turning instead to drugs, drink and wild parties. Till even her grandfather would have nothing to do with her.

Dario should feel nothing but contempt for her. And yet…

Her pale, pure skin, her wide-open cornflower eyes, her plump bow of a mouth, the voluptuous curves on that tiny figure…even her air of barely suppressed energy, comprised a feminine package that was far too alluring.

It infuriated him. It was not supposed to happen. And things which were not supposed to happen had a way of disappearing silently out of his life: bought off or simply banished by his superior power and strength of will. Dario had worked hard for what he had. He had no patience with things or people, or feelings, that did not comply with his plans.

'What I have to say isn't for public consumption.'

He punched down irritation at her contrary attitude in refusing to accompany him. What had he expected? Her previous actions, having her lawyer reject his more than generous offers out of hand, illustrated her selfish obstinacy.

He drew a breath, trying to block the rich scent of lilies and damp woman that played havoc with his concentration.

'Come. Let us find a better place for this conversation.' He'd be damned if he discussed matters of such importance in an echoing public foyer. She might have few scruples but he had more respect for himself than that.

He stalked across the vestibule and found an empty office. He held the door and waited for her to precede him.

His gaze strayed down over her compact, curvaceous figure as she entered, the sway of her pert bottom in the tight skirt. Even in a rain-stained suit, with saturated hair, her complexion milky with shock, she drew his unwilling gaze.

Despite those top-class legs, reason dictated she wasn't his type. Pocket Venus redheads with attitude and tarnished reputations weren't his style. Give him a brunette with a madonna smile and a docile nature any day.

Unfortunately the voice of reason stayed silent on this occasion.

'What is this place?' She stared at the desk before them. 'Are we allowed in here?'

He shrugged and closed the door. 'We are here. And we have privacy. That's all that matters.'

Her eyes widened and she opened her mouth as if to argue then clearly thought better of it.

Good. Things would proceed more easily when she learned to accede to his wishes. A shaft of anticipation warmed his belly at the thought.

'Your bridegroom—'

'What happened to Jason? Have you seen him?' No mistaking the concern in her voice. He catalogued the fact for later consideration. Perhaps, after all, their wedding hadn't been purely a convenient arrangement. Perhaps lust as well as greed had been a factor in her marriage plans.

He remembered Jason Donnelly's weak, handsome face— good looks but no substance. Was he the sort of man that attracted her? The idea was strangely disquieting. He had no interest in this woman's weaknesses, except insofar as he could exploit them to his advantage.

'I saw him this afternoon.'

'Is he all right? What happened?'

Dario felt a stirring of pleasure, remembering the ease with which this afternoon's interview had followed the map he'd laid out for it.

'Nothing happened. Your Mr Donnelly is perfectly well, though he is no longer *your* Mr Donnelly.'

Her brow puckered in a frown and Dario wondered if he'd let his satisfaction show. What did it matter if he had? There was nothing she could do about it. He held all the cards. No matter how much she protested, she'd find the only way forward was *his* way. After all the trouble she'd caused the knowledge pleased him.

'I don't understand.'

'He has decided he no longer wishes to marry you.'

'But why? And why not tell me himself? Why send a stranger?'

'He didn't send me. I chose to come.'

Her eyes widened as she met his gaze. Then she sagged back against the desk, shaking her head.

'Look, can't you just tell me? What's going on?'

'Mr Donnelly had a better offer. An offer he found it impossible to refuse. As a result he changed his mind about marriage.' Dario had made absolutely sure of that.

'An offer of what? Not marriage!'

Dario paced further into the room to stand before her, his feet planted wide, his hands finding his pockets as he enjoyed this moment of triumph.

'An offer of money, of course. That's the language the two of you understand best.' He watched her pupils dilate, darkening her eyes. Her jaw sagged to reveal even, white teeth and a glimpse of moist pink tongue.

Dario frowned. It was impossible that any woman should look sexy while gawping in disbelief, but somehow Alissa Mangano…no, Alissa Scott, managed it. That mouth was ripe, luscious, inviting. He felt a tingle of awareness, a tightening of muscles as his gaze zeroed in on the dainty curl of her tongue circling her lips.

He set his jaw. Lust for this woman was *not* on his agenda. His standards were higher than that.

'Money to do what?' She stood straight now, her momentary weakness sloughed. She stuck her hands on her hips, a picture of demanding femininity. Her neat chin jutted belligerently. 'And who made him this offer?'

Dario permitted himself a small, satisfied smile. 'I did. I offered him enough cash to ensure he gave up all thoughts of marrying you.'

It had been ludicrously easy. If Donnelly and this woman were lovers, there was no loyalty between them. Donnelly had jumped at the chance of cash in hand with no thought for the woman he'd jilt. It had been Dario who suggested he leave a message at the registry office.

Colour flagged her cheeks and her eyes sparked, giving her a vibrancy that had been missing before. A vibrancy that only enhanced her looks.

'Why would you do that?' She took a step closer as if to get a better look at him, staring straight into his eyes. Despite himself, Dario was impressed that she wasn't daunted as so many people were in his presence.

But then she didn't yet know who he was.

He shrugged and spread his hands. 'Because he was in the way.' And Dario had no patience for obstacles in his path. 'Because you will be marrying me instead.'

CHAPTER TWO

He meant it!

Unbelievably this stranger was in deadly earnest. Alissa shivered and curled her arms tight round herself. She stared up into that smirking, satisfied, gorgeous face and felt the bottom drop out of her world.

'Who the devil *are* you?' It emerged as a hoarse whisper, barely audible despite the stillness of the room.

For a heartbeat, then two, then three, there was silence.

'I am Dario Parisi.'

The words echoed in her ears like a death knell. Why hadn't she guessed before? The Italian accent, the outrageously handsome face, the arrogance, the air of discreet elegance only serious money could achieve. *The hatred in his eyes*.

But who'd believe he'd cross the globe to confront her in person? He'd been persistent. Now it seemed he was obsessed.

Alissa bit her unsteady lip. Looking into the intense burn of that stare was like looking into the scorching fires of hell. Dangerous, unforgiving and inescapable. She already knew this man was without mercy or finer feeling.

He had a reputation for ruthlessness and success the Press adored. In business he was without rival, letting nothing stand in his way when he wanted something. And in love…he had a reputation for being just as ruthless in acquiring and discarding gorgeous women.

'I'm delighted you remember my name,' he drawled, the

sting of sarcasm making her wince. 'I thought perhaps you'd put it from your mind.'

How could she when it had been imprinted on her consciousness every day? Her grandfather had been determined to marry her to Dario Parisi, alternately extolling his virtues and threatening her with retribution if she didn't obey. He'd taken special delight in reading out reports in the Italian papers describing Parisi's phenomenal success and his merciless tactics.

Her shivers grew to a shudder. A huge spider seemed to tap-dance down her backbone. She gritted her teeth and stood straighter, willing the trembling to recede.

It didn't matter how powerful he was, or that years of threats had turned Dario Parisi into a name to fear. He was just a man. Wealthy, ruthless, determined, but he had no power over her.

'You could have told me your name straight away. Or didn't it suit your desire for melodrama?' She refused to look away from that accusing glare. 'Was I supposed to faint at the realisation I was in your presence?'

Alissa wouldn't let him see how close she'd been to doing precisely that. Her heart pumped double time and her body was rigid from an overdose of adrenalin. But she had to stand up to him. She'd learned that was the only way to deal with a bully.

He scowled and Alissa experienced a fillip of delight that she'd chipped his superior air.

'But then,' he said in an easy voice as if she hadn't spoken, 'it's not surprising you remember the name of the man you were supposed to marry.'

'We were never—'

'Ah, but we were, Alissa.' He spoke her name like a slow, lethal caress, his emphasis on the sibilants giving it a whole new, provocative sound. 'It had been agreed.' The heat left his eyes, replaced by chilly hauteur.

'Not by me!' She drew herself up to her full height, glaring unabashed into his dark stare. 'Surely the bride has something to say in such circumstances.'

He shrugged those broad shoulders in a movement that was pure Italian male. She hated it.

'Not necessarily,' he murmured.

She stared.

Not necessarily.

That attitude summed him up. He was just like the old man: manipulative, domineering and chauvinistic. Yet he was only in his early thirties. What was it about Sicily that produced men like that, all ego and testosterone?

'In this century women have as much say in who they marry as men. And I didn't want to marry you.'

Shards of ice rayed out from his frozen glare.

'You thought I was eager to wed *you*?' His accent thickened, the only sign of emotion as he stood ramrod-straight. 'You think I delighted in the prospect of marrying a Mangano? That I wanted a bride of that tainted blood? A spoiled, irresponsible troublemaker who…' He reined in the thread of vitriolic accusation, his mouth flattening in a hard line of contempt.

'You know why I countenanced the match. It had nothing to do with desire for such a wife as you.'

That put her in her place! Alissa felt at a complete disadvantage, bedraggled and shivery, bruised by the sheer force of his personality. She dragged in a breath and slid clammy palms down her damp skirt, searching for a poise she was far from feeling.

'No, you wanted the Sicilian estate I'd bring as dowry. A crumbling castle and overgrown vineyards.' It was unbelievable that he set such store in stones, mortar and soil. Enough to agree to an arranged marriage to a woman he'd never met. Enough to collaborate with Gianfranco Mangano, the man he abhorred.

Dario Parisi was a tycoon with more wealth than he could spend in a lifetime, and still he wanted more. Her grandfather had been the same. They'd vied for the same property, using it and her to further their bitter feud.

His nostrils pinched and his jaw tightened till his neck corded with tension. Those were the only indicators of his struggle to restrain his fury. His face remained impassive, his gaze unreadable.

He obviously had a right royal temper, yet he knew how to control it. If it had been the old man, he'd have lashed out by now, incensed at her for standing up to him.

'I can't believe you bought Jason off.' She paced away from him, needing distance from his imposing presence. 'It must have cost you.'

'Your boyfriend is easily tempted.' Dario's gaze didn't leave her face, yet she had the uncomfortable feeling his attention trawled over her. Heat rose in her throat and she turned to pace again, avoiding that skewering stare.

'Obviously Mr Donnelly didn't feel your…charms were enough to entice him to go through with the deal.'

Her charms! Didn't he realise Jason was gay? But then Jason didn't wear his sexuality on his sleeve.

'You came all the way from Sicily just to stop my marriage?' She paused to shaft a glance at him. 'You must hate the Manganos very much.' The shudder ricocheting through her had nothing to do with her wet clothes.

He shrugged, and this time the movement was anything but insouciant. 'Your family stole from mine. Cheated mine. Deprived me of my birthright, thieving not only my family's home but also the opportunities that should have been mine. Did you ever think of that as you enjoyed your comfortable life? Did you spare a thought for those whose misfortunes laid the foundations for your luxurious lifestyle?'

Fury radiated from his glittering eyes, the steel-grey of a drawn sword. His posture was aggressive, like that of a man poised to destroy.

Alissa opened her mouth to tell him her life hadn't been one of luxury, but of punishment and fear. Yet he wouldn't believe her. He'd seen her grandfather's home, the grandest in that district of Victoria. He'd believe what he wanted to believe.

Just as the local townspeople had found it convenient to believe Gianfranco was a devoted old man who lavished care and luxury on his granddaughters. Far easier than facing the truth, that the pillar of society was a miserly sadist who spent a small fortune entertaining dignitaries to build his prestige but who thought nothing of sentencing his granddaughters to a week of bread and water for the slightest disobedience.

'Well? Nothing to say?'

She looked up into heavily lidded eyes, ignoring the flutter of tension in her stomach as she met his scathing glare. It wasn't her fault Dario Parisi was caught up in the destructive vendetta between their families.

'I'm not responsible for my grandfather's actions.'

'So you admit he did wrong?'

Alissa's lips firmed at the recollection of Gianfranco's crimes. The memories were so vivid she found her hands clasped together, white-knuckled and shaking.

Carefully she unknotted her fingers and let her hands fall. The past was the past. It was that knowledge which had enabled her to turn her life around, hers and Donna's.

'He did many things that were wrong. Perhaps now he's paying for them.' He'd been frightened enough by the looming prospect of death to leave his estate to the church, trying to atone for a lifetime of sins. All except the Sicilian property. He'd used that to try manipulating her one last time.

'Don't expect me to shoulder his guilt.' She stared back boldly, refusing to be intimidated. After what she'd survived a tongue-lashing was nothing. More important was the vital question of how to meet the terms of the will and get the inheritance she so desperately needed.

'Can I help you?' A disapproving voice made Alissa spin round. A woman in a navy suit glared at them from an open doorway. Alissa opened her mouth to apologise for intruding but Dario forestalled her.

'*Chiedo scusa.* We shouldn't be here, I know.' He lifted his shoulders and spread his open hands and smiled.

Even from where Alissa stood to one side, that smile was spectacular. It transformed his face from censorious and autocratic to warm, attractive and, she hated to admit it, downright *sexy*.

She blinked but the metamorphosis remained in place. He looked a completely different man. If she hadn't known what sort of guy Dario Parisi was she'd have thought him stunning. Even his eyes sparkled with charming, rueful apology. And that smile…

He was more dangerous than she'd thought!

The sheer force of his personality and his absolute determination to get what he wanted made him formidable enough. But with a charm that made even Alissa's pulse quicken? Definitely a man to beware.

The office worker didn't think so. Her frown melted and a smile hovered on her prim mouth as she heard his glib explanation, liberally peppered with Italian phrases. Cynically Alissa wondered if they were a deliberate part of the charming-Mediterranean-male persona he'd adopted.

It was only when he used the words 'my fiancée' and stepped close that she focused on the content of his spiel. She jerked out of reach as he explained how he and his fiancée needed privacy to discuss a personal matter.

Alissa glared, but her anger only corroborated the implication they'd had a lovers' tiff. Before she could set the record straight the other woman was actually apologising that she couldn't let them use her office as she had urgent work to do.

Unbelievable!

'No, no, you mustn't apologise. We have intruded here long enough.' He turned to Alissa. 'Come, *cara*.'

Alissa nodded at the now beaming woman and walked stiff-legged from the room, speeding up when she felt the proprietorial warmth of his touch in the small of her back.

She didn't pause as they walked outside. The rain had eased and she marched down the steps, too aware of Dario beside her. He was infuriating, impossible and an undoubted threat. Yet she couldn't ignore a tiny thrill of awareness at his long, lean body so close to hers.

She must be going crazy.

'In here, *fidanzatina mia*.'

'I'm not your little fiancée.' The words shot out of her mouth, indignation flaring anew. Her Italian was rusty but that she understood. 'We don't have an audience now so you can drop the act.'

She turned to see him inviting her to enter a limo, complete with tinted windows and a chauffeur standing to attention at the door. It was in a 'No Stopping' zone and the chauffeur, despite his suit, looked more like a burly bodyguard than a mere driver. More reminders of Dario's status and wealth.

'I'm not going anywhere in that.' Not with Dario Parisi. Especially not in a limo with blacked-out windows, driven by a goon.

'We have things to discuss.' The thread of almost-temper wove through his words, though his face gave nothing away. 'You know it. This isn't finished.'

Unfortunately he was right. Alissa would have loved to stalk away and never see him again. But that wasn't going to happen. Her shoulders slumped as weariness and worry took their toll. What choice did she have?

'OK.' She paused, thinking rapidly. 'There's a decent café two blocks away. We should find a quiet table.'

Silently he regarded her as if she were some unique specimen. Perhaps she was, refusing to kowtow to him. She'd bet a lot of women would just say 'Yes, Dario. Whatever you say, Dario', blinded by his wealth and fatal charm.

Even now the memory of his sexy smile warmed a shocked part of her.

'*Daccordo*. Come on, then. Lead the way.' He gestured her forward and paused to speak to the chauffeur.

You will be marrying me instead. His words resounded in her head as she walked. The words she'd steadfastly refused to think about for the last few minutes.

Could it be true? Could that be why he'd come to Australia? To claim her as his bride?

The idea sent a chill of trepidation through her. She tugged her shoulder bag on more securely and hugged her arms tight across her torso.

Dario Parisi's bride...the very fate she'd been so determined to avoid.

How she'd paid for her determination that last year in the old man's house. He'd never forgiven her refusal to comply with his scheme to link the two families.

She should have left home then, but she'd felt compelled to stay till Donna was legally old enough to leave home too. Donna had been her responsibility for as long as she could remember. She'd never leave her little sister alone to their grandfather's tender mercies.

Absently she rubbed at her wrist, remembering Gianfranco's reaction when she'd rejected the marriage he'd schemed to bring about.

'You're getting wet.' The deep voice curled like smoke through her memories, drawing her back to the present.

She turned her head to find Dario walking beside her, holding an enormous umbrella over them both. Heat from his body transferred the few centimetres to hers: her arm, her shoulder, her hip and thigh. And further, spreading through her shock-numbed body. Latent energy sizzled off him in waves, sparking tingles of awareness.

What was this man? Some sort of power generator?

Her pulse quickened and so did her pace. She didn't like

the illusion of intimacy as he sheltered her from the rain. The world beyond the umbrella was an anonymous blur, cocooning them together as the soft rain became a downpour.

It didn't seem to bother him, though the rain angled down so his legs must be getting wet. Had he chosen her left side to shelter her from a soaking? Surely not. This man was no protector.

'Thank you,' she murmured eventually, forcing the words through her tense lips, 'for the umbrella.'

He looked at her then. She could no longer see the gleam of anger in his eyes or stark impatience. But his expression made her stomach muscles spasm tight, her breath falter. She read speculation and something that looked almost like possessiveness.

No! Abruptly she looked away. There was no expression in his eyes. Nothing at all.

'Here. This is it.' Alissa didn't care if she sounded desperate to see the café. She plunged under its awning and pushed open the door, not waiting for him.

Dario shook the umbrella and followed her inside. She scurried in, spoke briefly to the waiter and took a seat with her back to the wall. The choice indicated Alissa Scott felt under threat. She had that much sense then.

Her jerky movements as she patted at her hair and fussed over her bag gave her away too. As did her furtive glances in his direction.

He dropped the umbrella inside the door, nodded at the waiter and strolled across the room, enjoying the way Alissa's eyes widened at his approach.

Obviously she hadn't bothered to discover what he looked like before today and his appearance was a surprise. The implied dismissal smarted. Yet though she tried to hide it, part of her response to him was feminine interest. Dario had been on the receiving end of female stares since adolescence. He could read those hot, guilty glances in a second.

One more piece of knowledge to use to his advantage. Who knew? Dealing with the recalcitrant Ms Scott might have unexpected bonuses.

He dragged out a chair and took a seat. His long legs tangled with hers till she shifted away.

What was he thinking? She was a cute little package, if one liked that sort of thing. But he was more discerning. Cheap goods weren't to his taste.

The waiter was there as he settled in his seat.

'Espresso,' Dario murmured, not shifting his gaze from Alissa's wide blue gaze. 'And...?'

'Hot chocolate.'

At his raised brows she muttered, 'I don't need a stimulant in my bloodstream.'

Why? Because she'd already taken something to see her through the day? No, she was sober enough. No sign of drug use. He'd scrutinised her carefully.

'I just want to get warm.'

Despite the streaks of hectic colour on her cheeks she was pale. Stress? Shock? Annoyance at having her avaricious scheme ruined? He felt no sympathy at all.

Leaning back, he stretched his legs and shoved his hands in his pockets. She'd go nowhere till he was ready.

The silence grew thick. Dario was in no haste to break it. He knew how to use it to unnerve an adversary. What was the point in rushing? The outcome was a foregone conclusion. Let her sweat a little longer.

Yet she didn't fidget. Her spine was straight and her gaze steady. Her attitude piqued his interest. She wasn't easily intimidated. That surprised him. He'd expected her to have little stamina and no grit.

The waiter left their drinks and Dario watched Alissa cradle her mug. She closed her eyes and inhaled on a sigh of pleasure that spiked heat straight through his belly.

Porca miseria! That wasn't supposed to happen. Not with

her. Just because he could imagine that Cupid's-bow mouth pouting under his, sighing out a very different kind of pleasure as those slim, neat hands caressed his...

'Are you going to tell me now, or are you enjoying trying to intimidate me?' she asked in a low voice.

Those remarkable eyes, the colour of the sea on a clear day, fixed on his. Her mouth twisted in a tiny wry smile that belied her defensive posture. She was a fighter.

'You know why I'm here.'

She lowered the mug, but kept her fingers wrapped round it as if needing its warmth.

'The Sicilian estate.'

'The Castello Parisi.' He nodded, using its proper name and feeling the inevitable surge of pride.

'You want it.' Her voice was flat, giving nothing away. Her gaze dropped to her hot chocolate.

'Can you doubt it?'

She shook her head once. 'No. You badgered the old man for it long enough.'

'Badgered!' He leaned forward till she raised her face. Her eyes were enormous, but if she expected sympathy she had the wrong man. 'To offer *more* than a fair price for what is rightfully mine? For what the unscrupulous old devil stole from my family? The home of my family for generations?'

The heat in his belly now had nothing to do with sexual awareness and everything to do with outraged pride and the desire for justice.

Until the *castello* was in his hands, once again the jewel in the crown of the now vast Parisi holdings, all his success was hollow. It was his home, his past, the family he no longer had. His identity, proof that he was worthy of his proud name. Dario had promised his father the day he died that he'd recover it. Nothing would make him break that oath.

'I know the story,' she said slowly. 'Gianfranco bought it

when your family fell on hard times, promising to sell it back when they recouped their losses.'

'He bought it for a fraction of its worth.' Hatred for the man who'd destroyed the Parisis sent adrenalin surging through his blood. 'Did he also tell you it was his underhand dealings, his dishonesty that ruined us in the first place? That he'd set out to destroy the family he'd once called friends?'

He didn't wait for an answer. 'Do you have any idea how it stuck in my craw to negotiate with that man? The niceties of business were too good for him. In an earlier time I would just have taken it from him.'

'By force?' Alissa looked into those metal-grey eyes and wondered how she'd ever imagined warmth there. His gaze was glacier-cold, frozen with a hate that made her shiver.

She shuddered and pushed her chair back from the table as dread curdled her stomach.

'I'm a law-abiding man,' Dario Parisi drawled, but his expression told her how he would have enjoyed inflicting a very personal vengeance on her grandfather.

Two of a kind. That's what they were. Just as she'd always suspected.

That was why Gianfranco had been so determined Alissa marry this hard-faced stranger. Partly for the satisfaction of seeing a Parisi marry his granddaughter. The feud had begun when a Parisi jilted Gianfranco's sister and he'd carried a chip on his shoulder ever since. But mainly because 'He'll put up with none of your nonsense, girl. He'll knock you into shape and keep you under control. A good, old-fashioned Sicilian husband with a hard hand'.

Her breath came in shallow gulps as she fought for calm. She was safe. Dario Parisi couldn't harm her.

'What's that?' She found her voice as he took a document from his suit pocket and spread it on the table.

'You need to complete it so it can be lodged today.' He reached back into his pocket and drew out a gold fountain pen, placing it neatly on the table beside the official-looking document.

Foreboding slammed into her. She couldn't sell him the estate, he knew that. So what was he asking her to sign?

Reluctantly she leaned forward and read the title.

Notice of Intention to Marry.

The breath whooshed from her lungs like air from a pierced balloon. She'd signed one when she and Jason had planned to wed. But this time the names were different.

Alissa Serena Scott and Dario Pasquale Tommaso Parisi.

CHAPTER THREE

'You can't be serious!' Alissa stared, heart sinking. Yet instinctively she knew Dario was absolutely serious about marrying her. Correction: marrying the Parisi estate.

She slumped, her energy draining away. She'd come full circle. After years fighting the old man's manipulative schemes, had she no choice now but to do as he'd always planned? Marry Dario Parisi and force his aristocratic family to accept a Mangano into the fold? Take as her husband a man every bit as dangerous as the old tartar who'd made her life hell?

'Your display of feminine vulnerability is charming,' murmured a deep, gravelly voice, 'but it's wasted. You could have made this easy. Instead you chose the hard way.'

Her head shot up. 'You blame *me* for this mess?'

'If the cap fits…' He looked so at ease, sipping his espresso, his dark suit parted casually, like a model in a glossy lifestyle magazine. Except no paid model would ever wear that lethally calculating expression.

'We could have married several years ago when I first agreed to the idea.'

Her grandfather's idea. Dario had only agreed after Gianfranco rejected offer after offer to buy the Sicilian estate. He'd vowed the only way a Parisi would get his hands on it was to marry her.

Alissa had refused. And she'd paid for her disobedience.

Absently she ran a finger over her wrist, a nervous gesture that stopped under Dario's scrutiny.

'I suppose your need for funds wasn't so urgent then. Your grandfather was alive to indulge you.'

Alissa almost laughed aloud at the idea of being indulged by the old man. 'Or perhaps I just objected to marrying you.' She put her palms on the table. She'd had enough of his jibes and his self-assurance. She wished she could find some vulnerability in him. But his only response was a quirk of the lips as if her riposte amused him.

'That doesn't bother you?' She lifted her chin.

'Our marriage isn't a meeting of minds. Or a consummation of romantic love. It's business. Otherwise I would not contemplate marrying a woman like you.'

He spoke through a chilling half-smile and Alissa shivered. *Ruthless.* That was Dario Parisi. She felt a net draw inextricably tighter around her, leaving no way out.

She'd thought she knew all about ruthless men. But the way his relaxed demeanour cloaked bone-deep obsession gave a whole new perspective on the type. Foreboding sliced through her. He was relentless, biding his time patiently for years as he waited to acquire the property he wanted. And acquire *her* in the process.

He leaned close, the smile sliding off his face. 'You should have accepted the offer I made after your grandfather died. Marriage, a quick divorce and a handsome settlement in return for your share of the estate.'

Except she'd wanted nothing to do with her grandfather's property. She'd had no qualms giving up her chance for wealth, especially with such strings attached. When her lawyer told her of Dario's second proposal after her grandfather's death, she'd rejected it instantly.

'I didn't want the estate then,' she murmured.

'No, you thought you could challenge the will and inherit

alone, without the inconvenience of sharing with me.' Suspicion darkened his gaze. 'Greed runs strong in your family.'

'You should talk!' She leaned towards him, recklessly disregarding the zap of electricity that sheared between them as their glares clashed. 'You'll do anything to get your hands on the *castello*.'

This close she saw the fine-grained texture of his skin, the shadow darkening his chin. She inhaled the scent of spicy male skin and citrus and her nostrils quivered.

Too close, screamed a warning voice in her head as each sense came alive to his presence. Alarm bells jangled as her heartbeat revved and her skin prickled.

Before she could move large hands captured hers, imprisoning them on the table. Long fingers linked around her wrists. Heat radiated from his touch.

'No doubt you also inherited a hatred of my family. You were determined to keep for yourself what's mine.'

She shook her head. 'No. I just didn't want the money.' Not until the news that Donna needed help.

The impact of his unblinking regard and his handsome, brooding face was devastating. She jerked her hands, trying to break free.

His encircling fingers didn't loosen. To an onlooker they'd seem like lovers. He was so intense, his wide shoulders crowding her in, cutting her off from the room.

'Don't lie. You grew up with money and you're feeling the pinch now you have to fend for yourself.' He paused. 'It must have been a shock to find Gianfranco had left most of his estate to charity.' One sleek, dark brow rose speculatively. 'You fell out with him.'

'You could say that.'

He shook his head. 'I know about your…habits. They don't come cheap.' His face hardened, grooves appearing beside his mouth. 'Even though you seem to have cleaned up your act lately, your record with designer drugs shows you have expensive tastes.'

Alissa goggled. He knew about *that*? Nausea churned in her stomach at the memories he'd dredged up. Bile choked her. This man knew about her past and judged her with such matter-of-fact contempt. Yet still he wanted to marry her!

How badly he wanted that land.

Looking into his wintry, judgemental eyes, she wanted to blurt out that she'd never taken drugs in her life. That she'd been innocent.

She couldn't. Only one other person knew the truth. The person she'd vowed to protect, even at the cost of her reputation. She'd gladly shouldered the blame and accepted the consequences. It was too late to change the record now. Besides, Dario Parisi was so biased he'd never believe her.

'You had me investigated,' she said flatly.

'Of course.' He slid a thumb along the side of her hand in a mockery of a caress. To her horror her skin drew tight and shivery. 'Even to gain my birthright, I would not walk into marriage without knowing my bride.'

He lingered over the last word with a deliberation that set her teeth on edge. She felt trapped. Claustrophobia gnawed the edges of her consciousness. She fought it, refusing to let it drag her under. She tried to slip one hand free, but his hold was implacable.

'Why wait till today to buy Jason off?' She hurried into speech, unnerved by his waiting silence.

'My staff contacted Mr Donnelly as soon as you sought permission to marry.'

'You organised this weeks ago?' Her eyes widened as she took in his satisfied expression.

'As if I'd leave it to chance! While you expected to marry him I knew exactly what your plans were.'

'And by having him jilt me today, you cut off my options.' The air was expelled from her lungs. 'I have to marry within a month to inherit.' She breathed deep, ignoring the acid taste of fear on her tongue. 'And in Australia we have to give a month's notice before marriage. Which means—'

'You just ran out of alternatives.' His smile didn't reach his eyes. 'Unless you have another bridegroom tucked up your sleeve?' He paused and stroked an insolent finger along her wrist. Her pulse jumped and she gritted her teeth, furious with him and with her traitorous body that didn't know the enemy when he sat before her.

'No one else willing to sign a document like this—' he nodded at the paper beneath her hands '—before close of business today?'

His sarcasm made her blood boil. 'You manipulative, arrogant, cocksure—'

'Now, now, Alissa. Is that any way to talk to the one man who can give you what you want?' His gaze roved over her with a provocative thoroughness that was the final straw.

'Take your hands off me. Now!' She didn't raise her voice but raw fury throbbed in each word.

His brows arched. His fingers loosened. She slid her hands into her lap and cradled them, trying to ignore the heat of his touch lingering on her skin. Trying to conquer her fear.

She wanted to shove her chair back and walk out, alone. Never see Dario Parisi's gorgeous fallen-angel face or hear his mocking, sexy voice again.

The trouble was she lived in the real world, with responsibilities she couldn't shirk. People she cared for. Cold iced her bones and she reached for her mug, seeking its residual warmth.

'By the terms of the will I have to live with my husband for six months before we jointly inherit.'

He nodded. 'We'll divorce as soon as the land is ours. Then you sell your share of the property to me, for the current market price, of course.' He sounded as if he discussed a routine financial transaction. Not marriage.

Alissa's heart beat fast at the idea of living with Dario Parisi. Could she survive six months with this man who looked at her with such condemnation, but whose touch turned her inside out?

'But it means *living together*.'

He watched her speculatively. 'That bothers you? Living with me?' If she weren't so keyed up Alissa would be insulted by his surprise. As if trusting herself to the care of a stranger was no big deal. What did he think she was? A tart as well as a drug addict?

'I knew Jason. I could trust him.' That seemed stupid since he'd duped her, but she'd known they'd be platonic flatmates and no more.

'Ah.' The syllable stretched out, like her nerves. 'You want assurance your abundant charms won't incite me to seduce you.' His gaze dipped to her jacket buttons and searing heat coiled in her stomach.

Alissa kept her mouth firmly shut against the protest that she'd never let a man like him seduce her.

'You have my word as a Parisi. I would never force a woman. Besides—' his lips curved in a half-smile that held no humour '—your type is not to my taste.'

Her type. Her *type*!

'I understand completely.' Alissa pasted on a saccharine smile, despite the protest of muscles taut with horror. 'I can't think of a man less appealing than you.'

It was minuscule compensation to see him taken aback by her statement. But, boy, it felt good.

Just as well he couldn't know she lied. Dario Parisi didn't appeal. But maybe with a personality transplant…that strong, lean body, the mobile, sensuous mouth and well-shaped hands… he was the sexiest man she'd ever seen. Fate didn't play fair.

'Excellent,' Dario murmured, thrusting aside annoyance at her insult. 'Then there will be no complications.'

He'd get what he wanted and dump Alissa Scott like lightning. Tying himself to a woman tainted not just by her Mangano blood but also by self-indulgence, avarice and low personal standards appalled him.

After the *castello* was safe he'd find the perfect wife. *That* Signora Parisi would be elegant, refined, sweet-tempered. Not a sharp-tongued virago who challenged with every stare, sidetracked his thoughts and stirred his hormones at inconvenient times.

They'd raise a houseful of *bambini*. He'd possess everything he'd dreamt of in the days when he had nothing but pride and determination. He remembered how it felt to be hungry and alone. *Never again*.

He'd have it all. Respect, wealth, power, the birthright he'd been denied. And a family of his own, flesh of his flesh.

Yet Alissa's jibe rankled. His looks and vast wealth made him irresistible to most women. She was no different. He'd seen the flare of awareness in her wide blue eyes.

Despite his strict code of honour that tempered the drive to succeed, he'd been accused of many things as he forged his way to the top of the corporate heap. Usually by unsuccessful competitors or journalists whose stock-in-trade was exaggeration. Why did her insult needle him like a splinter embedded deep?

'We know where we stand. *Si?* There will be no misunderstandings.'

The last thing he wanted was for her to try her feminine wiles on him. He had no patience with importunate women, even if they radiated sexual allure like this one. There was dynamite in the sway of her hips, her lush mouth and in the feminine curves her cheap suit couldn't hide.

Yet her huge, shadowed eyes looked vulnerable.

Nonsense. She was a calculating little piece. She'd deliberately stymied his chances to regain the estate, once when her grandfather proposed a merger and again after his death. She'd gone to great lengths to thwart Dario and keep the estate to herself and her weak-chinned boyfriend.

He had to remember Alissa Scott was his enemy.

* * *

No misunderstandings. Could she trust his word?

He despised her, so he couldn't want her. Could he? What about the sizzle of masculine speculation in his eyes? To her relatively inexperienced eye that looked like the stare of a man who was all too interested.

Was it possible his archaic ideas about family vendettas meant he wanted retribution? The *personal* satisfaction of seducing a woman he saw as his enemy?

No! Her imagination was out of control.

Alissa squeezed her eyes shut, wishing she could open them to discover this was a dream.

'Alissa?'

No one else said her name like that. A rumbling purr that made it sound interesting…seductive. That made her nape prickle and her breasts tighten.

Reluctantly she opened her eyes. Dario Parisi watched her with the attention a scientist gave a newly discovered species, missing nothing.

'A business arrangement.' She forced the words out.

He nodded.

'I suppose you've thought about where we'd live?'

'Naturally you'll come to Sicily. My home is there.'

'Naturally.' She doubted he noticed her sarcasm. It wouldn't occur to him that she had reasons to stay in Australia. A job, a home, a sister she loved and feared for. 'I'd have to give up my job.'

Grey eyes held hers. 'In six months you'll have enough money not to need a job.'

What would he say if she told him she loved her work? Enjoyed helping people plan their holidays? Had a flair for dealing with even the most hard-to-please clients?

It didn't matter. Nothing mattered except saving Donna. Even if it meant spending six months under the same roof as a condescending, manipulative Sicilian male.

Been there. Done that. Survived.

She looked at the paper between them. The details had been completed, even hers. He was frighteningly thorough.

Could she really be planning to agree? Shock held her rigid as she absorbed the enormity of what she risked. She was caught fast, she had no choice. But surely Dario was vulnerable too. His obsession with regaining the estate must give her leverage in this unholy bargain.

'If I agree—' she met his stare without blinking '—I want an advance. A third of the *castello*'s value on the day we marry.' Her heart thundered. The money meant nothing to him. He had plenty. To her it meant immediate treatment for Donna. The specialists said she had time, could wait, but this way there'd be no delay.

'Well?' Alissa lifted her chin, her palms growing damp. 'Your bankers could arrange it easily.'

'No doubt they could.' He left the sentence hang till her nerves shredded to tatters. 'You've inherited your grandfather's instinct for screwing cash out of people.' The deadly chill in his tone thrust her back in her chair.

His glare now was pure threat. Pure hatred. Each clipped word a shard of ice on her unprotected skin.

'Very clever, Alissa. You know I want the *castello*. I'll even marry *you* to get it.' His emphasis on the word made her feel like something that had scuttled from under a rock. 'But there I draw the line. I won't be manipulated any further by your family. Every man has his limit and I've reached mine. You Manganos have pushed me as far as I'm willing to go.' He leaned across and held her captive with a coruscating look.

'If you want any more you can whistle for it. I might be constrained by the terms of the will, but so are you, *fidanzatina mia*.' His lips curled in a smile that chilled her blood. 'This is the *only* deal on the table. If you want more, find some other man.'

Alissa shuddered. A lifetime's memories of fear and vulnerability flooded back as she met his merciless gaze. He had the upper hand because he was powerful and rich. Even if he had to wait for years and expend a fortune, he'd find a way to get the estate in the end.

She had no other options.

'It's an hour before the registry closes.' He glanced at his discreet gold watch. 'Then you miss the deadline.'

Alissa smoothed trembling hands over her skirt. She straightened her spine and reached for the pen, ignoring the voice inside that shrieked dire warnings.

This felt wrong. But it was the only way to make things right.

'Where do I sign?'

Dario paced the foyer, resisting the urge to check the time. She was on her way; he'd just had an update on her movements.

He strode to the entrance, fists deep in his pockets. He'd never been so keyed up before a deal. Regaining his family home meant more than buying or selling companies. This wasn't about mere cash, but about family, his very identity. This quest had been his sole purpose for as long as he could remember.

It went against the grain marrying a woman shallow enough to sell herself to acquire a fortune she could fritter away. But no sacrifice was too great.

His gaze fixed on a passing teenager, all fly-away hair and bare legs. Instantly the memory he'd repressed so often filled his mind. Alissa the first time he'd seen her. A few years ago, when he'd grown impatient of long-distance negotiations and visited Gianfranco Mangano. The old weasel had insisted only marriage would secure the Parisi estate.

Dario had sat in his car after the fruitless meeting, trying to find the bait to make Mangano sell. That was when he'd seen her, sneaking into the house in the dark.

He recalled the sultry length of her legs as she climbed out of the low car in her miniskirt. The throaty laugh of a woman sharing a joke with her lover. Her long hair flicked provocatively over one shoulder, a glimpse of pert breasts and a profile that stopped his breath.

His body had responded with a primal throb of hunger neither pride nor logic could prevent. The old man had let slip a thing or two about his granddaughter and her wild ways. He'd wanted her safely married and off his hands.

From that one glimpse Dario knew she wasn't the sort to have marriage on her mind. A judgement confirmed when he heard of her later drug conviction.

Yet he'd never been able to rid himself of that image of carefree, sensual beauty. Even now something about Alissa Scott made his hormones stand up and salivate. It was a reaction he wasn't proud of.

A blur of movement caught his eye and he turned.

Porca miseria! She couldn't be serious.

His lips thinned as she approached, his temper rising to boiling point. Had she no self-respect? She made a mockery of them both.

His gaze swept over his wife-to-be, climbing the steps towards him. Heads turned to watch. She wore satin and lace, a long white dress with a froth of skirts and a dragging train. A fussy veil obscured her face, no doubt hiding a triumphant smirk at his expense.

'I don't remember specifying fancy dress.' His provocative drawl slid across her flesh like ice. Alissa clenched her jaw and continued up the stairs, ignoring him.

She felt sick to her stomach about the wedding. The last thing she needed was sarcasm.

For two pins she'd…what? Run away?

She didn't have that luxury. The knowledge weighed her down, like shackles on a condemned prisoner. She drew a sustaining breath then wished she hadn't as the bodice, a size too small, constricted her lungs.

'Hello, Dario. As charming as ever, I see.'

He was too big, too daunting, too…unsettling. Tension squirmed in her stomach and her pulse tripped as she caught the scent of lemon and warm male flesh.

Her body conspired against her, responding to his overt masculinity with an excitement that appalled her. She lifted her skirts and hurried up the last of the stairs.

'What's the meaning of this?' He stepped in front of her so she had no alternative but to meet his steely gaze. Glacial ice couldn't be colder than the look he gave her.

'This?' She tilted her chin.

'The masquerade costume.' He spoke through barely parted lips and she had the satisfaction of knowing that no matter how terrible she felt wearing Donna's precious bridal dress, her bridegroom hated it more. Good. Let that be some small compensation for the distress he'd caused.

'Haven't you seen a bride before?' she taunted.

'But you're not a bride in the usual sense.'

For that she was thankful. The idea of a real marriage, of intimacy with Dario, was too devastating.

'What do you care?' She moved sideways but he blocked her, filling her vision, dominating her senses.

'Why do you insist on this charade?' he snarled.

Alissa slipped a hand under the veil and rubbed her temple where a tension headache throbbed.

'As I'm moving to Italy I had to explain to people I was getting married. There was no need when I'd planned to stay in Melbourne.' He said nothing, just stood, waiting. 'My sister is sentimental. She married recently. She believes in romantic love with all the trimmings.'

'So you lied about this marriage? To your sister?' There was condemnation in the deep timbre of his voice.

Alissa shrugged. 'It was easier to let her believe I'd been

swept off my feet. When we divorce it will seem a case of marry in haste and repent at leisure.' She wouldn't add to Donna's worries by revealing the true reason for the wedding. She'd be racked with guilt, knowing Alissa had married for her sake, and Dario Parisi of all men.

'That doesn't explain the costume.'

'Donna wanted to be here but I persuaded her not to.' Even her loving sister had seen it made more sense to save to see a specialist in the USA than cross the country for a wedding. 'She asked me to wear her dress. You know, something borrowed…' Her words petered out under his critical stare. 'I promised her I'd wear it. OK?'

'And you keep your promises?'

Did he have to sound so sceptical? It was a good thing she didn't care about his opinion. This was just a business deal. A charade to satisfy the terms of a will.

Yet, wearing her borrowed finery, dwarfed by his ultra-masculine presence, Alissa felt a thread of something unexpected weave through her. A tremor of awareness. Dario was still the sexiest man she'd laid eyes on.

Pity he was an arrogant jerk.

'If you've finished finding fault, can we go in? We don't want to miss our appointment.'

Silently he took her arm and escorted her inside, a parody of the solicitous lover.

After that everything was a blur. Nothing seemed real, not the weight of the dress, or the way her hand fitted snugly in his. When he produced a ring, a glittering proclamation of wealth and status, she wasn't even surprised that it fitted perfectly.

Only as the celebrant said, 'You may now kiss the bride,' did the comfortable illusion of unreality splinter.

Dario turned her round, his hands heavily proprietorial at her waist, and heat radiated through her. She read triumph in his eyes. Satisfaction.

That was when it hit her full force. She'd just married a man who could make her life hell.

Panic clawed at Alissa. She fought for oxygen, her breathing hampered by the too-tight bodice. Blood rushed so loud in her ears she heard nothing else.

Deft hands drew the veil up. Without its protection his scrutiny was razor sharp, his smile knowing. It was the satisfied look of a rapacious marauder, not a dispassionate businessman. And it confirmed what she'd feared.

This was personal.

Before she could protest his lips covered her mouth.

Instinctively she lifted her hands and pushed with all her might against the hard-muscled wall of his chest. It was warm, weighty, alive with the throb of his heart and as immovable as the building in which they stood.

His hands at her waist were deceptively loose. When she backed away they tightened possessively, holding her still. No mistaking that encircling grip for anything more tender than an imprisoning grasp.

His mouth touched hers. More than touched, it caressed, blazing a trail of molten heat across her lips. His kiss was slow, deliberate and provocative. Masterful. His lips were soft but insistent. Surprisingly seductive. He tasted of rich, honeyed darkness, of mystery. The musky male scent of heat and spice clouded her bemused brain.

Alissa's eyes widened as she registered pleasure at his skilful caress. A tiny spark of feminine appreciation. A rippling tide of awareness that heated her blood.

Ruthlessly she crushed it, ignoring too the sizzle of unexpected pleasure as his hands all but spanned her waist, making her feel dainty, feminine and delicate.

Desperately she focused on pushing him away. Yet her efforts had no effect. He swamped her senses till she was aware of nothing but his hot, heady presence and the current of desire threatening to drag her under. A slow-turning twist of unfamiliar tension coiled deep inside her.

Eventually he lifted his head and she stared, dumbfounded, at the man who was her husband. She hadn't expected him to kiss her. More, she couldn't believe his kiss had been so...disturbing. How could she have responded to a man she didn't want?

Dark grey eyes surveyed her as thoroughly as she scrutinised him. His gaze was unrevealing but for a shadow of expression that flickered for an instant.

A firm hand grasped her sagging jaw. 'Time enough to stare later, *moglie mia*.' His whisper was sardonic.

Moglie mia. My wife. Alissa's heart plunged in free fall as she absorbed the horrifying finality of those words. There was no going back.

He steered her to a desk so she could sign the marriage certificate. Absurdly she was grateful for his support. Her legs felt like cotton wool, her mind was muzzy with shock.

Why had he kissed her?

Because he can. It's a power thing.

Yet, watching his tight-lipped profile as he signed his name in a slashing script, Alissa could no longer read satisfaction on his face. He looked grimmer than ever.

Perhaps he didn't like kissing her. She tried to take comfort in the thought. But her brain was stuck in shocked awareness of how devastating his kiss had been.

It must never happen again.

Dario watched the witnesses sign the vital paper that finally secured his ownership of the family estate.

That bound him to Alissa Scott. Alissa Parisi now.

His wife. Distaste filled him. She sat motionless, bedecked in showy white satin and a froth of gauzy veil. Who did she think she fooled with that virginal outfit? She was no innocent.

Was the gown an obscure joke or had she been serious about

dressing to please her sister? The notion didn't sit well with what he knew of this woman.

Grasping, immoral, unrepentant. She'd tried so hard to deny him ownership of his home. She must have imbibed the Mangano hatred of Parisi blood with her mother's milk.

Yet he'd made her his wife.

The Parisi name shouldn't be sullied in such a way.

He ignored the turbulent heat that fired his bloodstream whenever their gazes met. The way his eyes strayed to her face. Her neat nose, bluer-than-blue eyes, her perfect mouth, the fragility of her slender neck.

He was merely taking her measure. It was anger he felt, not desire. He remembered the feel of her flagrantly enticing body, his hands encircling her tiny waist. The taste of her, rich and sweet. The tattoo of need that throbbed in his blood as he inhaled her skin's perfume. The pulse of need he couldn't suppress.

Triumph had tempted him to respond to the lure of her petal-soft lips. They'd fascinated him from the first. Now he knew they were lush, delicious, dangerously enticing.

The kiss had been an error.

It must never happen again.

CHAPTER FOUR

THEY EMERGED FROM the building into bright sunlight. Brilliant blue sky mocked Alissa's foreboding.

'Mr Parisi! Dario Parisi!'

Alissa faltered as strident voices called out.

'*Hell!*' Beside her, Dario gave vent to a stream of vitriolic Italian under his breath. Bewildered, Alissa saw a mob of photographers crowding close.

Dario turned, his shoulder blocking them from her vision. She read the sizzle of fury in his expression.

'That's why you wore the dress? Playing to the media?' His tone could cut solid ice. 'Enjoy it while you can, Signora Parisi. Your day in the limelight will be short.'

'Mr Parisi!' A shout cut across Alissa's denial. 'Have you got a statement about your secret marriage to an Aussie girl?' Cameras thrust close, their lenses threatening dark voids, the sound of shutter clicks aggressive.

'No comment,' Dario said brusquely, keeping her clamped against him as he shouldered his way down the stairs. His arm looped round her in an embrace like the bite of an unyielding iron chain.

'After you.' His clipped tone matched his tight hold.

Alissa stared at the limousine. At the door held open by a familiar chauffeur. The same tough-looking character who'd followed her this past month.

'No, thank you. I have my own car.' Her ancient red hatch-back was a block away.

'Nevertheless,' he paused on the word, his emphasis on the sibilant vaguely sinister, 'we'll travel together.'

Short of an embarrassing public tussle, she had no choice but to let him sweep her into the limo.

Alissa sat stiffly as he bent to tuck in the train of her dress, apparently oblivious to the clustering Press. She caught again the fresh scent of his skin, so warmly enticing. So unlike the rigid precision of the man himself. His black hair was combed severely, not a lock out of place. His collar whiter than white, the cut of his suit perfection, his visage as grimly beautiful as a stone god.

There was nothing soft about him.

As his eyes lifted under level black brows to meet hers, she was stabbed again by the chill of his disapproval. His distaste. And more. Hatred?

Alissa shrank back, heart fluttering. He had what he wanted, the promise of the old *castello*. He couldn't want a more personal form of retribution.

His silence as they sped off did nothing to dispel her unease. Tension built with each wordless kilometre.

'I didn't call the Press,' she finally blurted.

'Spare me your protestations of innocence.' He waved a disparaging hand. 'I have no interest in them.'

'Even if they're the truth?' Indignation sizzled at his presumption of her guilt.

His gaze bored into her, like sharpened steel against her soft flesh. 'I accept you are many things, but don't tax my credulity by pretending innocent is one of them.'

Hot denials trembled on her lips but she bit them back. Instinct told her he was as obstinate as he was self-satisfied. No amount of arguing would persuade him.

Alissa's pulse tripped at the flicker of awareness she read in his hooded eyes. A shimmer of heat flared in the pit of her belly. Despite his formidable control he had the look of a man well-versed in carnal pleasures. That sensuous mouth. Those hands...

Incendiary heat spread under her skin, over her breasts, her throat, to her cheeks.

She couldn't believe she had such thoughts about Dario. It should be easy to hate him for his brutal, domineering tactics, for his overweening pride, for the way he enjoyed her discomfort. Even for the pain he'd unwittingly caused with his first offer of marriage. Alissa had paid a high price for turning him down, enduring the worst ever of her grandfather's beatings.

But, to her horror, it wasn't hatred that stirred as she met his dark gaze. It was something far more primitive. Far more dangerous. Far more...feminine.

If ever Dario guessed, he'd make her life hell.

The setting sun turned the Mediterranean to liquid silk, indigo and pink shot with orange and shafts of gold.

It was beautiful, the exquisite colours, the rugged coastal outcrops, the ancient towns and villages. Yet a chill of trepidation lanced Alissa and she shifted uneasily on the limousine's leather seat.

Sicily. The island that had bred the manipulative, vicious man she'd had to call grandfather. The one place she'd never wanted to visit. The place that had also produced God's gift to himself, Dario Parisi.

Despite the first-class luxury of their flight and the doting attention of staff, Alissa had barely slept. She felt crumpled and stale. Worse, she couldn't shake her anxiety about Donna.

She didn't like leaving while her sister was ill. Yes, Donna was married now, but a lifetime's habit wasn't easily ignored. Alissa had been responsible for her since they were kids. She'd looked out for her, protected her.

She bit her lip, remembering how badly she'd failed her little sister when it really mattered.

Now Donna had David, a man who'd do anything for his bride. They'd be happy together. Donna deserved a chance at happiness after the childhood she'd endured. If only they could get the money for her treatment. Such severe liver damage was beyond the skills of the local medicos. Her only hope of survival lay in a radical new treatment overseas. Expensive treatment. They'd tried everything they could to raise the cash. Unsuccessfully.

Which brought Alissa to Dario Parisi. *Her husband.*

Through the long journey he'd been at ease amidst the extravagant luxury that, though she fought not to show it, unsettled Alissa. A man with that sort of money could get away with almost anything.

He'd slept soundly, as if he didn't have a thing on his conscience. He'd eaten heartily and been brusquely courteous in a way that reinforced his disapproval. Clearly he considered her undeserving of his exalted company!

He was an arrogant, macho dinosaur who considered his word law. His casual acceptance of lavish attention, his impatience at delay bespoke a man of enormous power and ego. Despite his handsome façade he was dangerous. She'd read about his cutthroat business tactics and how he crushed all before him. His reputation with women was no better. His progress was littered with beautiful, disappointed ex-lovers.

Dario sat back, surveying the landscape through narrowed, proprietary eyes as if he owned it all. For all she knew he might! The flight from Rome by luxury private jet was more proof of his stupendous wealth.

'How much further?' They were the first words either had spoken since they'd landed in Sicily.

Alissa could have kicked herself when she saw his mouth twist in a smirk of triumph. Had he hoped she'd snap under his silence?

If that was the worst he could do, he was in for a shock. She'd weathered far worse treatment, meted out by an expert.

When he spoke his voice was like smoky honey. Goose flesh rose across her arms and awareness sizzled. He'd probably spent years perfecting that deep tone. It was guaranteed to get under any woman's skin.

'What?' he purred. 'Aren't you enjoying the view? Most visitors are in raptures over their first sight of Sicily.'

Alissa met his scrutiny for only a moment before turning away. 'Most of them are willing visitors, looking forward to a holiday in the sun.'

'And you're unwilling?' He paused so long she fought the urge to look at him over her hunched shoulder. She was strung out, at the end of her physical and mental reserves. She didn't have the energy for a full-on altercation.

'No one forced you, Alissa. You came of your own free will.' The way he said her name, lingering over the sibilants, drawing out the vowels, made it almost a caress.

He was playing with her, enjoying her discomfort.

'That doesn't deserve an answer.' Dario Parisi and her grandfather had manipulated her into a position where the notion of free will was a joke.

Her husband relished the knowledge. He probably got his kicks out of bullying people who couldn't stand up to him. Or, in her case, besting the woman who'd spurned his offer of marriage not once but twice. No doubt his pride had smarted at the rejection. She'd bet he wasn't used to women denying him what he wanted.

From the corner of her eye she saw a blur of movement. Strong fingers cupped her chin. He didn't use enough force to hurt her, yet she had no option but to turn. His long frame crowded her into the corner of the back seat.

Her heart thumped an uneven tattoo as she inhaled the scent of ripe lemon and fresh man, a warm, earthy tang that made her nostrils flare and her pulse patter.

Heat flushed her body and she leaned back, trying to avoid contact. He shifted his hand, sliding his fingers down her throat, where she was most vulnerable, then round to cup her neck and hold her still. His thumb stroked the sensitive skin below her ear and blood roared, blocking out the hum of the car engine.

'Are you trying to make me feel *sorry* for you?' His dulcet tone was incredulous. 'Do you really think I should have any compunction about how I treat the woman who plotted to deny me my birthright?' He leaned close enough for his breath to feather her mouth.

Despite his leashed anger, there was something almost… erotic about the proximity of his long, mobile mouth with its sensuously full lower lip. She felt each word in puffs of air that ignited explosions of sensation along her own mouth.

It was anger that parched her throat and made her swipe her lips with her tongue. It couldn't be anything else, not when his every move, each piercing word, was a calculated insult.

His gaze flicked to her lips. The pressure of his hand increased. He pressed closer, thigh to her thigh.

'I did no such thing.' Her voice was breathless, shameful evidence of weakness. 'I just arranged to marry.'

'Arranged to marry.' He shook his head. 'That's what you call it? You refuse me yet connive to wed another so you can deprive me of what is *mine*? Did you get a kick out of that, Alissa? You didn't just want the money, you also wanted to hurt me.' His voice thickened to a low, dangerous whisper that sent a chill of anxiety along her spine.

'It wasn't enough that you've lived a life of indulgent luxury at the expense of my family. That you had every opportunity our money could purchase.' His searing gaze didn't release hers. 'You squandered those opportunities.' His lips thinned into a disapproving line. 'What have you made of yourself? You have a dead-end job, a well-developed taste for parties and a criminal record.'

His disdain triggered a rush of desperate energy. Alissa lifted her hands to his shoulders and shoved, desperate for space. But he didn't budge. He was as immoveable as the island along which the car sped.

Impotent, she could only brace her arms, hoping to prevent him from closing the tiny gap between them.

'You're so sure of my guilt.' Her voice was overloud in the cocooned silence of their private compartment. 'Did it never occur to you I'm as much a victim in this as you?'

More so. For Dario Parisi had turned the situation to his own advantage with the sure, quick wit and daring of a natural predator. He was beyond her league in that and so many other ways. But she refused to be cowed.

'A victim?' His eyes roved over her, his stare so intense she felt it, like the slide of burning ice on skin.

Her lips tingled as if singed by fire when his gaze dropped to her mouth. For a heartbeat, for two, he stared. By the third pulse beat the tingle had become a throb. By the sixth her breathing had constricted, coming in short, hard pants that made her breasts rise and fall mere centimetres from the solid, imposing strength of his chest. By the ninth her lips felt tender, swollen, as if bruised by his ravaging look.

She tried and failed to forget the taste of his lips on hers. The blaze of heat that had engulfed her as he marked her with the brand of his possession. Though he didn't care for her, he'd taken the time to remind her she was his wife. His chattel.

And, despite every instinct for self-preservation, part of her responded to that primitive claim!

Still he didn't move. His sleek brows arrowed down in a frown of diabolical concentration. With his deep widow's peak, glossy dark hair and spare, powerful features he was the epitome of danger, his elegance a façade to raw power and primal urges.

His gaze held her immobile, in thrall to this thing that sparked between them. It was something she didn't want to name. Something that scared her more than threats or promises of reprisal.

He looked away and Alissa almost sobbed with relief.

Till he moved again. He cupped her face, his thumb on her mouth, pressing open her lips. Darts of fire shot out from his slow, deliberately erotic touch, straight to her engorged nipples and her belly.

Horrified, she stared into his darkening eyes.

She tasted his skin on her lips. A salty, musky tang. His thumb pressed lower, dragging her bottom lip down till he could invade her mouth, swiping her inner lip and tongue. That small invasion was shattering.

She read the glitter in his eyes, no longer cold and indifferent but febrile with an unholy pleasure. He knew exactly how devastating she found his caress.

His thumb traced the ridge of her teeth and her eyelids flickered, heavy with the weight of this new and alien force. She wanted to bite down on his flesh. Suckle it, draw it into her mouth, make his body heat and writhe like the twisting coils of sensation flaring inside her.

How had her anger morphed into this?

His lips drew back in a smile of stark masculine satisfaction. He closed in on her and she was helpless to break the spell of his touch and her own surging desire.

It was only as his head lowered, his chest brushing her oversensitive breasts, that she regained her sanity.

With both hands she clamped hold of his sinewy wrist and pulled. The silky hair below his cuff tickled but she ignored it, just as she ignored the frantic messages of her brain. Messages of thwarted desire and soul-swamping need.

Once she'd thought Dario less of a threat than her abusive grandfather. She'd been wrong. Dario had only to look at her, touch her, and she turned into someone she didn't know. Someone ravaged by disturbingly primal needs that Alissa Scott had never experienced.

'We may be married but you don't have the right to paw me,' she gasped, thrusting his hand away and shoving at his chest.

Beneath his open jacket she felt hard-packed muscle. Heat and power and pure male energy.

She shut her eyes and prayed this madness would cease.

'You give me the right when you look at me like that.' His uneven whisper was a rough growl. 'If ever a woman invited a man—'

'Enough!' Her eyes snapped open. 'Read my lips, Signor Parisi. I—do—not—want—you—near—me!' She punctuated each word with a thrust of her hands, becoming more desperate as he remained stolidly unmoving. She was at his mercy, locked in this tiny space.

Her heart hammered a panicked beat that threatened to choke her. Claustrophobia, the old enemy, engulfed her, making her senses swim and her head spin. The world closed in, darkening her vision to a narrowing tunnel of fear.

'Please,' it was a hoarse whisper, 'I...'

An instant later she was free. Cool air brushed her cheeks from an open window. Light banished the encroaching shadows. She slumped. Dario's stare raked her. But as she gulped down sweet air even that didn't matter.

She was safe. For now.

Dario scrutinised her intently, searching her pale features for signs of satisfaction or triumph. Her play on his sympathy had worked.

Was she so good an actress? He frowned, noting the pulse hammering in her slender throat. Her breathing was ragged, as if strained by fear.

Moments before she'd been caught in the same heady sizzle as he. With an expert knowledge honed over thirty-three years he'd recognised it. Despite her denials she'd been so hot and ready he could have had her on the back seat of the limo. Anticipation had thrummed through him.

At first he'd assumed it was a trick, seduction to soften him up for another attempt to wheedle cash from him.

Except she hadn't initiated that erotic little interlude. He had.

Now she gave an excellent imitation of a woman overcome by fear. Could he have so misread her? Had she truly been unwilling? The idea gnawed at his belly. He would never force himself on a woman in that way.

Or perhaps she was chagrined to find her fake response to him was the real thing?

Dario had no false modesty about his effect on women.

Now he was stunned at the sliver of doubt puncturing his certainty. He'd closed in on her out of anger, wanting to punish her. He hadn't forgiven her for making this difficult. She could so easily have agreed to his proposal years ago and all this would have been long settled.

Dario wasn't used to being manipulated. He'd been forced to barter his name to acquire the *castello*, marrying a Mangano. Yet when he'd finally swallowed his pride this woman had thrown his offer in his face. She'd tried to make a fool of him by ensuring he didn't get his inheritance. She'd even had the gall to ask for money up front before the wedding. As if he'd finance her lifestyle!

Now his plan to punish her had backfired. She'd brought him to a fever pitch of arousal in moments.

He'd barely touched her. Hadn't even kissed her. Yet the taste of her was imprinted on his palate. Their kiss yesterday had been a necessity then a punishment and then, to his astonishment, a pleasure.

One taste and he craved more.

Dario sank back, his mind whirling. Despite all he knew about Alissa Scott she'd got under his skin.

It was not to be tolerated!

The sight of familiar security gates eased the tension between his shoulder blades. Soon he'd be home. This illusory link between them would snap once he resumed his usual routine—

Dario's eyes widened as the car swung up the approach to

the house. His gaze fixed on a cluster of people around a small figure in black at the foot of the entrance staircase.

Che diavolo! This was just what he'd hoped to avoid.

The car purred to a halt. Alissa looked out the window and gasped. She'd thought the end of this journey would bring some respite. How wrong she'd been.

Her eyes goggled as she took in the scene before her, lit by the setting sun. A masterpiece of minimalist architecture greeted her. Massive, soaring, stark white but for slender columns of polished steel and vast expanses of smoky glass wall. This couldn't be his house, surely?

Her gaze strayed from the huge bronze entrance doors, down the imposing steps to the group watching the car.

Alissa heard a burst of pungent Italian oaths that would have done her grandfather proud. Disconcerted, she slewed round to see Dario staring at his welcoming committee. The stern, lowered brow and the tight set of his jaw betrayed displeasure.

'Stay here!' he barked, then swung open the door and unfolded his length onto the driveway.

He stalked across the gravel and a resounding cheer echoed around him. He took the hands of a slight figure at the centre of the crowd. The woman was tiny but projected an air of authority. Alissa saw the woman's grey head nod as she broke from his grip, her hands gesticulating.

Abruptly the scene changed. Dario bent to kiss the woman on both cheeks, there was another cheer, then he strode back, his long legs eating up the distance.

There was no mistaking the grim annoyance in those grey eyes as he opened the door and held out his hand. His mouth was pinched in a straight line and his nostrils flared as if he took deep breaths to calm himself.

Reluctantly Alissa put her hand in his, and then almost withdrew it as a jangle of nerves cascaded up her arm and through her body. Her gaze flew to his, aghast, and she saw the almost imperceptible tensing of his jaw, the narrowing of his eyes that told her he felt it too—that instantaneous spark of connection.

'Come. There's someone waiting to meet you.' He tucked her arm in his, covering her fingers. She felt blanketed by his heat, yet she shivered. 'But take note.' His voice was a low, silky threat. 'Say as little as possible. You'll smile and nod and I'll do the talking. Understood?'

'Why?' Despite the exhaustion that made her sway on her feet, she had no intention of blindly kowtowing.

She caught his eye, hoping to look confident. Then she wished she hadn't. His look could freeze blood at fifty paces.

'Because if you don't, if you utter one word of disagreement, I'll make sure the next six months are the most miserable of your life. And that money you want from the estate? It might even be delayed.'

His voice was a lethal slash of sound. But worse was his expression. He wore a smile that from a distance must look charming. Up close it accentuated the feral anger in his eyes, the raw savagery of his tone. He looked like every nightmare her grandfather had ever conjured for her, evil intent cloaked by stunning good looks.

She could almost believe he'd like nothing better than an excuse to sink those strong white teeth into her tender flesh. Rapacious, fierce, deadly. That was Dario Parisi.

What had she got herself into?

'I…'

'Is that agreement? Speak up, woman.'

'Then stop looming over me!'

His eyes widened. Alissa even surprised herself. She'd thought she was too tired to meet his belligerence head-on, yet it wasn't in her nature to submit meekly to bullying. That was why she'd always been in trouble as a kid.

'Why can't you just *ask* me to cooperate?' She was sick of threats. Was that how all Sicilian men operated?

'Are you saying you would?' Disbelief coloured his voice.

He didn't wait for her to respond. 'You will do as I say.' It was an order, not a question.

'Since you ask so nicely.' She pasted a sickly sweet smile on her face. Better than letting him see how his threat to withhold the money for Donna unnerved her.

'Good. Follow my lead like a good Sicilian wife and things will be easier for you.'

Alissa opened her mouth to snap out a retort. If there was one thing she'd never be, it was a good Sicilian wife!

He forestalled her by draping his arm around her, drawing her against his warm, solid body. That sucked the breath from her lungs and the words from her mouth. She hoped he couldn't feel her shiver. His ego was huge. Proof that she wasn't immune to him would only fuel his conceit.

'Come, *wife*, and meet your household.' His voice dripped an icy contempt that belied his wide smile.

There was a chef, a housekeeper, gardeners, a secretary, security men, maids and more. Names and faces blurred as Dario introduced her and good wishes were pressed upon them. The smiles looked genuine, as if they liked him. He must pay a fortune in wages. That was the only explanation.

'This is Signora Bruzzone.' His tone softened but his grip tightened. 'Caterina, this is my wife, Alissa.'

Alissa wondered if anyone else noticed him pause before the word 'wife'. But the woman before her gave no such indication. She drew Alissa out of Dario's grasp. His hands dropped reluctantly.

Gleaming dark eyes smiled up at Alissa as the older woman kissed her on both cheeks. She was grey-haired and dressed smartly in black. Her face was strong with character and traces of great beauty, her smile genuine.

Alissa, used to being on the small side of average, felt ungainly and ill-dressed beside her. The dark trousers, cream blouse and caramel jacket that had seemed perfect for travelling were rumpled now.

'Alissa, welcome to your new home!' Her English was accented but clear, her welcome genuine.

Alissa didn't know how to respond, especially with Dario glowering at her. Tentatively she returned the older woman's hug, uncomfortably aware of his scrutiny.

'Thank you, Signora Bruzzone.'

'You must call me Caterina. There's no need for formality. I was Dario's housekeeper for years and now I hope to be your friend.' The older woman smiled. 'You will be happy here. I know Dario will work hard to ensure it.'

Alissa struggled to repress a bubble of hysteria at the thought.

'As you say, Caterina, it will be my business to look after her.' His smooth tones slid along Alissa's nerves as his hand skimmed her waist. She drew in a trembling breath then bit down hard on her bottom lip, fighting the instinctive need to shrug him off and flee.

Snapping dark eyes surveyed her face then Caterina spoke again, more sharply this time.

'Dario! Look at the poor little one. She's exhausted. You shouldn't have subjected her to the long flight so soon after the wedding. Not everyone has your energy.'

The older woman smiled again. 'I have told him he should have waited and brought you here to marry. Then it wouldn't seem quite so strange to you.' Her eyes flashed a rueful glance over Alissa's shoulder. 'But it is always the way with this one. He sees what he wants and he is impatient. He would never take no for an answer.' She shook her head, but Alissa read fond approval in her eyes.

'Come. Everything has been prepared. I've seen to it myself. Welcome to your new home, my dear.'

Alissa opened her mouth to respond but the other woman gave an order to the staff, who separated, creating a pathway up the wide steps.

Without warning strong arms curved round Alissa's back

and legs. She was swung high, coming to rest against the hard heat of an impressive male chest.

'What…?'

Her eyes clashed with dark grey ones under straight black brows. The intensity of Dario's scrutiny cut off her question and her heart dived.

He stood unmoving, looking at her. She was insidiously aware of the feel of his powerful arms, of splayed hands pressed intimately against her. A hint of spicy scent made her nostrils quiver and somewhere deep inside a spark of something horribly like excitement fired her blood.

Dario's expression changed slowly. Shock sizzled in her veins as a real smile curved his sculpted lips. The effect on that chiselled, handsome face stole her breath.

He strode forward and around them cheers broke out.

He was halfway up the sprawling staircase before Alissa found her voice. 'I can walk. I'm not *that* tired.'

'It doesn't matter.' His words feathered her forehead. 'They'd be disappointed if we broke with tradition.'

'Tradition?' Alissa told herself it was weariness that dulled her brain. That her slow thinking had nothing to do with the effect of Dario Parisi's arms about her.

'Of course.' His teeth flashed a smile of genuine amusement, edged with something else she preferred not to identify. 'Didn't you know it's Italian tradition for a groom to carry his bride over the threshold?'

'You have to be kidding! You know this isn't—'

His embrace tightened and he strode faster, his long legs eating up the distance to the massive front doors.

'You and I know what our marriage is, but it does not suit me that anyone else should know.' He paused and looked down into her eyes. 'Welcome to my home, *wife.*'

Her breath hissed as he shouldered his way through the open door to the sound of raucous cheering from below.

'Well! Now you've kept up tradition you can put me down.' Her nerves were shredded. She needed space.

He shook his head and crossed a vast atrium towards a curving marble staircase.

'Ah, but that's not all. There's more.'

'More?'

'Oh, yes.' This time the smile he bestowed betrayed a raw heat that reminded her of a hungry predator. 'Didn't you hear Caterina? She has already made the preparations.'

'Preparations?' Alissa didn't like the look in his eyes, or the jerky way her pulse galloped in response.

'Of course. She has prepared our marriage bed.'

CHAPTER FIVE

ALISSA'S HEAD SWAM as he strode through double doors and kicked them shut.

The room was huge, luxurious and private. The whisper of his breathing and the frantic thrum of her pulse were the only sounds.

A vast lake of smoky blue carpet spread like a reflection of the indigo sea beyond the enormous windows. The furnishings were few but impossibly expensive. The centrepiece was a bed: wide, low and far too large. It filled her vision and she couldn't look away.

Panic gripped her, fuelled by his menacing threats in the car, and more, the savage satisfaction she'd glimpsed in his eyes as he carried her up the stairs.

This man despised her, he couldn't possibly want...

'I'd like to stand on my own feet now,' she said as calmly as she could. 'There's no need to perform for your audience any more.'

'Ah, but you heard Caterina. You're exhausted.'

Alissa didn't look at him. She felt too vulnerable, here in his embrace. His searing gaze was too disturbing.

'Not that exhausted! Put me down. Now!' She welcomed the surge of anger. It beat the insidious chill of fear and the edgy awareness hands down.

Instead of answering he shifted his hold, drawing her closer, pacing slowly to the bed. Alissa's heart beat in time with each step as tension coiled tighter.

When he stopped the bed was an unending expanse below her. Blinding-white linen filled her vision, old linen, edged with ornate, handmade lace. The scent of lavender and sunshine emanated from it. Petals were strewn across the comforter. In the centre lay a plump, blush-pink rose.

'As you wish.' He lowered her.

Alissa was torn between wanting to tear herself from his arms and trying to scrabble back into them rather than be placed like some virgin sacrifice on his marriage bed.

The bedding cushioned her like an embrace. She held herself stiffly, sitting primly away from the luxuriously soft pillows.

'You can't mean for us to share this bed.'

'Why not?' His voice was a sultry murmur, his eyes glittering with a light she didn't want to decipher. 'We're man and wife. It *is* customary. Are you afraid there isn't room for two?'

Despite her best intentions, Alissa's gaze strayed over the bed. Its modern lines were designed for something less traditional than heirloom sheets. Satin perhaps, sinfully soft and caressing. She could imagine Dario sprawled here on black satin. Dario with a svelte, dark-haired beauty.

Alissa shot off the mattress, horrified at how vividly she pictured him naked. Her knees trembled as she faced him. He looked as implacable as a carved deity.

'Don't even joke about it, Signor Parisi. You and I both know you have no interest in sharing this bed with me.' She refused to dwell on the possibility that she was wrong. 'I'm sick of your innuendoes and accusations. I'm tired after the trip and definitely not in the mood for your point-scoring games.'

Alissa breathed deep, trying to calm her racing pulse. She'd been on a roller-coaster ride of anxiety too long. She needed to claw back some control.

'Now,' she said, squaring up to his unreadable gaze, determined not to let him sense her fear, 'I've gone along with this charade and I haven't disappointed your fan club out there. I've been *more* than reasonable, putting up with your he-man routine carrying me up here.' She paused and dragged in another deep breath, wishing she could rid herself of the shivery awareness.

'I'd appreciate it if you'd show some courtesy and give me privacy. I don't care how you explain it to your retinue but we will *not* be sharing this bed.'

She spun round and marched to the far side of the room. With each step she expected the heavy weight of his hand to descend on her shoulder and halt her in her tracks.

Her fingers were unsteady as she pushed open a door and found what she'd hoped for: a bathroom. Relief flooded her as she entered and clicked the door shut, snapping it locked behind her.

For a moment she gazed at the palatial travertine and gleaming glass. Then she slumped against the door and let her shaky legs give way till she sat, huddled on the floor.

Six months of marriage. How was she going to survive?

Her situation got worse by the hour.

Dario stared at the door and willed his taut muscles to relax. His palms prickled at the memory of her curvaceous form in his embrace. Her rich, sweet fragrance lingered in his nostrils. More, his blood pooled and thickened low in his body.

Damnation! He was aroused. Fully, painfully aroused. By Alissa Scott, his not-so-convenient wife.

It had been the feel of her, warm and luscious and soft in his arms, that excited him. But even more, the sight of her standing up to him fearlessly when ninety-nine women out of a hundred would have meekly acquiesced.

The blaze of hauteur in her eyes as she called his bluff had been nothing short of magnificent. The belligerent jut of her chin, like an Amazon queen who didn't know the meaning of defeat. Her precise, cut-glass diction as she challenged him.

The sizzle of defiance radiating off her. All had been superb. Glorious. *Sexy as hell.*

Even her dark red hair, tumbling around her shoulders as her rigidly upswept style disintegrated, had enhanced her splendour. It added a sensuous promise to her defiance. A reminder that beneath the glacial indignation every inch was warm, red-blooded woman.

The undercurrent of attraction had exploded into a tidal wave of wanting. He couldn't fathom it. He'd become accustomed to capitulation, not defiance. But this one woman, daring to confront him as no one had in years...

She'd been scintillatingly *alive*. Vibrant and real in a way few women were. She didn't simper or mindlessly agree or deliberately issue sultry invitations.

She hated him.

And he'd never been so turned on in his life.

The realisation was a shocking body blow.

She wasn't his type. She was everything he despised. She was his blood enemy. She was trouble with a capital T. She was nothing like the quiet, charming woman he planned to find and make his permanent wife.

Yet he was across the room, his hand on the bathroom doorknob, without any memory of deciding to follow her.

Horrified, he snatched back his hand and strode to the windows. The indigo waves, ceaselessly moving, reminded him of her. Of the way her brilliant gaze darkened as she faced him down.

He shoved his hands in his pockets and swung round, only to be confronted by the bed. Even now he saw her there, russet hair and pouting lips pure invitation against the pristine bedspread. Her full breasts rising and falling in her passion.

He'd wanted to push her back against the covers, cup that delicious flesh in his hands, taste her again on his tongue. Find release inside her.

But sex meant complications. He had enough experience of

importunate ex-lovers to understand that. Sex with his wife…
that would be a complication on a grand scale. Better to keep
this strictly business.

Suddenly the idea of spending half a year under the same
roof as Alissa didn't seem simple. Even in a separate room she'd
be a distraction. Knowing she was here in his home would be
a potent disturbance to his well-ordered life. His plan to make
the next six months as difficult for her as possible was back-
firing. He'd intended to enjoy her discomfort, enjoy making
her pay just a little for the inconvenience she'd caused and the
damage her family had done.

She was supposed to be at his mercy. Not the other way
around.

Dario tightened his fists. Perhaps it was enough to have the
castello in his grasp. He needn't sully himself with petty vengeance, despite the provocation.

He'd master this unwanted desire and forge ahead as he'd
always done. Only his total-focus determination had got him
where he was today, out of a nondescript orphanage and into
the rich lists. If he'd let himself be sidetracked he'd still be
nothing, nobody, not the worthy inheritor of his family pride
and prestige.

He turned. His gaze flickered to the bathroom door but he
headed for the landing. Alissa could wait. He had to straighten
things out with Caterina. She was far more than his retired
housekeeper. She was the one person who'd known him since
those early days in the orphanage. She'd believed in him, giving up her job to keep house for him as his quest to rebuild the
Parisi fortunes prospered.

He hadn't told her his plan to marry. His current housekeeper must have spilled the news so instead of arriving to see
his new wife installed in an apartment of her own he'd been
faced with Caterina's joyful excitement. She'd even made up
a marriage bed with linens inherited from her grandmother.

He tunnelled a hand through his hair. Going through the

farce of carrying his bride over the threshold had been easier than telling Caterina the truth.

She'd been at him so long to find a 'nice girl' and settle down. He hadn't had the heart to explain that this was all about business, property and a decades-old feud.

Now he'd have to. He squared his shoulders and strode out of the room. He ignored the small voice that warned his life, his foolproof plan to get everything he wanted, had suddenly become dangerously complicated.

It was the middle of the night when Alissa woke on the sofa in Dario's bedroom. She must have nodded off waiting for him to return. Jet lag and stress had exhausted her, yet she could scarcely believe she'd slept.

A blanket covered her and she was dressed but for her shoes. She darted a look at the massive bed.

It was empty. Her heartbeat notched up a pace when she saw it had been slept in. Where was he now? She sat up.

That was when she noticed the deep murmur. Not the sound of the sea—the roll of incoming waves was slower and more distant. She stared into the silver-grey moonlight, realising it was Dario she heard, his voice husky, rich and deeply male. It tingled across her senses like the prickle of approaching lightning, making her skin contract.

Alissa squirmed. She was too aware of the big, bothersome Sicilian. She tried to convince herself anxiety tensed her muscles but her restlessness had more to do with feminine awareness. It had been like that from the moment she met those clear-as-crystal eyes and felt a jolt like a fast-dropping elevator in the pit of her stomach.

If she could concentrate on Dario Parisi as her enemy she could fight him. But as she finally spied him, almost naked on the balcony, her determination to do just that slipped from her mind.

The moon revealed a sleek body of honed muscle, broad

shoulders and long, taut limbs. Her breath stopped then escaped on a whoosh of desperation.

How did she fight the devil when he had the body of an angel?

He paced, talking into his phone. Each powerful stride revealed leashed energy and supreme fitness, as if he were an athlete impatient for his event. Even the shadow of dark boxer shorts low on his hips promoted the fantasy.

She caught one word, 'Maria', as he turned near the open glass door. His girlfriend? Was that why he was impatient? He was stuck here with a wife he didn't want when perhaps he'd rather be with Maria, working off some of that sizzling animal energy.

Alissa swung her legs to the ground, shoving aside the blanket and leaning her elbows on her knees. Nausea hit her at the idea of Dario and another woman.

It couldn't be jealousy. That was absurd. She didn't even like him. She wasn't attracted to that…master manipulator. The man who'd shown no compunction and every sign of chilly contempt as he bent her to his will.

'Ah, you're awake. My apologies if I disturbed you.'

He stood before her, legs planted wide and hands on hips in a stance that was purely male and appallingly attractive. The fact that he wore nothing but a pair of silky boxers and an enigmatic smile obviously didn't concern him in the slightest.

He was so supremely self-confident.

Every cell of her body clamoured to alert. Not with fear but with something far more dangerous.

Alissa jerked her gaze to his gleaming eyes, pretending she hadn't just imprinted a stunning picture of raw male beauty onto the dazzled lenses of her eyes.

She refused to be attracted to him. No matter what her body thought. Her mind was stronger.

Surely it was stronger.

'Why didn't you wake me?' Her voice, high and breathless, sounded like a stranger's.

'Why disturb you when you were comfortable?' His tone had a satisfied, unsettling edge.

'Don't play games, Dario.' She paused, astonished at the shot of pleasure that speared her at the sound of his name on her tongue. The enveloping darkness had altered the atmosphere between them. The very air felt charged. 'I didn't want to sleep here.'

He lifted his shoulders and, despite herself, Alissa was enthralled by the ripple of muscle and sinew on his lean, hard body. Moonlight lovingly silvered each taut curve and plane.

'As you fell asleep and refused to rouse, I assumed you weren't serious.'

'You tried to wake me?' Her mouth dried at the thought of those long fingers touching her while she slept. A tickle of sensation feathered her waist, her hip, as if in response to the light brush of a hand.

Was it possible he *desired* her? Had he wanted her awake to consummate their marriage? Anxiety and outrage flared. And a thrilling undercurrent she preferred to ignore.

He stepped close and her fingers curled into the sofa's fine leather. His gaze pierced her, as if he saw the weakness weighting her bones. She strove to look away, horrified at the drift of her thoughts. The tang of the sea on the breeze tickled her nostrils and the scent of warm skin mingled with it. She tugged the blanket over her knees, wishing for a more substantial barrier.

'You seem very much at home in my bedroom.' His voice was deeper than ever. A deliberate taunt. Alissa's eyes flickered to the wide bed. Even in this light she could make out a scattering of rose petals.

The marriage bed they were supposed to share.

The thought was unnerving. A traitorous part of her wondered how it would be sharing that space with this man—fit, strong and no doubt practised in every sensual skill.

Madness!

Yet she recalled the dreamy look on her mother's face years ago when she'd described meeting Alissa's father. Like a bolt of lightning, she'd said. So strong she hadn't hesitated to marry him weeks after they'd met.

Instant attraction was appallingly dangerous. Her mother hadn't known what sort of man he really was. That he'd dump her just after the birth of their second child.

Alissa had more sense than to fall in love, especially with someone like Dario. But here in the warm night, where she felt the caress of his breath on her face, she wondered if women in her family had a predisposition to instant, all-consuming lust. To attraction that drove out logic.

Had that happened to her mother? Had Alissa inherited a terrible weakness for the wrong man?

No! It was a midnight fantasy, fuelled by anxiety. In the morning she'd feel nothing. She lifted her head and met the glitter of his eyes head-on.

'Don't get carried away by your ego, Signor Parisi. I was jet-lagged, that's all.' She busied herself, holding her breath while she folded the blanket. 'You can show me to my room now.'

He said nothing, just stood, arms akimbo, watching her. His eyes waited to trap her as she looked up. Once more she felt the shock of awareness shudder through her.

'I'll make a deal with you.' His voice was low and even. No sign that he felt anything except impatience. 'If you can live quietly for six months with no embarrassing scenes, no attempts to score points in front of others, I'll ensure you're comfortable till we inherit and divorce. You'll have the freedom of the estate and the local towns. I'll even provide a driver for you.'

Alissa stared, wishing the lights were on so she could fathom his expression.

'Why should you do that?'

He raised his shoulders and spread his hands palm upwards in a gesture that was pure Sicilian.

'A truce is easier for both of us.'

'What do you get out of it?' He wasn't obliged to provide anything but the roof over her head. After her grandfather's mean ways and a taste of Dario's dislike, she wouldn't have been surprised if he'd charged her board.

'Contrary to what you think, you're not my top priority.' His voice dipped into sarcasm. 'I have major commercial projects underway, more important things on my mind than continually sparring with a Mangano.'

'I'm not a—'

'No, how could I have forgotten?' The soft chill of his words stopped her. 'You're a Parisi now.'

It was true. For the next six months she was no longer Alissa Scott. The realisation unnerved her. As if in acquiring his name she'd somehow mislaid something of herself. Something vital.

'I'll never be a Parisi,' she said in a rush. 'I'm a wife on paper only, not your possession.'

Her fingers clenched. She'd had enough of men shoving her into moulds of their making, treating her as a chattel to be bartered and negotiated over, like a lifeless piece of property. His stare grazed her but she didn't look away.

'You're right,' he said at last. His husky voice rasped across her nerves. 'You'll never be a Parisi.'

Odd how his dismissal jarred. As if she cared what he thought, cared whether he believed her good enough to grace his oh-so-special family tree.

'But meanwhile you are my temporary wife. Why not accept my hospitality graciously? All I ask is that you behave with propriety.'

'Propriety?' Lava-hot anger coursed through her blood. She shot to her feet and paced away from him, needing an outlet for her simmering temper. 'What? No wild parties, you mean? No drugs?' She swung round to glare at him from the other end of the room. 'Is that what you're worried about? That I'll contaminate the illustrious Parisi name?'

His stillness told her that was exactly what he meant. Disappointment swamped her. Why was she surprised? He knew about her conviction. That she was intimately acquainted with the less salubrious entertainments awaiting young girls in a big city. She shuddered as she remembered those nightmare days.

'Don't sound disappointed, Alissa.' Her name in his mouth was a lethal weapon, carving through even her fury to burrow deep inside her flesh. A weak part of her responded even now to the sexy promise of this man.

She clenched her jaw, horrified to find she fought two enemies: Dario Parisi and herself. Never had she reacted like this to any man!

'Definitely no drugs,' he said. 'No wild parties.' He paused and she lifted her chin. 'But I was thinking more of romantic liaisons. You will not see other men while you are my wife.' His voice dropped to a rumble that reverberated across her skin. *His wife.* She rubbed her hands over her arms, smoothing away the sensation.

'Publicly we'll maintain the fiction of marriage but in reality we need have little to do with each other.' He paused. '*If* you can behave with decorum. And believe me, there will be people checking that you behave.'

Minders. Spies. He'd employ a private detective or bodyguard to watch her every move. It was like the past all over again. But she sensed Dario Parisi's authority was even more potent than Gianfranco's had been.

For a moment the darkness pressed down on her, stifling, heavy, like a velvet weight that muffled the senses and impeded her breathing. Her chest tightened and blood rushed in her ears. Finally she forced down the welling void of fear.

'And you?' she said into the waiting silence. 'Will you also behave with decorum?'

'*Cosa?*'

She stalked towards him, anger driving her on. She revelled in it. Better that than fear. 'Will you give up your indulgences? Give up your women, your pleasures, so people believe we're married?'

Dario shifted his weight. He loomed taller, ominously threatening. Alissa stood her ground, noticing the sharp line of his jaw and the tendons taut in his neck.

'Careful, *cara*. It's dangerous to pick a fight with me.' His words were a whisper. 'Goad me too far and I may decide the best approach is to make this marriage real in every sense. Perhaps then you'll be more amenable.'

Time stood still as he held her gaze, letting his threat sink in. Her insides curled at the hint of anticipation in his tone. At the scent of sexual danger in the air. As if he'd like the excuse to seduce her. At this moment he might even succeed. Despite her fear and her wariness, she responded to him in the most appalling way.

'I just want to ensure you play your part in this charade.' Her voice wobbled.

Finally he nodded, a bare fraction of movement, and Alissa breathed again. 'For the next six months no one will have cause to think I'm interested in any other woman. They'll believe we're devoted.'

'That wasn't what I meant! You don't have to pretend we're...'

'Intimate?' Suddenly he was right there before her, filling her senses, invading her space.

Silently she nodded, fearful of the quicksand of hidden desires and emotions beneath her feet.

'Perhaps you're right. That would be too much.' Yet he didn't move, just stood, a living, breathing masterpiece of maleness. Alissa sucked in a deep breath then wished she hadn't. He smelt like sun shining on lemon groves, like the sea's salt spray, like hot sexy man.

She broke away, needing distance. 'So we behave impeccably and live separate lives?'

'Precisely. We'll need to be seen together sometimes. At civic receptions, that sort of thing. But that won't be often. You'll have your own rooms.'

Tendrils of relief spread and flowered inside her. 'Perfect. Why don't you show me now?'

'Your suite isn't ready. Tomorrow will be time enough.' For the first time his words were rushed, as if he was uncomfortable.

What was he hiding? Something about her room? That wasn't likely. Or perhaps about the old lady, Caterina, who'd welcomed her so warmly and made up the marriage bed?

'You didn't tell her the truth, did you? Signora Bruzzone. You let her believe this marriage is real!'

Again he shrugged, but this time the movement was stiff, as if she'd hit a sore spot. 'It's only for one night. Tomorrow she'll be gone.'

Alissa stared, sensing his tension. Her mind whirled. Caterina thought they'd married for love. Had he withheld the truth because he didn't want to disappoint her? Because he cared for her good opinion? The knowledge stunned Alissa. Had Dario lied, sharing a room with a woman he distrusted, for Caterina's sake?

That made him suddenly…human. Flesh, blood and feelings. Warm, compassionate feelings, caring for someone else. This the man who'd chastised her for dressing as a bride so as not to disappoint her sister!

She stood still, stunned to realise his aloof exterior perhaps hid a chink of finer feeling. Who'd have guessed?

But why was he so sensitive of Caterina's good opinion? She was his ex-housekeeper, not his mother.

Suddenly Alissa realised the significance of that scene when they'd arrived. Not one member of Dario's family had been present. She frowned.

Had he fallen out with them all? It was odd, when he talked so much about family honour. Maybe his sense of honour was of the destructive variety, like her grandfather's.

'What are you doing?' she asked as he crossed to a set of doors on the other side of the room.

'Getting dressed.' He disappeared into a huge dressing room. 'You can spend the rest of the night here.'

When he emerged, he was dressed all in black. It suited him, far too much.

'I'll see you at breakfast. I have work to do.' He didn't even glance her way as he strode from the room.

Instantly Alissa felt that tiny spark of warmth vanish. She fooled herself if she believed he was motivated by anything other than self-interest.

Was he already breaking his promise to behave discreetly? Did his 'urgent work' go by the name of Maria?

Alissa grimaced as anger and nausea swamped her.

The suspicion that he'd gone to meet his lover in the night should be nothing to her. She should welcome his departure. So why did she feel sick at the thought of Dario spending the rest of the night in another woman's arms?

CHAPTER SIX

THE SOUND OF feminine laughter on the sea breeze curled insidiously into Dario's consciousness. Evocative, familiar laughter. The sound of his wife enjoying herself.

Not that she laughed around him. Then she was stiff and careful, as distrustful as he of the undercurrent of desire that rippled, strong as the tide, between them.

His brows drew together. He had to concentrate on this contract. He jabbed a finger at a clause then slashed it out and scribbled his initials in the margin.

A murmur of voices from the garden replaced the laughter and the next clause blurred.

Who was it this time? In just a week his bride had charmed all the household staff. She'd even broken through the grim professional barrier of the security staff rostered to accompany her when she left the premises.

At the crackle of paper he looked down and smoothed the contract that had crumpled in his fist. It was impossible to work.

Grimly he faced the unpalatable truth: Alissa intruded into his thoughts too often. Each day he received a report on her activities. Even that, short and factual, tugged his mind away from important business.

She swam, explored the estate, visited quaint towns and took scenic boat trips. She had cooking lessons with his chef, shopped for souvenirs and spent evenings in her room. He didn't know whether to be pleased or annoyed that she'd done exactly as he'd demanded.

She'd behaved with perfect propriety. If you could call it propriety to charm every male she met!

When he worked at home, like today, her presence was everywhere. From the daisies in the hall where once there'd been formal floral arrangements, to the sound of her laughter, breathless and enticing, drifting inside.

He'd waited for her to step out of line, show her true colours. But she'd deprived him of that satisfaction.

He barely saw her, rarely spoke to her. Yet she haunted him. He dreamed of her as he tossed in his empty bed. He woke with the taste of her in his mouth, imagining her exotic lily scent on his sheets. Despite his attempts to ignore her, this attraction gnawed at him incessantly.

Dario looked at his white-knuckled fists, felt the heavy throb of frustration low in his body and wondered how he could go another twenty-five weeks without decent sleep. He wouldn't seek sexual relief elsewhere. Even though this marriage was just a convenient merger, he had more self-respect than that. And he couldn't sleep with his wife. Giving in to this desire would hand her power on a platter.

Which left him furious and frustrated. He never gave in to weakness, no matter what the provocation.

A gurgle of laughter interrupted his thoughts.

Dario shoved his chair back from the desk.

Alissa's smile faded as a frisson of awareness crept up her spine. It didn't take Giorgio's wide-eyed look or the sound of footsteps on the path behind her to let her know Dario was approaching.

That telltale tingle was enough. It never failed.

Time and again she'd felt that delicious shiver and found him watching. Usually he turned and left without a word and each time her gaze followed hungrily. She couldn't help it.

There was something about Dario. Something she'd never experienced with any man. Something dark and strong and irresistible. She fought it with her mind but her body hadn't got the message. He was dangerous. Yet something stirred inside whenever he came near.

Even concern for Donna couldn't prevent Alissa's alarming reaction, especially since her worries had been allayed a little by regular phone calls and by knowing she'd get the money her sister needed.

With a smile for Giorgio she turned down the path to the sea. She'd reached the shade cast by a stand of pines when Dario's voice stopped her.

'Running away, Alissa?'

She froze, her hand on the railing at the top of the steps to the beach. He was close, his voice soft in her ears. Her body tensed in awful anticipation. She hated that he could do this to her. She avoided him when she could but her reaction to him had only intensified, like a blade honed keen to razor-sharpness.

'Why should I run? I haven't done anything wrong.'

She turned, grateful for the railing as her knees threatened to buckle. She'd grown accustomed to him in tailored suits that emphasised his suave leanness and complemented the strong contours of his face. But in jeans that hugged long, powerful thighs and a white shirt with the sleeves rolled to reveal sinewy, golden forearms, he was devastating.

Despair threatened. The craving grew stronger each time she saw him. She should hate him, and yet…

'Why indeed?' He frowned as he paced closer. 'Feeling guilty at being caught flirting with my gardener?'

'Flirting?' Alissa's eyes widened. 'All we did was chat! He was telling me about his daughters.'

She liked Dario's staff. She enjoyed their hospitality in introducing a newcomer to Sicily. What surprised her was their enthusiasm for Dario. Their loyalty and admiration went beyond lip-service. They genuinely liked and respected him. Just as Caterina Bruzzone's affection had been real. There'd been tears of happiness in the old lady's eyes as she wished them well when she left for her home on the mainland the day after Alissa's arrival.

The locals Alissa met were pleased when they discovered she was from the Parisi estate. Her husband was respected. People spoke of his generosity, his support for charities and his schemes to rejuvenate the region.

It was as if there were two different men—the chilling manipulator who'd turned her life upside down and the generous man, admired by all. The dichotomy only increased her wariness and confusion.

Did something in her bring out the worst in him? Whenever he drew near every instinct warned of peril. Yet even that couldn't douse the thrill she felt deep within when they were together.

'If you say so. I'm sure you found the subject fascinating.' Dario's eyes were dark as storm clouds as they raked her. She wished she'd worn something other than a short denim skirt and singlet top. Something more substantial so she couldn't feel his gaze on her. Armour perhaps. She clung to the railing, tilting her head to meet his stare, ignoring the way her nipples tightened. Hoping he hadn't noticed.

He stepped near and automatically she paced back, only to find her foot dangling in mid-air.

'Careful!' Strong hands encircled her arms and pulled her close. A shaft of heat scorched her as she inhaled the unique scent that was Dario. A second later he moved away to stand looking out to sea, as if the sight of her pained him. As if touching her contaminated him. Her heart squeezed in indignation and distress.

'You don't want to fall and break your leg. That would impair your activities.' His tone was sardonic.

'Activities?' Was he still worried she yearned for a wild

nightlife with good-looking guys and designer drugs? Stupid how the idea hurt.

'Your swimming and sightseeing.'

'I see.' She stared at his grim profile. So her 'chauffeurs' had reported her movements. She'd suspected it but the confirmation disappointed her. He didn't trust her an inch. She felt hemmed in, restrictions binding her tight. She was in limbo, unable to get on with her life, forced to live here on sufferance. Try as she might she couldn't pretend this was a holiday.

'What do you want, Dario?' Steadfastly she ignored the tiny thrill that came from saying his name.

'Must I want something?' He slanted a look her way. The banked heat in his gaze stoked unwilling need deep inside her.

'Yes. You spend most of your time avoiding me like the plague.'

'Does that disappoint you, Alissa?' The devil was in his eyes and in that slow, provocative curl of his sensuous lips. She shivered, imagining she saw an answering flare of sexual interest in his expression. 'Would you rather I danced attendance on you?'

'I couldn't think of anything worse.' She crossed her arms tight over her chest, telling herself it was only half a lie. The thought of being with him filled her with excitement as well as trepidation. That worried her sick. If only she could detest him as thoroughly as she ought.

'As it happens I do have a reason for interrupting your morning—to tell you we're invited to a business reception. I assume you have something formal to wear.' His gaze skated down her bare legs as if the sight annoyed him.

'Do I have to go?' Just ten minutes in his company unnerved her. How would she survive an evening? The air zapped and crackled with the energy pulsing between them. Yet, she hated to admit it, she'd never felt more alive than when she sparred with him. It was scary.

'I told you we'd need to be seen together. If we don't go the curiosity of the Press will mean no more pleasant outings for you. We give them some pictures and we satisfy local interest. It will only take a few hours.' His eyes narrowed as if he read her turmoil. 'Don't worry, I'll look after you.'

Alissa couldn't think of anything calculated to disturb her more.

'What sort of clothes?' she said quickly. 'I haven't got a cocktail dress.' Her wardrobe wasn't extensive.

His brows climbed. 'I'll have one of my staff drive you to a suitable boutique. Aim for classy rather than provocative if you can.' Again his gaze dipped disapprovingly.

'Since you asked so nicely, I'll try.' Saccharine dripped from her tongue. She had a good mind to buy something outrageous to provoke him. But the thought of his gaze on exposed flesh deterred her.

'You do that.' He stared across the bay, obviously dismissing her. She'd turned to leave when his deep voice stopped her.

'You haven't been out to inspect the *castello* you'll inherit. Why?'

She swung round, her gaze following his to the grim, squarish castle of sand-coloured stone climbing up from the rocky headland at the end of the beach. It was forbidding with its turrets and crenellated walls.

'*That's* the *castello*?' It hadn't occurred to her. She'd expected something less mediaeval. Not a real castle. That explained Dario's autocratic attitude. If the place had been in Parisi hands for generations his family was local aristocracy. He'd be used to deference and immediate compliance with his wishes. No wonder she made him scowl when she refused to acquiesce to his every whim.

'That's the Castello Parisi. Home of my family.' His voice was rich with possessiveness and pride. Alissa watched his face set in determined lines.

But what fascinated her was the glimpse of raw emotion in his expression. His eyes held a yearning look she'd never

noticed before. It surprised her. It made him appear almost…
vulnerable.

Dario really had a passion for the place. This was deeply
personal to him. It wasn't just about acquiring real estate. What
did the *castello* mean to him?

From the look on Dario's face his determination was about
far more than besting the Manganos. She couldn't imagine
any property being so important she'd sell herself in marriage
to acquire it.

Nothing was that important to her. Nothing except her family.

Alissa flicked a look at the modern masterpiece that was
his current home. Despite its unusual style it was homey and
comfortable by comparison.

'You don't mind living so close? Overlooking what your
family once owned?'

'Mind?' He gave the villa a cursory glance. 'I built here so
I could see my birthright every day till I possessed it.' There
was a chilling hint of obsession in his voice.

'I suppose you spent time there as a child.' He'd have happy
memories of it. Though the *castello* had belonged to her grandfather he'd left it empty—the perfect place for an adventur-
ous boy to explore. The idea lessened the unnerving impact
of Dario's absorbed stare.

Dario shook his head. 'I've never set foot inside, nor will
I till it's mine.'

'But surely you lived somewhere close and—'

He swung round and his eyes, gleaming grey like the bar-
rel of a gun, pinioned her. 'Didn't your grandfather tell you?'
He paused as if waiting for her to respond. The intensity of his
stare grazed her skin.

'No, I can see he didn't.' His brow puckered as he met her
confused gaze. 'Strange. I thought he'd revel in the story.' Dario
shrugged, turning towards the sea and the distant mainland.

His broad shoulders hunched as if against a chill wind only he could feel.

Something about his stance made Alissa want to reach out to him, despite the danger he embodied. He looked so solitary. Like a man in pain. Even his skin seemed taut, stretched across the angles of his face.

'I didn't grow up here.' He hefted a deep breath then another. His broad chest rose and fell but the tension in his corded muscles didn't slacken. She felt its echo in her own rigid limbs. 'I grew up over there, on the mainland.'

'Your family left Sicily?' That had never occurred to her. She knew Sicilians lived close to their roots, with generations staying in the same village. Her grandfather had only left because his nefarious practices made it too hot for him to stay. 'They haven't returned with you?'

'My family?' Dario's mouth twisted in a grimace that tugged at something inside her. 'I have no family. Not any more.' He flung out an arm towards the brooding castle. '*That* is all I have left of my family.'

Alissa opened her mouth to question him, but didn't get the chance as he swung round to face her. His eyes flashed with possessive fire.

'The *castello* belongs to me by birth, by right, by tradition.' His eyes narrowed and her pulse thundered as his hot gaze raked her. 'Now it's mine by marriage too.'

For a moment grey eyes meshed with blue, tension spiked between them like an arc of high-voltage energy. The air sizzled and her heart pounded.

Was he claiming the *castello* or her as well?

With a raw gasp Alissa spun round and stumbled up the path, uncaring what he thought of her sudden flight. He frightened her. He had the driven look of a man who didn't mind what rules he broke as long as he won. The sort of man she'd learned to fear and despise.

Yet there was something else in his eyes, some strong emotion that squeezed her chest tight just at the tiny glimpse of his passion. Was it pain? Grief? Regret?

She shook her head. Why go to such lengths to acquire a place he'd never set foot in? This wasn't about mere avarice, she understood that much at least. This was about something more fundamental.

What had he meant, that the *castello* was all he had of his family? Surely he exaggerated. She couldn't imagine a Sicilian with no family. More, she felt a dull ache of distress at the idea of anyone deprived of family. Her grandfather had been appalling but her sister meant everything to her.

Alissa catapulted to a stop just inside the house, her mind reeling. Trepidation shivered through her as she remembered Dario's steamy, proprietorial look. The look that curled her toes and stopped her breath.

She had an unnerving premonition her peaceful stay, safe from his attention, was going to end in calamity.

Alissa scooped the plastic bucket through wet sand and plonked it on the lopsided sandcastle. Giorgio's little girls, Anna and Maria, crowed with delight when she lifted the bucket, leaving a perfect round turret. The toddlers clambered close, their hands full of shiny pebbles and shells, ready to decorate it.

'Careful!' Alissa grabbed one of the twins as she wobbled and lost her footing. 'There you are, sweetheart.' She sat Anna before her so she could reach the tower.

Their chortles made her smile, especially when Maria turned and draped strands of seaweed over Alissa's hair.

'A mermaid, am I?'

'With that hair there's no doubt about it.' The deep voice rumbled out of nowhere, dragging her round to face the sea. Her breath slid out and for a moment she forgot to breathe.

'Dar-yo, Dar-yo.' The twins erupted into movement, wriggling to their feet with an urgency that spelled ruin for their sandcastle.

His stride was fluid. She watched the bunch and release of muscles in his chest, abdomen and long legs as he cleared the waves. He wore low-slung swim shorts that revealed the perfect interplay of sinew and muscle. Each tiny movement mesmerised her, as if she'd never seen a man before.

She'd never seen one like Dario.

From his water-slick coal-black hair to the perfection of his body and the grin he directed at the girls hurtling towards him, he was breathtaking. The glint of water on his flesh gilded him in the early-morning light. He looked like a sea god, powerful and potent. Alissa's insides contracted in shivery delight just watching him.

Then he was on his knees, arms outstretched to the girls. 'You'll get wet,' he warned, but they catapulted into his arms, babbling in excitement.

Alissa sat back on her heels, stunned, as she absorbed the sight of Dario, who'd manipulated her so remorselessly, laughing with the children. Obviously they knew him well. He understood their lisping baby talk far better than she.

She blinked, remembering his ice-cold enmity in Melbourne, the contemptuous tone as he'd spoken of her family. She'd never have believed him capable of such unfettered joy or such patience as she saw now as the girls draped him with seaweed and shells.

'You must be a merman too,' she whispered, unthinking.

Instantly dark grey eyes met hers and heat throbbed between them, blocking out the sound of the girls' chatter. The world around her eclipsed into a void as the connection between them intensified. He hadn't done anything but look at her, yet his potent attraction tugged at her.

Abruptly Alissa turned away and her tension eased a fraction. She stumbled to her feet, brushing sand away.

'You're not going swimming, are you? There are strong currents.' His voice, with its husky edge, made her pause, but she didn't meet his eyes.

'No. I've just learned to wear a swimsuit when I'm here with the girls. I end up getting wet and sandy.'

Yet it wasn't the fine grit that bothered her now, it was the sensation of his eyes roving over her body in her violet Lycra one-piece. The swimsuit covered everything that ought to be covered but it fitted like a second skin. Flames licked her body as his intense gaze scorched her.

She shook her hair so it fell across her breasts then grabbed her sarong and tied it high, letting the fabric drape round her. Still he watched. That should bother her. But what she felt as she met his stare was more like triumph, like excitement.

What was happening to her?

He knew. The glitter in his eyes, the tight, knowing curve of his lips told her he understood completely.

But it couldn't be. It was impossible. She couldn't be susceptible to a man who embodied everything she most hated. He was power-hungry, ruthless, selfish.

Except now, with the girls, his arms curved protectively around them, his head bent to their chatter, he seemed like a different man altogether. A man of gentle, teasing humour and tenderness. A man who, despite his gruelling work schedule and his mega-millions, still had time to know and play with his gardener's young children. The sort who might even one day tempt her to shed her wariness and hurt and trust a man.

Dario was a puzzle. Whenever she thought she knew him he revealed a new facet that intrigued her.

'Come,' he said to the girls, getting to his feet and taking their hands, 'Alissa is waiting.'

She couldn't prevent the smile tugging her lips as she watched him: six feet plus of sheer masculine power, gently leading the chubby twins. There was seaweed in his hair and a large shell on the wide plane of one straight shoulder. A suspicious melting sensation squeezed her chest. Hurriedly she looked away, gathering buckets and spades.

'It's time we went. Breakfast will be ready.'

'You breakfast with Giorgio and his wife?'

'Do you object?' They lived on his estate, where his word was no doubt law. She glanced at the cottage up the hill. The friendship she'd found here meant a lot since she was cut off from her sister and home. It was a delight to spend time with Giorgio's family now and then and it felt good to help out, giving them a break from the girls' restless energy since they had a newborn to care for.

'If they wish to invite you into their home, that is a matter for them.'

Instantly defensive, Alissa thought she detected disapproval in his voice. Her spine stiffened and her chin lifted. For a few moments she'd forgotten his low opinion of her. Now that knowledge stabbed her through the middle.

'Don't let us hold you up.' She gestured in the direction of his villa. 'You've probably got early-morning meetings. I'll see the girls home.'

He stood motionless so long she thought he'd ignore her dismissal. Finally he hunkered down beside the girls and said something in the local dialect that made them burst into giggles.

'Enjoy your breakfast, Alissa.' His husky, deep voice swirled around her, making her skin prickle with unwanted awareness. Then he turned and walked away along the beach, his stride easy and assured, owner of all he surveyed. Despite her best intentions she followed every step, avidly drinking in the superb picture he made.

Grimly she warned herself to be sensible.

So he liked children.

So he was gorgeous.

So his smile made her heart flip over.

He'd never smile like that at her. Dario and she were destined to be enemies.

Pity they were also man and wife.

CHAPTER SEVEN

DARIO WRENCHED THE tie from his throat and tossed it onto a chair. His cufflinks followed, then his shirt as he strode onto his private balcony. The sultry air was so still he could taste the impending storm on his tongue.

But it wasn't the weather that got under his skin. He'd been unable to concentrate all day and had come home early. All because of Alissa. He'd taken in barely one word in ten at his meetings. His mind had been fixed on the woman who kept him awake night after night. His wife.

He couldn't shake the images of her on the beach today. Skin lustrous as pearls. Hair seductive fire, spilling round her. Body all feminine curves, lusciously rounded at hips and breasts yet such a tiny waist.

More, he grappled with the shock of seeing her happy and carefree with Anna and Maria. He'd pegged her as a woman who'd have no time for children. Yet she'd been careful of them, joining their fun while keeping a watchful eye on them. Her pleasure had been genuine and the sight of her had stopped him in his tracks as he emerged from his swim.

His body had responded predictably to the picture she made: a sexy, gorgeous, half-naked woman in the role of nurturer. Grimly he'd realised nothing could appeal more to a man's most basic instinct: to mate.

Meanwhile he struggled to adjust his assessment of her. This woman was more complex than he'd first thought. Dangerously complex. Something about her made him yearn for things he couldn't quite grasp. Yearn for things other than the carefully orchestrated future he'd set as his goal a lifetime ago to fill the yawning void in his life.

He tunnelled a hand through his hair, noting the encroaching storm clouds. A flash of white out to sea snagged his attention. Someone was out on a sea kayak. Someone in a white shirt with dark red hair. Too far out, with this storm coming in so fast. The bay grew dangerous when the wind was up, a lethal trap for the unwary.

Seconds later Dario was racing to the beach.

Alissa clung to the kayak, straining to drag herself up. But the strength had seeped from her arms. They were like jelly. She'd ventured too far out, only realising it was time to turn around when the rumble of thunder alerted her to changing weather. She'd raced back as fast as she could, but she'd grown exhausted as she struggled against unfamiliar currents and the suddenly massive sea.

A freak wave had toppled her over. Now all she could do was hang on. Fear swamped her but she refused to give in to it, despite the lashing spray that bit her skin and the surge that tossed her like flotsam. So long as she held on she had a chance. But her numb fingers were loosening.

A movement made her yelp as something slid against her. Were there sharks? Panic swelled and she swallowed water, half submerged beneath the waves.

Something hard encircled her arm, biting into her frozen flesh. It pulled and she came up for air, spluttering and gasping. Her heart was ready to burst and her lungs worked like bellows to draw in oxygen.

Swearing. She heard swearing. In Italian. Her befuddled brain barely took that in before she was grabbed beneath the arms and hauled from the sea.

'Hang on tight,' a barely audible voice instructed over the roar of the sea.

Dario. She recognised that husky-edged growl, even through the sound of the storm. She felt warmth beneath her and realised she was lying across his legs. He'd climbed onto the kayak and dragged her up too.

Relief swelled as she clutched his solid body. She'd be safe now. She couldn't imagine anything defeating him. If any man could battle the elements and win it was Dario. His determination, his sheer strength, would see them through. Besides, imagine his temper if she drowned before they inherited his precious *castello*!

It was the cessation of noise that roused her. The storm's full-throated roar died to a muffled rumble. The needles of rain on her skin stopped abruptly. Alissa's eyes fluttered open to an awareness of being held against something hot and solid. She nuzzled her head against her makeshift pillow and heard the steady thud of a heartbeat.

Dario! For a moment she allowed herself the luxury of sinking against him. Any longer would be dangerous.

'You can put me down.' Her voice cracked.

'Why, so you can run off and do something equally stupid?' he growled. His grip tightened. She looked up to see his chin jutting above her like the prow of a warship.

'I'm sorry. I didn't realise how fast the storm was coming in.' Remembered fear choked her throat and she bit her unsteady lip as he lowered her onto a fabric-covered surface. She blinked and looked around the gloomy interior. They were in the boat shed, jet skis and other craft stored around them. Alissa looked down to discover he'd sat her on a canvas day bed.

'Here.' Thick towelling draped her shoulders and strong hands rubbed her back, her hair, her arms. Slowly she felt the blood circulate, tingling through her body.

'I'm sorry,' she mumbled again. 'I didn't mean to put you in danger.'

'Me!' The towel was stripped away to reveal him full square before her, feet planted wide, like a warrior ready for battle. This warrior wore nothing but saturated boxer shorts and a gold watch. His chest heaved—with emotion, she suspected, rather than exertion. His glare could cut solid rock. Right now it sliced into her.

Alissa tugged the massive towel round her shoulders, her movements weak and uncoordinated after her desperate exertions. She tried not to feel intimidated by the blast of anger and undiluted testosterone he projected.

'You're worried about *me*?' His voice rose incredulously. 'Didn't I say the bay had dangerous currents? Didn't you see the storm approaching?'

She shook her head, feeling every kind of fool for putting herself in a situation where she needed rescuing. She'd been so distracted by thoughts of Dario, trying to make sense of the complex man and his motivations, she'd forgotten basic safety precautions like checking her distance from the shore.

'I apologise.'

'You apologise!' His voice was like thunder, welling around them. 'You could have been killed.' His hands were bulging fists, the muscles bunching ominously in his arms. 'Do you have any notion how close you came to drowning?'

Alissa didn't feel safe any more. The fury in his tone sparked recognition. A lifetime's lessons in violence stiffened her sinews. She scented the anger on his skin and instinctively she slid along the day bed, out of his reach. She swung her legs to the floor and forced herself to stand. She swayed but held herself upright with one hand clutching the metal bed frame.

'What are you doing, woman?' His forehead pleated, dark brows jamming together. 'Sit down before you fall!'

Dumbly she shook her head, her eyes never leaving his.

She didn't have the strength to run. All she could do was try to anticipate his first move.

He strode forward and fear clawed up through her chest. But instead of raising his hand he grabbed her and dragged her hard against his chest. His heart slammed a rough tattoo against hers as he lifted her off her feet.

'You have to be the most obstinate, difficult woman—'

The accusation ended as he bent his head and took her mouth in a plundering, voracious kiss that drew her into a storm of unrepentant desire. He swallowed her instinctive protest, clasping her close to his slippery body.

Shock held her immobile. In that instant before she could gather her wits he vanquished her incipient protest as his mouth softened. Now his lips and tongue caressed, invited, tempted. One hand slid down to cup her bottom and draw her close to the hard urgency of his body.

Excitement shivered through her. Sweet desire. Need. Her exhaustion was forgotten as she drank in his kisses, returning them with an untutored fervour that would have astonished her if she'd been capable of thought.

Nothing was real but this. His body straining urgently against hers. His mouth an instrument of pleasure. She cupped his jaw in her hands and felt a thrill of delight as this powerful man shuddered against her.

What was he doing? From somewhere a shard of reason pierced his non-functioning brain.

Alissa suffered from shock and exposure. She'd almost lost her life in the sea. The damnable treacherous sea that had been his enemy for so long. It had stolen everything that mattered to him. Everyone.

His arms tightened instinctively around her.

Was it any wonder he shunned love in favour of the future he planned, with a carefully considered marriage to an appropriate woman? No more emotional relationships for him. No love. Not when soul-destroying loss was the cost. Not when happiness was so easily wrenched away by greedy waves.

The sight of Alissa battling to stay afloat had brought back too many tragic memories. His heart squeezed as he realised he'd almost lost her too.

Finally he found the strength to lift his head, dragging raw breaths into his labouring lungs.

Dazed azuré eyes stared up at him. Her lips were ruby-red and plump from his kisses. Hectic colour streaked her cheekbones, testament to the sudden passion between them.

What sort of man was he, letting emotions drive him to such lengths? His fury resulted from their near-death experience. Was that the cause of this almost unstoppable desire too? And the fear that made his heart clatter against his ribs?

He felt…he felt…too much.

Shame washed through him. She was traumatised. He had no right to treat her like this.

More, now that he knew her a little better he began to doubt his first assessment of her. What he'd discovered he admired. His instinct was to protect her.

He swung her up in his arms, noticing with grim pleasure the way her hands automatically rose to link at the back of his neck.

'Come on, Alissa. It's time a doctor checked you out.'

Five days later Alissa stood beside her husband at a reception in a magnificent old palazzo and tried to understand the change between them. There'd been no mention of that passionate kiss, no reference to the rescue, yet since that day Dario's attitude had altered. He didn't avoid her as much. Nor had there been more barbed remarks. They lived a wary truce.

Sometimes she looked into his eyes and glimpsed a flash of the incandescent fire that had almost consumed her that day in the boathouse. The fire that, to her shame, she couldn't help but miss.

Whatever Dario felt, he kept it to himself.

So much about the man she'd married was inexplicable, from his obsession with regaining the old estate to his fiery passion and his sudden withdrawal. She longed to ask about his family, hoping he'd exaggerated about having none. But she hadn't found the nerve to query him. Then there was the esteem in which he was held locally, his comfortable relationship with Anna and Maria—more like a kind uncle than a world-weary tycoon.

He'd flummoxed her the day of her rescue. She'd seen his simmering fury and smelt his anger with the preternatural awareness of an animal hunted by a predator. She knew the signs of untrammelled anger since she'd lived most of her life with its violent consequences. But, despite his wrath, he hadn't taken out his temper on her. Instead he'd given her the sweetest, most desperate kiss she'd ever known. One that left her wanting more.

Now tonight, the goalposts had shifted again.

Dario went out of his way to touch her, keeping her close as they circulated through the throng of dignitaries. His arm at her waist was possessive. The feather-light weight of his breath on her hair and cheek was a stealthy caress. His husky voice was intimate, binding her to him with invisible ties.

The intimacy was for public show. Yet that didn't prevent the warmth spreading and sizzling under her skin.

Her face ached from plastering on a smile. Her body was stiff from trying to maintain a distance between them. It was a losing battle. That casual drape of his arm tightened whenever she prised herself away a fraction.

She'd known he had a way with women and the looks that followed him round the room proved it. Yet it wasn't the young and lovely who received the full blast of his attentive smiles. The smiling, elegant pair they'd just left were in their seventies at least.

Dario was no longer the man she knew and distrusted. That unnerved her.

'You said we had to be seen together,' she whispered, 'not that we'd be like conjoined twins the whole evening.'

'Don't worry, Alissa. No one will mistake us for siblings.' His long fingers stroked the dark velvet at her waist and she sucked in a shocked breath. Such a tiny movement yet waves of pleasure radiated from his touch.

'Now we've been seen and congratulated, perhaps we can leave?' She stood rigid, locking her knees against the melting sensation that made her legs wobble as his hand idly circled.

His arm dropped. Instantly she felt bereft.

'No. I still have people to see.' His expression was suddenly grim. Had she annoyed him? 'If you would prefer not to accompany me...'

'Yes.' She sounded far too eager. 'I'd prefer.'

With a nod and a narrowing glance he turned and headed through the crowd. Alissa released her breath on a sigh. When she was with Dario she felt so unsettled. Even now she couldn't tear her eyes from him. Yet it wasn't distrust that kept her attention locked on him.

It was something more primal. More personal.

Her pulse revved as he turned and smiled at someone. His spare, sculpted good looks, his dark colouring might have been the inspiration for whoever invented the tuxedo. Surely no man had ever looked more elegant, more handsome, more dangerously powerful in such formal attire.

'Your husband is very handsome, Signora Parisi.'

Alissa blinked and looked up into the face of a gorgeous, elegant woman. Golden hair, stunning face. Eyes that were sharply assessing.

'Thank you, Signorina...?'

'Cipriani. Bianca Cipriani.' She paused. 'Your husband has a reputation for being ruthless. Many women would think twice before marrying such a man.'

Alissa caught her breath. This woman was trouble, that was obvious. But how to escape her without making a scene?

'All successful entrepreneurs are single-minded.'

'But Dario is in a class alone when it comes to getting his own way, no matter the cost.'

'What is it you want?' Better to get this over quickly. She didn't want a scene with a jealous ex-lover.

'Just to give a friendly warning.' The blonde's eyes narrowed. 'If you're wise you won't trust him with anything you value, like your heart or your life. He cares for nothing but his precious Parisi estate.'

'Is that what happened to you?' Despite her better judgement Alissa couldn't quash the need to know.

'Me?' Bianca laughed. 'Hardly. *That's* the sort of woman your husband has always preferred.' With a leaden sensation in her stomach Alissa followed her gesture.

There was Dario, in intimate conversation with a gorgeous brunette. The woman looked like a model: tall, slim, with an air of fashionable languor and the serene face of a madonna. In her gown of silver gauze she was the perfect foil for Dario's dark suit and lean good looks. He stood close, his body language proclaiming his interest.

Bile rose in Alissa's throat. She pressed a palm to her roiling stomach. The sight of Dario, fascinated by the dark-haired beauty, made her nauseous. Her breath shallowed, her hands grew clammy.

These last weeks he'd sneaked under her defences, shattered her preconceived notions and made her doubt what she knew of him. More, he'd given her a taste of passion and foolishly she craved more. She was jealous of the brunette who so obviously intrigued him.

'Are you all right?' Bianca's words dragged her from her horrified stupor. 'You're very pale.'

'I'm OK.' Alissa turned her back on the perfect couple. She

crushed stupid regret that she'd never be tall and glamorous, the sort of woman Dario found attractive.

She should thank her lucky stars! An intimate relationship with him would be disastrous.

'Why do you hate him?'

The other woman straightened. 'He killed my father.'

'He *what*?' She searched Bianca's face but she looked utterly genuine. A chill slid through Alissa.

'My father owned a company that once belonged to the Parisis. Dario was obsessed with acquiring it and everything else in the old Parisi estate.' Her gaze flickered to Alissa. 'When my father refused his offers Dario used other means to acquire it.'

'What do you mean?' The hairs stood up on the back of Alissa's neck.

Bianca shrugged. 'Your husband is powerful. Suddenly there were problems on site, loan extensions cancelled. Pressure mounted from all sides. What was once a thriving business was reassessed at a fraction of its value. My father had to sell but he got a pittance for it. He felt he'd failed us. That's when he took his life.'

Dario's skin prickled, senses alert as he felt her eyes on him. After weeks of repressed desire he recognised this heightened awareness instantly.

Casually he turned. Their gazes connected and his heart accelerated. He took in her creamy skin, the swell of her breasts beneath the square neck of her black velvet dress. She wore no jewellery, but with her sapphire eyes and fiery hair she needed no adornment. Her dress clung to her curves but was puritanical in its simplicity. Perversely it made him more eager to remove it. Her legs in sheer stockings and high heels were incredibly sexy.

It took a moment to notice the woman beside her. Bianca Cipriani. Was she dripping poison into Alissa's ears? Dario was surprised to find he wished the two women hadn't met. As if he cared for his wife's good opinion.

'Dario, are you listening?' His companion pouted. Automatically he apologised, realising he'd barely listened to her chatter. Dario frowned. For months he'd considered her a contender for the position of permanent wife after Alissa left. She was sophisticated yet eager to accord with his wishes. She had breeding, beauty, brains. She wanted children. She was Sicilian. She was perfect for the role.

And yet… His gaze strayed to Alissa, demurely dressed to kill. His temperature rose and his groin tightened. It annoyed him to find he was more interested in his unwanted wife. He excused himself and went to fetch her.

She stood alone now. Her eyes were a blaze of colour, lips a plump, perfect invitation, at odds with her rigid posture. Tension stiffened his every muscle and sinew as he approached. Anticipation weighted his limbs, stirred his pulse to a heavy, needy throb.

Tonight. He'd deal with this tonight, he decided as their eyes locked and fire scorched his blood. He'd spent weeks pretending abstinence could master this unwanted desire. The time for denial had passed.

He'd do whatever it took to get her out of his system for good.

CHAPTER EIGHT

'Signora Parisi. There was a long-distance call for you. A message to ring your sister.'

Instantly the low-level anxiety Alissa had lived with for so long rocketed to the surface, morphing into fear. Donna had been fine last night, or so she'd said. Had something changed?

'Thank you.' She nodded to the housekeeper and hurried towards the stairs.

'Alissa.' Dario's voice, low and resonant, made her pause. Even through her worry the sound of his husky, deep tone could stop her in her tracks.

'Yes?' She turned but didn't meet his eyes. She didn't need that challenge.

'We need to talk. When you've made your call I'll be in my study, waiting.'

Startled, she looked straight at him but couldn't read his impassive expression. He had the face of a poker player. Of a man who wheeled and dealed in multi-million-dollar enterprises. And yet…there was something about the way he held himself, like a predator waiting to pounce…

A tremor rippled through her. No! She was being fanciful. Worry over Donna made her imagine things.

'All right.' She turned and headed for her room, praying with each step that bad news wasn't waiting.

Dario poured himself a single malt, and then, in a move unusual for him, another.

The potent alcohol did nothing to soothe his tension. He was wound too tight, his body burning up with a hunger so rampant he felt like a raw adolescent. Except this attraction was nothing like the spike of physical desire he'd experienced as a callow youth. This was more intense, more disturbing, an omnipresent awareness that hijacked his mind as well as torturing his body.

It was enough to make him question his judgement. He wanted to believe she was all she seemed, feisty yet sweet, innocent even. Yet he had proof enough of her wild ways, her reckless carnal pleasures. She'd tried to steal his birthright, refusing his generous offers while conniving to wed another. She'd acted as his enemy.

Frustration and anger hummed through him. These growing doubts weren't like him.

He'd had his fill of decadent socialites. Of shallowness and avarice. Yet his gut instinct urged him to believe in her. More, something about her tugged at emotions he'd almost forgotten. That made him vulnerable.

He burned at the thought of her sharing her favours with other men. He couldn't repress a surge of jealousy at the memory of her ex-lover, Jason Donnelly. Dario's yearning made a mockery of his pride and his standards.

He swallowed the last of his Scotch, barely noticing it burn his throat. He poured himself another, furious that with her alone his formidable control was nonexistent. Just the sound of her voice, a whisper of her scent on the air and his mind blanked. His hands shook as he poured the whisky. Savagely he swore. He *would* conquer this weakness.

A breath of air feathered the back of his neck as the study door opened. It couldn't be reaction to her presence. No woman had that sort of power over him.

He turned. She stood inside the closed door, silhouetted by lamplight that caressed each dip and swell of her hourglass figure. His throat tightened as need, instantaneous and all-consuming, devoured him.

God, how he wanted her!

He'd expected her to flaunt her abundant charms. Instead she'd tortured him in a dress that covered her arms, her shoulders, her thighs. It should have been demure. But, in a devious twist of feminine power, that hint of cleavage and the way the fabric wrapped itself round her like a lover's caress turned demure into sinfully sexy.

'Dario, we need to talk.' His jaw tightened. The sound of his name in that breathless voice made him hard.

'Precisely what I had in mind. Drink?'

'No, thank you.' She walked further into the room and he read determination blazing in her eyes. Her posture was rigidly perfect. His wife had something on her mind.

Something in her set face tripped his internal alarm system. Something not quite right. Instantly he was alert.

There was nothing warm about her expression. Dario felt his ardour cool as his mind clicked into gear. Part of him loathed the suspicion but it rose with devastating inevitability.

Would this be the moment she showed her true colours? When she tried to persuade him to alter their agreement? Would she again try milking him for the wealth she'd grown accustomed to and now missed? From the moment she'd signed the prenuptial agreement along with the notice of intention to marry, he'd wondered.

Something stirred deep in his belly. Disappointment?

'I want to renegotiate our arrangement.' Her look seemed direct, honest and just a hint wary.

The stupid, fragile hope that he'd been wrong died instantly, leaving a queer hollowness in its place.

'There's nothing to renegotiate. When we inherit I'll organise the divorce and your payment.'

She stepped closer and he got the full impact of that wide-eyed look. For all his cynicism he melted a little under her soulful gaze. That stirred his resentment. He didn't take kindly to being played. He'd long ago developed armour against the wiles of avaricious women.

'Something important has come up.' She drew a slow breath, a predictable feminine ploy but effective. His gaze slid down to her full breasts.

'Really?' He kept his tone noncommittal.

'Yes.' She paused, as if hesitant. 'I need money now. The money from the sale of the *castello*. So I thought…'

What? That he'd give it to her? He owed her nothing. To the contrary, she'd grown up with the fortune and opportunities that should have been his. His fingers wrapped tighter round the glass as the old wrath took hold. He'd almost forgotten it these past weeks as he'd let her lull him into half believing he'd got her wrong.

Had that touching scene on the beach with the girls been window-dressing? Part of an elaborate ploy to allay his suspicions? Women had gone to greater lengths before now to win his attention. Could he have been that gullible?

No one made a fool of Dario Parisi.

'We could sign an agreement, a contract. I'll agree to sell you my share of the estate when we inherit and in return you give me my share of its value now.'

Dario shouldn't be surprised, yet the sour tang of disappointment filled his mouth.

'That's not possible.' He downed his whisky. The blaze of heat rocketing down his throat couldn't rival the flare of anger in his belly. Anger at himself for ever thinking he'd been wrong about her. Fury with her for not being what he'd hoped.

'Of course it's possible.' She paced closer and her scent, like an invitation to paradise, filled his senses. 'Your lawyers could draw up such a document.'

'I've no doubt you're right. But what good would it be when there's no guarantee I'd ever own the estate?'

'I don't follow you.' She tilted her head, the picture of innocent confusion.

'It's simple, *moglie mia*. Once you have my money, what's to stop you leaving?' For a moment an image of Alissa, shackled to his bed, wearing nothing but a beckoning smile, distracted him. Heat twisted in his gut. It would be one way of keeping his wife close. Pity he was supposed to be an enlightened twenty-first-century man.

'You'd have our contract.'

'Much good that would do when you desert me. I can't claim the estate unless we live together for six months.'

She spread her hands, palm up. 'But that wouldn't change. Don't you see? I'd stay here. The only difference would be that I'd have my share a little early.'

'A little?' He tilted a derisory brow. 'More than a little. Besides, I'd have no guarantee you'd remain.'

'You'd have my word. And a contract.' She approached and his body stirred.

'Contracts can be broken. So can promises.' He put his glass down. He had to steel himself against the shudder of need that ripped through him as he looked down at her. Even now, when she tried to squeeze cash out of him, the hunger didn't abate. What would it take to exorcise this woman?

'But…this is important!'

'I've no doubt you think so—'

'It *is*. Really.' Her fingers touched his sleeve, then she jerked her hand away as if she too felt the jag of electricity that sparked from the point of contact.

He'd never known such awareness.

'It's not for me.' Her voice was urgent, her eyes pleading. She raised her clasped hands to her breasts and he felt a primitive surge of satisfaction at the picture she made. The beautiful woman poised as a suppliant.

He wondered how it would be to have her beg him, not for money, but for pleasure. For the release and ecstasy he could give her. Heat steamed off his skin as dangerous excitement scored his soul.

'It's for someone else.' She paused and he watched her hands clench tight against her breast. 'You don't know about my sister—'

'I do know. I made it my business to know.' He watched her eyes widen. 'Donna. Younger and with your colouring. Left school early. Recently married.'

Her eyes widened. Obviously she hadn't expected him to be so well acquainted with her circumstances, despite the background check he'd ordered.

'That's right.' She licked her lips with a delicate pink tongue and Dario almost groaned. Another blatant tactic, yet he wasn't immune.

She baited him, deliberately torturing him in the hope he'd weaken. Her tactics were so obvious they should be amusing. Except they worked. His libido roared into rampant life as he watched her.

'Well, it's for Donna. She needs money, a lot of it.'

His raised palm stopped her. He'd been angry before. Now fury hummed through him. She dared use her sister as an excuse for her greed? Only someone like him, who no longer had a family, could appreciate the depths she'd sunk to with this despicable lie.

She didn't appreciate what she had. She didn't deserve it.

Dario recalled the private investigator's report. Her precious sister had been found nightclubbing while under age, including the night of Alissa's drug bust. Now this woman had the temerity to paint herself in the role of caring older sibling! She hadn't been a decent role model when her teenage sister needed her. Any normal woman would have protected the girl, not led her astray.

'What's that to do with me?'

'You have money. Plenty of it. And Donna needs this cash

desperately.' Her wide eyes looked so innocent even now he felt a tremor of response. Damn her.

'I know all about her need for money,' he said slowly, remembering the rest of the investigator's report. The younger woman had married a cattle farmer in the middle of one of the worst recorded droughts. The bank held an enormous mortgage over their heads. But he knew there was no danger of foreclosure. The drought had broken while he was in Australia. The bank wouldn't call in debts now there was every sign of a bumper year to come.

No, Alissa was using this as an excuse.

'You do? You've known all this time?' Eyes dark as the sea met his.

He nodded. 'I've read a comprehensive dossier on you and your family, remember?'

She stared silently, her face curiously blank, as if from shock.

'Well, then.' Her voice trembled a fraction. She really was a talented actress. 'You understand why I need to get hold of this money as soon as possible.'

'Then by all means find a way to help her. But don't expect me to give you a handout.'

Alissa gaped at the man before her. So powerful, so arrogant, so unfeeling. How could he look her in the eye and refuse her request? How could anyone be so inhuman?

He'd known about Donna's need for cash all this time! She could barely believe it. Her mind reeled at the thought. Yet Dario's calm face revealed a horrible truth: he'd known and he hadn't cared. Any decent man in his position wouldn't wait to be asked, he'd offer to help straight away.

Something inside withered at this appalling revelation about the man she'd almost convinced herself she cared for. She'd thought he was different. Thought she'd somehow been wrong about him. What a pathetic fool she'd been, letting herself fall prey to his powerful allure. She should have learned her lesson about heartless men years ago.

'It's not a handout! It's only what I'm entitled to. What I'm due to inherit.'

'After we've lived as man and wife for six months.'

Alissa jammed her fists on her hips and glared at him, impotent fury igniting. 'You're something else, Dario Parisi. You're a callous, selfish bastard.' Pain tore at her, clogging her throat so the words emerged thickly.

She'd been a naïve innocent. Despite the harsh realities of life with her grandfather she had little experience of dealing with men and none of dealing with anyone like Dario. She'd let his surface charm, those glimpses of a warmer, caring man, lull her into believing she'd somehow been mistaken in her initial estimate of him.

Under the spell of his potent sexual allure she'd forgotten the one thing that counted above all else—his hatred of her family.

So what if he was pleasant and polite to the elderly people at tonight's reception? If his staff liked him? That he had a soft spot for children? Maria and Anna were his people, living on his estate.

Alissa was an outsider. Worse, she was a Mangano, member of a family he abhorred. She knew first-hand about the tight-knit bonds of Sicilian families and their feuds. How could she have forgotten when it was obviously part of what made Dario tick?

She caught her breath on a stifled sob. She'd been ready to believe the best of him too because, despite his fury the day he rescued her, he hadn't resorted to violence as an outlet for his anger. How pathetic could she get?

Her first assessment of him had been right. He was a callous manipulator, more interested in property and ownership than people. Only tonight he'd been accused of causing the death of a rival.

'How do you sleep at night?' she whispered, anguish choking her.

Glittering eyes stared at her from a face pared to stark lines. 'This really matters so much?'

'Of course it matters!' What sort of unnatural sister did he think her?

'You'd do whatever is necessary to help her?'

A tide of hope rose. He was human after all. He'd find a way to help them. He *had* to.

'Of course.'

His lips curled in a dangerous smile. It sent a discordant jangle of premonition through her. 'Then I have a solution to your sister's problem.'

Relief surged and Alissa realised her hands were clamped together so tightly they were numb. Carefully she unknotted her fingers and wiped her clammy palms on her skirt. Dario followed the movement and a *frisson* of unease shivered through her. His gaze was like a hot caress, as real as the touch of a hand.

'Thank you.'

'You haven't heard my solution.'

'As long as there *is* a solution.' Her voice shook.

'Oh, there is.' Her nape prickled at his tone, a soft, predatory growl. 'It occurs to me we're not fulfilling the terms of your grandfather's will.'

'What do you mean?' One moment they were talking about Donna and now the will. 'We're married, living together.'

'But not as husband and wife.'

Alissa's pulse slowed to a dull thud as she looked up into a face devoid of expression, but for the hint of satisfaction that curled the corners of his mouth.

'We're living under the same roof—'

'But not as husband and wife.'

His words sank into her bemused brain. At last she understood that masculine smirk. She froze.

'You want sex!' Her voice was strident with shock.

'Don't sound so surprised. It's what husbands and wives do.'

'But not us! We're not—'

'Married? Ah, but we are, *cara*.' His eyes glittered and that devilish smile widened. 'Here's my proposition. Live with me as a proper wife, in every sense, for the rest of our six months and I'll advance half your share of the money now. The rest you get at the end of our marriage. I need a guarantee you'll stay.'

Alissa opened her mouth to object. No sound emerged.

'I'll see my lawyers and organise the transfer of funds tomorrow…' his voice was a rumble of sensual anticipation '…if you start by satisfying me right now.'

'You're out of your head!' Shock and outrage glued Alissa to the spot. 'You don't even like me.'

Slowly he shook his head, his ice-bright eyes never leaving hers. 'Don't pretend to be so innocent, *cara*.' He stroked her cheek in a caress that detonated explosions of exquisite sensation. 'What's between us has nothing to do with liking.'

He crowded closer and the air between them sizzled. 'I don't have to *like* you to bed you,' he murmured, his voice dropping to a deep suede caress. 'In fact, I'm beginning to think mutual dislike might add a little extra piquancy.'

'You're sick!' she spat back. Yet it was all she could do not to lean closer, to narrow the tiny gap between them till their bodies touched. She turned her head to avoid his hand but he simply wrapped his fingers around the nape of her neck. Tendrils of fire slid through her veins.

'No, not sick. Just a man.' His gaze dropped to her breasts that seemed to swell and tighten under that heavy-lidded look. 'With a man's desires.'

Bemused, she stared into the face that had haunted her dreams. A face so beautiful yet bereft of tenderness. Bereft of everything except unvarnished, unapologetic lust.

Alissa wrenched herself away and strode across the room. Her chest heaved and her legs shook as she forced herself to stop and stare out at the long sweep of the bay, striving for calm. The silver-grey moonlight was chill and stark, like Dario's eyes as he spoke of bedding her.

Her stomach squeezed against the roil of emotions. Disbelief, fear, worry over her sister. And…anticipation.

No! She couldn't want Dario. She wrapped her arms round herself, trying to think clearly. It didn't matter that he'd somehow inveigled his way beneath her defences these last few weeks. Surely she had more self-respect.

'Is this how you get your kicks, Signor Parisi? Playing games with innocent women?' She swung round to face him. Even from half a room away, the intensity of his stare turned her knees to jelly.

'Innocent? The woman who deliberately connived to stop me retrieving what's rightfully mine?' He crossed his arms over his chest in a movement that emphasised the latent power in his big frame. 'The woman whose supposed innocence led her to parties where sex as well as money was traded for designer drugs?'

'I never—'

'Enough!' For the first time Dario raised his voice in a roar that silenced her instinctive protest. It echoed the thunderous beat of her pulse. His eyes meshed with hers, holding her immobile. 'One more denial,' he continued, his voice a lethally quiet whisper, 'and I withdraw the offer.'

'But…'

At the sight of his narrowing eyes and raised brows, Alissa's words petered out. He was utterly implacable. Her stomach dived and her throat closed in a spasm of horror. The dull, metallic taste of fear seared her tongue. The truth didn't matter, not now.

Frantically her mind whirred, but she found no way out. 'You really are as bad as they say, aren't you?' A shudder rippled down her spine as she faced him. 'Cold, clinical, calculating. Completely without remorse.'

Only the knot between his brows hinted at his displeasure. 'I see my fame precedes me. But your views on my character are of no importance.'

Alissa shook her head. Had she hoped even now he'd deny it? 'You're some piece of work, Dario Parisi. I thought I knew all there was to know about unscrupulous men, but you're something else.'

Dario frowned as if finally her words had punctured his self-absorption.

Despair wrapped around Alissa's heart. There was no uncertainty in his eyes. Just hunger.

It hurt to draw breath. She reached for the back of a nearby sofa, needing its support as the world crashed into splinters around her. Her hand was a stiff claw sinking into the plush upholstery.

She thought she'd known powerlessness and humiliation. The night her grandfather had knocked her off balance and down the staircase when she'd refused to marry Dario. The night she'd had her fingerprints taken by the police.

But this…

This was the ultimate insult. The ultimate power play.

Grimly Alissa pushed herself straight, angling her chin higher. She wouldn't give Dario the satisfaction of seeing her pain. Instead she'd remember Donna's voice on the phone tonight, her brave attempt to hide her worry and despair. That would keep her strong.

'If I agreed…' She curled her fingers into her palm till the nails scored her skin and she found the nerve to continue. 'If I sleep with you, you'll pay half my share of the inheritance straight away with no arguments?'

His smile was grim, as if her words both pleased and angered him. 'You'll do more than sleep with me. I want satisfaction. I want to come deep inside you.' His voice dropped to a pitch that resonated in her very bones. 'I'll have you, whenever I want, however I want, until we divorce.'

A cold trickle of despair slid down her back as his words fell between them. And yet…in the pit of her belly a tiny swirl of something hot and urgent coiled into life at the idea of Dario, deep inside her.

Dumbfounded, Alissa stared, not seeing his harsh, gorgeous face, but instead the pair of them tangled on his bed. It shamed her that a small, wayward part of her found the idea exciting.

She was losing her grip. She'd never been with a man. Never found the courage or the desire to trust a man so intimately with her body, her private self. Yet here, now, his words attracted as well as repelled. She fought self-loathing as well as desperate anxiety.

'No bondage. Nothing rough.' She winced as the words erupted from her mouth. They sounded like capitulation.

'I don't get my kicks that way.' He looked haughty.

'Some men do.' Her voice was uneven but firm.

'You have my word as a Parisi; there will be nothing like that. There are plenty of other ways we can find pleasure together.'

Alissa almost laughed at his certainty. His belief she'd find pleasure with him. She ignored the tiny, traitorous pulse beating at the juncture of her thighs.

'And if I…agree, you'll give me the money tomorrow?' She couldn't believe she was saying this.

'I promise.' He inclined his head.

It would almost be a pleasure to teach him one woman at least wouldn't succumb to his magic touch. She swung round to face the window. By the time she saw the coast by daylight she'd have given herself to Dario.

Panic and disbelief petrified her. Her jaw ached and she realised she'd clenched her teeth so hard her head began to pound.

Could she do it? Her hands twisted as she groped for an alternative. *Anything* to avoid Dario's cold-blooded proposition. But she'd been over her options so many times. There *was* no alternative.

Donna needed treatment sooner than they'd expected. This was the only way to get it. Her options had narrowed to this. Letting him…

Her shoulders slumped as she realised there was no other way. She couldn't even refuse on the grounds that he wouldn't keep his promise. Everything she'd learned about Dario indicated that, though he was merciless, he had enough pride never to break his promise.

Which left her no escape. No alternative but to give herself to him.

CHAPTER NINE

DARIO STOOD, RIGID with anticipation, watching her.

What had got into him? Promising money for sex? He'd never stooped so low in his life.

Something had snapped as he listened to her try to gull him out of his money, appealing to his sympathy. He'd expected something of the sort, but when it came to the crunch, nothing had prepared him for the tidal wave of wrath and disappointment that washed over him when she lived down to his expectations. That she should use her own family as an excuse to get money! That, above all, rankled.

His self-control had shattered under the lethal combination of fury and frustrated desire.

He grimaced at the thought of his lawyers drawing up the contract. Yet not even burgeoning shame at his tactics doused the flare of expectancy as he waited for her answer. The keen blade of desire that ripped through his soul, his conscience, his belief in himself as an honourable man.

His first assessment of her had been right. Strange he felt no vindication at the knowledge. In this one thing he'd rather have been wrong.

His hands bunched in his pockets as she stood staring at the moonlit bay. Suspense gripped him in a vice.

Despite her protests, he'd read her responses. Her gaze followed him when she thought he wasn't looking, her lips parted a fraction in unwitting invitation when he got close. This would be a mutual pleasure.

As long as she agreed. He scowled as still she kept her back turned. Anxiety juddered through his muscles. This show of reluctance wasn't amusing.

She turned and he held his breath, trying to read her face. Her eyes avoided his. Not a promising start. Dario was stunned to discover he was nervous.

'All right.' Her voice was tight. 'I'll do it.'

Instantly his face relaxed, as if her words eased his tension. That was impossible—it would imply he'd worried she wouldn't agree. Yet this was a game to him, an exercise in domination. He didn't care for her. The knowledge chilled her to the marrow. She'd never be warm again.

'Good.' His lips curled into a slow, sultry smile that, despite everything, made her insides turn over and her heart patter. Was she going mad to react so?

'Come here, *cara*.' His voice was a stroke of velvet, barely concealing an immutable will.

'Now?' She couldn't prevent the catch in her voice as fear overcame desperate bravado. Her fingers clutched frantically at the back of the sofa.

'Now.' He held out one hand.

Looking into the steely depths of his stare, Alissa read an intent that panicked her.

'Not here!'

'Here. Now.' He gestured imperiously, commanding her presence.

He couldn't be serious! She flicked a horrified glance at the door. 'Anyone could come in.'

'My staff have retired for the night. Besides, no one enters this room without my express permission.' He paused and Alissa swallowed as she read the predatory hunger in his face. She'd never felt so small, so vulnerable.

'Unless you wish to back out of our arrangement.' His face tightened, making him look more austerely remote than ever. And more compelling.

He meant it. Absolutely, unequivocally.

That was all it took for cold, hard fury to fill her.

Damn Dario Parisi and his unholy bargain, his superior air and his demands for satisfaction. She'd give him satisfaction all right. Somehow, despite her inexperience she'd manage and in the process she'd show him how much she despised him. Then when she had his money, when Donna was on her way to the U.S., she'd...

'Alissa.' It was a breath of air, a whisper of sensuous promise. A command.

Gleaming eyes held hers and awareness pulsed between them. She ignored it, delving into the well of indignation that lent her strength to stalk across the room.

Dario barely had time to register satisfaction at her capitulation. Suddenly there she was, soft curves pressing close, her evocative lily scent drugging his senses. Thought atrophied as his libido roared into top gear and every drop of blood rushed south.

She snagged his silk bow-tie in one hand, tugged it undone then ripped it off. The action sucked his breath from his lungs in startled delight. His body tightened predictably as her hands moved to his shirt.

Buttons followed. She was like a dynamo, a whirlwind. He read savage intensity in her small, set face. Not once did she raise her eyes to his. Yet the feel of her neat hands yanking his jacket from his shoulders, reefing his shirt free, aroused him more than he'd thought possible. Only a supreme effort of will held him still, letting her have her way instead of reciprocating. Soon...

She ripped his shirt open and pushed it from his shoulders. Her hands, warm and erotically supple, paused. Her palms slid down, following the swell of muscles. There was a sharp intake of breath and she snatched her hands away as if singed.

It didn't surprise him. He was burning up. Never had he stood passive as a lover stripped him ruthlessly, almost desperately. It was profoundly arousing. His desire was a voracious hunger, an explosive force.

Dario reached out, unable to wait to claim her. It didn't matter what she'd done or why she'd agreed. All that mattered was that she was his. This was more than revenge, more even than desire. This was raw and elemental.

The velvet at her waist was exquisitely soft, but not as soft as her skin. He clamped his hands round her tiny form and dragged her up till she was plastered against his bare chest. She felt like the promise of paradise.

She'd feel better naked.

He smiled as he bent to claim her mouth. That lush, siren's mouth he'd dreamt of so often.

'No!' She wrenched her face from his hold.

She was refusing him! In that instant he felt he'd implode, so all-consuming was his craving.

Then she planted an open-mouthed kiss on his collar-bone and he quaked. Her hands slid down his chest, scraping his nipples and dragging out a groan of longing. Fire shot to his belly. He was so hard, just at the touch of her lips and hands on his bare flesh. He teetered on the verge of losing control.

He fumbled to drag up the skirt of her dress. Velvet bunched in his fingers then slipped as her hands went to his trousers. Lightning shot through him. At the touch of her fingers on his belt his belly contracted. His lungs were on fire, each breath scouring his chest.

He'd expected their union to be spectacular but he hadn't been ready for this cataclysm of sensation. It was exquisite torture as she slipped his belt undone, her fingers provocatively hesitant as she reached for the fastening of his trousers.

Her face was obscured as she kept her head down, watching her hands at work. Finally the fabric fell and he sucked in a thankful breath. He lifted his hands to tug her hair undone but she was too fast. Before he could touch her she was kneeling, undoing his shoelaces.

Potent, erotic images filled his brain as he watched her slide off his shoes, socks, trousers. Images of her pleasuring him with her luscious mouth, her delicate, nimble fingers. He choked back a growl of need, feeling his body race into overdrive.

She'd bewitched him. That was the only explanation. The longer she knelt, head bowed, the harder it was to wrest his mind to any sort of cogent thought. When he had mastery of himself again he'd resent the power she wielded over him. For now he intended to enjoy it.

He grasped her shoulders and pulled her up. His eyes closed as he cupped her neat, rounded bottom and pulled her close. His pelvic thrust against her feminine softness was urgent, instinctive. Bliss.

'Let your hair down.' It was a hoarse plea that emerged as a growled command. He couldn't manage it. It was all he could do to hold himself still. He wanted this to last more than the twenty seconds it would take to rip her underwear off and thrust inside her.

The drumming beat of his need was the only sound as she reached up and dragged out hairpins. Seconds later her hair, long tresses of fire, coiled around her shoulders and further, to rest like a silken invitation across her breasts. How would it look against her pale bare skin? He had to find out.

Drawing on every scintilla of strength he'd once taken for granted, he stepped back half a pace. He shuddered at the loss of body contact. But soon…

He reached for her zip, reefed it down in one desperate jerk, then gathered her skirts in his fists and lifted the dress over her head. His breath ceased as velvet spilled to the floor. He lowered his hands, drinking her in.

She was perfect. Skin like moonlight. So pale and luminous he was almost scared to touch her with his big hands. Her breasts were high and full, her waist a bare hand span, her hips a swell of invitation. Her hair fell in glorious waves around her breasts.

She looked like a mermaid, a Venus, an angel.

Women came to him in silks and diaphanous laces. In sexy bustiers and suspender belts. Alissa wore unadorned cotton. In a deep indigo, it was the perfect foil for her milky skin. And on her legs, lace-topped stay-up stockings. The sight of silky white thighs above sexy dark hosiery was so erotic. She had spectacular legs. She was spectacular everywhere. Satisfaction thrummed in his blood.

'Look at me, Alissa.' Slowly she raised her head. Her lips were firm, rosy curves. Her chin tilted regally, baring her slender neck. Her eyes blazed azure fire.

It took a lust-hazed moment to realise it wasn't the burn of desire. That the angle of her jaw was a challenge, not an invitation. That her lips were primmed, not pouting.

Disbelief tugged at his consciousness. Something like guilt burned acid in his gut. No, not guilt, he assured himself quickly. Alissa was here by choice. She wanted what he had to offer. He wasn't taking advantage of her.

And yet...

And yet everything revolted at the idea of her deigning to pleasure him. This connection between them was mutual. From the first he'd known it. Even now, despite her air of icy self-possession, she couldn't conceal the rapid pulse at the base of her throat, nor her uneven breathing. She felt it too, though she tried to hide it.

And she was going to admit it.

'On the sofa.' The words were a rough order. It was a blow to his ego that he'd stood, a shaking, desperate man, putty in her hands, while she'd kept her mental distance.

He stooped to retrieve a condom from his wallet then took

off his boxer shorts. The slide of fabric over his groin exacerbated his anger and his determination. He was so aroused one touch from her would send him over the edge.

He turned and stalked to where she sat primly, knees together, hair a glowing curtain concealing her breasts. That was even more exciting than if she'd been spread naked before him.

Dario pulsed with need and saw her eyes widen as she took in the sight of him, completely bare and hungry for her. Did he imagine it or did she shrink back? No matter. Soon she wouldn't shy from his touch, she'd beg for it.

He felt his smile as a taut stretch of muscles when he knelt before her and put the condom within reach.

'What…?' Her voice petered out as he wrapped his hand round her ankle. So slim, so delicate.

He lowered his mouth to her leg as he unbuckled the tiny strap. Silk stockings and even silkier skin that contracted in shivery ripples as he slid his lips along it. Deftly he slipped off her shoe, taking her foot in his hands as he kissed her calf all the way to her knee. She shifted but he held her, massaging with his thumbs as he kissed back down to her ankle.

Her breathing changed, became deeper. The tension in her muscles eased as his massage relaxed her, made her more aware of physical sensation. He smiled against her instep then moved to her other foot. This time as he progressed with hot kisses up her leg he heard her gasp of pleasure, quickly stifled.

Now both shoes were discarded, he allowed himself access to her thighs. With just a little pressure they fell apart before him and he had to take a moment to focus on his plan. Not to seize immediate gratification but to pleasure her till she relinquished the last of her obstinate self-possession.

Yet it was a moot point who got most pleasure as he trailed caresses up her thigh. His heart pounded so loud it was a miracle she couldn't hear it. At the top of her stocking he slipped a finger under the elastic and swiped his tongue along the lace mark, pleased at her tiny jump of reaction. She tasted honey-sweet. Her single mew of pleasure urged him on, upwards, till the scent of feminine musk tingled in his nostrils.

Resisting temptation, he pressed only the lightest of kisses against flesh-warmed cotton, before caressing her other thigh with his lips, tongue and fingers.

Her languorous ease vanished. Her muscles grew taut. Smiling, he moved up again, lingering a moment to tease her through the fabric of her panties, before sliding his mouth up over her belly to her navel and higher.

It was heaven here, enfolded by her smooth thighs, right at her centre. He buried his face in her long hair, revelling in its fine texture and fresh scent. It spilled through his fingers, an erotic caress against palms already sensitised by contact with velvet-soft skin.

But beneath it was treasure. He released her bra and pulled it away, nuzzling those long tresses aside to discover her pink and white flesh.

The ruched peak of her nipple was beneath his tongue then in his mouth as he suckled strongly. A rapier blade of need sliced through him. He was lost in pleasure.

The swell of her other breast enticed him. He tugged at her nipple with thumb and forefinger while he bit down gently on the other one and was rewarded with a shiver of response. Did she know she thrust herself higher into his embrace with each lap of his tongue?

'Do you like that, Alissa?'

Her eyes glittered feverishly as she struggled for breath. Was she ready to admit to this force between them?

'Yes.' It was a sob and it was music to his ears. He'd needed to hear her say it and know this was mutual.

Only after he'd drawn sighs of shuddering pleasure from her did he lift himself higher. Her breasts cushioned his chest as he kissed her hair, her closed eyes. He licked the outline of her ear and nipped its sensitive lobe.

Dario hoped she felt half the excruciating pleasure he did

from this druggingly slow lovemaking. His body strained to breaking point as he leashed his urgent lust. Never had it been so difficult to restrain himself.

Finally he felt the slide of small fingers at his waist, his back, his shoulders. Triumph and relief warred as he bent again to do homage at her breasts. Her hands tunnelled through his hair, grabbing him close.

Alissa shifted restlessly under him and he arrowed a hand down, beneath the indigo cotton, now satisfyingly damp to the touch. Unerringly he found her sensitive nub of pleasure, teasing it with light strokes till she rose helplessly against his every touch.

Never had a woman's response been so powerfully erotic. So satisfying. So arousing. She clamped his face to her breast and her body curved up to his in abandon as if all she thought, all she knew was him.

Yes!

Alissa moaned a protest as he dragged himself back, gulping breaths into his air-starved lungs.

She was the most glorious sight, eyes narrowed to gleaming, provocative slits. Her lips were parted and swollen even though he hadn't yet tasted them. Her hair splayed, a wash of copper and rust streaked with gold, across the dark blue upholstery. And her breasts…

'Please.' Even her voice was a throaty invitation.

Reluctantly he pulled back. 'Patience, little one.'

Swiftly he retrieved the foil package, fitting the condom with a speed born of urgency. He tugged down her panties. She shimmied her hips to ease the way and his belly cramped in excitement. Soon…

When he rose again she was naked, a triangle of russet hair hiding her feminine secrets. The scent of her arousal filled his senses. Very soon he'd learn those secrets. Lowering his head, he dragged his tongue over the path his fingers had followed.

She shuddered into desperate life, her legs clamping his head then falling away as if abandoning the effort.

'Please. Dario.' She urged him higher. He caressed her again, exulting in her response as her hips tilted and she shivered all around him.

'Dario!' It was a low, keening sound but he recognised the desperation in her cry. Didn't it echo his own need?

He rose, about to tell her to stretch full length on the settee so he could blanket her with his body. But even that would take too long. He needed her now.

Instead he clamped her hips and dragged her to the very edge of the seat. He leaned in, hard against her softness, full and ready against her openness.

Lightly he tilted his hips and she rose to meet him. The slide of her slick flesh against him was almost too much. His eyelids flickered as lightning sparked behind them. No, too soon.

With a smile that must have been more grimace, he slid a hand between them, circling, probing, entering. Her eyes widened and heat flared in their blue depths. Again he stroked and she lifted to meet him, her gaze clinging.

How he wanted…no, how he *needed* her.

Her face revealed wonder, as if she'd never known such pleasure. An illusion, of course, but a heady one. He was at breaking point when she reached for him.

'Dario. Now…please.'

His heart gave a huge surge that sent his pulse out of kilter. He dragged her hand up to cup his face and turned to nuzzle it. The scent of Alissa, sweet and salt and absolute temptation, filled him. He licked her palm and her eyes closed.

'Watch me,' he whispered.

She opened her eyes as he lifted her legs round his hips and positioned himself at the entrance to paradise.

'Yes.' It was a hiss of sensual need.

Slowly, inexorably, he surged forward. His shoulders, his

buttocks and thighs, every inch of him strained with tension as he entered that tight, slick space.

Such was the force of will needed to restrain himself he almost missed the tiny sensation of resistance and the breathless grimace that contorted her features.

'Alissa?' Did she hear him? For a moment that looked like distress on her face. He paused, shocked at the message his brain sent him, unable to comprehend it. Then she lifted her hips and thought fled as he slid forward.

Instinct took over as he withdrew then pushed again, more strongly this time. She moaned in pleasure and tension spiralled. He stroked her face, her breasts, encouraged her to stretch up so they were flush together, skin against skin. Heat against heat as he filled her and she welcomed him home with tiny answering movements.

She linked her hands round his neck as she stared into his eyes. His heart swelled to bursting point. A second later, with the first rapid spasm of her body round his, he felt the spark flare in his blood. She cried out as if in surprise and her body clenched around his.

He knew a moment's satisfaction at her climax before he plunged into a vortex of fire. It racked him with pleasure, sent flame racing along his veins. Light exploded in his numbing brain and filled him with ecstasy.

It seemed forever before he slumped forward, pulling her close. His chest heaved as he buried his face against her but the instinct to hug her to him was so strong he didn't care whether he breathed freely or not.

He was too spent to think, to do anything other than ride the aftershocks of cataclysmic orgasm and stroke her hair with fingers that shook.

He'd just had the most fulfilling sexual encounter of his life. With his wife.

A wife who had been a virgin until five minutes ago.

CHAPTER TEN

ALISSA WOKE TO a feeling of well-being pervading even her bones. She sensed daylight, yet her limbs were weighted, her body relaxed and replete, her mind empty of everything but the recognition of comfort.

Dimly she realised this was different from other mornings. There was no tension, no anxiety gnawing her vitals the instant she woke to a new day.

Luxuriously she stretched, wondering what—

She froze. The pillow she'd nuzzled was a cushion of living muscle dusted with masculine hair. Her shin had slid between two solid male thighs and one hand was clamped around the curve of a very solid shoulder.

Dario! She was sprawled across Dario like some...

'Morning, *cara*.' His voice, gravel and satin, evoked delicious memories of pleasure. 'I trust you slept well?'

He stroked her spine, making her shiver and arch her back so her breasts pushed into his torso. The friction of skin on skin brought her fully awake. She recognised the pulse of arousal quickening her blood, beating in that tender place between her legs.

She sucked in her breath, drawing with it the rich, addictive scent of Dario's skin. Her bones melted as her body, conditioned after just one night to pleasure at his touch, softened in anticipation.

'I—'

He swallowed her words in an open-mouthed kiss, lifting her up so she stretched full-length against him. As his tongue stroked hers the taste of bitter chocolate and honey, of Dario, filled her mouth. He kissed with the leisurely expertise of a master.

Last night he'd turned the tables, seducing her so thoroughly her angry energy had transformed into erotic abandon.

He'd been so gentle as he wiped away the tears of release and wonder from her eyes. He'd tucked her close and carried her to his suite. Relying only on the moonlight, he'd bathed her with warm water and gentle hands before depositing her, dazed and exhausted, in his bed. He'd spooned close, wrapping himself round her like a blanket. In the night she'd woken to his coaxing voice and it had seemed natural to turn to him. Allow him access to her body. Allow herself the ecstasy of his lovemaking.

He cupped her face and kissed her, his skin with its morning roughness gently abrasive. The stroke of his tongue, the caress of his mouth, the slide of one restless thigh between hers awoke delicious sensations. She craved again the mindless ecstasy, the tenderness, the feeling of warmth that excluded all cares.

'Cara.' His voice dropped to a low note that made her shake with desire. It was enough to make her forget...make her forget...

Donna! The blinding flash of remembrance blasted her. She jerked in his embrace as realisation hit.

How could she have forgotten, even for an instant? Her sister was counting on her. Alissa had only gone through with this because... The skein of thought frayed as he tugged her close and deepened their kiss.

Had she submitted to Dario simply for Donna's sake? Or had that been an excuse? A voice in her head accused her of hiding behind Donna's problems so she could reach out for what she'd secretly wanted from the first.

Had she been motivated by altruism or selfishness? And

now Dario's ruthlessness, bargaining with her sister's life, came crashing into her brain.

Suddenly her night of unexpected joy was a tainted, guilty pleasure.

'No.' Breathless, she pushed against his shoulders, levering herself away, till she could look down at him.

That was a mistake. His dark hair was rumpled from her touch, his eyes slumberous, sizzling with the concentration he gave to physical pleasure. His jaw was shadowed, giving him a potently sexy bad-boy look. His lips... Alissa looked at that perfectly sculpted mouth, remembering the bliss of his kisses.

'Stop!' Her voice was uneven and her chest heaved against his. She squeezed her eyes shut, torn between self-disgust and delight at the erotic sensation of her nipples against his powerful chest.

'What is it, *cara*?' Dario relaxed his hold and she shuffled away, dragging the sheet across her chest.

Her head bowed as guilt speared her. How could she have forgotten her sole reason for being here? It didn't matter that last night had been the most wondrous experience of her life. What a few moments ago had seemed a short, blissful respite from care now condemned her as heartless and selfish. And condemned Dario as...she didn't want to think about it.

Alissa sat up, focusing on the clock beside the bed. She didn't trust herself to look into the silvery depths of his eyes.

'You promised to transfer the money this morning.' She drew in a sustaining breath. 'The banks are open now.'

Dario couldn't believe his ears. He reared back as if she'd struck him.

Minutes ticked by as he stared at Alissa. The woman who'd given him more passion, warmth and pleasure than he'd ever had. Who'd made him question everything he'd been so sure of yesterday. Not with clever words, but with the apparent honesty and generosity of her body's responses. He'd actually believed she couldn't be the mercenary little go-getter he'd thought her. He'd decided that, despite all the evidence, he'd somehow been mistaken.

His mouth tightened as he fought down rising bile. His bed reeked with the musky scent of sex. Of her deviousness and his gullibility.

When he'd discovered her to be a virgin he'd felt guilt at pressuring her into his bed. He'd felt like the lowest slime ball that had ever slunk out of a gutter. Until his senses overrode his conscience. After that he hadn't been able to stop himself, for the ecstasy surpassed everything he'd known.

Afterwards he'd believed his view of her character flawed. She couldn't be all he'd thought her. Yet his guilt hadn't stopped him reaching for her again. His scruples were no match for his need.

He'd told himself that this morning, in the clear light of day, he'd discover the truth.

But the truth was, despite her virginity, she'd played him all along. There'd been no connection between them, no melding of souls that went beyond the boundaries of physical pleasure. He'd imagined that as he'd reeled from the most erotic, satisfying experience of his life.

Shame flooded him that he'd let himself imagine there was anything more between them. She'd laugh if she knew.

'I said the banks are open now.' Her chin jutted up, her mouth settling in a firm line.

His hands clenched as he surveyed her. She looked like a queen refusing to acknowledge a dirty peasant, despite the fact they were in bed together.

Was she trying to put him in his place? After last night's intimacies?

Ingrained memories of condescending looks and arrogant words rose instantly. For years he'd endured the stigma of not fitting in, not being good enough. He'd been too independent to please prospective foster parents. They'd wanted him to forget his past and his family and pretend to be theirs. When he hadn't he'd been labelled difficult, a kid who'd never amount to anything.

He thought he'd obliterated any sensitivity to such things. He *had* done. Until Alissa played havoc with his libido and his judgement. Until she'd awakened emotions long forgotten. *That* was what he couldn't forgive.

'Probably not the best way to greet your lover,' he drawled, trying not to react to the seductive picture she made, her hair a sensuous curtain around pale, perfect shoulders. The sunlight outlined her sweet curves through the linen.

'Why not?' Her voice was sharp. So different from last night's throaty purrs and moans of delight. He wished he could have her now as she'd been then. Pliant, eager and so responsive. 'It's the only reason we're in bed.'

Fury surged, stirring an unfamiliar turmoil of emotions. How could he be disappointed that she was motivated by money? That last night had been about hot sex and mercenary gain?

'You'll need to improve your bedside manner, *cara*, or your next lover mightn't be so generous.'

'Generous?' It was a squawk of outrage. 'You've got a hide.' Her eyes flashed fire that scorched his bare skin. 'There's nothing generous about you, Dario. You'd sell your grandmother if you thought you could turn a profit.'

A shaft of anger pierced him at her accusation. She couldn't know how much family meant to him.

'I earned every penny of the money you owe me.' He watched her swallow hard. Her eyes flicked away as if the sight of him offended her sensibilities. 'No doubt you'll make sure you get your money's worth over the next months.'

A chill descended with her words. Part of him cringed at the truth of what she said. Even now, nothing would keep him from taking her to his bed again and again. Despite his lacerated pride, one night with her wasn't enough. The realisation made him lash out.

'Then it's as well you have a natural talent for pleasure, isn't it, Alissa?'

Satisfaction was an inner glow as he watched a blush rise in her throat. Surely at least some of her responses had been genuine. He recalled her wide-eyed wonder as he'd brought her to the brink of climax again and again. The sweet pulse of need in her body, the clumsy yet entrancing way she'd taken her turn at pleasuring him.

Hell! He was hard just remembering.

'Why were you a virgin?' He'd blurted the words without thinking, still shocked by the discovery.

Her brows arched. Energy sizzled between them at the intensity of her glare.

'Because I don't like men,' she snarled.

Stunned, he registered a plunging sensation in the pit of his belly. She couldn't be... No, not when she'd responded to him the way she had.

'At least not enough to want to go to bed with one of them,' she added, as if reading his thoughts.

'Why not?' He had to know.

'I've yet to have a close relationship with one who doesn't want to control my life.' Her eyes flashed. 'Can we cut the chat while you organise my money?' Her words might have been chipped from glacial ice. Just like her profile of regal disdain.

Deliberately Dario stretched and linked his hands beneath his head. He'd promised so he'd deliver on the money. But it went against the grain to jump to her tune.

'Congratulations,' he murmured. 'You have to be the most blatantly greedy woman I've met.'

'You expect me to apologise?' She leaned forward as if spurred by feelings so strong she couldn't sit still. 'You think I should be ashamed, when you *know* why I need it?' To his astonishment tears glittered on her lashes before she blinked them away.

They were back to that. Suddenly he'd had enough of this conversation, sickened by the way, even now, she tried to play on his sympathy. He flung back the sheet and stalked to the dressing room to tug on some jeans.

'Don't think you can walk out on our deal.' She'd followed him. He swung round to find her, swathed in a trailing sheet, hair in disarray and a mutinous expression on her face. The hunger for her grew in him anew.

What did that say for his judgement? He turned his back so she wouldn't see how she affected him.

A small, firm hand arrested his movements, dragging at his arm, trying to tug him around.

'You *owe* me, Dario!'

He swung back, face taut as he battled the urge to silence her with his mouth. Disgust filled him at the predictability of his need for this woman.

'Enough! Get me your bank details. By lunchtime you'll have enough cash to keep a dozen farms afloat.' Or, more likely, spend it on herself.

'Farms? What farms?' She frowned as if he spoke a foreign language.

Had she forgotten the excuse she'd used last night? The need to save her sister's cattle station? He shook off her hand, zipping his jeans and reaching for a T-shirt. 'You said you want cash for your sister.'

'That's right.' She stood behind him. He felt her warmth, smelled her skin. 'But she's not buying a farm.'

'Saving a farm, then.' He flung out one hand in a dismissive gesture. 'Wasn't that your excuse for wanting to cut a new deal? To save her from foreclosure?'

Silence. Except for a hissed intake of breath.

'You thought that's why I wanted the money?' Something about the quality of her voice made him still. He turned to find her white-faced. 'You said you'd had us investigated, that you knew all about us.'

He nodded. 'I paid an Australian detective agency. They were thorough,' he said, thinking of the dirt they'd dug up on her past.

'Not thorough enough,' she murmured. 'They didn't check medical records, did they?' He watched her press one clenched hand to her breast.

'Not that I know of.' There hadn't seemed a need. 'Why?'

Alissa lifted her chin to meet him stare for stare. 'Because my sister is ill. Her only hope is a radical new treatment in the U.S. Without it she'll die.' She breathed deep. 'It costs a fortune. Money Donna and her husband don't have. Money I could only get by marrying you.'

The world tilted and spun crazily off its axis as he met her unwavering gaze.

It couldn't be. And yet…it would be easy enough to check. She must know that.

Dario's lungs laboured. His chest constricted under the impact of an invisible blow that shoved him back against one mirrored wall, leaving him stunned.

Could the investigators have missed something so crucial? He'd employed the best. But perhaps the best hadn't been enough. He should have used his personal staff.

He met her unflinching gaze, read the shock in her face, the horror in her eyes. His certainty cracked.

It was possible.

A yawning chasm ripped open inside him as the implications struck home.

Che diavolo ha fatto? What the devil had he done?

'Tell me.' His voice was strained and his features set in a mask that hid his emotions. Only his searing eyes hinted he felt anything at her news.

Alissa told herself she didn't care what he thought. All she cared about was saving Donna. If she concentrated on that she could ignore the crazy yearning for the comfort of his strong arms about her. Tremors of fatigue and reaction ran through her and she slumped into a chair.

'Tell me.' The words were stronger now. He planted his feet wide. He'd dropped the T-shirt and stood bare-chested, his hair all dark, tousled locks, his arms at his sides.

She couldn't stop a thrill of appreciation at his male perfection. She hated herself for it.

'There's nothing to tell.' She lowered her gaze. Even his feet, strong and sinewy, reminded her of how she'd abandoned care and duty and given herself to pleasure in his embrace. Self-disgust was bitter as aloes in her mouth. 'The specialists in Australia can't help and our health system won't fund her treatment overseas.' She fisted her hands in the cotton at her breast.

'When did this happen?'

'We got the news a couple of months ago.'

Alissa saw emotion flicker in his eyes. Did he believe now that she'd only gone through with a marriage for Donna's sake? That, after refusing to marry him when her grandfather was alive and then again immediately after the old man's death, this was why she'd agreed? She bit her lip. She shouldn't care what he believed.

'You didn't ask me for money then.'

'Ask you?' Fury surged. 'Why would you help? From the first you made it clear you hated me because of my grandfather's plans for us to marry.' She sucked in oxygen, trying to calm her racing pulse as she remembered the contempt in Dario's eyes, the mocking chill in his tone. 'I had everything planned with Jason until you stormed in breathing fire and brimstone and wrecked everything.'

'You could have told me.' His voice was low.

'As if that was likely!' She fixed him with a glare. 'You gave the impression you'd revel in our misfortunes.'

'You believed I'd ignore the fact that your sister was dying?' His jaw hardened. 'That I'd stoop so low?'

'What? Lower than forcing me into bed when we hate each other?' Her voice broke and she looked away, wrapping her arms tight round her torso. She lashed out at Dario but it was she who felt guilty. She who'd let herself wallow in pleasure when she should have withstood his seduction. She who'd forgotten her responsibility to her sister.

'You thought I'd let her die. That I would negotiate such a bargain knowing all the circumstances.' His voice held a strangely distant note that made her turn.

What she saw made her suck in a stunned breath. A stranger looked back, eyes devoid of life, lines etched deep around his mouth. An unnatural pallor greyed his skin.

'Dario?' Shock held her rigid. He looked as if he'd been dealt a fatal blow, sheer willpower keeping him on his feet. She'd been so ready to believe the absolute worst of him last night. It seemed now she'd been wrong.

Regret streaked through her. Could she have convinced him of the truth last night? He'd been implacable. But then she'd been so ready to judge him badly. She'd let her prejudices blind her. She'd judged him her grandfather's equal, reviving old fears and mistrust.

She opened her mouth to speak when he forestalled her.

'What's wrong with your sister? Was it an accident?'

'No, nothing like that. Donna has liver damage and other complications. It's a result of…problems. She went off the rails for a while.'

'Define "off the rails".' His gaze narrowed.

Alissa stared at one mirrored wall, seeing Dario, tall and imposing, and herself, huddled in a swathe of white.

'Drink. Guys. Drugs.' After a lifetime of obedience to their grandfather, Donna, the quiet one, had finally rebelled in spectacular fashion. Alissa hadn't been able to stop her. Familiar guilt scorched her conscience. It was as if Donna had sought the quickest way to destroy herself: sex and drugs at seventeen, rehab at eighteen. Married and dying at barely twenty.

A deathly chill ran up Alissa's spine.

'She was under age at the time. Yes?'

Alissa turned to find Dario watching her, something like understanding in his eyes. 'How did you know?'

'The investigator got some of it right.'

'I worked two jobs, making ends meet after we left home. Donna was old enough to live with me, but not old enough for clubbing.' But that hadn't stopped her. 'I didn't realise she'd used my ID to get into nightclubs and bars until it was too late.'

'That explains it. She was mistaken for you. Her behaviour, the drugs, the men…it was her, using your ID, pretending to be you.' His expression was grim as he held her gaze till she assented.

'And the night of the drug bust?'

Alissa couldn't look away. That invisible connection she'd imagined last night was back, drawing her into his power. 'I went looking for her.'

'Did she have drugs?'

Alissa nodded. She'd been desperate to get Donna out, away from the guy with the sweaty, possessive hands who was all over her kid sister, away from the poison she'd been putting in her body. Even now, if Alissa shut her eyes, she could imagine the throb of mind-numbing music, smell the rank scent of crowded bodies, see Donna…

'You took the drugs from her when the police raided, didn't you?'

'What else could I do? She's my little sister!' For a moment longer she met his piercing grey eyes then turned away. 'It was best in the long run. The shock of my arrest convinced Donna to get help. She's been clean ever since.'

Much good that would do now she's dying.

Alissa's lip wobbled and she bit down fiercely, refusing to

give in to fear. They'd find a way. Donna would get her treatment. She'd survive.

'Alissa.' His voice tugged her back from her thoughts. 'I'm sorry. Sorry for everything. I—'

'No!' She leapt to her feet, staring into a face etched in slashing, spare lines that might even signify pain. Into eyes shadowed with regret. 'I don't want to hear any apologies. Not now.'

Her emotions were too raw, too confused for her to cope with any more. She ached with disappointment and fury. Against them both: him for discovering her carnal, selfish weakness and her for giving in to it, despite the dictates of self-respect and duty.

'All I want is the money I earned last night.'

CHAPTER ELEVEN

'YOU LOOK MUCH better now, sweetheart.' Alissa smiled into the
wan features so like her own and gave thanks. Even now, so
soon after her treatment, Donna was much improved. It was
everything Alissa had hoped and prayed for.

'Don't exaggerate.' Donna smiled weakly from her hospital
bed. 'I've seen the mirror.'

'I know what I see, and it's all good. David is as smitten
now as he was four months ago when you married. He thinks
you're the most beautiful girl in the world.'

Donna's eyes softened at the mention of her husband, just
as his did whenever she was around.

It must be wonderful to share that kind of love. A squiggle
of emotion stirred inside Alissa, the same sensation she felt
whenever she saw her sister and brother-in-law so blatantly in
love. It wasn't jealousy. She didn't begrudge them their happiness. Yet Alissa couldn't help wishing she too could experience that sort of devotion.

Inevitably her mind turned to Dario, the silent, distant, ultra-
efficient man who'd arranged Donna's treatment. He'd seen
to it she jumped to the top of the specialist's patient list. He'd
organised everything, including a nearby apartment for David
and a manager for the property in their absence. He'd hired
a luxurious house for himself and Alissa a short walk from
the hospital.

Donna and David thought those were the actions of a besotted husband. Only Alissa knew they were the result of a guilty conscience.

Dario would never look at her with wonder in his eyes. He didn't want a long-term lover, at least not one like her. His tastes ran to tall brunettes, not short, sassy redheads. Their night together had been an aberration. He hadn't touched her since. One night was all it had taken to cure him of his desire. Pain scoured her at the thought.

'Just like the way Dario looks at you,' Donna said.

Alissa dredged up a smile, playing along with the fiction. 'Dario has too much control to wear his heart on his sleeve.'

'That's what you think. You don't see how he looks at you when you're not watching.' Donna shook her finger knowingly. 'His eyes go all hot and hungry. Honestly, it makes me burn up just seeing it. Especially since he's such a hunk. No wonder you couldn't resist him.'

Alissa stared at her sister, her automatic denial disintegrating on her tongue. How she longed for that to be true. Even knowing Donna was exaggerating, Alissa felt her heart give a fillip of excitement.

Much as she tried to despise her husband for the unholy bargain he'd forced on her, she couldn't deny her attraction to him. It was as strong as ever.

Stronger. For now she knew the ecstasy to be found in his embrace. The tender way he treated a lover, as if she was the only woman in the world.

The fact that he was driven now by remorse, so attentive to her needs, to her sister and her husband, revealed him as a man trying to atone. There'd been no mistaking his shock when he'd learned about Donna.

'You should spend more time with him, instead of spending your days with me.'

'Why do you think I'm in the States?' Alissa smiled, thinking how great it was to have Donna well enough to fantasise about her older sister's non-existent love life. 'It's for *you*, 'sweetie.' She brushed a lock of hair from Donna's face. The maternal gesture was completely natural. Alissa had been looking after her since their mum died.

'But you could fit in a second honeymoon with your gorgeous husband.' Donna waggled her eyebrows.

Alissa forced a laugh past her choked throat. Weeks ago, when she'd confronted Dario after their night of passion, she'd thought she'd never want to be intimate with him again. Now the knowledge that he slept in the massive suite next to hers tortured her with guilty longing. She wished he'd return to Sicily instead of working here with two secretaries and a barrage of phones.

Surely if he wasn't here she wouldn't feel this edginess? This hunger for his touch?

Was it because she'd never been with another man? She hadn't known how spectacular sex could be. She recalled Dario's taunting voice, telling her she had a talent for pleasure. Heat flared in her cheeks. Could he be right?

Right or not, it was clear she no longer held any appeal for him. He was scrupulously distant and reserved.

'Alissa?'

'Sorry. I was miles away.'

'But not happy thoughts. Don't you want a second honeymoon?'

Did she? Alissa bit her lip, realising she did. Despite his managing ways and their disastrous relationship to date, she wanted Dario. Desperately.

It was desire but it was more too. An unbreakable connection. When he entered a room she shivered, hoping and fearing he'd take her in his arms. The comfort she'd found in his embrace was magical, though she told herself she should despise him. She even missed their verbal sparring!

He was her guilty secret.

'Alissa? What's wrong?' Donna's voice was sharp. 'It's about the marriage, isn't it? I *knew* there was something you weren't telling me.'

Alissa met her sister's penetrating stare and silently cursed. Donna was far too acute sometimes.

'Why should there be anything wrong? As you say, I've married a gorgeous hunk who swept me off my feet.'

'Except you're not the sort to be swept off your feet. You always had guys trying to catch your interest, but you ignored them. Men have never been your weakness, not like me.' She hung her head.

'Don't!' Alissa squeezed her hand. This wasn't the moment to revisit the past, when rebellion had led Donna into promiscuity with the worst sort of guys. 'That's over. You have David now.'

'I have, haven't I?' Her quick smile faded. 'But what about Dario? Your romance was so sudden. And I always thought you wanted to live alone after Granddad.' She paused. 'Dario just burst onto the scene around the time you said you'd find a way to…' Her words ended in a gasp.

'You're imagining problems where there are none,' Alissa began. 'Dario and I—'

'He's the one, isn't he? The one Granddad wanted you to marry? The mega-rich Sicilian!' Horror dawned in Donna's voice. Tenaciously she gripped Alissa's hand. 'Tell me you didn't marry him for my sake. For the money.'

'Of course not. I…' Under Donna's stare, she heard her words peter out. Alissa had never lied to her sister. Except about this. 'We just…'

The door to the private room swung open and Donna's doctor, flanked by a phalanx of junior medicos, entered.

'Mrs Kincaid. I'm glad you're awake. I have the results of your tests.'

Dario strode to his bedroom. He'd worked past midnight again, hoping to dull the emotions swirling inside him and upsetting his equilibrium. Guilt and regret as well as desire. The unabashed hunger for the woman he'd manipulated and, in his arrogance, abused.

For the first time ever he was ashamed of his actions. Yet even shame couldn't blunt the keen edge of his need. She despised him. Hell! He despised himself. Yet he craved her. Her spirit, her strength, her firebrand attitude, the way she stood up to him and refused to be dominated.

The way she gave herself so unstintingly to physical passion. *The way she made him feel.*

He worked nineteen-, twenty-hour days, trying to exorcise her from his mind. Yet it was fruitless. For the first time, rebuilding the Parisi fortune and prestige held no allure.

He didn't understand how she fired this craving in the blood. Despite her guts and beauty, she was nothing like the woman he'd planned to take as his life partner.

His footsteps slowed as he passed her room. He hadn't seen her this evening. She'd stayed late at the hospital and he'd kept to his office.

He paused. That was when he heard muffled weeping. Instantly he tensed. Through everything she'd never cried. Except when he took her virginity. He'd convinced himself then that she'd wept in ecstasy.

This sounded like despair. His gut twisted. What could make his courageous wife cry as though her heart had broken?

He shoved open the door and stepped inside. She was hunched on the window seat, arms wrapped round her knees. Her feet were bare, her hair a tangled swathe of coppery red burning like fire in the lamplight. She wore a shapeless sleep shirt that was downright ugly with its inane cartoon characters printed on pale cotton.

She looked perfect.

His insides clenched at the sight of her. Desire, need and something more. Something…warm and protective.

'Alissa.' In an instant he crossed the room, hands in pockets to prevent himself reaching out. She'd feel contaminated by his touch. Helplessly he watched her shake as a tremor racked her. 'What is it? Speak to me.'

Hearing Dario's voice, Alissa gulped down the salty knot of emotion filling her throat and scrubbed her hand across her eyes. She hadn't seen him for days and now he had to find her like this.

'Alissa! Tell me what's wrong.' His voice was rough, that gravel-over-satin tone she'd last heard in his bed. Something unravelled inside and her breathing snared like a bird in a hunter's net.

'Nothing's wrong. I'm fine.'

'It doesn't look like nothing.' Long fingers clasped her chin and turned her face up. Tendrils of forbidden delight wove out from his touch. She was so susceptible.

She scowled. Had she interrupted his sleep? But a glance showed he wore dark trousers and a white shirt. Her gaze dropped from his intense expression to the V of golden skin at his collar-bone. She breathed deep but only succeeded in filling her lungs with his scent.

An instant later he hunkered beside her, his heat enfolding her as he wrapped his arm round her back.

'Is it your sister? Is it bad news?'

Alissa shook her head, feeling more foolish than ever. 'N-no. She's all right. The doctor came with the f-final test results.' Desperately she tried to master her voice. 'It will take her a long time to recuperate but the treatment was a success.' Her lips pulled tight in a trembling smile. 'She's going to live.'

A large palm circled slowly between her shoulder blades. 'Then what's the matter?' He was so close Alissa could feel the puff of his warm breath on her cheek. She bit her lip. 'Alissa?'

'I d-don't know!' It was a wail of despair. She should be ecstatic. She *was* ecstatic. This was the best news. What was wrong with her that she couldn't just rejoice?

She'd shared a celebratory dinner in the hospital with Donna and David then made her excuses, knowing they needed time alone. She'd been fine as she entered the elegant house Dario had hired with its discreet smell of money and its plush, indifferent silence. Her smile had waned on the way up the magnificent empty staircase. By the time she'd soaked in the travertine spa there'd been a curious ache in her chest. Then something had cracked inside and she'd collapsed, bawling her eyes out.

'I never cry,' she sobbed. 'Never.'

'Shh. I know. I know.' His arm tightened and she burrowed closer.

She felt as if a dam had split, smashing under the force of a welter of emotions. Through everything she'd been tough, never giving up hope. She'd been strong for Donna even in the darkest hours, first with their grandfather, then during Donna's addiction and illness. She'd fought Dario's demands too, every step of the way.

But now…Alissa had lost the strength that had sustained her for so long. She was confused and afraid.

Strong arms drew her up against a hard chest.

'What are you doing?'

'Putting you to bed. You can't stay there all night.'

Alissa didn't mean to snuggle against him. He was the enemy, the man who'd put her through hell and somehow bewitched her soul. Yet she couldn't resist leaning into him as he scooped her up. She wanted to revel in the illusion that she was protected and cared for. Cherished.

Minutes later she lay huddled at the centre of her too big bed. Shivers racked her until he slid in behind her and pulled the covers up.

'No. Don't!' She tensed and scrabbled to escape. 'I don't want—'

'Shh, Alissa, I'm going to hold you. Nothing more.' He wrapped his arms round her and pulled her against the furnace-like heat of his bare chest. Caution told her not to let down her guard but something deep inside urged her to trust him.

Her need for comfort was too strong. She slumped against him, grateful beyond words that he was here. She didn't understand what was happening. Never had she experienced this loss of control. She sniffed back the despised tears and turned her head into the pillow.

'You're overwrought. You need to get warm.'

Overwrought! She'd never had the luxury of giving in to nerves. She was the strong one, the protector, even sometimes the scapegoat, putting herself between Donna and the old man when his temper grew dangerous.

'What's wrong with your arm? Have you hurt yourself?' She looked down to find she'd been rubbing her forearm. It was a nervous gesture she hardly noticed now.

'It's an old injury. It doesn't hurt any more.'

'What happened?' His words feathered her ear and a sliver of heat pierced her, warming her from the inside.

Alissa stared across the room, stunned to be sharing a bed with Dario, soaking up his warmth and reassured by his presence. It was insane, but it was real. It felt so good.

'Alissa?'

What did it matter? There was no point in secrets now.

'I broke my arm a few years ago when my grandfather knocked me off balance and I fell down a flight of stairs.'

The sudden spasm of Dario's arms around her midriff robbed her of breath.

'*Dio buono!* You could have been killed.'

'I was lucky.' She watched his hand curl round her wrist, stroking as if to soothe the long-dead pain. The sight of him touching her, the sensation of his caress, unknotted some of her coiled tension.

'How did it happen?'

'One good, hard push.' Her lips twisted on the memory.

'It was deliberate?' His voice was a husky croak of disbelief.

'With my grandfather it was always deliberate.' There was a sense of release at sharing the truth. Residual anger against the old man was enough to banish her teary weakness, for now at least. 'He made my mother's life hell when she brought us to his home after our father deserted us. When she died the old man turned his attention to me and Donna. *Necessary chastisement* he called it.' The bitter taste of memories coloured her words.

Dario's iron-hard arm around her waist tightened even as his touch on her arm gentled. Alissa suppressed a sigh as that simple, tender caress eased her bone-deep tension. He had such power to heal as well as to hurt.

'No one saw?'

She snorted in disgust. 'No one wanted to see. I tried to get help when I was young, when I was worried for Donna. But it was easier to turn a blind eye, especially as my grandfather was an important man. He had money, power and reputation. No one wanted to know. He ensured the town believed I was ungrateful and unruly, causing trouble.'

Alissa drew a shaky breath. 'He was obsessed with controlling our lives, from who we met to how we dressed. The worst wasn't the beatings but the mind games, the manipulation, the continual battle for dominance. If he'd had his way we'd never have made a decision for ourselves.'

Each word plunged into Dario's brain like a stiletto blade. His meeting with Gianfranco Mangano had confirmed the old man was the sort of snake with whom he'd never normally do business. Only Dario's vow to his long-dead parents, his vow to retrieve what they hadn't been able to, had made him swallow his pride and deal with such a man.

He remembered the glitter in Mangano's eyes as he'd complained of his granddaughter's wild ways and her need to learn obedience. The vengeful twist to his mouth had been ugly as he'd declared his intention to marry her to a 'strong man' who'd keep her out of trouble.

At the time Dario had believed the unscrupulous old swindler had simply reaped what he'd sown in the form of a granddaughter as appalling as he.

Dario slid his fingers over the soft skin of Alissa's inner arm, amazed at the strength of this tiny woman. His stomach clenched at the history of abuse she'd revealed.

Wrath, white-hot and untrammelled, fired his blood. Animals like Mangano didn't deserve the blessing of a family. Especially not when others, loving and responsible, were denied the chance to grow old with their children.

Alissa felt so small and defenceless cocooned in his arms. He hated the thought of her hurting. Of her fighting such battles with no one to protect her.

Ice clamped his chest as he recalled the stark anxiety in her eyes when he'd confronted her in the boathouse. His fear for her had made him lash out and she'd withdrawn, dragging herself to her feet. Had she thought he'd strike her?

Dario's heart hammered as guilt scored him.

'What made him hit you?' The thought of her, crumpled at the foot of the staircase in Mangano's ostentatious mansion, made him ill.

'I stood up to him,' she murmured in a voice so low he barely heard. 'A friend had a party and for once I was determined to go. It was a 60s retro night, everyone wore miniskirts or flares. But it wasn't wild. Her brother even drove me home.' She paused and he felt her draw in a deep breath. 'I'd hoped to slip in quietly but my grandfather was up late because you'd visited unexpectedly.'

Memory blasted Dario. Of how he'd sat in his car outside the Mangano house, seething at the old man's insistence on marriage to his granddaughter. Dario had seen her, bare legs and long, loose hair, smiling at the guy who'd driven her home. Even in the gloom she'd been breath-stoppingly gorgeous. He'd been jealous as hell of the youth, just because he'd been on the receiving end of her megawatt smile. The memory had infuriated him ever since because of its unfailing ability to stir his libido.

'So, it was punishment for being out without permission. But you weren't a child.' There'd been no mistaking her for anything but a full-grown woman.

'I lived there till Donna was old enough to go too. I couldn't leave her with him.' Alissa shifted as if to move away and he firmed his hold till she subsided against him. Did she have any idea what it did to him when she wriggled like that? Her perfectly rounded bottom was pure invitation against his groin. His boxers were no barrier to desire. Jagged darts of heat speared him as he fought not to react.

It took a moment for her next words to penetrate his rapidly fogging brain. 'He was angry about the party. But what really did it was our argument about you.'

'Me?' He shook his head, trying to clear it of subversively potent images of Alissa inciting him to take her. 'You argued about me?'

She nodded and her hair slid against his bare chest, a silken caress that loosened all the power in his limbs.

'He demanded I marry you. He'd talked about it before but I don't think he believed it was a real possibility until you visited.' The uninflected way she spoke chilled Dario to the marrow. He sensed the pain it hid.

'He was so excited, so determined that I obey. He wanted it arranged as soon as possible.' The chill became a hoar frost of tension.

'What happened?'

'We argued. He demanded I sign a marriage contract and I refused.' Alissa paused long enough for Dario to count the blood pulse three, four, five times in his ears. 'The old man lost his temper and lashed out. I went to hospital with a broken arm and a cracked rib.'

Her words, so matter-of-fact, revealed a horror he'd never guessed at. He felt contaminated, dirty, realising he'd unwittingly been culpable in injuring her. If he'd continued to refuse Mangano's scheme as he had originally, this wouldn't have happened.

'I can't breathe,' she gasped and Dario discovered he was squeezing her in a vice-like grip. Instantly he loosened his hold, his body trembling with the force of a fury that had no outlet.

'I'm sorry, Alissa,' he whispered against her velvet-soft cheek. 'So sorry.'

How much damage had he done to this woman?

No wonder she avoided him. Understanding hollowed his chest. He could barely imagine the stress she'd been under. Only now, with the easing of fears for Donna, had Alissa's defences weakened. Her formidable control had shattered.

What a burden she'd carried. And for so long. Trying to protect her sister against their monstrous grandfather, and against Donna's foray into drug abuse.

Then he, Dario, had come on the scene. Another man with money and power. Another man determined to bend her to his will. Determined to believe the worst.

His gut twisted as he realised how he'd compounded her pain, how he'd compounded her fear of being manipulated and abused by a man.

At least he hadn't beaten her as her grandfather had.

No. Instead he'd forced her, a virgin, to give herself for his pleasure. Self-contempt was a scorching brand burning his innards as he remembered her shock and defiance that night.

By all that was right he should release her instantly.

But he couldn't relinquish his hold.

Guilt, shame, regret, even his well-honed sense of honour was powerless against the force of his desire—his selfish need for the woman who despised him.

He cradled her close, arms tightening possessively.

He couldn't let her go. Not yet.

CHAPTER TWELVE

ALISSA'S EYES FELT puffy when she woke. The salt tang of tears was still on her tongue.

How long since she'd cried? Years. Soon after her mother died Alissa had learned that, perversely, her grandfather enjoyed her fear and pain. She'd bottled up her emotions and pretended to be stronger than she was.

Until tonight when her worst fear had miraculously been removed and she didn't need to be strong any more.

Weeping had left her numb and empty. No, not empty. There was effervescence in her blood, a tingle of relief. Donna was safe! The words rang over and over in her brain.

After the heavy, dreamless sleep she felt warm and weightless as if she floated on a tropical sea.

Yet it wasn't the ocean that cradled her. It was the sinew and flesh and hard muscle of a man. In her sleep she'd snuggled closer to Dario till she lay across him, breast to breast, one foot tucked between his bare knees, one hand in the softness of his luxuriant hair. She threaded her fingers deeper into his locks, overwhelmed by the sense of rightness here in his arms, her lips against the steady pulse at the base of his throat.

Her heart turned over as she remembered how he'd held her, simply held her when she needed comfort. His soothing words, his gentle caress. As if the stranger with the harsh, judgemental expression had never existed and there was only the man who'd made such surprisingly sweet love to her in Sicily. Who'd rescued her from the sea. Who'd organised Donna's life-saving treatment.

As if, despite what had gone before, he was the one man she could rely on. The one man she could trust.

Which was the real Dario?

His circling thumb at the small of her back made her breath catch. Whorls of pleasure erupted from the spot, twisting with devastating accuracy to all the erogenous zones he'd discovered that night in Sicily. Her lips parted in a gasp that brought the tang of male flesh to her mouth.

In an instant comfort transformed into desire.

All it had taken was one tiny, almost innocent caress.

Last night's storm of emotion had left her defences shattered. She couldn't even pretend to indifference. She arched into him like a cat stretching to a caress.

This was right, she knew it in her bones. Logic would call her a fool, but now, bereft of every barrier she'd used to keep the world at bay, this craving wouldn't be denied. *For Dario.* For the ecstasy he'd brought to her untutored body. For the potent sense of connection they'd shared, as if, for a few moments, their twin souls joined.

It was irresponsible but she didn't care. Not now when everything in her confirmed he was the one, this was the time. No matter how short-lived the moment.

She pressed her lips against his neck and slicked her tongue along his hot, salty skin. She almost purred aloud at the taste of him in her mouth.

The thumb at her back was replaced by a hand slipping down, squeezing her bottom till she pressed against him. There she found the rigid proof of his answering need. He felt so *good.* Restlessly she circled her pelvis. Instantly his hand clamped her motionless against him.

'You're barely awake, Alissa.' His voice was a harsh rumble vibrating in his neck, against her open mouth. 'You'd better stop.'

Why? In case she changed her mind? Hardly, not when need thrummed through her like a life force.

Or was it that he didn't want her? He hadn't wanted her in weeks. Yet there was no mistaking his desire. She rotated her hips again and was rewarded by a surge of power, bringing his erection hard against her. His fingers tightened on her buttock.

'Alissa.' It was a warning growl. The timbre of his voice, low and rough, stirred her senses. He was so very, very male. For only the second time in her life, that knowledge was a potent aphrodisiac.

This might be her only chance to experience again those wonderful sensations. Through all the worry over Donna and outrage at Dario's actions, nothing had suppressed her yearning for his lovemaking.

Life had taught her that happiness was rare. She determined to seize what she wanted now.

Raising her other hand, she bracketed his skull with her fingers and pulled herself up to plant a kiss on his mouth. His next words were muffled as she slipped her tongue between his lips and kissed him as he'd taught her.

Instantly desire became marrow-deep need. He was big and warm and luscious. She cupped his jaw. The texture of his roughened skin against her sensitive palms sent a jolt of fire to her womb. He tasted…perfect, like dark, bitter chocolate, rich and strong.

Alissa shifted, straddling him as she stretched high. She delved deeper, tongue stroking, till finally, with a rippling shudder of reaction that vibrated through them both, Dario came alive. His tongue tangled with hers, his head angled to access her mouth better. His hand slipped under the stretchy cotton of her nightshirt to mould bare buttocks with long fingers.

His other hand tugged down those silky boxer shorts and Alissa gasped as his erection rose under her. She squirmed and his hand tightened, holding her still as he deepened their kiss. Now his other hand covered her breast through the cotton, stroking, squeezing, then flicking across her nipple.

She groaned and gave herself up to the assault of pleasure. Energy roared through her, spiking with each caress of his hands and mouth. Yet she was filled with a weighted laxness that made her putty in his hands.

It wasn't enough. She needed him. With a supreme effort she managed to co-ordinate her fingers enough to fasten on her nightshirt and drag it up. He grabbed the hem from her and ripped it over her head.

Alissa wanted to look down at him then. To see the desire in his crystal-grey eyes, to see his hunger for her.

Yet…would his need match hers? Or would it be tainted with pity? Pity he'd felt as she'd told him about her past and her grandfather's abuse. Pity for the desperation she couldn't conceal. He wanted her, but surely not with the soul-deep yearning she felt.

Coward that she was, she kept her eyes shut, telling herself it was only physical release she sought. Knowing it for a lie, but unable to face him. Not yet.

'Alissa.' The hoarse whisper, the light touch of his fingers at her breasts, almost cracked her resolve. She wanted again that connection, as if they shared their very souls, watching each other as they gave themselves.

But this was enough. It had to be.

With a whimper of pleasure she pressed close, absorbing his sultry heat, kissing him desperately. He matched her lips to lips, tongue to tongue, breath for breath. Her lungs were ready to burst, her blood pounding a desperate rhythm, when he lifted her up away from him. She made to protest but stopped as she felt the blunt, velvety nub of his arousal. She moved back and was rewarded by the feel of him sliding, long and powerful, against her.

'Dario.' It was a choked gasp, part plea, part wonder.

Strong hands steadied her, holding her safe as her legs trembled. She planted her hands on his shoulders, gripping tight as the tremor became a shudder of anticipation that shook her whole frame.

'Come to me, Alissa.' His voice was a throaty purr. 'Come to me now.' He urged her higher. Willingly she rose, felt him there, where she most needed him, then let his gentle guiding pressure bring her to meet him.

Her lips parted in a gasp of ecstasy as they joined. Even the first time he hadn't filled her so completely. His power and sensuality stole her breath.

He moved and a cry of delight broke from her. Dario clasped her hips, urging her to move. Lights blazed behind her closed lids and spasms of greedy pleasure rippled through her.

'Please, Dario.' Her fingers curled into his flesh but he didn't stop. His movements grew stronger, sharper, coiling the tension to breaking point till with a single smooth thrust he flung her into ecstasy.

Rivers of molten delight filled her, starbursts of sensation as she pulsed in his arms, completely lost to all the world but him. He surged up, higher than she'd thought possible, and flooded her with his warmth. The instant of mutual pleasure grew and expanded as they shared ecstasy.

Finally, shaking, he drew her down, wrapped his arms round her and held her against his juddering heart.

His lips moved against her hair, nuzzling her ear and a belated blast of sensation burst through her. She stiffened then collapsed, boneless.

Dario scooped her close, astounded by the perfection of what they'd shared. Sex had never been this good. Something about this woman was different—beyond his experience.

Alissa had turned to him. Even after what he'd done to her, taken her virginity to satisfy his lust, misjudged her in the most appalling way. That she should invite him so boldly was a wonder. He'd been hard-pressed to hold back long enough to give her pleasure in return.

Was it just stress, the need for comfort, that prompted her to seduce him? Or desire, strong as his own?

He remembered how she'd kept her eyes shut, as if she couldn't bear to look at him, even as he pleasured her. Regret was a slow-turning stab of pain low in his belly.

Had she simply used him for the physical release he could provide? He couldn't blame her if she had.

Yet he wanted more than a frantic coupling in the dark. He wanted her again, and, he realised with a certainty that stunned him, he wanted more than her body.

He wanted all of her.

This was utterly new territory. It defied every certainty he'd constructed for his life and he had no idea where it would lead.

Alissa shifted and his body stirred. That ripple of awareness so soon after satiation was unprecedented. But everything about her was different from previous experience.

This possessiveness was a new phenomenon. He'd never shared his lovers but nor had he felt such a primal sense of ownership. Was it because she'd come to him a virgin? He slid his hands over her curves, hauling her close.

The knowledge he was her first, that all she knew of physical intimacy she'd learned from him, fired his blood. He felt like a conqueror who'd won the best prize.

He wanted… His hand paused in its proprietorial sweep over her hip and thigh. Unseeing, he stared into the cool light of dawn as he realised what they'd just done.

Unprotected sex.

It was unthinkable. Unbelievable. He'd never in his life so lost control that he'd forgotten a condom. Never.

His jaw clenched and his groin tightened as he relived the pleasure of that release, hot and vital with no barrier between them. Pleasure such as he'd never known.

There was no danger of disease, but there was the risk of

pregnancy. He waited for the inevitable sense of entrapment to surface.

Alissa sighed and nuzzled his neck. All he felt was satisfaction that he might have planted his seed in her.

What the hell was happening to him?

Three hours later Dario had showered, shaved and dressed while Alissa slept. He should tackle the mountain of work awaiting him, yet he didn't leave. He sat in an armchair and pretended to read a report.

His gaze strayed to the woman curled in the centre of the bed. The curve of her bare shoulder and the spill of long, bright hair fascinated him, drawing his attention from fiscal details. Her face, so beautiful in repose, looked relaxed for the first time in weeks, though smudges of tiredness were visible beneath her eyes.

He watched her wake and stifled rising tension. How would she react? He'd given up all pretence of indifference. Somehow, without him understanding how, she'd become important to him. He needed her. At least till this…fascination wore off, as it eventually would.

'Hello, Dario.' His body responded to the huskiness of her just-awake voice. 'I didn't expect to see you here.'

Typically, she'd tackled the issue of his presence head-on. His lips quirked appreciatively. It wasn't just her body he admired.

'Good morning, Alissa. You slept well?' He saw her cheeks flush. Remembering her high colour as she'd climaxed only a couple of hours ago, he felt his body harden.

'Yes, thanks. About last night…'

He had the impression she chose her words with care. Tension dragged at his sinews, stiffening his muscles. He put the report aside and crossed his ankles, projecting an air of relaxed attention.

'Yes?' He watched her sit up, drawing the sheet over her

breasts. The sight of her, tousled, pink-cheeked and naked beneath the fine linen, was disconcertingly provocative. He gripped the arms of the chair tight.

'Thank you,' she murmured, her blush growing rosier as her chin tipped higher. 'I'm grateful.'

Grateful! She was grateful to him for making love to her? Unable to remain seated, he sprang to his feet. Of all the responses he'd imagined, gratitude wasn't one he'd considered. He shoved his hands in his pockets and strode across to stare out the window.

'There's no need for gratitude,' he said through gritted teeth. It had been his pleasure. All pleasure.

He didn't want thanks as if he'd done a trifling favour. He wanted her to need him as he needed her.

'Of course there is.' Her sincerity made him turn. Her eyes blazed and she held his gaze without blinking. 'I want you to know I'll keep my part of the bargain. I'll be your *proper* wife, as we agreed.'

Blue fire flashed in her eyes and he knew what she meant by 'proper' wife. His senses clamoured, knowing he'd have her just as he'd desired these long weeks.

But, searching her face, he discerned no excitement. She looked like a woman talking only business. No sign of passion. The realisation cut the ground from under him. Disappointment welled like blood from torn skin. Yet he wouldn't refuse her offer.

'Thank you, *moglie mia*,' he said, summoning restraint. He had to go before he did something stupid, such as let her see how much he needed her. 'I appreciate your reassurance. And now, forgive me but I have business to attend to.'

Unable to resist, he drew her hand to his lips, pressing an open-mouthed kiss on her palm. There was fierce satisfaction at the sound of her indrawn breath and the sight of her pulse racing at her wrist.

She was as vulnerable to this passion as he.

Yet gratitude had prompted her promise to share his bed. That shredded his pride.

Surely a flame that flared so bright must burn itself out soon. This was a temporary aberration. In time his reaction to her would dull. Then he could find a docile Sicilian wife to bear his children. To restore the Parisi family in fact as well as name—those goals had sustained him for so long.

That was what he wanted, the perfect life with no untidy emotions to trap the unwary.

Unless Alissa was already pregnant.

A thrill of possessive pleasure sideswiped him. Till he realised how slim was the chance she'd conceived.

He forced himself to drop her hand.

He ignored the whisper of conscience that warned he acted out of pride as much as need. That for the first time he desired a woman more than she desired him.

The notion was unsettling.

No, this was a matter of mutual passion. He would make amends for the wrongs he'd done her. He'd care for her as she deserved. And, he vowed, he'd give her more pleasure than she'd ever known until the time came to part.

Alissa stared at the closed door and her heart plummeted. When he'd kissed her hand with barely leashed passion, heat had risen again between them. Hope had risen too. Hope that he felt that spark of connection.

But when he'd raised his head and looked at her with eyes like winter he'd doused her hope. Was the magic she'd felt with him one-sided? Had he felt nothing more than physical release? The sort of release he'd had with countless women?

His expression when he'd thrust aside her gratitude had been forbidding. But he'd saved Donna's life and last night he'd offered Alissa the comfort of his embrace, no strings attached. He'd listened, he'd held her close and she'd felt as if nothing could hurt her again. She'd never felt so cared-for in all her life.

Had he no idea how special that was? How incredible and fragile was that tender bud of trust she felt? Apparently not. He'd refused to acknowledge her thanks.

Perhaps her gamble was sheer folly. After all, what did she know of intimacy between a man and a woman? Only what she'd learned with Dario. Maybe what seemed extraordinary to her was nothing of the sort.

Yet her feelings were so strong they couldn't be denied. She'd turned to him this morning wanting comfort and that sense of belonging she'd discovered in his arms. His tender response was everything she'd wished for.

She'd made up her mind to continue their bargain, hoping that by the end of their allotted time she'd discover what these raw new feelings meant. Perhaps even discover that Dario felt them too. Despite his ruthless streak, she knew there was another side to him. A tender, caring, compassionate side.

She remembered how he'd pulsed within her and how, as she realised they'd forgotten a condom, there'd been no panic. Just acceptance and a thrill of pleasure.

Had she taken leave of her senses? *Wanting* to stay with the domineering man who'd disrupted her life?

It was crazy. It was asking for disappointment. Yet Alissa could no more keep her distance from Dario than she could ignore him.

CHAPTER THIRTEEN

IT WAS EARLY evening. The square of the tiny Sicilian village was packed when Dario gave in to the clamorous roar of the crowd and got to his feet.

Alissa watched him on his way to the gaily decorated dais where the mayor had already given a speech. Dario paused here and there at the tables to exchange greetings.

Her husband was the centre of attention. It wasn't simply his superb looks, or the lithe grace of his ultra-fit body that held everyone's gaze; an aura of power crackled around him like static electricity. Beaming faces, wrinkled and smooth, old and young, followed his progress.

Alissa's Italian had improved in the months since their return from the States. She followed the mayor's speech, littered with references to Dario's vision in rejuvenating traditional local industries like olive oil and ceramics production in what had recently been a depressed area. How he'd endowed schools, backed cottage industries and offered work. To these people Dario was a hero. Nor was that new. Whenever she accompanied him to community events she was overwhelmed by the affection in which he was held.

Who was the real Dario Parisi? A civic hero? Absolutely. Plus he had the absolute devotion of his staff. They genuinely respected him.

He'd moved heaven and earth to save her sister and ensure she and David were financially comfortable. He'd been under no obligation to do that, but he had. Because he felt guilty for his actions? Perhaps that was why he grew stiff and formal whenever she attempted to thank him.

He loved children, shedding his formidable reserve whenever Maria and Anna were around, becoming tender, fun, the sort of man who made a woman dream of the future.

How did she reconcile his generosity with the coldly conniving man so obsessed with recovering his family estates? Who had, if the story was true, caused the death of a competitor? That man seemed no longer to exist. She saw few traces of him.

Alissa still didn't understand what motivated him.

Sometimes she felt she was almost close enough to know him. When he made sweet love to her through the night, or just held her in his arms when her period started. He hadn't known how desperately she'd craved his tenderness then. It was crazy, her disappointment when she had learned she wasn't pregnant. She should have been thankful there'd be no baby from their marriage. Yet she'd felt bereft.

Even then he hadn't chosen to sleep elsewhere. As if it wasn't just sex he wanted. As if he too wanted more.

Did he feel that strong link between them?

Some days she was sure he did. Days when, to the amazement of his staff, he took a holiday from his all-consuming work and spent the day with her. They swam, explored local sights, or lay in bed and made love.

Yet whenever it seemed they were on the brink of an understanding, he withdrew. There was a barricade around him that no one breached. Except perhaps Caterina Bruzzone, the old woman who was as close to Dario as family.

Alissa's gaze lingered on Dario, masculine perfection in a dark suit, holding the crowd in the palm of his hand.

The man who, she finally admitted, held her happiness in that broad palm too.

'He is a fine man, Signora Parisi.' A middle-aged stranger

leaned close, nodding approvingly. 'We are lucky in your hus-band's patronage.'

Blindly she smiled and nodded, tears blurring her vision. She was too emotional these days. With the destruction of the defences she'd used to protect herself from her grandfather, and later, the man who'd bought her in marriage, she had no reserves left.

She watched Dario, stepping from the podium to rousing applause. Her heart swelled. With pride? Longing? Love?

She pressed her lips together to prevent a gasp. No, not love. Gratitude for saving Donna. And affection. After all, Dario had introduced her to wondrous physical passion. They said a woman kept a soft spot for her first lover.

She wasn't so foolish as to fall for her husband. That would be disaster. He didn't want love, would be horrified if his con-venient wife became sentimentally attached.

'It was a good day when he returned,' the stranger contin-ued. 'We were doomed with old Cipriani in charge.'

Yanked out of her thoughts, Alissa turned and stared.

'Old Cipriani?' Bianca's father? The one driven to suicide. 'What was wrong with him?'

The stranger shrugged. 'Best not to speak ill of the dead.' Then he turned to shake hands with Dario, who'd forged his way back through the throng.

'Are you ready to go now, *tesoro*?' The rare endearment took her by surprise. Dario leaned close, the warmth of his smile encompassing her.

'The celebration's not over.' She struggled to control her racing pulse and look unruffled.

He shrugged, spreading his palms wide in that habitual gesture which once had so annoyed her. Now she enjoyed the wry curl of laughter on his gorgeous mouth. 'The party will go into the night. We can stay if you wish.' He bent nearer. 'Or we could go home and celebrate privately.'

His voice was a husky burr that melted her insides. The

knowing look in his eyes and the promise of pleasure sent heat flaring along her cheeks.

Alissa put her hand in his, enjoying the touch of his fingers, firm and familiar. 'Let's go home.'

A gleam darkened his eyes, then his face smoothed into the unreadable mask he wore so often. 'I hoped you'd say that.'

Fifteen minutes later they sped along a winding road with spectacular views of the coast. The Lamborghini's engine growled as Dario manoeuvred the car expertly round a bend.

With his jacket slung across the back seat, his sleeves rolled up and pleasure curving his lips, Dario looked sexier than ever. Almost carefree.

How rare that was. Usually he was busy, driven by business responsibilities and other cares he didn't share with anyone. He was so self-contained.

'What is it?' He didn't take his eyes from the road but he knew she watched him. Just as she could tell when he entered a room by the tingle of awareness at her nape.

She shook her head. 'Nothing.'

Dario swung the car round another curve and they swooped down to the coast. The Castello Parisi loomed on its promontory, a reminder that they'd soon be home.

Home for the next couple of months, Alissa reminded herself with a twist of regret. Not once had Dario hinted he wanted her to stay beyond their six months. Ruthlessly she squashed her hurt.

'More than nothing. You've been watching me since we left. What's on your mind?'

She hesitated, then decided to take the plunge. 'Tell me about Signor Cipriani.'

Dario's hands tightened on the wheel, his shoulders hunched so slightly she might have imagined it. The speedometer flicked to the right as they sped faster.

'What do you want to know?' he said finally as he swung the car off the road into a narrow lane running straight for the sea.

'I've heard things. And I wondered—'

'Whether it's true he killed himself because of me?' There was no inflection in his voice but the carefree aura had disappeared. Regret swamped her as she took in his white-knuckled grip and the taut angle of his chin.

Did she really want to know? Wasn't it more comfortable not knowing?

'No. I…'

'Of course you do.' His voice was flat as he pulled up. He switched off the ignition and the sound of waves invaded the still interior of the car. 'Come. Let's walk.'

It was only when they got out that Alissa realised they were on Dario's private property towards the end of the beach nearest the *castello*.

He held her hand as they picked their way down the path to the beach. His grip was impersonal. Gone was the closeness they'd shared today. Had she imagined that?

She blinked back hot tears. She didn't know where she was with him. She only knew she wasn't ready to leave him.

When they reached the firm-packed sand he let go and stooped to remove his shoes. Silently she followed suit.

'It's true,' he said in a sombre voice as they walked down the beach. 'He died because of me.'

'No!' She grabbed his hand, curling her fingers round his. Instinctively she knew he wasn't to blame. Her heart thudded in distress till finally he returned her grip.

Relief bubbled up. The fact that he'd accepted her touch and he held her tight made something soar inside. Warning bells jangled. She was in so deep. She cared for Dario too much.

'How can you know it wasn't my fault?' His gaze held hers in the gathering darkness.

'I just do.'

There was no sound but the shush of waves as he stared down at her. A breeze played in his hair, but Dario didn't move a muscle. After endless minutes he turned and led the way further down the beach.

'Guido Cipriani had something I wanted—a business started by my family. It was the last asset my parents kept before Mangano, your grandfather, ruined them.'

Dario picked up his pace till they strode. 'He deliberately destroyed them. It took years of bribery and corruption, plus some unfortunate investments and a downturn in the markets. His hatred of us was blood-deep.'

'I know.' She remembered his gloating pleasure in triumphing over the Parisis.

Dario sent her a swift sideways look but kept walking.

'I determined to get the company back. I've made it my life's work to recoup all the assets the Parisis owned.'

Alissa shivered as the square battlements of the *castello* loomed ahead. In the fading light it had a threatening air. She'd bartered her freedom so Dario could obtain that medieval symbol of power and family pride.

'You're cold.' He tugged her close. 'We should go back. The temperature is dropping.'

'No. I'm OK.' She needed to understand this to understand Dario. 'What did you do?'

'I offered to buy but he wouldn't sell. He'd put in decent managers who'd kept it profitable but eventually even they couldn't keep it in the black.'

'Why not, if it was profitable?'

'Cipriani was a gambling addict. He wasn't just siphoning off profits, he stole from the business to pay debts to people who…enforced payment.'

Alissa shivered, imagining who those people were. 'What happened?'

Dario's arm tightened and she leaned into his solid warmth. 'When the time was right I offered again.'

'Bianca said you offered less than its value.'

'Much she'd know,' he said under his breath. 'All Bianca

Cipriani knew was the business supported her luxury life-style. She's typical of her set. Never had to sully her hands with honest toil. When the cash dried up she looked for some-one to blame.'

Dario stared at the *castello* rising above them. 'Cipriani had no choice. It was sell to me or let the authorities uncover his theft.' Dario smoothed a hand back through his hair, a gesture she'd never seen him use. 'He signed the deal then went and shot himself. He couldn't face the loss of honour, no longer able to support his family.'

Dario's profile was grim, flesh pulled taut over bone. The sight of his pain made her chest ache.

'That wasn't your fault.'

'Wasn't it? If I hadn't badgered him to sell, if I hadn't been there ready to jump in—'

'Someone else would have.' She touched his arm. 'Did you lure him into his gambling debts?'

'Of course not.'

'Or use underhand tactics to ruin him?'

Dario drew himself up. 'No! I'm a Parisi, not a...'

Not a Mangano, that was what he'd been going to say.

'If you didn't ruin him, how can you blame yourself?' For Dario did blame himself, it was there in his grim face.

He shook his head. 'I should have seen it coming and pre-vented it. His wife...'

Alissa heard the tightly controlled emotion in his voice and pressed closer. He wrapped his arms about her and she was surrounded by his spicy scent and heat. His heart pounded near her ear.

'I don't understand. If your funds just covered his debts, where does Bianca get money? She doesn't look short of cash.'

Dario's hand palmed her hair. 'Of course I topped up the sale price to ensure his wife was provided for. Her husband was dead. She had no one else. It seems she's foolish enough to let Bianca squander it.'

'Of course.' Alissa stifled a shocked giggle. There was no 'of course' about it. Judging by the couture cut of Bianca's outfit and her lavish jewellery, Dario's idea of 'topping up' the sale price had been absurdly generous.

Was there anything more ridiculous, more utterly unfathomable, than this man's code of honour? To blame himself for a death that wasn't his fault, then make amends in the most generous way? He had such an inflated sense of responsibility.

Alissa stood on tiptoe and pressed a kiss to his lips.

'What's that for?' he growled as if taken by surprise.

She shook her head, not ready to examine her reaction. 'Come and sit out of the wind.' Alissa led the way to the sheltered rear of the beach. She had too much on her mind to go back yet.

After a moment he sat beside her, his legs stretched out on the sand, his arms propped behind him.

For a long time they were silent. Finally, encouraged by the gathering dusk and Dario's earlier revelation, she asked the question that had been on her mind so long. This seemed her best chance to understand.

'Dario, why is it so important you get back everything the Parisis owned?'

'It's my birthright, my obligation to my family,' he shot back without pause. 'What man wouldn't wish to restore his family's fortunes?'

'Surely your wealth is more than your family ever owned.' She knew he had controlling interests in ventures right across Europe and North America.

'I promised to restore what was ours,' he said in a tone that made her slip him a sideways glance. His profile was hard and sharp as volcanic glass. 'I won't stop till I've done it. It's a matter of honour. Of duty. The rest is a bonus.' He flicked his fingers as if the millions, or perhaps billions, he owned were a mere bagatelle.

'Promised whom?' His family? Had he really no one of his

own? Despite the affection in which he was held locally, he was the most alone person she'd met. Totally, frighteningly self-possessed, except for the rare occasions he let down his guard with her.

The waves rolled in and ebbed back again and again. When he didn't answer, her throat closed.

It didn't matter that he wouldn't confide in her. After all, she wasn't his real wife. She was a temporary bed partner. Resolutely she blinked moisture from her eyes and planted her palms on the sand, ready to rise.

Long fingers encircled her wrist. 'My father. I promised him before he died.' Despite the clipped words, his voice was resonant with deep emotion.

'I'm sorry, Dario. I take it he died before you approached my grandfather about the *castello*?'

Even in the gloom his scrutiny was so intense it was like a touch. 'He didn't tell you?'

'I know nothing about your family except Gianfranco hated them because a Parisi jilted his sister.'

Slowly Dario nodded then turned to watch the waves. His free arm lifted and a pebble arced into the water.

'It happened when I was seven.'

'I'm sorry,' she repeated inadequately.

'My father was determined to recoup his losses. Some of them, like the *castello*, had been in our family for generations. Generations of proud tradition, plus blood, sweat and hard work.' Not by the slightest inflection did he give a hint of emotion. It was as if he recited a rehearsed piece. Yet his bunched muscles and the tendons straining at his neck told another truth. He lobbed another pebble into the water, the movement one of perfect grace and restrained savagery.

Alissa shivered as a chill wind brushed her skin.

'He'd take me on his knee and tell me about family traditions built over centuries. About our history and our obligations to the land and our people.' His lips curved but it wasn't a smile. 'He planned to regain it all. The lost family honour as well as the assets. To rebuild the Parisi name till it commanded the respect it once had.'

Dario's voice held a note that filled her with foreboding. Another stone splashed in the shallows. 'There was an opportunity to start again, a venture in northern Italy. If it worked he'd have enough to return to Sicily and start again.'

'But it didn't happen.' Alissa's heart was in her mouth, anticipating the tragedy she knew must come.

'No.' He drew in a breath so deep his chest expanded mightily. 'There was a storm. The ferry was overcrowded. The authorities said later there should never have been so many people aboard.'

Alissa slipped her fingers from his loosened grip and covered his hand. It fisted, rock-hard in the sand.

'There wasn't enough room in the lifeboats. Papa wouldn't let me stay with him. He said it was my duty to go. He made me promise…'

For the first time she detected a tremor in Dario's deep voice. She leaned in, resting her head on his shoulder, hoping to bring some small comfort. Her heart plunged at the picture his words conjured: father and son ripped apart in the mayhem of a sinking vessel. She should never have asked about this.

'He demanded you carry on his plans if he couldn't?' It made a horrible sort of sense. Dario had been a kid when he'd shouldered this burden. No wonder he was so driven, so implacable in his quest.

'No, I offered that freely. As his son it was my duty to restore the family honour.'

When he spoke of honour she heard an echo of her grandfather and his obsession with righting past wrongs. But now she understood the difference between Dario and the old man. Dario's pride wasn't rooted in hate but in love. Love for his family and a deep-seated sense of duty.

'He made me promise to look after the others.' Dario's voice was so low she barely heard him.

'Others?' His body stilled as if he stopped breathing. Fear clamped her chest.

'My little brother, Rocco, and my mother. It was late in her pregnancy and she wasn't feeling well.'

The words echoed into a silence so profound Alissa couldn't even hear the sea. Only the sound of his words thudding like bullets into her flesh.

'And they…did they…?'

'The lifeboat was overcrowded,' he said once more in a colourless voice that froze her blood. 'It capsized in the rough seas. I held on to Rocco as long as I could. But I couldn't save him.'

'It wasn't your fault.' The words were automatic as she struggled to comprehend the enormity of his loss. How had he coped with such an appalling tragedy?

'I should have been able to save one of them. Just one.' His voice thickened and he drew another mighty breath. 'Their bodies were never recovered.'

Alissa turned blindly and wrapped her arms tight round him as if she'd never let go. It didn't matter that he was big and strong and stoic. She'd heard the pain in his voice. Her heart broke at the thought of that little boy losing everyone who loved him. Believing it was his fault.

How could his father have put that responsibility on him? It wasn't fair. Then she remembered Dario saying he hadn't wanted to leave his father. She'd guess even at seven Dario had seen himself as a man, willing to stay like his father and take his chances on the sinking ferry. Perhaps the promise to care for his mother and brother had been the only way to get him onto the lifeboat.

Her silent tears soaked the fabric of his shirt as she hugged him close. His body was rigid.

'Where did you go…afterwards?' Her words were choked.

'An orphanage on the mainland. I lived there till I was old enough to strike out on my own.'

Alissa sucked in her breath, her mind reeling. Never had she suspected anything like this. She'd assumed Dario had grown up with privilege if not with the money he'd accused her grandfather of stealing. Dario had such an unconscious air of command she'd figured he'd honed it through years of haughty condescension.

Yet he'd grown up alone, without anyone of his own to love. How wrong she'd been.

'And then?' She had to know the rest.

'I returned to Sicily. I began as a labourer but discovered I had a talent for business. After a few years I was working for myself, employing others. I brought Caterina over. She'd been house mother at the orphanage and promised to be my house-keeper when I set up my own home.'

Alissa felt a flash of relief as the grimness of his tone abated a fraction.

No wonder he'd kept the truth of their marriage from Ca-terina. He hadn't wanted to hurt her, the one person he cared for. He hadn't wanted her to know he'd married in order to wrest back his family's past glory.

And no wonder he hated the Manganos.

'You blame my grandfather.' Her tone was flat.

'If he hadn't swindled my family we'd never have been on that ferry,' he growled with awful simplicity. 'He didn't just steal the *castello* and the money, he stole my family, the life we should have had together. Of course I blame him.'

Now so much made sense. Dario's accusation that she didn't deserve the advantages she'd had at his family's expense. He'd thought her a privileged bimbo like Bianca Cipriani. That she'd had family, wealth and security when he'd had none. Gianfranco had stolen his future, his very family.

Even as she dragged his stiff form close and rose on her knees to cradle his head against her breast, Alissa knew the comfort she offered could only be transient. He might find ease, release, even pleasure, with her. But in his mind her grandfather's sins would always taint her.

These past weeks, despite the warmth and pleasure they'd found together, there'd still been unspoken barriers between them. Now she knew why. Dario would never look at her without remembering.

The hopes she'd secretly cherished splintered like fragile spun glass. There could never be a future for her with Dario.

He pulled her to him and something melted inside.

It was the worst possible time to realise she loved him.

CHAPTER FOURTEEN

'SHE CAN'T COME to the phone, Donna. She's still asleep.' A smile tugged Dario's mouth as he thought of Alissa, sated and exhausted after a long night of loving.

Last night he'd bared his soul to her. He didn't understand what had prompted him. But for the first time ever he'd known an overwhelming urge to share himself.

It had felt *right*.

She'd stripped him to the bone, scoured away everything till he'd been exposed and naked, more vulnerable than he'd felt since he was seven and they'd told him he'd lost everyone.

Now he felt renewed, reborn, with a strength and wholeness that made his blood sizzle. Alissa had done that for him.

They'd made love on the beach with a desperate ardour that barely slaked his need. He'd been insatiable, for her touch, her body, and more, that sense of completeness only she gave him.

Back home they'd barely made it to the bedroom before they'd turned to each other. The wild yearning hadn't been his alone. Alissa had matched his passion with a desperation that stole his breath.

Finally their frantic need had been assuaged and he'd lain with her in his arms, marvelling at the incredible sense of contentment filling his parched soul.

Alissa was...special. She was...

'Pardon?' His musing ceased abruptly as he took in his sister-in-law's words. 'What did you say?'

'I said Alissa can come to us when she moves back to Australia. Now we're financially secure, thanks to you, she can holiday here before returning to Melbourne.'

Dario's brows furrowed. He spoke slowly, as if one wrong syllable might shatter something vital. 'What makes you think she's returning to Australia?'

'It's all right, Dario. You don't need to pretend. Alissa explained the arrangement: six months then you go your separate ways. It won't be long till the time's up. I know she's looking forward to picking up her old life…'

Donna's words faded to a background buzz as his mind whirred into top gear. Alissa had told her sister *that*? Had talked about relocating as soon as possible?

Searing pain banded his torso, a fiery loop tightening till finally he remembered to breathe. His heart hammered against his ribs, pounding out a desperate protest.

From the jumble of his emotions he identified the one that hollowed his bones.

Fear.

He was terrified by the idea of Alissa leaving. Of losing her.

Dario put out an arm and caught the corner of his desk. Winded, disbelieving, he stared at the contracts stacked for his signature. He felt a powerful urge to swipe them off the table and into oblivion.

How insignificant they seemed in the face of this brutal revelation. Suddenly the world shifted into focus, revealing a truth he'd never suspected.

The momentary weakness passed and he straightened, sure of himself again. He was used to snap decisions and trusting his instinct. He was used to taking charge.

He had no doubts about his course of action.

'Things have changed, Donna. Alissa won't be going to Australia except on visits. We're staying married. Permanently.'

* * *

Anguish scooped out the place where her heart had been. In his mind she'd always bear the stain of her grandfather's role in his family's ruin.

She had to save herself while she had the strength.

Quietly she stepped inside and snicked the door shut, determined to face him before her resolve wavered.

Alissa marvelled at his arrogance as he spun Donna more lies. Anger sparked and she welcomed it. Anything was preferable to the helpless yearning that had tormented her since she'd woken in his empty bed.

She crossed her arms over her chest and waited. He ended the call and turned to stare out the windows, his gaze fixed on the *castello*. Why wasn't she surprised? It was all he really cared for. Old stones and dreams of past glory. Not the love of a real flesh-and-blood woman. He yearned for the past, for what he'd lost. And who could blame him?

The knowledge pumped her blood faster. Her mouth twisted. She was jealous of a pile of rocks and mortar! The disturbing realisation lent her the strength she needed.

'What do you think you're doing, lying to my sister?'

He spun round and Alissa had the momentary satisfaction of seeing shock stark on his handsome face. Then the shutters came down. He looked as warm and approachable as a marble statue.

His aloofness stiffened her resolve. She could cope with that. It was the hidden Dario, real, vulnerable and hurting, who shattered her barriers with his tenderness and passion.

'Come in, Alissa, and sit down. We need to talk.'

'We sure do,' she muttered as she paced across the room. 'You've got a nerve, feeding her that story.' Yet even as she lashed her anger her weaker self longed for him to pull her close and say it was true: he wanted them to remain man and wife because he loved her.

She wanted it so badly she trembled.

'Here.' He gestured abruptly to the long lounge.

The place where they'd first been intimate. Piercing bittersweet memories surfaced.

'No, thank you.' She halted before his desk, keeping a safe distance between them.

Eyes the colour of winter rain meshed with hers. The dangerous undertow of desire tugged at her. She looked away. 'Tell me,' she demanded.

'Your sister's call pre-empted a discussion I'd planned to have with you.' He sounded relaxed, as if he were discussing anything but their future. 'I've been considering our marriage…'

'And?' Her heart hammered in her throat.

'All things considered, it seems logical to make our arrangement permanent.'

All things considered… Suddenly Alissa wished she'd taken his offer of a seat. Her legs were rubbery, her knees quaked. She braced her palms on his desk and breathed deep. 'All what things?'

He took a stride towards her then halted, jamming his hands deep in his pockets.

'We got off to a rocky start.' He ignored her stare of disbelief. 'But we've settled into a good relationship. You like the life here. Sicily suits you.' His gaze snared hers again and she read approval in their glittering depths. Heat corkscrewed in her stomach.

'You've fitted in perfectly, coping with society events and local gatherings like the one yesterday. Fitting in with *me*. With my lifestyle. We're good together.' She waited, breathless for him to say the one thing that mattered, the one thing she needed to hear.

He remained silent and something cracked inside her.

Alissa licked her lips and discovered the rusty taste of blood where she'd bitten down too hard. Had she really expected him to make a declaration of love?

She'd known from the first Dario wasn't for her. Stupidly she'd let her emotions blind her to that. The surging pain that cramped her stomach and tore at her throat was testimony to the danger of false hope.

Her feelings for him were so different now she knew the real Dario. But, though he knew her too, he still viewed her as nothing more than a convenience. Pain scored her heart. Had he any idea how he hurt her?

'I fit your lifestyle.' Her voice was a rasp of anguish. 'You mean we're good in bed.'

Those broad shoulders lifted in a fluid shrug and his smile tugged at her belly as he leaned close over the desk. 'That goes without saying, *tesoro*. The passion between us is out of this world.'

His satisfied smirk reminded her that while she'd made love he'd had sex. Last night heaven and earth had moved and her soul had soared as she gave herself to the man she loved. But he'd simply craved oblivion after the wrenching memory of past grief. For him it had been a physical and mental cathartic, no more. She'd known it then and she knew it now. That didn't make it easier to stomach.

She'd given herself willingly. Her heart had ached for the vulnerable boy he'd been and the driven man he'd become. But now the pain was for her foolish dreams, the impossible yearning for a man who could never return her feelings. Staying with him to be used in that way would destroy her. She might even begin to hate him.

'Was there anything else?'

His eyes widened at her abrupt tone. 'Of course.'

His brows arrowed down as if he was puzzled by her lack of excitement. Dully she supposed women were usually more enthusiastic about Dario's propositions. Her knees wobbled as she remembered how enthusiastic she'd been just hours ago. The ache of unshed tears filled her mouth.

'I can give you everything, Alissa. Jewels, money, luxury

holidays. You'll never have to work again. You'll never have to worry about anything. I'll take care of you.'

'Like a kept woman?' He still thought she cared about those material things? How little he understood her. It wasn't his wealth she craved. It was *him*: obstinate, gorgeous, passionate and challenging.

'No! Like my *wife*.' His tone made it clear this was the highest possible honour. 'You want children. I've seen the way you are with the little ones. You'll make a marvellous mother.' His voice dropped an octave and a thrill of delight ripped through her. 'I want to start a family, Alissa. Soon.' His eyes darkened in promise. 'If you agree we could start trying straight away. Today.'

Alissa trembled at the temptation of his words. He had an unerring ability to find her weak spots. An image filled her mind of Dario on the beach with a little dark-haired tot. Their child.

She sucked in a breath of dismay at how badly she craved the future he painted. Almost enough to forget he'd never love her. Or that he wasn't interested in *their* children, his and hers. She saw it with a sickening clarity that wrenched her heart. He wanted babies to replace the family he'd lost. This was part of his plan to restore the Parisi clan.

'Any woman could give you a baby, Dario. It doesn't have to be me.' Yet she wanted it to be her. Wanted it desperately.

'It's *you* I'm asking, Alissa. Doesn't that mean anything?' He strode round the desk so there was no barrier between them. This close she felt the inevitable desire to nestle in his arms and give him whatever he wanted.

'It's not enough.' She forced the words through stiff lips. It was the hardest thing she'd ever said.

'What?' The single syllable boomed in her ears. He drew himself up to his full, imposing height and stared down his long, perfect, aristocratic nose at her. 'What more do you want?

I offer you my name, my honour. I promise you luxury, a life of comfort and ease. The children I know you want.' He scowled.

'Is there nothing else, Dario? No other reason to remain married?'

He was silent so long Alissa couldn't repress a rising bubble of hope. Was it possible he loved her? That he just couldn't say the words? She remembered how he'd cut himself off from emotion, converting his loss and pain into a drive to succeed and an aloofness that set him apart from everyone. Could it be…?

Slowly he nodded, his expression reluctant. She waited, rigid with expectation.

'You must know I feel responsible.' He paused, breathing heavily through flared nostrils. His gaze was brilliant, pinioning hers. 'I misjudged you. I pressured you. I forced you to give me your virginity and—'

'No!' She stumbled back, a palm to her racing heart. She didn't want to hear she should marry him because of some antiquated nonsense about him soiling her 'innocence'. If his strongest feeling for her was guilt, what sort of marriage would it be? Her heart plummeted, her hopes splintered into fragments. 'Don't say any more.'

He closed the gap between them. His scent, his heat, his presence undermined her resolve to remain aloof.

'We're good together,' he purred in the bedroom voice that made her traitorous body tingle even now. 'Admit it, Alissa. You want me as much as I want you.'

He lifted a hand and she jerked back. 'No!' She summoned all the defiance she could muster and glared into his heavy-lidded eyes. 'No,' she said again more quietly. 'I agreed to stay for six months, that's all. I want my freedom when the time's up.'

Dario's face was grim, taut skin over jutting bone. Slashing frown lines scarred his forehead and bracketed his mouth. Defiantly she met his eyes. She read doubt there and determination too. Dario wasn't the sort to give up anything he wanted and right now he wanted her. The irony of it appalled her.

'You're lying,' he murmured, eyes narrowing. 'I know you want me. Your body tells me so.' He wrapped an arm around her, hauled her close and claimed her mouth. His kiss was short and hard. It turned her world upside down and sent desire corkscrewing through her trembling body. Her knees were jelly, her breathing ragged as he pulled back and scrutinised her hot face.

'You can't hide the truth, Alissa. You're mine.'

For one crazy instant she revelled in his proprietorial mastery.

She stumbled back till a wall blocked her escape. 'We're good in bed.' Her voice cracked. 'But I'm sure there's no shortage of women who could satisfy you.' She hid a wince at the idea of Dario with another woman.

He was hers, a silent voice screamed. But Alissa had to stop fooling herself. He could never be hers. Not in the way that counted.

'Once our divorce comes through you can take your pick of women. No doubt you'll find one more suitable than me.' Excruciating pain stabbed her chest as she said it.

'You don't mean that.' There was arrogant certainty in his face. What did she have to do to make him release her?

'I've never been more serious in my life. Staying here would…' Her voice wobbled and she stopped, trying to shore up her defences. She swung round, pretending to stare out the window so he couldn't see the tears brimming.

'You know I never wanted to come here, Dario. You *know* I didn't want marriage. I was manoeuvred into it. Now you think it's convenient to stay married and you're trying to force me again, telling Donna I'm staying. But I'm not a pawn on a chess board. I'm a woman with thoughts and feelings of my own. I make my own decisions.'

'You believe I'm manipulating you?'

'Aren't you? It feels like it.' Her voice was dull. Pain blunted the sharp edge of her indignation. She wanted to hide somewhere and grieve in peace.

'You believe I'm trying to control you. Like your grandfather did.' His voice seemed to come from a distance. 'That's what you're saying. That I'm like him.'

Miserably she shook her head. Dario and Gianfranco were poles apart. Dario was an honourable, caring man, though proud and blind to love. He stood head and shoulders above scum like her grandfather.

'I just—'

'Stop.' The single word cracked like a gunshot, jerking her to a halt. 'Don't say any more. You've made your feelings abundantly clear.' His voice was as cold and haughty as on the day so long ago when he'd hijacked her wedding. She cringed inside, grateful she couldn't see his face.

'I won't detain you. You can consider our arrangement at an end.' Stupidly she held her breath as if that might stop the pain that lanced her chest. 'There will be a car waiting as soon as you're ready to leave and a ticket on the first flight out.'

Silence. Thick, accusing silence. Then the sound of the door opening and closing as he exited the room.

He'd taken her at her word and left her alone.

It was over.

Alissa drew a raw breath as tears slid down her cheeks and her knees crumpled. She huddled on the floor as grief engulfed her.

She had her freedom.

It was a hollow victory.

Half an hour later she sat on the wide back seat of the limousine as it purred along the coast road.

Through a glaze of tears she saw the forbidding outline of Castello Parisi on the next headland. It mocked her. It would be here, a permanent part of Dario's life long after he'd forgotten her.

The past had triumphed. She'd met her match in a crumbling pile of ancient masonry.

It was only after they'd passed it that Alissa's numbed brain began to function. Shock clawed her as she realised what Dario had done. He'd sent her away before they'd been married six months. They couldn't inherit the *castello*.

He'd deprived himself of his one chance to acquire the prize he'd worked all his life to win.

CHAPTER FIFTEEN

DARIO STOOD ON the beach, hands jammed in his pockets, staring at the restless sea. It reminded him of Alissa, the way her eyes danced with pleasure, her quicksilver quality, the energy she brought to everyday living. The passion she'd bestowed on him.

His chest constricted at the idea of never seeing her again. Never holding her or watching her eyes light with passion. Never sharing those silent moments when the world faded and there were just the two of them, connected by a force so strong it defied everything he'd ever known.

He'd fooled himself into hoping she felt it too, the wellspring of emotion and need that drew him to her. It had been a false hope.

A tide of despair swamped him.

She'd broken the seals on emotions he'd buried a lifetime ago. Emotions he'd forgotten and new feelings he'd never before experienced.

If he hadn't met Alissa he'd still be that remote, diffident man, isolated by pride and lack of emotion.

She'd left him raw and wounded, horrified by the man she'd revealed. Her absolute refusal to countenance a permanent relationship forced him to take stock of who he was. It wasn't a pretty sight.

He'd treated her like a whore, demanding she sleep with him for payment. He'd stolen her virginity then not had the decency to release her. He'd used her to sate his lust, regardless of her own needs. He hadn't stopped to find out what she wanted, had just assumed what they had was as good for her as it was for him.

He'd learned nothing. In the end he'd been so desperate to keep her he'd tried to bulldoze her into staying. Manipulate her into agreeing. She, who'd fought most of her life against her domineering grandfather.

His shoulders slumped as the truth pummelled him, like waves on a high sea.

He had nothing to offer her. All he had was his quest to recoup past glories. But now he understood no wealth, power or prestige could make up for the emptiness inside him. The emptiness now she had gone.

She'd been right to leave. Yet already he found himself planning to follow and fight for her. He had no notion how he'd convince her to return, no leverage he could use, but he *couldn't* give up. He—

'Dario.'

Hairs prickled his nape as he imagined her voice on the surging waves. By now she'd be halfway to the airport, eager to be gone.

He should give her time before he pursued her, time for her righteous anger to abate. Time for him to develop a plan. But his desperation was too great. He spun round and almost slammed into the figure blocking the path to the villa.

'Alissa.'

Was that his voice? That raw, hungry gasp? He was beyond caring how much that revealed. He cared only that she was here.

Her hands were small, capable and *real* in his grasp. He felt her warmth, looked down into her cornflower-blue eyes and still couldn't believe. *She was here.*

It was all he could do not to drag her into his arms and kiss her doubts away, blotting out the world.

But that hadn't worked before. He had to make this work between them. There was no other alternative.

'Dario.' His name tasted perfect on her lips. She wanted him to tug her close and kiss her doubts and questions away, take her to that special place they alone shared. But he held back.

Suddenly her idea seemed too crazy even for words. Had she made a terrible mistake? She shivered as ice covered her heart. Her tongue froze as she looked up into his set features.

'I came back because I realised...'

'Yes?' His tone gave nothing away. Only the hammering pulse at the base of his throat gave her hope. That and his grip, tight enough to make her blood pulse hard and slow in her fingers.

But he had himself in hand. Dario Parisi, careful and in control. His expression was unreadable.

She hesitated, hearing her blood pound in her ears. She was afraid to lay herself bare but she had to know. She couldn't leave him while there was even the remotest possibility...

'I realised you wouldn't get the *castello* if I left.'

His iron-hard grip on her fingers slackened and her hands slipped free, falling to her sides.

'You came back because of the *castello*?'

His eyes turned gun-metal grey, blank and devoid of light. The sight doused her last hope. Suddenly she wished she was in the limo, cocooned from everything by the tinted glass that concealed her misery.

She'd made an awful mistake. The realisation numbed her brain.

'I said you were free to go. I do not hold you to our agreement. I forced you into that bargain unfairly. I won't do it again.'

He raised a hand to spear through his sleek, perfect hair. Was it imagination or did his fingers tremble?

'But you need the *castello*. I understand what it means to

you.' She paused, horrified to realise how badly she wanted to stay. If acquiring the place would bring him peace after a lifetime of pain she was prepared to swallow her pride and help him. And it would give her a few more precious weeks with him. 'It's only for a short while. I could move into a guest room and…'

'No! It's impossible. Do not even suggest it.'

Alissa's eyes prickled and her throat jammed as roiling emotion engulfed her. He wouldn't even let her help him achieve his dream. She really had destroyed whatever affection he'd had for her. Desperately she told herself it was for the best. She swung round to leave.

'Alissa.' His voice stopped her. It wasn't a command but a hoarse plea. 'Please understand that I will not dishonour you any more.'

Dishonour! What did she care for honour when her heart was breaking? The blue Sicilian sky dimmed as despair pressed down on her. She lifted one leaden foot to walk away.

'If you had come back for any reason but the *castello*…'

She stumbled and strong arms wrapped round her before she could find her feet. Dario hauled her back against him and she shut her eyes at the exquisite sensation of their bodies locked together.

To be held by the man she loved, feel his heart beating behind her, his arms like warm steel, supporting her…

It was delicious torture, pleasure so poignant her poor heart welled and overflowed.

'But the *castello* means everything to you,' she whispered when at last she found her voice.

'You're wrong, *tesoro*.' His words were muffled in her hair as he nuzzled her scalp. Tremors of reaction vibrated through her and she arched back against him. 'Once it did. But not now, not for a long time. Not since I fell in love.'

Alissa heard the words but couldn't take them in. He can't have said—

She turned so swiftly she bumped her nose on his chin. She tried to back away to see his expression but his arms locked relentlessly round her. He hauled her close and she heard the thunder of his heart pound against her, matching her own galloping pulse.

'The *castello* is just a place.' His voice rumbled up from deep in his chest. She felt every word. 'A special place, but not nearly as important to me as you, *carissima*. That's why I had to let you go. It isn't worth the pain you were suffering, being here with me. I've abided by my promise to my father, but he wouldn't expect me to destroy the woman I adore to get it.'

'You love me?' Had he really said it?

'I love you, Alissa. I've never known anything like this feeling.' He grasped her hand and pressed it to his heart. The pulse of his life force beneath her palm, his words a hot caress against her forehead, made the unbelievable real. Excitement sheared through her.

'For months I told myself it was lust, but from the first it was far more. You are such a woman, *my* sort of woman. Strong, independent, but caring and gentle.'

He put his hands on her shoulders and stepped back till at last she could see his face. His silvery eyes shone overbright. She'd never seen that expression before, of joy and fear mixed together. Hope sang in her breast.

'Dario.' Her voice was choked as she reached up to cup his jaw. 'I can't believe it. You're so—'

'Stubborn? Unwilling to see what's under my nose?'

'Of course not.' A smile broke on her lips as she met his eyes and saw the tenderness there. An expression of love so real, so honest, for a moment words were beyond her. 'I never guessed. You never hinted…'

'That's because I didn't know myself till I'd sent you away.' He turned his face into her palm and pressed feverish kisses there, sending her body into meltdown. 'I thought it was my pride you'd injured, till I realised the truth. I'd become like the man I hated most in the world. I'd become as ruthless as he, desperate to get what I wanted no matter what the cost. When I saw how deeply I'd hurt you I knew I'd do anything to make it better, even let you go.'

Regret shimmered in his eyes. An agony of self-hate that evoked all her protective instincts.

'Shh, Dario. You're not like him at all. You could never be. You're honourable and generous. You genuinely care.' She drew a shaky breath and bared her soul. 'I love you too. But I thought you'd never feel the same. That's why I had to leave—'

His plundering mouth stopped her confession. He snagged her close and tilted her head to accommodate his sweet invasion. It was all there in his kiss, the heady emotion, the shared passion, the trust and promise for the future. Everything she'd ever dreamt of. And more.

'Tell me again,' he whispered against her lips. Heaven was in his hoarse command. In the way he held her, as if she was the most precious treasure in all the world.

'I love you, Dario. I'd trust you with my life.'

He crushed her so close she could barely breathe, yet she smiled as she looked up into the earnest features of the man she adored. He was as handsome as ever. But never had he looked so gorgeous as now, with love shining clear and bright in his eyes.

'*Bella* Alissa. Will you marry me? A proper wedding this time. In a church with all your friends and family. A wedding with all the trimmings and a reception in the town square for everyone to join in.' His voice resonated with the depth of his feelings. 'I want everyone to hear when I promise to love and honour my darling wife.'

Alissa knew no hesitation at all as she leaned close and murmured, 'Yes, Dario. I will.'

* * * * *

COMING NEXT MONTH from Harlequin Presents®
AVAILABLE MARCH 19, 2013

#3129 MASTER OF HER VIRTUE
Miranda Lee

Shy, cautious Violet has had enough of living life in the shadows. She resolves to experience all that life has to offer, starting with internationally renowned film director Leo Wolfe. But is Violet ready for where he wants to take her?

#3130 A TASTE OF THE FORBIDDEN
Buenos Aires Nights
Carole Mortimer

Argentinian tycoon Cesar Navarro has his sexy little chef, Grace Blake, right where he wants her—in his penthouse, at his command! She should be off-limits, but Grace has tantalized his jaded palette, and Cesar finds himself ordering something new from the menu!

#3131 THE MERCILESS TRAVIS WILDE
The Wilde Brothers
Sandra Marton

Travis Wilde would never turn down a willing woman in a king-size bed! Normally innocence like Jennie Cooper's would have the same effect as a cold shower, yet her determination and mouth-watering curves have him burning up all over!

#3132 A GAME WITH ONE WINNER
Scandal in the Spotlight
Lynn Raye Harris

Paparazzi darling Caroline Sullivan hides a secret behind her dazzling smile. Her ex-flame, Russian businessman Roman Kazarov, is back on the scene—is he seeking revenge for her humiliating rejection or wanting to take possession of her troubled business?

You can find more information on upcoming Harlequin® titles, free excerpts and more at www.Harlequin.com.

#3133 HEIR TO A DESERT LEGACY
Secret Heirs of Powerful Men
Maisey Yates

When recently and reluctantly crowned Sheikh Sayid discovers his country's true heir, he'll do anything to protect him—even marry the child's aunt. It may appease his kingdom, but will it release the blistering chemistry between them...?

#3134 THE COST OF HER INNOCENCE
Jacqueline Baird

Newly free Beth Lazenby has closed the door on her past, until she encounters lawyer Dante Cannavaro who is still convinced of her guilt. But when anger boils over into passion, will the consequences forever bind her to her enemy?

#3135 COUNT VALIERI'S PRISONER
Sara Craven

Kidnapped and held for ransom... His price? Her innocence! Things like this just don't happen to Maddie Lang, but held under lock and key, the only deal Count Valieri will strike is one with an *unconventional* method of payment!

#3136 THE SINFUL ART OF REVENGE
Maya Blake

Reiko has two things art dealer Damion Fortier wants; a priceless Fortier heirloom and her seriously off-limits body! And she has no intention of giving him access to either. So Damion turns up lethal charm to ensure he gets *exactly* he wants....

You can find more information on upcoming Harlequin®️ titles, free excerpts and more at www.Harlequin.com.

HPCNM0313RB

REQUEST YOUR
FREE BOOKS!

2 FREE NOVELS PLUS
2 FREE GIFTS!

YES! Please send me 2 FREE Harlequin Presents® novels and my 2 FREE gifts (gifts are worth about $10). After receiving them, if I don't wish to receive any more books, I can return the shipping statement marked "cancel." If I don't cancel, I will receive 6 brand-new novels every month and be billed just $4.30 per book in the U.S. or $4.99 per book in Canada. That's a saving of at least 14% off the cover price! It's quite a bargain! Shipping and handling is just 50¢ per book in the U.S. and 75¢ per book in Canada.* I understand that accepting the 2 free books and gifts places me under no obligation to buy anything. I can always return a shipment and cancel at any time. Even if I never buy another book, the two free books and gifts are mine to keep forever.

106/306 HDN FVRK

Name _____ (PLEASE PRINT)

Address _____ Apt. #

City _____ State/Prov. _____ Zip/Postal Code

Signature (if under 18, a parent or guardian must sign)

Mail to the **Harlequin® Reader Service:**
IN U.S.A.: P.O. Box 1867, Buffalo, NY 14240-1867
IN CANADA: P.O. Box 609, Fort Erie, Ontario L2A 5X3

**Are you a current subscriber to Harlequin Presents books
and want to receive the larger-print edition?
Call 1-800-873-8635 or visit www.ReaderService.com.**

* Terms and prices subject to change without notice. Prices do not include applicable taxes. Sales tax applicable in N.Y. Canadian residents will be charged applicable taxes. Offer not valid in Quebec. This offer is limited to one order per household. Not valid for current subscribers to Harlequin Presents books. All orders subject to credit approval. Credit or debit balances in a customer's account(s) may be offset by any other outstanding balance owed by or to the customer. Please allow 4 to 6 weeks for delivery. Offer available while quantities last.

Your Privacy—The Harlequin® Reader Service is committed to protecting your privacy. Our Privacy Policy is available online at www.ReaderService.com or upon request from the Harlequin Reader Service.

We make a portion of our mailing list available to reputable third parties that offer products we believe may interest you. If you prefer that we not exchange your name with third parties, or if you wish to clarify or modify your communication preferences, please visit us at www.ReaderService.com/consumerschoice or write to us at Harlequin Reader Service Preference Service, P.O. Box 9062, Buffalo, NY 14269. Include your complete name and address.

SPECIAL EXCERPT FROM

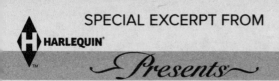

HARLEQUIN

Presents

*These two men have fought battles, waged wars and won.
But when their command—their legacy—is challenged by
the very women they desire the most...who will win?*

*Enjoy a sneak peek from HEIR TO A DESERT LEGACY,
the first tale in the potent new duet,*
SECRET HEIRS OF POWERFUL MEN,
by USA TODAY bestselling author Maisey Yates.

* * *

CHLOE stood up quickly, her chair tilting and knocking into the chair next to it, the sound loud in the cavernous room. "Sorry, sorry." She tried to straighten them, her cheeks burning, her heart pounding. "I have to go."

Sayid was faster than she was, his movements smoother. He crossed to her side of the table and caught her arm, drawing her to him, his expression dark. "Why are you running from me?" he asked, dipping his face lower, his expression fierce. "It's because you know, isn't it? You feel it?"

"Feel what?" she asked.

"This...need between us. How everything in me is demanding that I reach out and pull you hard against me. And how everything in you is begging me to."

"I don't know what you're talking about," she said.

"I think you do." He lowered his hand and traced her collarbone with his fingertip, sliding it slowly up the side of her neck, along her jawbone.

She shook her head, pulling away from him, from his touch. "No," she lied, "I don't."

She didn't understand what was happening with her body, why it was betraying her like this. She'd never felt this kind of wild, overpowering attraction for anyone in her life. But if she was going to, it would have been for a nice scientist who had a large collection of dry-erase pens and looked good in a lab coat.

It would not be for this rough, uncivilized man who believed he could move people around at his whim. This man who sought to control everything and everyone around him.

Unfortunately, her body hadn't asked her opinion on who she should find attractive. Because that was most definitely what this was. Scientific, irrefutable evidence of arousal.

* * *

Will Chloe give in to temptation? And will she ever be able to tame the wild warrior?

Find out in *HEIR TO A DESERT LEGACY*,
available March 19, 2013.